CAROLINE HEMINGWAY

THE DESTINY CHRONICLES BOOK 4

CARROWAY

ISBN   978-0-9942028-3-3

Published in Australia in 2017 by Carroway

"You have plenty of courage, I am sure," answered Oz. "All you need is confidence in yourself. There is no living thing that is not afraid when it faces danger. The true courage is in facing danger when you are afraid, and that kind of courage you have in plenty."
— L. Frank Baum – The Wonderful Wizard of Oz

Courage comes in many forms. Sometimes we cross paths with people who impact us profoundly.

This book is dedicated to a courageous school friend who battled breast cancer. Although we weren't "besties" at school, I got to know her more the last few years via Facebook. Her journey to beat this disease was fought bravely, she fought hard and through it all she loved life, encouraged everyone she knew and smiled despite her pain. Her legacy inspires me to find courage when things get tough and to always believe there is hope, no matter what the circumstances. Di, thank you for showing me how to be grateful for every moment in life. You won't be forgotten.

To my brother Peter and my cousin Jeanette – your courage in the face of loss is incredible – I love how you both realize that love and kindness are all that matters in this world. Keep on making a difference.

As always, I dedicate this book to my awesome family, who cheer me on and give me so much to be grateful for. Kids, I love you and Hamilton, you are my best friend and lover - let's continue having adventures together.

"Being deeply loved by someone gives you strength, while loving someone deeply gives you courage."
Lao Tzu

PROLOGUE

THE air was humid but somehow she shivered uncontrollably. She stood rooted to the spot, as he looked her over critically, his eyes lingering on all her womanly curves. She pushed down the urge to vomit, the urge to flee. She knew she would not get far – there was no escape from this dark, awful place. She'd heard the women refer to this place as the golden cage, but there was nothing golden about it. She flinched as he ran his finger up her bare arm toward her shoulder and he laughed at her discomfort.

'You are beautiful Süheyla,' he said in his foreign accent. 'Don't worry you will get used to it all.'

'Please,' she said weakly. 'There's been a mistake. It is not my choice to be here.' The room seemed to swim and she felt off-balance.

He laughed, louder this time as though she had said something amusing. She looked confused.

'That is no concern of mine,' he answered. 'The Valide Sultan handpicked you out of all the girls and that is all that matters. You should be honoured to be with an officer.'

Honoured she thought angrily. *To be a prisoner – a slave!*

'You cannot force me to stay here,' she challenged, her last ounce of courage surfacing.

He slapped her hard across the face and her cheek throbbed as she held it. She was shocked. She had never seen a man treat a woman this way before. She held back the tears as she bit down on her lip. She would not give him the satisfaction of her fear.

'Don't ever speak to me that way again,' he growled cruelly. He looked her up and down and subconsciously licked his lips. 'You will do nicely,' he said sliding his hand under her robe, invading her personal space, touching her breast in a way that left her ashamed.

Don't let him touch you, her mind screamed but her body refused to cooperate – her limbs felt dead and incapable of retaliation.

'Please don't,' she whispered again.

He ignored her pleas, pulling her closer and kissing her roughly on the lips as he held her arms pinned tightly to her sides. Then he spun her around and pushed her against the brightly tiled mosaic wall. The beautifully ornate patterns would have enthralled her once, but now they were a terrible reminder that she was alone in a culture she did not understand, amongst people who did not value her.

She closed her eyes and let her mind wander to happier times. She started to hum a lullaby her mother sang to her as a child, shutting out the horrible reality of what was happening to her, of what he was doing to her. She would not let him take anything more from her – she would separate her heart from her body – she had to or she would die in this place – this golden cage.

THE GOLDEN CAGE

ONE

❦

CHILDHOOD

GRISWOLD - AUTUMN 1671

SHE giggled into her hand as she huddled behind the tree. She peered tentatively around the mossy bark, the forest quiet. She couldn't see them. His face suddenly appeared around the thick trunk and she squealed with fright.

'Got you,' he yelled as she tried to escape. They tumbled to the ground, their clothes getting covered in damp leaves and soil as they rolled down the mossy slope.

They both lay panting as they giggled, their game of hide and seek almost over.

'Ssh,' he said putting his finger to his lips. 'We have to find Griff before he wins.'

They scrambled to their feet and spent the next while looking for the elusive young man. Eventually they had no choice but to concede defeat.

'Where could he be, Summer?'

'I have no idea,' she giggled. 'Let's forget about him and go back to the castle for hot chocolate.'

'Summer, Cam, I'm up here,' he called from the tree under which they were standing.

They looked up to see Griffin sitting on the branch smiling at them victoriously. Cam looked at Summer and she smiled, knowing exactly what he had in mind. Griffin was trapped in the tree. He may have won the game, but they weren't going to let him off so easily. They picked up chestnuts and started pelting him till he begged for a reprieve.

'So you surrender then?' Cam asked.

Griffin clambered down the tree, red blotches forming on his skin where the chestnuts had hit him.

'I surrender,' he said hugging his cousin and sister.

⌘

There were only two years between Summer and Griffin Sveinsson. Cameron Hamilton was their second cousin, born to Struan and Catriona nine moons after Griffin. The three of them had been inseparable growing up. They spent every summer together exploring their surroundings at Griswold Castle. Other times they would all terrorise the servants at Ebondeen Castle. They were nicknamed the "Terrible Trio" by the castle guard. Cam enjoyed spending time with his cousins, as he was an only child. His father had contracted mumps as an adult, leaving him unable to have any more children and Cam would have been lonely had it not been for Summer and Griffin's company.

Struan did his best to give Cam as much attention as he could, but with one leg he tired quickly and could only be so active before his stump became inflamed and painful. Cam loved visiting Griswold – his uncle Erik, a huge Northman, fascinated him with stories of Kaldakinn and the raids he had participated in. Cam was in awe of him. Then there were his cousins. It was the one time he felt what it would be like to have a brother and sister and secretly he envied them both. Although Isabel was actually his first cousin, he

4

thought of her more as an aunt, since their age difference was so vast. She was so much fun. She loved nothing more than getting out into Grimwood Forest to hunt with her bow and arrows. He wished he could be half as good as her.

His mother was more restrained and refined – she spent her days doing needlepoint and playing music. As much as he loved her, Cam hoped that one day he would marry someone more like Isabel than his own mother. That's what he liked about Summer – she was carefree and full of adventure. She didn't mind if her skirts got dirty, she refused to ride sidesaddle and she was always up to mischievous pranks. She was twenty now and rather beautiful. She had her mother's blue-grey eyes and her hair was a rich chocolate brown, not quite as dark as Isabel's raven locks and not as light as Erik's. Griffin was the more serious of the two – his dark brooding looks taking after his father Phoenix. Isabel had done well to talk to him about his father, reminding him of the man that he was. Griffin did not know whether to be proud of his heritage or embarrassed by the evil that was part of his history. He was grateful to Erik for accepting him as his own – in truth he viewed him as his father and loved him deeply. Phoenix was just a name, a fantasy to him; yet he still felt an overwhelming responsibility that one day he would rule Griswold. The thought terrified him.

⌘

Erik too, was thinking of Griffin's future as ruler of Griswold. He felt responsible for ensuring his son was ready to take on the task.

'Isabel, the time is drawing close for Griffin to rule Griswold. He's a young man and we need to step aside and allow him rule his kingdom. We must ensure he is ready for it.'

They were eating breakfast in the parlour and Erik licked his fingers as sweet honey dripped from the hot bread he ate.

'I agree,' she said sipping the hot brew they called "tee". It was a brew made from leaves brought to Griswold by Holtlanders who had initiated trade with them.

They had always known the day would come when they would no longer rule Griswold, as it was Griffin's birthright. They knew he would do a fine job, but they wanted to ensure that he would be ready for the responsibility of leading a kingdom that was increasing in both influence and wealth. Working together with the Northmen of Kaldakinn had benefitted their kingdom tremendously. Both clans had enjoyed greater wealth and prosperity as a result. It also gave them greater strength in their fighting force as no other kingdom dared to take on Griswold or Ebondeen now that they were aligned with the Northmen.

Griffin had spent the last winter in Kaldakinn learning survival and warfare tactics with his grandfather Earl Thorfinn. He also learned how to build ships. It had been a valuable time for him as he soaked up the knowledge. The warrior women had tried to convince him to stay and bed them but he had simply shrugged off their advances. His father had warned him about these women.

'What more does he need to learn?' Isabel asked.

'I have taught him how to fight with a sword and he knows how to shoot a bow thanks to you. He has mastered survival in harsh conditions. What he really needs to learn now is how to govern wisely and with strength. The threats of the future will not come from the North or the

THE GOLDEN CAGE

surrounding kingdoms – I fear they will come from the continents to the east of Griswold. These kingdoms are becoming giants in the civilized world and I have heard many tales of the Bourbon King trying to expand their influence and rule.'

'What should we do then?'

'I'm not sure Isabel – let me think about what would be the best for Griffin. It is our duty to make sure he is ready to take on this responsibility, or it could break him.'

They finished their breakfast and headed down to the Great Hall to listen to the tenants' disputes for the day. They expected to see their son as they had decided to involve him in the decision-making and resolution process. It was all part of his education. Summer would attend her lessons with her tutor and although she was an avid reader and extremely bright, she preferred to be either out riding her stallion, Hawk, or painting. They had discovered her incredible talent for art when she had painted them a family portrait one Christmas. Her brush strokes and ability to capture their expressions had astounded them. She had even managed to get a few commissions and her artistic reputation was growing.

⌘

She looked out the window, her mind a thousand miles away.

'Summer, did you hear me?'

She did not respond, her expression glazed.

'Summer,' her exasperated tutor said more firmly. Finally she turned her eyes to the young monk who tried his best to educate her.

7

THE GOLDEN CAGE

'Sorry,' she mumbled turning her focus back to the numbers in front of her.

'One day this stuff may save your life,' the young monk teased.

'Yeah right,' she muttered under her breath. As much as arithmetic did not appeal to her, needlepoint and music lessons appealed to her even less and so she forced herself to concentrate and get it done.

The sooner I get this over with, the sooner I can go for a ride on Hawk.

TWO

HISTORY

SUMMER was working on a very special painting and she needed it to be perfect. It was a gift for her grandmother Aislinn's birthday. She looked critically at the charcoal drawing on the dirty parchment. It was an old drawing – at least fifty years old but it had been lovingly cared for and somehow there was an authenticity to the scene depicted.

She remembered the story her great grandmother, Imogene, had told her. Some evil men burnt their home down many years ago in an attempt to kill their whole family. During her escape from the fiery cottage, she had grabbed the only thing she could as they fled– a drawing a passing traveller had done as payment for their generosity in giving him food and a bed for the night. It was a sketch of the whole family as they sat around the hearth – Mac had Maddy on his lap while Mitchell slept in Imogene's arms. Aislinn and Struan sat at their feet playing a game in front of the fire. It was a picture of contentment and Imogene had kept it treasured all these years. Now she had given it to Summer to use as inspiration for her painting. Summer ran her finger over Mac's face. Her great –grandfather held a special place in her heart. She had been so close to him growing up and she smiled remembering how he'd nicknamed her Summerbee. When she was just six he and her great grandmother moved to Ebondeen Castle at Struan's insistence. She spent every summer with him and he had taught her how to ride.

She missed him desperately – seven years ago he had been taken from them after falling from a roof. At seventy-eight he should never have been up a ladder, never mind on the roof, but when a tenant on Ebondeen's lands developed a leak in their thatch he had taken it upon himself to check it out. Imogene had been devastated by his death and Summer had taken it equally hard.

It took her a long time to come to terms with his absence. Holidays at Ebondeen were never the same again. She would spend hours at his grave and talk to her Papa-Mac, as she called him. It was where she began to draw, as she sat telling him all about her days. She would leave the pictures she drew under a small rock for him.

She finally stopped going when her pictures became wet and damaged. She could not understand why Papa-Mac had not taken them. Her mother and father had found her weeping in her chambers after a visit to his grave one day.

'What's the matter Summer?' Isabel asked stroking her daughter's hair.

'He doesn't like them,' she said in broken sobs.

'Who doesn't like what, sweetheart?' Isabel and Erik looked at one another confused.

'Papa-Mac doesn't like my drawings. He hasn't taken any of them.'

They exchanged concerned glances over her head.

'It's not true Summer. Papa-Mac cares very much about you and he would tell you how much he loves your drawings if he were here.'

'But you said that he can see everything and that he is still with us,' their thirteen year old daughter sniffled.

'And he can. Papa-Mac has gone to a place called Lionsgate to be with the Great One and Ziah. It is a beautiful

THE GOLDEN CAGE

place – your father and I both went there once and I can tell you that Papa-Mac is very happy there.'

'But why can't he come back like you did?' she persisted.

'Not everyone who goes to Lionsgate wants to come back here Summer. Papa-Mac lived a good, long life and he made us all very happy. We all miss him, but one day we will see him again. We can look forward to that. While he sees all the beautiful drawings you have done, he can't get them. Why don't you keep a special book of all the drawings you do, and one day, maybe, when it is your time to go to Lionsgate, you will be able to give them to him. Leaving them outside under a rock will just destroy them. Papa-Mac is not in that pile of dirt anymore – he's in a much better place.'

She felt her disappointment wane and relief that he was not alone replaced it. He had the Great One to love him. She would make a special book of her drawings and maybe one day when she visited Lionsgate she could show Papa-Mac all her drawings. Cam and Griffin had seen how she had struggled and had made an effort to include her in their games. It was this empathy that forged a solid bond between them and turned them into the Terrible Trio.

⌘

She worked on the family portrait at every moment she got – it was imperative that she capture each of them perfectly – it was her responsibility to preserve their family line in paint for the future generations. She furrowed her brow as she worked, her concentration intense.

Her brush flew over the canvas creating magical strokes as she worked and each of their faces came more

11
THE GOLDEN CAGE

and more to life with each application of paint. She loved painting outdoors - the light and fresh air inspired her. She could not work shut in a dark chamber. Her father had built her a conservatory to paint in during the winter months. It was the best gift she had ever received. Even when it was icy cold outside, the warm hearth kept the glass box warm and she still felt part of the bleak landscape as the natural light flowed in. Painting was her escape, her private world that she could retreat to and be lost in.

'Summer,' her mother called coming into the conservatory. She laughed seeing her daughter's beautiful face smudged with blue paint, her tongue just resting on her lower lip as she scrutinised her work critically.

'Here, you ragamuffin,' Isabel said affectionately wiping her daughter's cheek with her handkerchief.

'Don't look Mama,' Summer scolded covering her work. 'It's not done yet.'

'Ever the perfectionist,' Isabel smiled. 'I have just received a letter, and you won't believe who it is from.' Isabel waved the letter in the air mysteriously.

'Well, don't keep me in suspense Mama.'

'It's from the King of Hexagonia. He's heard about your paintings Summer, and he's requested you to paint his portrait.'

'Are you serious?' she squealed in delight. 'Mama that is the wildest thing I have ever heard.'

Hexagonia was across the seas to the east of Griswold and it was becoming well known as a cultural icon in the modern world.

'He's willing to pay you handsomely Summer, and he's also offered you the opportunity to be part of court for a few moons. This is an amazing opportunity for you to meet many influential people. Just think how many commissions you would get if you paint the King's portrait?'

A look of fear crossed her face. 'I can't possibly do it Mama. What if I can't capture him and he is dissatisfied with my painting? I could lose my reputation, or worse, my head,' she said dramatically. 'Besides, I don't have dresses suitable for court and I can't possibly leave you and Papa and Griffin. I have my lessons too and I could never leave Hawk...' she rambled.

'It sounds to me like you are getting cold feet and are fabricating every excuse under the sun why you should not go,' her mother said. 'Next you'll be telling me that Friar Thomas will miss you.'

'Well, that is true Mama. What would Friar Thomas do if he could not tutor me daily? He would be out of a job,' Summer said earnestly.

Isabel laughed loudly. 'I'm sure he will manage just fine Summer. As for the other excuses they can all be solved. We will make quite sure that you have dresses for court and your father and I will be fine while you are gone. As for Griffin, we have an idea. We are hoping to negotiate with King Louis to allow both Griffin and Cam to accompany you. We wish for them to join the Musketeers while you are there to learn as much as they can. Your father believes Griffin needs to learn how to lead men. It would be a win-win situation for everyone and if Griffin can build a relationship with the King's court we would have a powerful ally from the east.'

'So I wouldn't have to go alone then?'

'No Summer, we would never allow you to go to Hexagonia alone. You would certainly need a chaperone.'

THE GOLDEN CAGE

Her enthusiasm returned when she heard that Cam and Griffin would accompany her. It would be their adventure – the three of them together – taking the world by storm.

Watch out Hexagonia, here come the Terrible Trio.

⌘

Erik and Isabel thought it through carefully. This was a golden opportunity for both their children and Cam. If they could get the King to agree to Griffin and Cam escorting Summer, then it could be a way to ensure that he form an alliance with Griswold and Ebondeen. They were both aware of King Louis' desire to extend his influence and although Hispania was in his immediate sights, their kingdoms further to the west would eventually capture his attention. If Griffin and Cam could form a relationship with the King's guard, the King would become aware of Griswold and Ebondeen's alliance with the Northmen. They doubted even King Louis would take on three kingdoms, especially since the Northman's' reputations as fierce warriors was well known throughout the world. Even Hexagonia had experienced invasions by the northern clans in years gone by.

Not only would Cam and Griffin learn greater skills from the Musketeers, they would also ultimately protect their own kingdoms.

'Do you think the King will be willing for Cam and Griffin to join the Musketeers?' Isabel asked.

'I think we have the winning hand,' Erik chuckled. 'If he is as arrogant as rumour has it, he will want the best portrait possible, and Summer has made quite a name for herself. I think we can negotiate something.'

Erik drafted a letter to the King outlining their terms of Summer's contract. Then they sealed it with the Griswold stamp and sent a rider to dispatch it as fast as possible.

THREE

❧ ⟨◊⟩ ❧

KINGS

PALAIS DU LOUVRE - FRANCIA

'IT has to be splendid, Monsieur Mansart. I have taken on the task of converting my father's hunting lodge into a palace and this magnificent piece of architecture will stand forever in Francian history.'

'I understand King Louis. I have a vision for the large hall that will make this palace the talk of all Francia and even beyond its borders. We will make a grand statement by using mirrors; interspersing them between the green marble pillars right up to the vaulted ceiling that will be covered in artworks,' he waved his arms as he described his masterpiece. 'What do you think?'

'It sounds truly spectacular.'

The architect and the King pored over the plans for the new Palace. King Louis was well known for his love of art and architecture. He had established numerous academies during his reign that included painting and sculpture, architecture and science. He was passionate about incorporating the arts into the Francian culture. This Palace would not only showcase numerous beautiful artworks, it would be magnificence itself in proportion and design – a veritable architectural dream.

He had chosen Monsieur Louis Le Vau to make that dream come true – to design a Baroque Palace and the architect had not disappointed him. It was just a pity that he would never see it completed as he had succumbed the previous year and now his business partner Jules-Hardouin Mansart had taken over the project. King Louis could not wait for the day he could get away from the capital, Lutèce, and its political games. This was the reason he had decided to convert the simple chateau on the land his father had hunted on, into a vast and sprawling estate, as far from the city as possible. He would make it the official palace of Francian Kings for generations to come. It was a massive project but necessary. Since he had become his own chief minister when Cardinal Mazarin had died he had caused quite a stir at court. Cardinal Mazarin had done a good job ruling when he was too young to do so himself, but now he did not want others making choices for him as King – he wanted to govern himself. It had not been well received initially but he had stood his ground. Moving his court to Château de Versailles would give him even greater control in the future.

'I am hoping to have a new portrait done in the next few months,' King Louis said to Jules. 'There is a superb artist who I hope will accept the commission.'

'I will keep that in mind Your Majesty. I will make sure that we have the perfect place for it when Château de Versailles is complete.'

The architect gathered his papers together, bowed and retreated from the King's chambers. Their business was done for the day. Louis stretched out in front of the fire and closed his eyes. He dreamed of how Versailles would look when it was complete. The first phase of the building was truly magnificent. There was still a way to go and already it had cost a small fortune.

You can't put monetary value to beauty he thought.

She giggled at the door and his eyes flew open, lust filling them as she swayed into his chamber, kicking the heavy door closed behind her.

'What are you doing here, my dear?' he asked. She giggled again and fluttered her lashes at him pretending to be coy.

'I am merely here to serve my king. I thought he may be hungry or need some exercise,' she teased. 'I believe I am able to assist with both those needs,' she smiled seductively.

'Does Queen Maria know you are here?'

'I believe the queen has a migraine and is lying down. Poor dear.'

'Sophie, you are truly wicked,' Louis laughed as he grabbed her pulling her into his lap. He kissed her and his hands pulled at her dress in urgency.

⌘

King Louis was known as 'The Sun King' in court and it was not only for his power as king and that everything rose and set with his decisions. It also referred to his virility and his desire to create life wherever he went. It was not a secret that had an eye for the ladies and preyed on them. He had bedded most of the servants and ladies in waiting but his latest favourite was Sophie. She was his wife, Maria's, chief lady in waiting and she was a delicious little thing. He had known the moment he had seen her that he wanted her in his bed. Maria always pretended that she did not know what was going on but deep down she knew that Louis could not keep his trousers on or his hands to himself. It hurt her deeply but to retain her dignity she feigned complete ignorance. They may be sport for Louis but she was the Queen of Francia. She would provide the legitimate heirs to the throne and any other little bastards would never rule.

FOUR

✣

ADVENTURE

GRISWOLD

SUMMER and Griffin stood beside the carriage. Goodbyes were always hard. Isabel tried to keep the tears back and she swallowed hard.

It's only a few moons they will be away she thought as she hugged her daughter tightly.

'Take care of yourselves,' she said to them both. 'Griffin I am trusting you and Cam to ensure that Summer is safe while you are in Hexagonia.'

Cam leaned out of the carriage window with a grin. 'Don't worry Isabel; we will make sure no Hexagonian sweeps her off her feet. As Musketeers we will defend her honour to the death,' he chuckled.

'Don't worry Mama,' Griffin reassured her. 'We will keep her safe. Thank you for making this possible – we will learn so much.'

Erik pulled the young man into a bear hug. He loved his son so much. 'You will be ready to rule Griswold when you return Griffin. This is a golden opportunity to make alliances and learn some new things. We are proud of you both,' he said kissing his daughter on the cheek. 'Now get going before you miss your ship.'

They waved as the carriage rolled out the castle gates and down the winding hill toward the river. The castle would be so quiet without the three of them wreaking havoc. Erik wrapped his arms around Isabel and drew her close against his chest.

'They will be all right, won't they?' she asked.

'They will be fine Isabel. It's hard letting go but we have to let them discover their own path.'

'I know,' she smiled, 'but it doesn't stop me worrying.'

'Let's go hunting this afternoon. It will keep your mind off them and we could have a secret tryst under a certain oak tree,' he winked.

'What oak tree?' she said, feigning ignorance.

'The oak tree near the river, where you took my innocence and my clothes,' he laughed.

'Erik!' She giggled remembering the day they had ridden to the river. It was not long after she had declared her love for him and become his wife in the true sense. They had spent every moment together and discovered every inch of one another's bodies. That day she had stolen his clothes and hidden them when he had gone for a swim after their lovemaking.

'I haven't forgiven you for that,' he laughed. 'It was awkward explaining to Balfour and his men why I was standing naked on the edge of the riverbank.'

Isabel remembered hiding in the reeds alongside the river, trying not to giggle when the soldiers came by on a routine patrol.

She had to stop herself from laughing out loud when she heard Erik lamely explaining that he had the urge to get out of the castle and swim naked as he missed the freedom he had in Kaldakinn.

'Your excuse was priceless,' she said. He smiled.

'What else could I say? They already thought I was a savage from the North so I just went along with that. It was less embarrassing than admitting that my wife had stolen my clothes.'

'I'm sorry,' she laughed. 'Let's go for a ride and do some hunting and I might even let you woo me under that oak tree, but I promise I will never steal your clothes again.'

'How can I resist such a beautiful woman,' he said pulling her close and kissing her.

⌘

Summer stood on the deck of the boat, her hair billowing in the breeze. They were about to set sail and their adventure was beginning. King Louis had sent a ship to collect them. It was a grand vessel, with huge sails and beautiful carved woodwork. It was much larger than the longboats she was used to seeing in Griswold. She had spent many summers on the longboats as a child, as she had wanted to learn as much as she could about her father's people in the North. She stroked the wooden rail and imagined life in Hexagonia.

'It's beautiful isn't it?'

'Yes it is,' she said shyly, turning as a young man in uniform joined her at the rail. He wore the uniform of a Musketeer, the large silver cross brandished boldly across his broad chest. His tabard was deep blue and displayed a sun under the silvery cross. He was tall with thick dark wavy hair that just touched his collar; a small moustache and neatly trimmed goatee gave him a regal look. It was his eyes however, that were captivating. They were deep green– the colour of emeralds.

THE GOLDEN CAGE

'Forgive my manners Mademoiselle Summer. My name is Tristan Chevalier. I am a Dragoon in the King's Musketeers.' He swept off his large brimmed hat and nodded his head gallantly as he half-bowed.

'Pleased to meet you,' she said as he took her hand. 'What is a dragoon?' she asked curiously.

'I'm in the cavalry – a Grey Musketeer trained on horseback and in fighting. It is an honour to escort you to Francia.'

'Don't you mean Hexagonia?' she asked a little alarmed.

He smiled at her worried expression.

'Don't worry; I assure you I am not abducting you. Hexagonia is an ancient name for Francia – we don't refer to ourselves as Hexagonians anymore – now we are known as Francians who reside in the great city of Lutèce, Francia. King Louis wanted to give our kingdom a new image, hence the new name.'

She blushed at her mistake. He must think her an ignorant fool.

Why am I bothered by what he thinks of me? she mentally chided herself.

'Well, thank you for taking the time to educate me and to escort us safely. How long will the journey take?'

'If the winds are good it should only take a few weeks.'

Cam and Griffin joined them at the rail. It seemed clear that they would all get on well together. Tristan spent the remainder of the evening telling them stories about Francian court and life as a musketeer. It sounded exciting and terrifying all at once. It was dawn before they all fell into their beds, exhausted and ready to dream of adventures in this foreign land called Francia.

THE GOLDEN CAGE

The rolling motion made Summer feel sick. The ship creaked and groaned as it cut its way through the steel grey ocean. She felt fine for the first few days, but now she was desperate to plant her feet back on solid ground and everything swayed constantly. She tried to distract herself by painting but focussing on the canvas just made her feel sicker. She hung over the side of the boat and retched once more. The sea sprayed her face with a fine mist.

'Here,' he said handing her a handkerchief. She wiped her mouth and smiled weakly at Tristan who looked very concerned. 'I know how you feel,' he said kindly. 'The first time I went to sea I spent the whole first week vomiting. Come, I have made you some weak tea with ginger and lemon. It will help with the nausea.'

She followed him down to the galley. She sipped the steaming liquid and felt her stomach settle.

'Thank you,' she said gratefully.

'We have made good headway – it won't be too long till we see the Francian shore,' he encouraged her.

'Music to my ears,' Summer said.

⌘

FRANCIA

Louis was ambitious. At twenty-nine years old he was a young king and had ruled from the age of six when his father had died. He wanted to advance Francia's influence

24

and marrying Maria Theresa of Hispania had been a start, but he wanted more. He was ambitious and wanted to expand his country to be one of the most powerful nations of the new world. He had followed the expansion of the Anatolians with great interest. They had successfully conquered many people and built a strong and powerful nation that had grown and strengthened over the centuries. Francia had a reasonable relationship with the Anatolians thanks to an alliance that King Francis had made with Sultan Suleiman the Magnificent in 1536. This alliance had rocked the western world, as it was an alliance of two very different belief systems. King Francis had been criticized for his decision, but he had persevered with the alliance as it was in Francia's best interests to work with the Anatolians in fighting the House of Habsburg that threatened them both. Louis learned much from his predecessor and kept a watchful eye on how the sultan ruled his kingdom. They had an amicable relationship and occasionally envoys travelled each way to maintain the relationship. Francia had even provided some of the slaves for Topkapi Palace as a sign of goodwill.

Louis smiled – things were going well – he was building a palace that would be as magnificent as Sultan Mehmed's Topkapi Palace. Francia would stand in history and be as well remembered as the powerful Anatolians – he would make sure of that. He was the Sun King after all. His thoughts were interrupted by a messenger at his door.

'The ship has docked, Your Majesty. The carriage has been sent and the guests will arrive later today. Their quarters have been readied.'

'Thank you, Felipe,' he replied. 'Please make sure that Mademoiselle Summer has everything she needs. Appoint someone to act as a lady-in-waiting to her. The success of my portrait depends on how well she is treated here. She must lack nothing while at court.'

THE GOLDEN CAGE

'Yes Majesty,' the messenger replied, scurrying off to make the final arrangements.

⌘

The ship bumped against the dock gently. Summer, Griffin and Cam stood side-by-side taking in all the sights and smells of Lutèce. They could not believe the sheer size of the city. Traders unloaded their wares on the cobbled streets. Women stood on the corners calling to the men, flashing their cleavage or thighs at the sailors, offering some comfort for a fee.

'It's incredible,' Summer breathed. 'It has a life of its own.'

'Yes, and a smell of its own too,' Cam laughed wrinkling his nose.

'Look at the architecture – its magnificent,' Summer gushed pointing at the Pont Neuf Bridge that spanned the river Seine. As an artist her senses were in overdrive as she marvelled and appreciated the beauty of the buildings around her. Griswold castle seemed almost crude in comparison.

'Don't let Lutèce fool you Mademoiselle,' Tristan said seeing her delight. 'It is also known as La ville lumière which means the city of lights, but it's not all beauty and splendour, I can assure you. There's a lot of poverty in amongst these grand buildings which leads to thievery – watch your purse at all times and keep it hidden under your cloak. Thieves have a talent at cutting purse strings in Lutèce. They may also pretend to be sick or crippled to get your sympathy and money.'

Tristan helped Summer down the gangplank to the awaiting carriage. Little children tugged at her cloak, their eyes pleading in their dirty faces, their palms turned upward.

'Allez-vous en,' Tristan said sternly and the children scattered, afraid of the tall Musketeer in uniform.

'Oh Tristan, don't frighten them,' Summer cried dismayed. 'They are just children who have nothing. What harm are they doing?'

'Even if you give them some coins Mademoiselle Summer, they will not get to keep them. They are sent out onto the streets by adults to beg, and they will take the money off them and spend it at the local tavern tonight. Children are used as pawns, as the wealthy are more sympathetic to them and they earn more money.'

Summer looked horrified at this.

Who would ever exploit a child in such a way? Life certainly is different here, she thought.

In Griswold, people helped one another in the community if there was difficulty. Lutèce obviously did not care whether people were starving on the streets. She had been here only a few hours and already she could see the difference between the desperately poor and the wealth of Kings. She was not sure she liked the chasm she saw. She knew what it was like to live a privileged life as a lady of Griswold, but her parents always made sure that their villagers had enough food and lands to support themselves. They ruled fairly and with compassion. Tristan was right, this was not just a city of lights; there were corners of darkness that spilled out onto the cobbled streets and the residents pretended not to notice them.

The carriage rolled along the streets toward the Palais du Louvre where she would live the next few months and

THE GOLDEN CAGE

the further she travelled the more she determined to embrace the adventure and enjoy every moment of it. This was an opportunity of a lifetime and she was grateful for it.

Tristan watched the emotions cross her face. She was like a child discovering something new for the first time. She was beautiful and he felt his heart stir in his chest.

You are not good enough for her Tristan. She's the daughter of a Lord and Lady. You are just a soldier, he mentally chided himself.

FIVE

ACCUSATIONS

KING Louis planned a welcome feast for Summer, Griffin and Cam's arrival. Frankly, he did not care too much about the young gentlemen – Summer was the only person he was interested in, but he'd made an agreement with the Lord and Lady of Griswold that involved all three of them, so he would have to keep up his end of the bargain.

He was captivated the moment he saw her. She was nothing like he imagined. He had expected an older woman, a spinster who put her art ahead of anything else. His jaw almost hit the floor when she was introduced to him. Not only was she deliciously young, but she was incredibly beautiful too.

The chandeliers glittered in the ballroom as the orchestra played a waltz. Couples danced and wine flowed as servants offered delicacies on silver platters. Summer felt self-conscious in her ball gown. It seemed almost simplistic in design compared to the rich and ornate fabrics the Francian women flaunted. Her dress was sea green and flowed and followed the curves of her body in soft voluminous waves. The sleeves were soft chiffon that fell to her wrists in transparent folds. The green fabric highlighted her chocolate locks and blue-grey eyes. She felt plain, but there was more than one man who could not take his eyes off her. Little did she realize that the simplicity of her dress simply highlighted her natural beauty.

'May I have this dance?' Tristan asked bowing before her.

She giggled at his gallant gesture and took his hand. She did not notice his admiring glance.

'I'm afraid my dancing skills are not terribly polished,' she said apologetically, 'but if you are willing to take the chance of getting your toes stepped on, then I am happy to oblige.'

'Don't worry, just follow me – my dancing skills are quite adequate,' he smiled. 'My mother insisted we all learn to dance before we came to court.'

'We?' she asked.

'My sister and brother. We all came to court at different times but mother made sure we were well prepared. I think she hoped we would all wed nobility,' he laughed.

'Where are your sister and brother now?' Summer asked as he swirled her around the floor with ease.

'My sister Louise, is married to Lord Dubois. She met him at court and they have land outside of Lutèce. My brother never quite took to Francian court. He believed it to be superficial so he joined the clergy instead. He spends his days feeding the poor and endeavouring to bring equality in Lutèce.'

'Good for him,' Summer said. 'Where do your parents live?' She noticed a brief look of sadness that crossed his face.

'My father stays in a small village near Versailles and my mother is no longer with us. She died a year ago from sickness.'

'Oh I am so sorry Tristan, I truly am.'

He smiled at her genuine concern that she may have upset him.

'All the more reason to show her how well she taught me to dance,' he teased. Summer relaxed in his arms. 'I'm pretty sure she's watching and critiquing my performance.'

Summer laughed. 'What made you join the Musketeers?'

'Becoming someone important at court is rarely possible for commoners, despite Mother's grand ideas. Francian rules are very clear on who joins the nobility. Our family was not considered wealthy enough to purchase titles and lands. That left me the option of becoming a servant or messenger at court and it would have been my lot had fate not looked kindly upon me. I saved the King from an untimely end. It was simply luck that I was in the right place at the right time and I discovered a plot to harm him. As a reward I chose to become part of his Musketeers. He also rewarded me with some land of my own.'

'That is quite a tale,' she smiled. The song came to an end and they moved apart.

'May I cut in and have the next dance?'

Tristan looked annoyed, then bowed graciously when he realized it was King Louis who made the request. One did not deny the King. Summer blushed, unsure what to do in the King's presence. She curtsied awkwardly and then held out her hand. Louis pulled her close and she was sure he could feel her heart hammering against her ribs. She felt uncomfortable being so close to him. He was a married man and she wondered how his wife felt watching him touch her more intimately than he should. She tried to pull away slightly but the king would not release his grip.

'Your time at court is very important to me Summer. If there's anything you need you simply have to ask,' he whispered intimately in her ear.

'Thank you your Majesty, but I am sure that I won't need anything more. You have been more than generous already.'

They finished the dance and Summer curtsied again. She was relieved when he moved off to talk to some of the nobles. She breathed out heavily and moved off the dance floor. She was shaking.

'Can I offer you some wine Mademoiselle,' a young girl approached her.

'No thank you,' Summer responded as the girl stumbled and emptied the goblet of red liquid down the front of her gown.

'Oh Mademoiselle, I am so sorry,' the young girl cried distressed. 'Let me help you get cleaned up. I have ruined your beautiful gown.'

'It's all right,' Summer said following the young girl down the hallways toward her chamber. Once the door was closed the young girl's demeanour transformed.

'You need to watch out Mademoiselle, if you know what is good for you,' she snarled.

Summer looked surprised. 'What do you mean?' she asked trying to remove the wet dress.

'Don't play coy with me. The king is off-limits. He's my lover and I will not stand by while you try to woo him into your bed,' Sophie spat.

Summer was shocked. To learn that the King had a mistress was bad enough, but to be accused of trying to seduce him was another. Indignation rose up as she faced her accuser.

'I have no intention of bedding the King, thank you,' Summer said coldly. 'Now if you would leave, I think I can manage myself.'

THE GOLDEN CAGE

'You've been warned –the next red stain on your dress won't be wine,' Sophie threatened as she left the room.

Summer pulled off her dress and filled a basin with cold water. She feared the red stains would never be removed from the beautiful gown. It felt like a scarlet letter of red wine and she felt sick to her stomach. She felt dirty even though she had done nothing to be ashamed of. It wasn't a good start.

There was a knock at her door. She pulled on a robe and tightened the belt at the waist.

Who could it be?

Tristan stood at her door looking apologetic.

'I'm sorry to disturb you Mademoiselle Summer, but I just wanted to check that you were all right.'

'I'm fine, thank you Tristan,' she said putting on a brave face.

'I saw Sophie spill the wine on you and it didn't look like an accident to me,' he pressed.

So that was her name – Sophie!

Summer was about to brush off the incident as a silly accident, but as she opened her mouth the words refused to come. She turned away, embarrassed as sobs wracked her slender frame.

Tristan was surprised and shocked at her distress.

'Mademoiselle Summer please don't cry. I'm sure that the kitchen will get the stains out of your dress.'

'It's not the stupid dress Tristan,' she sobbed. 'I've not even been at Francian court for a day and already I have been accused of trying to become the King's mistress.'

Tristan frowned. He was angry. He knew that Sophie had indeed not spilled the wine on Summer by accident. Everyone knew she was sleeping with the King and when she saw Summer dancing with Louis her jealousy must have gotten the better of her. Part of him knew how Sophie felt. He too had felt jealous when Louis had pulled her close on the dance floor, but it was inexcusable that the girl had threatened her.

'Here,' he said handing her a handkerchief. She blew her nose and smiled at him.

'Thank you again – it seems you are forever handing me handkerchiefs.'

He laughed and bowed. 'It is my pleasure Mademoiselle Summer.'

'Oh for goodness sake Tristan, stop calling me Mademoiselle – please! We're friends and friends call me Summer.'

'Then Summer it is. Will you be all right now? You know you should not worry about Sophie's threats – I would never let anything happen to you, but she is right about one thing. The King does have his eye on you. Be careful Summer – he has a reputation as a womaniser.'

'Well he can just find some other woman – I am not willing to be one of his conquests,' she said emphatically.

'I'll leave you then,' he said backing up to the door. He took her hand and kissed it before turning on his heel. 'Goodnight Summer.'

She stood at the door for a while after he left, a half-smile on her face.

She had never met anyone who intrigued her quite so much. He was a gentleman, but not in the usual foppish, conceited manner that many Francian men possessed.

THE GOLDEN CAGE

Rather, he was rugged, yet sensitive at the same time. She had to admit that his kiss on her hand had sent butterflies circling through her midriff in gently fluttering waves. She liked him – she really liked him.

⌘

'Did you enjoy that Majesty?' Sophie asked as she lay back on the pillow, her bare breast peeping out of the sheets. Louis smiled satiated.

'There is plenty more where that came from Louis, if you keep your hands off the portrait princess.'

'You're jealous,' he laughed pulling her ankle and revealing a creamy thigh.

'No, I'm just protecting what is mine. I'm serious Louis; I won't be cast aside when a new piece of flesh comes along.'

'You have nothing to worry about Sophie,' he placated. 'Your flesh is more than enough for me.'

What you don't know won't worry you, he thought slyly.

Queen Maria had already berated him for dancing too intimately with Summer and he would have to be careful not to upset the apple cart. He had not realized just how beautiful she was when he had engaged her services. Now he was interested in more than just her painting talents.

If I play my cards right I may just have my cake and eat it too, he thought lustfully.

⌘

35

Queen Maria sat in her chamber – alone again. She played solitaire and it kept her resentment from overflowing. She was not oblivious to the whispers of the nobles and servants in the palace and Louis had humiliated her once again by fawning over the young artist. She was exquisite and Maria knew she could never hope to compete with her youth and beauty. At thirty-two she was older than Louis and certainly not as lithe as the young woman. Pregnancy and childbirth had seen to that. Maria had endured her fair share of pain and loss. The heir to the throne was Louis the Dauphin and he was nine years old. Maria thought of her other children and sadness threatened to engulf her. She had borne three daughters, of which only one had survived. Anne Élisabeth had only lived six weeks after she was born. Maria had been heartbroken at the loss. She thought it might bring her and Louis closer but it did not. She had to face her pain alone. Marie-Anne was born two years later and Maria was delighted – she felt that the Great One had given her another chance. Almost exactly six weeks after the birth Marie-Anne was found lifeless in her crib. Maria was inconsolable.

The Great One must hate me, she thought angrily.

She not only had to endure grief but the rumours that circulated around her daughter's deaths.

Mostly, it was the accusations and insinuations that she had suffocated the infants in their sleep that really ripped her soul. She vowed never to have another child and she kept Louis from her bed for a long time. She could not bear the thought of losing another baby. Finally she had capitulated when Dauphin Louis got sick. She was terrified that he might die too and that there would be no other heir to succeed the king. She decided to put Francia before her own feelings. She had borne Marie-Thérèse three years after she buried her last child. The little girl was a delight to her and Louis and they both doted on the four year old.

THE GOLDEN CAGE

Eighteen months after Marie-Thérèse was born she had given birth to another son, Philippe Charles. He was a handful at two years old and he kept the nursemaids busy and on their feet. As much as Maria loved her children, they were not the companionship she longed for. She yearned for the passion she and Louis had shared when they were first married. They had hardly spent a moment apart and now they hardly ever saw each other. She wanted to be his wife and give herself to him without reservation, but somehow her resentment to his philandering ways prevented her from doing that. She blamed herself for his womanising – she had driven him away with her fears and yet she wished at the same time that his love and devotion had been strong enough to withstand temptation. Occasionally he would visit her bedchamber but it was usually when he was drunk. She had made the mistake only once of going to his chamber at night. She had heard moans coming from within before she could knock. A woman's cries had sent her scuttling back to her own rooms, furious and hurt. Now she dared not seek him out – it was easier pretending that nothing was amiss.

She sighed and dealt another hand of solitaire.

SIX

DISCOVERY

GRIFFIN, Summer and Cam found their new life at court quite an adjustment. It seemed that the palace never slept, that there were secret trysts behind every door – whether they were lover's trysts or politics, it made no difference. It was evident to them that this was a rather superficial place. One's word meant nothing and deceit seemed a normal part of Francian court. It was nothing like the open honesty they had experienced back in their own kingdom. Griffin did not enjoy the backstabbing that seemed commonplace in Francia.

Rulers here may behave this way, but I have no intention of becoming that kind of ruler.

His father was right – he would learn a lot here and equally he would learn what not to do.

Their first week was spent acclimatising to the culture. King Louis wanted Summer settled and comfortable before they began working on the portrait. It had to be perfect. They spent their days doing archery in the palace gardens or taking in the sights of Lutèce. Tristan was delegated responsibility for their wellbeing.

She stood with her arm drawn back, her eye lined up against the string as she aimed at the target. Archery was not difficult for her; after all, her mother had spent many hours teaching her how to shoot a bow. Although she would rather be handling a paintbrush, she was quite at ease with the weapon. She released the string and the

THE GOLDEN CAGE

arrow flew silently and swiftly through the air hitting the target perfectly in the centre.

'Incredible,' Tristan said surprised at Summer's accuracy.

'I'm not just a pretty face,' she teased.

'I can see that,' he whistled in admiration. 'Where did you learn to shoot like that?'

'My mother taught me,' she laughed seeing the surprise on his face. 'Oh yes, she is quite the archer.'

'Remind me never to get on your mother's bad side. So how are you settling in?' he asked seeing the wistful look on her face when he mentioned her mother.

'It's very different from home and I would be lying if I said I didn't miss my parents, but it is an opportunity that I am extremely grateful for.'

'I meant what I said Summer. If you ever feel overwhelmed or afraid here, you just have to say so and I will be there for you.'

'Thank-you Tristan,' she touched his arm gently in appreciation. 'You have made this so much easier for me.'

King Louis watched from the parapet of the castle. He did not like what he saw. He felt a pang of jealousy when she touched the young Musketeer. He would have to get her alone, and soon.

Summer dreaded the end of the week. Cam and Griffin would move out of the palace and into the barracks with the other Musketeers, as their training would begin. She would still see them, as their barracks bordered the palace, but it would not be as often. She would be kept busy enough working on King Louis' portrait and the weather was beginning to turn cold, the trees almost bare of their leaves as winter approached. She felt a little anxious about being left at Francian court alone, especially after her run in with Sophie. She had avoided the young girl ever since her attack after the ball. She had also made it impossible for the King to be alone with her, making excuses every time he tried to get her to take a walk. It was becoming increasingly difficult and her apprehension at having to spend hours painting him increased daily.

At least he will have to sit still and keep his hands to himself while I paint, she thought trying to make light of it.

The Musketeers of the Guard were mostly aristocrats or noblemen. Very few commoners were ever enrolled in the guard. Tristan was the exception after his discovery of the Huguenots plan to kill the king. It was a religious war, both sides fighting for their beliefs to pervade Francia. Cam and Griffin would be the first outsiders to join the Guard and Summer knew it was because her parents had only granted her permission to paint Louis' portrait if the King would train them. She felt the weight of responsibility for all of them. If she angered the King then Cam and Griffin would also suffer. Diplomacy was going to be called for and she was not quite sure how she would juggle it all.

⌘

LIONSGATE

The Great One felt Summer's burden. She was so talented and she would do a magnificent painting of Louis, he was in no doubt about that. What concerned him was her innocent trust in the goodness of all men. She had been thrown into the cesspool of Francian debauchery that was a part of court life. He was pleased that Tristan was there to watch over her. It had been no coincidence that he had

THE GOLDEN CAGE

been the one to uncover the plot to kill the King. The Great One had made sure he was in the right place at the right time. He had great plans for the young man that went beyond being a servant in the palace. Being a Musketeer was just the beginning.

⌘

Cam and Griffin carried their bags on their shoulders. Finally their adventure was beginning. They would become soldiers just like any other musketeer in the King's guard. They stood waiting for Tristan, nervous and excited.

'Here we are,' he said waving to the stone barracks. He ushered them through the solid wooden door into a large room. The stone floor was spotlessly clean and the beds were lined up in perfect rows like wooden soldiers ready for battle.

'You are at the end,' he said indicating the two unmade beds. Each bed had a pillow and some blankets folded at the end. 'There is a trunk to store your things under your bed,' he added.

They unpacked their items and awaited further instruction. Tristan handed them their uniform.

'It's not the full musketeer uniform, but it's what you'll wear while you train,' he said. 'You have to earn the right to wear the full uniform,' he smiled. They changed into the plain blue tabards and trousers each admiring their new attire.

'Let the good times begin,' Cam laughed.

'I hope Summer will be all right,' Griffin said. 'I don't like leaving her alone at court. Some of those nobles seem just a little too lecherous for my liking.'

THE GOLDEN CAGE

'She'll be fine Griffin. Your sister knows how to take care of herself – your mother and father have seen to that,' Cam assured him.

It was true. Isabel and Erik had taught them both how to fight and defend themselves. It was imperative in the times they lived. Summer was not a delicate flower. She may appear pretty and feminine to outsiders, but underneath was a fierce tomboy who loved nothing more than to get out into nature on horseback and let the wind blow through her hair as she stormed the countryside.

'You're right,' Griffin laughed. 'Nobody makes Summer do anything she doesn't want to. Friar Thomas knows that only too well.' Both men laughed loudly as they thought of her exasperated tutor and the number of times she had tricked him.

⌘

Summer took a deep breath – the time had come. She could no longer avoid the King. He had summoned her to the library where they would be working. She checked her reflection in the mirror and brushed a stray strand behind her ear. She wore a simple gown of yellow silk. It had a high neckline and long sleeves. She wanted to wear something that gave the King the impression she was there to work – no revealing necklines or distracting curves for him to gaze at – it was all business today. She picked up her bag that held the tools of her craft and headed out the door. She made her way to the library, praying she would not get lost in all the corridors of the palace. She had been here just over a week and still she found the huge passageways confusing. Finally she found the huge room that housed thousands of books. She knocked lightly on the door before she entered.

'Come in Mademoiselle Summer,' the King said in a lazy voice. He was settled comfortably in a leather wingback chair, his wig slightly crooked on his head. Summer tried not to smile. The French idea of wearing wigs was somehow comical to her – she imagined Cam and Griffin in wigs but the thought of her father, Erik, in a wig almost made her collapse in fits of laughter.

Summer stop it, she mentally chided herself. She curtsied to the King as she tried to regain her composure. She gazed around the room and gasped, delighted to see floor to ceiling shelves stacked with books.

'It's quite something to behold, isn't it?' Louis said seeing her reaction. 'Sit down please,' he said waving at an armchair opposite him. She sat balanced on the edge of her seat as though she were ready to flee at the slightest moment.

'Relax Summer. May I call you that?' he asked although she knew it wasn't really a request but rather a statement she could not refuse.

'Certainly Majesty,' she replied politely.

Polite but official, she reminded herself.

'I thought it would be good to get to know one another before we begin the portrait. Tell me about yourself.'

She was surprised at his desire to make small talk but she indulged him telling him all about her family and life growing up in Griswold. His eyebrows raised when she mentioned her father was from the North.

Was that a measure of respect in his eyes or was it fear?

'I've heard some very good things about your paintings,' he complimented. 'People say that you capture

43

THE GOLDEN CAGE

the heart of your subjects rather than just their appearances. This is the kind of portrait I want – one that shows who I truly am.'

Summer had to halt her thoughts from going into overdrive.

How do you paint a lecherous, pompous ass?

If he could read her mind she would be guilty of treason. She did not fancy losing her head. The rumours of the King's infidelities were well known, although people kept them from the King and his wife. To do anything less would be hazardous for their wellbeing. She squashed down her thoughts and tried to concentrate.

'I will do my best your Majesty,' Summer said humbly. 'Usually I begin a portrait by doing sketches of my subject in their daily life so that I get a feel for who they are underneath their posed persona. This way I can capture your true personality before you select the pose you think is best.'

'What a genius idea,' he said clapping his hands like an overgrown child. 'No wonder your portraits exude more than those we've seen in the last few centuries. How very innovative. Where would you like me to sit first?'

Summer could tell this was going to be tedious. He just didn't understand the concept. She smiled patiently.

'I thought that you could just continue your day as normal and I will follow you around. Getting a natural portrait is possible if you are not overly conscious of posing. Every other king has a posed portrait. I was hoping you would prefer something more natural and unique.' She did not want to offend him.

'Oh,' Louis sounded disappointed. He envisioned himself sitting regally on a throne while she painted him.

Still, her work was phenomenal and unique and he wanted a portrait unlike any other Kings.

'You are the master - or mistress I should say,' he laughed winking mischievously at her hoping she would get his meaning, 'and whatever you think will produce the best end result is fine with me,' he said.

Summer felt her cheeks turn crimson but she refused to give him the satisfaction of her discomfort. She ignored his insinuations.

'Well let's get to it then. Just pretend I am not here and continue as you normally would,' she said formally.

The rest of the day was spent with Louis dealing with court business and entertaining the nobles. Summer sketched furiously trying to get various angles and expressions of the King. By the end of the day she felt exhausted but satisfied with the work she had done. She had captured him with a serious expression on his face, a reflective expression and one of him laughing. It was a good place to start.

'Thank you my dear,' Louis said kissing the back of her hand lingeringly when she was ready to leave.

Summer tried to extract it but he would not let it go. He stroked her fingers intimately, which made her increasingly uncomfortable.

'I will see you tomorrow to begin our portrait,' she said.

'Won't you be coming to dinner in the hall tonight?' he asked surprised.

'No, I think I will have a tray sent up. I have a lot to go over with the sketches and I need to write a letter to my parents.'

'That is a pity, but I understand. Don't let work and no play become a habit for you Summer. I can offer plenty of

THE GOLDEN CAGE

leisure time between our painting sessions,' he said winking at her once more.

Summer felt nauseous. He was outrageous and had the subtlety of a bull in a china shop.

'I am sure I will find time to enjoy other pursuits besides just our work Majesty,' she said curtly.

'Till tomorrow then,' he said kissing her hand again.

Summer could not move fast enough to get away from him. He disgusted her, and the arrogance of the man that he actually believed any woman he bestowed his affection on would fall at his feet in wonder, infuriated her. She had to get away. She raced down the corridor, her skirts swirling around her as she fled. She rounded the corner far too fast, connecting heavily with another coming in the opposite direction, sending her smaller frame flying as inertia came into play. She lay on her back, dazed momentarily, out of breath.

'Summer, are you all right?'

Tristan rushed to her side, becoming aware that the folds of yellow silk he had collided with, contained Summer.

'Nothing damaged other than my ego,' she laughed embarrassed.

He pulled her to her feet effortlessly and she brushed her skirts down.

'You're limping,' he said distraught. 'We should have that checked out.'

'No please, I really am fine. I think I just twisted my ankle when I fell. It was my fault. Can we please just get out of here for a while?'

They went for a walk in the garden - evening was just descending and it was beginning to get colder now that winter was approaching. The frogs and crickets sang in a symphony of sound that became louder as the sun waved goodbye for the day. Pink and orange hues filled the sky in a fiery mass that was breathtaking.

'It's beautiful,' she breathed and he nodded in agreement.

'Yes it is.' He was not referring to the sunset. 'May I ask why were you in such a hurry?'

'I'm not sure I should be telling the King's guard any of this.' She hesitated.

'Then don't tell me as the King's guard – tell me as your friend. You can trust me Summer. I am not like those other nobles who curry favour and then stab one another in the back to win the King's affection.'

'He made a pass at me,' she said indignantly.

Tristan's face reddened. He was angry.

How dare he abuse his power? It wasn't enough that he had bedded half the young women at court – now he wanted his way with Summer too.

Tristan recognized his anger was more than just indignation – it was jealousy that consumed him. He knew right then that this beautiful woman meant more to him than he realized.

'I'm sorry Summer. You have every right to be angry. Many women at court would be honoured to have King Louis woo them – in fact becoming his mistress is a highly sought after position here in Francia, but I know that you are not familiar with this world and the practices that happen at court. I'm glad you got away so fast,' he teased. 'I can tell you Louis cannot run that fast.'

'I was doing so well too, until a handsome young musketeer literally knocked me off my feet,' she teased.

'I'll have to have a word with him then,' he said stopping and taking both her hands in his. 'It is important to me that you are safe while you are here Summer. I will not let anyone harm you – not even the King.'

'Why are you being so kind to me? Why do you even care?' she asked, her eyes earnest.

'I care more than you know,' he said softly staring into her eyes.

He longed to kiss her – to grab her and never let go, to taste her and protect her, but he did nothing, unsure of how she felt about him.

'Besides I gave my word to your brother and cousin that I would ensure your safety.'

Summer felt the moment vanish. She could not understand why she felt such acute disappointment. Perhaps his only interest was to keep his word to Griffin. It hurt.

'We should get back,' she said reluctantly.

'Yes,' he agreed.

Was that disappointment in her eyes?

They made their way back to the palace and he escorted her to her chamber door.

'Goodnight Summer.'

'Goodnight Tristan,' she replied.

He turned away as she opened her door. He had taken three steps when he heard her say, 'Wait Tristan.'

She ran up to him and hugged him.

'Thank you,' she said kissing him on the cheek, 'I care more than you know too,' she said blushing as she ran back to her chamber.

Tristan smiled as he walked back to the barracks.

She cares about me too.

SEVEN

HEART STRINGS

KING Louis was frustrated. He was not used to being ignored by a woman he set his sights on. The more elusive and standoffish Summer was, the more he desired and wanted her. She was driving him crazy. Even Sophie had complained that he was distracted and no fun anymore. He placated her by telling her that he was just tired. She did not believe him. She pouted and withheld herself from him but he didn't seem to care. It made her all the more determined to break his infatuation with Summer.

'You know she is spoken for?' Sophie said when she had once again tried unsuccessfully to seduce him.

'Who?' he said disinterested.

'The artist, of course,' she enthused. 'It's the talk of court – how she has found love here and how happy she is.'

Louis' spirits rose.

I knew she was attracted to me, he thought arrogantly.

It was as though Sophie could read his mind. She saw him sit up and take note of what she was saying. He puffed out his chest subconsciously like a peacock during mating season.

He thinks I'm talking about him, poor fool.

'Oh really? Who is the lucky man?'

'Tristan Chevalier. It seems she is quite smitten with him and they have been spotted taking intimate walks,'

Sophie exaggerated. 'He is rather handsome, I must admit,' she rubbed salt in the wound.

Louis was seething. He waved Sophie out of his chambers using the excuse of a headache. Really his pride had been hurt, and he struggled to deal with the thought of Summer with another man. No one would have her but him – he would make sure of that. Tristan Chevalier may have saved his life once, but that debt was paid. He owed him nothing.

⌘

Dear Mama and Papa,

Life at court continues to shock and enthral me simultaneously. The ball gowns worn by the women must cost a pretty penny and could probably feed a small village. Still, I don't feel completely out of place here although the brazen morals of some of the people at court still manage to shock me. My painting of the King is coming along slowly and I am satisfied with how it looks – which is quite surprising, as you know how critical I am of my own work. Cam and Griffin are having a whale of a time as Musketeers and they both look extremely dashing in their uniforms even though I have been told time and again they are not true Musketeer uniforms as yet. Their training has been intense and I do miss them but I try to see them as often as I can. I miss you both so much and as much as I am enjoying this experience, I long for the day I can see you both again. Take care and au revoir as the Francians say.

All my love

Summer.

She sealed the letter and handed it to her lady in waiting to dispatch. She missed them so much. Life in Griswold was simple and honest and that is what she truly missed. The grandeur and magnificence of this place seemed almost a farce, as though reality was hidden by games of pretence and facades. The only person she truly believed and trusted here, besides Griffin and Cam, was Tristan. Her heart fluttered at the thought of him. She had debated whether to mention the King's inappropriate behaviour to her parents in the letter, but the thought of her father sailing into Lutèce with half of Kaldakinn to confront him made her decide against it. She had to fight her own battles.

A knock at her door brought her back to reality.

'The King requests your presence in his chambers Mademoiselle Summer.'

'His chambers?' she spluttered as though she had misheard. All her bravado at fighting her own battle quickly evaporated.

'Yes, his Majesty is feeling a little under the weather today and thought you could paint in his chambers today.'

Summer did not know what to do. To refuse the King would be an insult.

'I will be there shortly,' she said to the messenger.

She grabbed a shawl and wrapped it across her shoulders covering herself to her neckline. It was ridiculous how she had to dress like a nun to keep his eyes off her. Despite all the tactics she used, he still always made her feel like he could see her body right through her clothing. She resented him for that.

She followed the messenger to his chambers. He ushered her in and then left them together. The door closing sounded like a prison cell clanging shut – its echo a

THE GOLDEN CAGE

final barrier to her route of escape. Summer's heart began to hammer in her chest, fear clinging to her like an unwelcome parasite.

'Don't look so alarmed my dear,' Louis said seeing her discomfort.

'Why are we working here today?' she managed to utter.

'I was not feeling too well and thought some quiet time would enable us to both get what we want.' He left the innuendo open.

'Well let's get to it,' Summer said all business-like as she set down her paints and brushes. It was then that she noticed the large canvas she was working on was nowhere to be seen in his chambers. 'Where is my canvas?'

'All in good time my dear. You are such a workaholic, which I truly admire; but without some fun time and a little indulgence life would be so tedious, don't you think?'

'I have nothing against fun Majesty, but I do believe procrastination is an equally loathsome quality when there is work to be done,' Summer said sweetly.

'Touché,' he laughed. 'I am not chiding you Summer – in fact I have heard that you are certainly having some fun in your spare time. It has come to my attention that a certain young Musketeer of my guard has swept you off your feet.'

Summer blushed. 'It seems the rumour mill in Francian court works overtime Majesty, as I'm sure you are quite aware. Would you have me believe every rumour I have heard here in court,' she subtly insinuated.

It was the Kings turn to blush. 'Of course not my dear.'

'Well then, I wouldn't believe everything I hear if I were you,' she dismissed the rumours.

'Now, are we going to stand here all day chatting or are we actually going to get some painting done?' she challenged.

'I'll have them bring the canvas immediately,' he said resigned.

How has this little slip of a girl outwitted me? She's far more intelligent than I thought.

Summer had managed to deflect the king's advances but it was only temporary. What she did not realise was that she had made him more determined than ever to tame her.

⌘

Cam and Griffin worked tirelessly at their training. They gave everything in the exercises and it left them exhausted at the end of each day. They were even too tired to attend any court functions and so they seldom saw Summer. Griffin felt guilty about neglecting his sister and he kept telling himself that he would soon get used to all the training and would have more time for her in the near future. Even Cam had given up chasing the pretty single ladies at court. They ate dinner, cleaned their boots and muskets each night, then flopped into their wooden beds to catch some sleep before the next day's training. Tristan smiled seeing how fatigued they were. He recalled the early days of training and how exhausting it was. It would get better in a few weeks. In the meantime he would keep an eye on Summer and reassure Griffin of her safety.

He made his way toward the palace, excited to see her. They had agreed to have an evening walk each night after dinner. It was Summer's way of keeping up to date with her brother and cousin's news, although they both knew deep

THE GOLDEN CAGE

down it was far more than that. He waited in the gardens under the wisteria pergola for her. The purple blooms were long gone and the green leaves fell to the stone floor forming a soft green carpet. There was a chill in the air as the season was rapidly changing. Before long this terrace would be blanketed in snow.

'You're deep in thought,' she said as she approached.

'Summer, you look lovely as always.'

She wore a pale ice blue gown that highlighted her dark locks. He wished he could wrap her in his arms and tell her how he felt.

'How is the portrait coming along?'

'Too slowly,' she sighed. 'The king had me summoned to his chambers today to paint and yet there was no canvas to paint on.'

'He did what?' Tristan said outraged. 'Summer, this will initiate all sorts of rumours at court.'

'I know, but don't worry; I made sure he understood it was all business. I had my canvas in no time and the door wide open while I painted.'

Tristan laughed. 'I think the King has met his match.'

'He did mention that he had heard rumours about us,' she said shyly.

Tristan seemed alarmed. 'What rumours?'

'Apparently you have swept me off my feet with your dashing personality and good looks. It's all the talk I believe.'

'Well, have I?' he asked half earnestly.

Summer blushed, looking down at the floor. She had been teasing him but he looked at her with such intensity she knew the moment had shifted from light-hearted banter to something deeper. It was the moment of truth and they both knew it. Their half-hearted flirting over the weeks had brought them to this point.

'Summer?' he took her hands in his.

'Yes,' she whispered so softly that he almost missed it. 'He certainly has swept me off my feet.'

He drew her close as his arms engulfed her, whispering into her ear, 'Not half as much as she has swept me off mine.'

She pulled away and looked at him, surprise on her face.

'I have?' Her wide-eyed naivety only further endeared her to him.

He nodded. 'You couldn't tell?' he teased. 'I'm not just out of my depth Summer. I am drowning in my feelings for you and praying that you will save me.'

She laughed, 'You can climb into my lifeboat anytime – there's room for you.'

He tilted his head and kissed her sweetly on the lips. Her heart hammered and she felt like the one who was drowning. Never had she imagined that a kiss could turn her world upside down. It was pure art – more beautiful than any painting or sculpture she had experienced. She closed her eyes as he explored her mouth, drawing her closer. If this was love, she never wanted it to end. Finally they drew apart, each a little breathless at the intensity of their emotions. She shivered and Tristan wrapped her in his cloak.

'You're cold,' he said pulling her close once more. She rested her head on his chest and shook her head. Her voice was husky 'No, just shaking from happiness.'

He smiled. 'I am a lucky man,' he sighed.

'No, I am the lucky one,' she said looking into his sparkling green eyes. 'I never expected to ever meet anyone like you.'

'Summer, we must keep this a secret. We cannot let our feelings become public knowledge,' Tristan said concerned.

'Why not?' She felt her euphoria evaporate. She wanted to shout her feelings from the castle parapets.

Does he regret this? She wondered.

'I don't believe the King was asking about the rumours out of curiosity. I think he was fishing for information because he has his eye on you as his next mistress.'

'All the more reason for him to believe I am not available,' she said emphatically.

'Summer, he is the King of Francia. If he feels threatened by someone else, he will pursue you even more forcefully. He'll do anything to remove anyone who stands in his way. The king gets what he wants.'

'Are you saying that he would harm you?' she asked shocked. 'Surely he would not go that far?'

'Oh no, he is too devious to do it himself. He would send me off to some battle and let the enemy pick me off. Either way, I would not be able to protect you. For now it is better for him to think the rumours are false. We must find a more secure place to meet. Don't come back here until I send you a letter with a new rendezvous.'

'Be careful Tristan, I could not bear it if anything happened to you.'

He pulled her into an alcove along the ivied wall and kissed her again, lingeringly. She clung to him, excited but afraid at the same time.

'I must go now my love, but I will see you soon.'

EIGHT

DECLARATIONS

Dear Mama and Papa,

So much has transpired since I last wrote and I just had to tell someone. The most wonderful, unexpected thing has happened. I've met someone and I think he is the man I am going to marry one day. He is a Musketeer in the King's Guard, but more importantly, he is kind and generous and is my best friend in Francia, besides Cam and Griffin of course. I think I love him, but for reasons I cannot yet explain, I cannot tell anyone – not even Cam and Griffin. I feel so happy and this wild delirium is about to make me explode so I figured that you are the only people I can tell, as you are outside of Francia. I know you will wish to know more and soon I hope you will meet this man who has made me feel safe and happy here. In the meantime, please keep my secret safe – I will let you know when things change. The King's portrait is coming along nicely and I hope it won't take too much longer. I love and miss you both and send my love.

Summer

She sealed the envelope and set it on the tray for her lady in waiting to give to the courier. It was a weight off her shoulders, being able to tell someone her secret. She and Tristan were meeting twice a week outside of Lutèce at his sister's country house. Lady Dubois was a delight and had agreed to help her brother keep his romance a secret until it was safe for them both. The time they spent together was too short, but Summer looked forward to every visit. She escaped from the castle by using the excuse of needing exercise after hours of painting. King Louis had offered to ride with her but she had told him that she needed time alone to clear her head. Instead he had offered her the use of one of his finest mares. The first week she'd gone riding just to make sure he was not having her followed. She was dismayed to realize that he indeed was having her trailed by one of his men. She and Tristan had no choice but to wait a little longer before they met. It took three weeks before Louis called off his watchdog and they could finally be together.

She stood up from her writing desk, stretched and gazed out of the window across the palace gardens. Despite the beauty of the immaculate garden, there was something too ordered about it all. She wished there were wild flower gardens instead, because those were the type of gardens that were full of surprise and natural beauty.

She moved away from the window. All she wanted was to soak in a steaming hot bath. It had been a while since she'd eaten dinner at court, as she wanted to give Louis a wide berth, but tonight was a special event and he had all but commanded her to be present. A delegation, from Sultan Mehmed, the Anatolian ruler was visiting court and King Louis was hosting a banquet for them. Summer showed reluctance to attend until Louis told her that Cam and Griffin would be there. She wondered if she would see Tristan. It would be hard pretending they were just friends when she would want to touch him, kiss him and be close to him.

Finally she pulled herself from her bath - she could delay no longer. She readied herself for the banquet, pulling on the beautiful gown her mother and grandmother had worn on their wedding day. She loved this gown – it had an incredible story attached to it, and even after all these years, it was still beautiful. She was reluctant to bring it to

THE GOLDEN CAGE

Lutèce, but her mother had insisted she have at least one exquisite gown at court. She thought of the gown King Louis sent to her room as a gift – a beautiful vivid red velvet dress with a neckline that was obscenely low. It screamed wanton woman and Summer was furious with him.

The absolute nerve of the man!

She would not wear anything from him, especially a dress that would have half of Francia believing she was a harlot who was bedding the King. She immediately penned a diplomatic note of appreciation to him declining his generous gift. The messenger looked mortified when she handed the dress back with her note. He looked terrified and Summer felt a pang of guilt at putting him in such a precarious position.

She looked at her reflection admiring the beautiful gown she wore. The sleeves fell in waves to her arms and the silver thread that ran up from the bottom sparkled in the light, the embroidered butterflies dancing on the soft fabric. She felt beautiful in this gown. Her hair fell in waves around her shoulders and she pulled the sides back and fastened it with a slide. She thought of Tristan and the stolen moments they shared – somehow it gave her courage to endure the evening.

⌘

The banquet was a lavish affair and Summer could not help noticing that Louis had sandwiched her between himself and the emissary of the Anatolian Sultan. She felt isolated from her family, as Cam and Griffin were placed further down the table. She was annoyed – King Louis had enticed her to this banquet by inviting her brother and cousin and yet it was clear that he didn't really want her spending time with them. Tristan was there, but he was placed at the furthest point from her and she wondered if the King were making a point.

Well I won't give him any reason to question our relationship.

'You did not like my gift?' Louis said leaning over toward Summer, whispering in her ear.

Summer blushed, quite aware of what it must look like to others watching them. She pulled back slightly to break any intimacy.

'Not at all Majesty, the dress was truly one of a kind,' she replied politely, *that only a courtesan would wear,* she thought. 'It is my policy not to accept gifts from those I am commissioned by. The agreed upon payment before I begin a work is all I will take once the painting is complete. My father taught me to keep business as business and it is a rule I never break.'

'I see,' he said sullenly, then he smiled, changing tactics. 'I am not disappointed though – your gown is simply magnificent, unlike any dress I've ever seen before.'

'Thank you Majesty.' She had no intention of elaborating on the beautiful gown – she did not want to share such a personal story with him.'

She felt Queen Maria's icy gaze as she sat on the other side of Louis. Summer felt compassion for the woman. He had completely ignored his wife the entire evening and she could sense her deep humiliation.

She listened, pretending to be interested as the King and the Sultan's emissary discussed politics and art. Only once did she falter when Sophie entered the hall, glaring at her with daggers in her eyes. The King was oblivious. She let her gaze linger toward Tristan more than once and their eyes met across the room. They knew exactly what each was thinking.

'Summer.... Summer, where have you gone off to dear girl?' King Louis said snapping his fingers and bringing her back. Summer blushed.

'I'm sorry Your Majesty, I was thinking about the portrait,' she lied.

'She works too hard – extremely dedicated she is,' he said to the emissary. She did not fool him. He knew she had been gazing at Tristan Chevalier. It irritated him.

Finally when dinner was over she made her escape and sought out Cam and Griffin.

'Summer,' Griffin growled lifting his sister in a bear hug and swinging her around. 'I've missed you.'

'Not half as much as I have missed you boys,' she laughed.

They caught up, sharing their news. Summer decided not to worry her brother and cousin by telling them of the king's advances. They had enough on their minds and after Tristan's warning she did not want to endanger them in any way. It seemed an eternity before Tristan made his way over to them. His conversation and tone did not give anything away, but his eyes spoke volumes. She could see the desire smouldering beneath his lashes and she wanted nothing more than to whisk him away and cover him with kisses. It was pure agony pretending there was no chemistry between them.

It seemed an age before King Louis and the Sultan's emissary retired to his chambers to discuss politics. Summer breathed a sigh of relief – finally she could be herself. She went out into the gardens with her brother, cousin and Tristan. Some of the young women at court followed them, flirting outrageously with the two new musketeers. Cam thrived on the attention – he was a prankster and ladies' man at heart and the women loved his easy-going nature as he teased them. Griffin was quieter and more reflective, but his mysterious demeanour was equally attractive to the women. Tristan and Summer lagged behind the group, watching as the woman fawned over the two men.

'Looks like the boys have their hands full,' Tristan observed.

'I'm sure Cam is loving it, but Griff probably finds it uncomfortable,' Summer said. 'He's always been a bit shy around the ladies.'

'Yes, Francian women can be quite brazen, I assure you,' he laughed.

'Is that experience talking?' she teased.

He laughed and brushed her hand lightly with his before placing it into his pocket.

'I'm only interested in attracting one woman at Francian court,' he said softly. Their flirtation was subtle but powerful.

The party began to get jovial when one of the women suggested paddling in the fountain.

'Are you insane,' Cam shouted. 'It's freezing. That water practically has icicles in it.'

They lifted their skirts and splashed like children oblivious to everything around them, giggling and screaming at how cold it was.

'Are you afraid?' one of them called to the two men on the side. 'We thought musketeers were tough.'

The jibe was taken and before long Cam and Griffin joined them. It was this opportunity that Tristan took to pull Summer into the garden greenhouse. The silence of the glasshouse and the abundance of plants that engulfed them gave them a moment of privacy they desperately wanted.

He pulled her to himself and kissed her, their passion growing.

'You don't know what agony it has been to look at you all evening and not be able to touch you. I wanted to throttle the King when he was whispering in your ear.'

'Trust me I do know,' she replied. 'You had your fair share of ladies swooning over you at dinner,' she teased.

'Oh, so you noticed,' he jibed in return. 'There is only one woman's attention that means anything to me. You look exquisite,' he breathed huskily looking her up and down.

'This was my mother and grandmother's wedding dress,' she said.

'It was? Promise me you'll wear this dress the day you become my wife,' he said earnestly.

'What are you saying Tristan?'

'I love you Summer, and I want to spend the rest of my life with you. Marry me?'

'Yes, yes, yes,' she said breathlessly.

He kissed her again, slowly as though to make their intimacy last longer than their stolen moments.

'Meet me tomorrow at the usual spot.'

'I'll be there,' she said.

They joined the rest of the crowd, putting on their friendship faces once more. Summer felt delirious with excitement – she wanted to be with him and although he had proposed to her, she knew they could not get married until her commission was over and she was away from court. King Louis once again dampened her dreams – he was a petulant child who would throw his toys out of the crib if he could not have his way. So they had another secret to keep – the list was growing ever longer. She could be patient now that she knew how much he loved her. Besides, she wanted her entire family to be part of their special day.

⌘

She carried the letter to the King's chamber. He had instructed her to bring him any correspondence her mistress had; and although she felt guilty for betraying her, she knew her first loyalty had to be to her king.

Now she handed over the letter Summer had written to her parents. He steamed it open, so as not to destroy the seal completely and quickly read the contents of the letter. His face darkened as he read her declaration of love for Tristan.

So she lied to me – her heart is with Tristan Chevalier.

Somehow he knew it, but he had hoped he was wrong. He quickly sealed the letter again and handed it back to the servant. 'Make sure this letter gets delivered,' he said curtly. She took the letter and curtsied as she left.

Louis cursed under his breath. It wasn't simply about having another woman to warm his bed or satisfy his appetite – he could have any woman in Francia to do that. He admitted to himself that Summer challenged him and the more she rebuffed his advances, the more he desired her. She did something to his heart that no other woman had been able to do since he first married Maria years ago. The feeling of passion and desire was so strong that he had to have her. Tristan Chevalier was just in the way.

THE GOLDEN CAGE

He waited for Lucas Beaumont, his trusted confidant. Lucas was a commander in the King's guard, but he also handled things for Louis that would be considered confidential and not entirely ethical. He was Louis' fixer when problems became too great. Lucas had taken care of numerous wenches who professed to carry Louis' bastards and he conveniently got rid of anyone who posed a threat to the king or Francia – quietly and quickly.

'You called Majesty.'

'Lucas, I have some business for you to take care of.'

⌘

Summer kicked the mare into action and headed out the stables. She could not wait to see Tristan. Since he had declared his love for her the previous evening she had hardly been able to eat or sleep. She had barely been able to focus on the canvas and King Louis had eventually called a halt to their session.'

'Your heart is simply not in it today, Summer. Is everything all right?'

'I'm fine Your Majesty. I'm just a little tired after the banquet and seeing my brother and cousin. I got to sleep very late last night as we had so much to catch up on.'

'Perhaps you should go and rest.'

She had been delighted to escape as her mind and heart were in another place.

She'd made a decision and she rode like the wind before she lost her courage.

She did not see the rider that trailed her horse at a distance.

⌘

LIONSGATE

Mac looked down on his beloved great-granddaughter and he wanted to shout out to her, to warn her of the danger following her, but he could not – he was in Lionsgate and had no way to contact her. He had a bad feeling in the pit of his stomach.

'She's not going to be all right, is she?' he asked the Great One.

'It depends,' the wise old man answered. 'People think I am this control freak who has every path and event planned out. Well I'm not, as you know Mac, from your own journey. That Golden book does not have its pages filled – it is each person who writes their own story. Summer will make choices that possibly may affect her, but this is her opportunity to write her own story.'

'But what of the things that are beyond her control – what about the man following her?'

'We all have things that are beyond our control Mac. If I intervene every time an event happens I would not be giving people the opportunity to make their own choices, to grow and believe in their ability to overcome – their opportunity to become better and kinder people. I have to trust those I love, as much as they have to trust me.'

'It's hard watching and not being able to do anything about it,' Mac said.

'I understand how you feel,' the Great One said draping his arm across Mac's shoulders. 'Summer will find her way Mac – as you all did, despite some severe hardships.'

NINE

TENDERNESS

FRANCIA - EARLY WINTER 1671

HE opened the door before she could knock and pulled her in spinning her around. Her face was flushed from the cold and she was breathless. She surrendered against the wall as he kissed her hungrily.

Finally he pulled away gazing lovingly at her.

'Where's your sister?' she asked.

'She's gone to Lutèce for the day; we have the house all to ourselves.'

She smiled, it was meant to be. The decision she had made was right. He took her hand and led her into the parlour. A roaring fire crackled in the hearth and she noticed a tray with two wine goblets. There was crusty bread and cheese on the tray with strawberries.

'Where on earth did you get strawberries at this time of year?' she exclaimed.

'I thought you might be hungry after your ride,' he said seating her on a cushion in front of the flames. 'My sister has connections far and wide,' he said lifting the ripe red berry and teasing her lips open with it.

'Thank you. I'm ravenous and freezing too,' she laughed as she swallowed the delicious fruit.

They ate with gusto and drank a rich red wine. Summer felt herself relax as she began to thaw. She suddenly felt anxious at what she was about to do, but somehow the red liquid gave her courage.

'We can't go on like this,' Tristan said. 'How much longer will the portrait take, Summer?'

'About another moon if I work day and night on it. I wish I could get it done quicker, but there is still so much work to do and I dare not do a poor job. I could barely concentrate today.'

'I fear for you,' he said. 'Louis is honing in on you – I saw it last night at the banquet, the way he looked at you and leaned in to you.'

'I can't bear being around him and I feel so sorry for Queen Maria, but I have a job to do Tristan. Besides Cam and Griffin's training is dependent on me. If I mess this up, it is not only me who will suffer.'

'I know. I'm just being selfish because I want to be with you so badly – to make you my wife,' he said tucking a stray strand of her hair behind her ear.

'I want to be with you too,' she said, 'which is why I made a decision last night.' He waited for her to continue. She looked down her lashes as she spoke softly.

'I don't want to wait.'

'You want to get married now?' he asked expectantly. His heart lurched in his chest. He wanted to wed her more than anything, but he knew that this would enrage Louis and endanger them all. What she proposed was risky.

'Of course I want to wed you, but that's not possible right now. That's not what I mean,' she blushed.

'I don't understand Summer.'

THE GOLDEN CAGE

'I want to give myself to you as though we are married.'

He was surprised by her admission. This was a huge decision for her to make. He felt touched that she would do this for him.

'Summer this is not something I expect you to do. You know I love you and I want more than anything to be with you completely – you drive me crazy and keeping my hands off you is sheer agony; but I am willing to wait for you, no matter how long it takes. I know how important your belief in the Great One is, and I would never do anything to compromise your beliefs. I would rather wait than make you choose between me and your faith.'

She smiled. He truly was one of a kind. She thought she might feel ashamed admitting her desire to make love to him, but somehow she did not. She wanted to be one with him, whether they were married or not. She knew her heart would never change – that she had already given it to him. Marriage was just a ritual to reaffirm what was in her heart already.

'I love you for considering my faith Tristan, but I also believe in living in the moment and enjoying life – this is something I have learned from the history of my family and the Great One. We have no way of knowing what the future holds. Louis has the power to separate us and I am not waiting for that to happen. I understand we can't get married now, and I am fine with that; but I also know that I have a choice to make and I don't want to wait to love you and feel you love me in return. I don't feel guilty about this because I know how much I love you. I know that I want to make every moment we have together count.'

He could see the determination in her eyes, the passion that emanated, and the genuine love that flowed.

'Tristan Chevalier, I don't need a priest to pledge myself to you. I know how I feel - I will love you the rest of my life, I promise never to go a day without declaring my love for you and no matter what obstacles we face, I will fight to keep what we have alive and protect it with all I have. Will you let me give myself wholly to you – my body, soul and heart?'

'I will,' he said a lump forming in his throat. 'I promise you Summer, that I will protect you from anyone who tries to harm you, because without you my life would never be the same.'

He removed a silver medallion from his neck and placed it around hers. 'This is a token of my love for you. My mother gave it to me when I joined the King's Guard as she believed it would protect me. Now, it will protect us both.'

She fingered the medallion. She knew how precious it was to him, the last remnant of his mother's memory.

'I love it. I won't ever take it off.' She kissed him. 'I want to love you the way we should be free to love one another.'

'You are unlike anyone I have ever met - brave and beautiful – sometimes I feel I don't deserve you.'

'Well you do,' she said drawing him closer.

He kissed her with little kisses that slowly deepened as their desire became stronger. He moved to her neck and she groaned slipping her hands into his shirt, feeling his muscles beneath her fingertips. Although she had no experience with a man, she instinctively knew what to do. She felt safe with him, like they belonged together.

'Are you sure Summer?' he asked once more.

'Completely,' she said unlacing the front of her bodice to reveal her sheer undergarments.

She was surprised how in control she felt – perhaps the wine had taken the edge off her nerves. This just felt so right and any thoughts of what her parents or her beloved Papa-Mac would think, left as she gazed at the man she loved.

Tristan spread a rug in front of the hearth for them. Then he pulled his shirt off, revealing the body she had only imagined beneath her fingertips. He watched as she dropped her garments to the floor, leaving her naked.

She's the most beautiful thing I've ever seen.

He swallowed hard and held out his hand to her. She knelt on the rug beside him, shivering.

'Are you cold?' he asked worried about her.

'No, just a little nervous,' she admitted. He slowly began to trace a finger across her shoulders and down to her breast. She gasped.

Tristan held back. He had bedded women before, but none had captured his heart and none were as inexperienced as Summer. He did not want to do anything against her wishes.

'Are you all right?' he asked concerned.

'Don't stop,' she whispered.

He leaned over and kissed her once more as his hands traced a path down her belly. She could feel his desire and she closed her eyes absorbing every moment of this pleasure.

The sensations were delightful as he explored her body and Summer realized why this act had such a powerful effect on a man and woman. The fact that King Louis would cheapen it by using it as a means to satisfy his flesh made her despise him all the more.

How can one give oneself so wholly to another without giving your entire heart and soul? I will never give myself this way to any other, she thought fiercely.

She barely felt any pain as they melded together perfectly and expressed their love rhythmically as they moved in front of the crackling fire. Summer had never felt so complete, so safe and loved in all her life.

⌘

She rode back to the castle in a dream. Nothing would take her joy from her, not even the icy wind that blew. It had been hard to say goodbye when she felt so close to him, and if they had actually been married they would have been starting their life together. She vowed that day would come.

She tethered her horse in the stables and watered the animal.

'Did you have a good ride Mademoiselle?' the young stable boy asked. He always readied her horse for her and he was quite besotted with the pretty young artist.

'Yes, thank you Loys, it was the best ride I've ever had,' she said smiling at her play on words. She felt momentarily wicked.

'You seem different today Mademoiselle, if you don't mind me saying,' he added quickly hoping it did not sound too intrusive.

She laughed. 'I certainly feel different Loys. The world is simply a beautiful place.'

⌘

King Louis was livid. Lucas Beaumont had just delivered the news of Tristan and Summer's rendezvous.

'You're sure she wasn't just visiting Lady Dubois?' he asked hoping that Lucas was wrong.

'Lady Dubois was not at home Majesty. She was in Lutèce today. I have confirmation from her servants who had the day off.'

'So you saw them together?'

'Yes Majesty and it was not simply as friends, if you know what I mean. Mademoiselle Sveinsson and Tristan Chevalier are lovers.'

Louis felt a stab to his heart. He should hate her and want her punished, but instead she had cast a spell on him and now he wanted her more than ever. He had hoped to be her first lover, but that was not to be. He was the King and nothing was inaccessible to him. He would show her what a real man was like between the sheets. He would make sure this ridiculous infatuation with Tristan Chevalier was nipped in the bud.

⌘

She lay in her canopied bed, dreaming with her eyes open, remembering every caress and moment she had spent with him. Her heart swelled at the thought of being his wife one day. She still did not feel any shame at what she had done. How could expressing her love for him be a sin? She could not understand why the Great One would be disappointed at her actions.

Surely showing love is the most beautiful thing in the world – the thing that makes living worthwhile? she thought dreamily.

THE GOLDEN CAGE

As she dreamed of a perfect world full of love, plans were being set in motion – plans that would affect not only her but everyone who loved her.

TEN

SEPARATION

HE could not believe what he was hearing.

How could fate be so cruel?

He stood in front of his commanding officer, Lucas Beaumont. He had just delivered the news to Tristan that there were rumours of a Hispanic attack on the western border of Francia.

'But it's winter and everything will soon be under thick snow. Do you really think they would attack now?' Tristan asked surprised.

'This is exactly why they would attack from the sea and not cross the border on land. The snow is already too thick and we have troops at the Franco-Hispania border. They know we will not be expecting them to attack via the coast when the weather is so poor and visibility so bad. It's why we cannot take this lightly. It's no secret that the Hispanics have wished to extend their kingdom, hence King Louis' alliance with the Anatolians. Even a Hispanic Queen on our Francian throne does not safeguard us from their attack. Queen Maria may be able to find out what they are planning, but it could be too late for that. We need intelligence right now and King Louis has asked for someone he can trust to command the mission. You are that man Tristan. You saved his life once. I would like you to take the young men from Griswold with you. This will be an important part of their training as musketeers and an opportunity for them to learn about reconnaissance. Take two other men with you, so that you can take turns to keep watch. Set up camp along the shores and let us know if any threat is imminent. We have dispatched a man to Spain to keep us posted on their movements. We will let you know when we receive word from him. Just because it is winter does not mean they will not try to catch us off-guard.'

Tristan nodded. 'When do you want us to leave?'

'As soon as you have your supplies and horses ready. There is no time to waste.'

I have to see Summer before I go, he thought numbly as he left the barracks.

⌘

'It is done,' he said to the man sitting at the desk. 'Your problem is taken care of.

'What about the other problem?'

'That too is taken care of. You have free reign,' he smiled at the use of the term.

'I am indebted to you, if this plan of yours works.'

'Oh it will work, I assure you.'

'For your sake, I certainly hope so.' King Louis smiled wickedly.

⌘

She cannot be disturbed as she is painting the King.

This is what Tristan had been told, and he cursed under his breath. He had to leave right away and yet he had been unable to see her. He scribbled a note, his quill

THE GOLDEN CAGE

scratching over the parchment as he hurriedly wrote. Then he sealed it and slipped it under her chamber door. He prayed she would receive it and understand why he had left without saying goodbye. His heart was torn in two – his love and fear for her and his loyalty to Francia.

He headed out to the stables to gather his men for the King's mission. He was glad that Griffin and Cam would be accompanying him. Reconnaissance was often a tedious and lonely mission. It would be good to have friends with him although he worried about Summer being left alone at court. He would miss her and there would be no one to watch out for her.

⌘

She found Tristan's note under the door. She quickly put it into her pocket and exited the room. She knew the letter was important, but for now it would have to wait, as she had to get to the King. She felt a measure of guilt as she heard it rustling in her pocket. She would love to read it, but no one kept the King waiting and he would be furious if he found she had kept secrets from him.

He may be the king, but he's an arrogant, pompous fool at times, she thought as she hurried to find him.

⌘

The painting session was over for the day and Louis had found it difficult to sit still or concentrate. Summer drove him insane with desire - the way she furrowed her brow in concentration as she painted, her tongue resting on the lips he wanted so badly to possess. Her complete

THE GOLDEN CAGE

oblivion to his desire made him want her even more – there was innocence in her that was so appealing, but her desire to flee so quickly each day hurt him.

She's not as innocent as she looks, he reminded himself. Once again she had departed abruptly after their session.

He looked up as Summer's maid-in-waiting entered his parlour.

'You have something for me?'

'Yes Majesty, another letter.' She held out the parchment to King Louis. He noticed Tristan's seal immediately.

'She has not seen this I trust?'

'No My Lord, I found it under her chamber door on the floor.'

'You have never seen this letter, do you understand?' he said sternly.

'What letter are you referring to Your Majesty?'

'Good, then we understand one another perfectly. You will be handsomely compensated for your loyalty.'

'Thank you Majesty,' she said curtsying before she left. Louis opened the letter reading the words that Tristan had penned.

My darling Summer,

I so wanted to see you, but circumstances have prevented that from happening. I have had a continual smile on my face since we were last together – I can't believe that you love me. I am so grateful we had that time together. I regret to tell you that I have been sent away, west of Francia, to scout the shores as there is word that an invasion could be imminent – Cam and Griffin are with me, so do not worry about them should you not see them at court. I may be away for many weeks and the thought of not being able to touch and kiss you weighs heavily on my heart but know that just as we promised I will declare my love for you every single day. You will know just how much I love you every time you look up at the stars and see how vast they are – that is but a portion of my love for you. Stay safe Summer – remember what we talked about, the dangers in court and keep alert – I am not there to protect you and the things we fear are real. I will send word as soon as I can.

All my love

T

Louis scoffed under his breath, *Romantic sop!*

He folded the parchment and placed it into one of his books. Once Tristan was neatly disposed of, he would have ample opportunity to sweep her off her feet. Tristan would certainly try and send word to her and he had to ensure that did not happen. She had to believe that he had forgotten her, that there was no hope for their future. He had the perfect plan.

ELEVEN

SUBTERFUGE

WINTER 1672

TRISTAN, together with his band of men, rode to the coast, west of Francia. There were some places that were more conducive to ships landing on their shores. Tristan knew exactly where the Hispanics would arrive, should they choose to invade. He was still not convinced they would attack Francia in winter. They set up their camp, sheltered by a grove of trees atop a cliff. The snow was thinner here, as they were further south than Lutèce. They could see the bay and ocean for miles as it stretched out, a glistening grey mass of water. They huddled around their campfire preparing their dinner. They drank rich mead to keep warm from the icy air, as a couple of quails roasted over the red-hot coals. Their breath formed clouds of vapour as they talked in hushed tones. So far there appeared to be no signs of an invasion. They took turns through the night to keep watch and stoke the fire. Tristan hoped that this mission would not linger too long. If they did not die of boredom, they would surely freeze to death. His real desire was to get back to Summer as soon as possible. He could not pinpoint why, but he felt afraid for her and the fact that none of them were there to protect her made him all the more anxious. He had to trust that she would not allow Louis to get too close or to put her in a compromising position. He would feel much happier once he was back at court. He would write to her as soon as he could.

⌘

'Where are we going?' she asked alarmed, as Louis ushered her out the palace to a waiting carriage.

'Just a little excursion for inspiration my dear,' he replied sensing her unease. 'You work too hard and today I thought we could go somewhere that will surely inspire you and send your creative senses into overdrive. Besides I want you to meet another creative genius. You will have a lot to discuss with him.'

Summer did not feel comfortable with his idea, but how did one say no to the King of Francia. She noticed two footmen on the carriage as well as three Musketeers who would ride with them.

Surely I will be safe with all these men around – it's not like he can maul me in front of a myriad of witnesses.

She let herself relax when her lady-in-waiting arrived to accompany them on the trip. She had her arms piled high with books as she balanced them carefully. Summer could just see the young woman's eyes over the top of the pile.

'Do you need a hand,' she asked concerned.

'I'm fine thank you Mademoiselle Summer,' she mumbled.
Louis made no effort to help the young girl and eventually one of the footmen helped her by packing the books into a trunk.

'What are the books for?' Summer asked curious.

'Just some of my favourite books I am transporting to a new venue,' Louis said nonchalantly. 'Hop in my dear,' he said taking Summer's hand as she ascended the carriage steps. He climbed in after her and duly flopped down next to her, rubbing his thigh against hers. Summer blushed but pretended to ignore his obvious attempt at intimacy. She straightened her skirts placing the thick fabric in folds next to her to ward off his body. Then she invited her lady-in-waiting to join them in the carriage.

'Thank you Mademoiselle but my place is on the front with the other servants,' she stammered taken aback.

'Nonsense,' Summer said before Louis could agree. 'It is no place for a woman out in the cold air. I insist you sit with us – I could not in all good conscience sit in this carriage in the warmth while you are seated out there freezing.'

The servant looked alarmed, glancing at King Louis awaiting his dismissal.

Louis could barely conceal his annoyance. The last thing he wanted was this servant sharing their carriage, but if he sent her out into the cold Summer would think him a heartless brute. He forced a smile, but his displeasure was not lost on Summer or the young servant.

'Of course you must sit inside with us,' he said trying to appear gracious.

Summer sighed inwardly. She would not have to be alone with him. She shifted over to let the young woman in. Finding creative ways to fend off the king's advances was becoming a full-time job and it was exhausting.

⌘

Queen Maria heard via the grapevine that Louis had left the castle with Summer. Not long after their departure she had seen a second carriage leave containing two trunks.

One was clearly Louis' trunk and the other she assumed was Summer's.

What is he up to now?

She felt sadness and rage overcome her.

How can he leave at a time like this?

Their young son, Philippe Charles had come down with a fever and for the last two days she had fretted over the child's discomfort and struggle to breathe. Not even the palace physician could give her an answer. She had hardly slept a wink but Louis had appeared not in the slightest concerned. She resented that his libido took precedence to their child's wellbeing. She felt her usual disdain for him return. He was a selfish pig as far as she was concerned.

She looked down at the flushed child and the usual dread she felt when one of her children became ill returned in full force. She had been in this place before – too many times and she had the same sick feeling that it wasn't going to be all right.

⌘

The carriage rambled out of Lutèce and Summer felt her anxiety return.

Where is he taking me?

It took a couple of hours before they arrived at a building that took her breath away. It was the most magnificent palace she had ever seen. It stood like a huge stone artwork, rising from the white snow that reflected off its walls. They passed through huge golden gates that reached up into the grey skies.

'Where are we?' she breathed in wonder.

'This is the work of art I was telling you about. Is it not the most beautiful thing you have ever seen? Welcome to Château de Versailles Summer. It's not finished yet, but soon I will be able to move here. Come, you must meet the architect.'

Summer forgot her inhibitions as she explored the many rooms, gasping at the Baroque architecture. She loved the large curved forms, twisted columns, high domes, and complicated shapes that gave the building a personality and presence of its own. King Louis was right – it was an artist's inspiration. She gasped at the enormous glass chandeliers that hung from the roof like embedded jewels.

'This is where your portrait will hang for generations to come Summer. I thought you should know,'

She looked shocked. Of course she knew that her portrait would hang in a palace, but to imagine it would hang in such an incredible building – a palace beyond any other palace, left her speechless and a little intimidated. Her portrait would hang in the same room as the great artist Le Brun's fantastic scenes that were being painted on the ceilings between the arched walls.

'I'm not sure my portrait could do such beautiful architecture justice,' she stammered.

'Nonsense,' he said catching her hand in his. 'I have seen your work and this building will simply be the perfect backdrop for a perfect piece done by a perfectly beautiful woman.' He kissed the palm of her hand intimately as his eyes held hers. She felt breathless, not because she was aroused, but because she felt trapped once more.

'Thank you,' she murmured as she tactfully removed her hand.

THE GOLDEN CAGE

'I thought we could stay here a few days and work on the portrait. I assume that being in these surroundings will unleash your creativity and that with fewer distractions we can get more work done, so I've taken the liberty of having a trunk with some clothes brought from the Palais du Louvre.'

Summer felt sick. She understood his ploy and all Tristan's warnings came flooding to her. He'd duped her into a false sense of security and made her believe they were on a day outing. Now he had turned the tables on her and she had no way of returning to Lutèce. Her fear bubbled and she fought it down. She was a grown woman and she had her rights. Just because he was a king did not give him the right to treat her as a possession. She would not allow it. She was the daughter of a powerful Lord and Lady, not some peasant girl who had to bow to the king's whims. She thought of Tristan and how angry he would be. She'd tried to find him earlier that morning but he was nowhere at court. She had been a little surprised that he had not sent her a message after the day they spent together. Now she worried that he might wonder where she was. She had no way to let him know her whereabouts.

'Do you not think people at court will wonder where we are and talk?' she asked him, keeping her tone even. 'I would hate for Queen Maria to get the wrong impression.'

Louis laughed. 'Let all of Francia talk my dear – I am the King and no one would dare say anything against me.'

But what about my reputation, Summer thought bitterly.

'Besides,' he added, 'It will only be for a few days and I have brought your lady-in-waiting to attest to your safety and retain your reputation.'

Somehow Summer did not believe him.

THE GOLDEN CAGE

She declined dinner with him citing a headache after the long carriage ride as the reason. The truth was that she could not bear to look at him. She was so angry at his deceit. He did not push her. He wanted her, but he was patient – he would earn her trust over the next few days at Château de Versailles. This was his first night in his beautiful castle and it was fitting that Summer was here. She was the mistress he envisioned filling his bed over the years to come at Versailles. This was just the beginning. He would bide his time.

⌘

Summer gazed out her window at the stars – they were so bright out here, away from the city lights of Lutèce. She felt just like one of them – one lost in millions of others. For the first time since she arrived in Francia, she felt alone and isolated. She shivered.

Tristan, are you wondering where I am? I'm afraid my love, Louis is closing in like a lone wolf.

She remembered her vow to him.

'I love you,' she whispered to the night sky. Every day I will declare how much I love you.'

She pulled the shutter closed and climbed into the huge canopied bed. She still felt lonely and afraid.

⌘

Summer woke, frightened and unsure of what had disturbed her. Her heart hammered in her chest as her brain tried to recall what she had been dreaming about. A clock ticked in the background, its rhythmic noise sounding eerily loud in the quiet room. She willed herself to turn her head, to challenge the monsters that hid in the recesses of the room. There was nothing there. She sat up and slowly expelled the breath she had been holding. It was all in her imagination. Nothing was amiss. She felt cold so she reached for her robe that she had placed at the foot of her bed. It was not there. The fear flooded back as she wriggled down beneath the covers, closing her eyes and her mind to the possibilities.

⌘

He'd tried so hard to resist, but he couldn't help himself. He told himself that he was just checking she was safe and sleeping well. He sat at the foot of her bed for quite a while watching her beautiful face as she slept. He wished he could kiss her but he knew it would be a mistake. He held her robe in his hands and then lifted it to his nostrils, smelling her scent and dreaming of taking her to bed. He was not sure when exactly he became aroused, simply that he had, and he knew he needed to leave. He took two steps from her bed before he turned back and snatched up her robe. He needed to sense her tonight, to draw in her fragrance as he relieved himself. Then he silently left her room and headed back to his own chamber – a desperate king who had everything, except the one thing he wanted most of all.

⌘

Tristan dozed under the stars around the campfire. He woke alarmed, fear creeping over him. He shivered and he knew it was not from the wintry weather that closed in, nor was it for him and his men. It was for Summer that he feared and he did not know why – only that he sensed she was in danger, and there was nothing he could do about it.

TWELVE

CHECKMATE

GRISWOLD

ERIK and Isabel missed their children. The castle seemed devoid of life and the silence wasn't welcome. Winter was upon them and light snow fell, the bleak landscape mirroring their emptiness. Erik knew Isabel felt Summer's absence – her bright, breezy, almost mischievous personality no longer a part of their day. They had received a few letters from their daughter and she sounded happy. Clearly she had lost her heart to the young musketeer. Erik wished he could be there to protect her and everything in him as a parent wanted to eye the young man out, but he trusted his daughter. She had a level head on her shoulders and she certainly knew what she wanted in life – that was the one trait all the women from Isabel's line shared and it gave him a measure of peace.

'A letter's just arrived,' Isabel beamed as she breezed into the parlour waving the parchment.

She severed the seal, excited to hear from her daughter. It wasn't from Isabel but rather from Griffin.

Dear Mama and Papa,

I have to apologise for the silence but training has kept Cam and I so busy – we've hardly had a moment to catch our breath. Things are going exceptionally well for us both – my only regret is that I don't see Summer as much as I would like to. She seems well and word is circulating at court that her portrait is coming along nicely and is quite magnificent, although knowing Summer she will want it to be absolutely perfect before she is happy with it.

Isabel smiled reading this – Griffin was right, Summer was a perfectionist with her work. She continued.

Cam and I have been given our first assignment and it's an important one. We are being sent out on a reconnaissance mission, as there have been rumours of an imminent Hispanic invasion. This will teach us some valuable skills. I have no idea how long we will be away from Lutèce but do not worry if you do not hear from me for a while. I will send word when I am able. I hope you are both well – I miss you both.

Griffin

'I hope he will be safe,' Isabel worried.

'They are simply scouting and keeping watch for the Hispanics Isabel – he will be fine. He's had valuable training with the men of Kaldakinn and knows how to use a sword. Now stop worrying your pretty little head,' he said reaching for her and pulling her into his arms.

'You're right of course,' she said kissing the giant of a man she had married. He was close to fifty and yet he did not look a day older than forty – his strong frame still muscled and his hair a deep honey blond. He wore his hair shorter now that he lived in Griswold, which Isabel liked. He still had the sexuality of a Northman but without the brutish, fearsome look his kin had. The scar alongside his eye had faded but was still visible – a reminder of their first meeting and the passion that existed between them. She loved him deeply and was so grateful for having the opportunity to make a life with him. It almost hadn't been so and every time she thought of how close she had come to losing him, it left her with an ache in her heart. Losing her first love had been devastating enough, but without that pain she would never have known what joy it would be to be loved by this man. He had been a magnificent father and husband.

'So...' he said keeping her close. 'I have a very good idea how to distract you.'

'Erik, it's the middle of the day,' she laughed.

'There's no time like the present,' he laughed. 'Besides it's not my fault you make it very hard to keep my hands off you. If you weren't so desirable I would be able to get some work done.' He scooped her up into his arms and carried her to their chamber.

'You're impossible,' she giggled, 'but I'm willing plunder.'

⌘

CHATEAU DE VERSAILLES

Summer was exhausted. She slept badly after she'd woken up afraid. She tossed and turned and every little sound had her on edge. She had finally fallen into a fitful doze early in the morning. She struggled to wake when her lady-in-waiting opened the shutters and brought her a breakfast tray.

'Good morning Mademoiselle Summer.'

Summer grunted unappreciatively from under the covers.

'I'm afraid I had to wake you, it is already mid-morning and King Louis is getting most impatient to start the portrait. He's had me packing all those books he brought into his library, but now he has nothing else with which to keep himself entertained so he demanded that I rouse you.'

She sounded apologetic and Summer felt guilty at her lack of graciousness.

It isn't her fault Louis is a spoiled brat.

'I'm sorry Celeste,' Summer said. 'Thank you for the breakfast.'

She pulled herself up and swung her legs over the side of the bed, moving to the fireplace to warm herself.

'I seem to have misplaced my robe. I was sure I left it at the end of my bed but I can't find it. Please see if you can find it for me today?'

'Yes Mademoiselle,' Celeste responded.

Summer ate quickly and then pulled on one of the dresses Louis had brought for her. She was annoyed that none of them were her own; instead he'd obviously had dresses made for her. They all had plunging necklines, although not as vulgarly low as the red velvet dress he had given her for the ball. Still, she would have felt more comfortable being covered a little more around him. It was not that she was prudish – if he were anyone else she would have had no problem with her attire, but Louis did not have the ability to be diplomatic or gentlemanly when it came to staring at a woman's breasts.

She made her way to his library ready to work on the portrait that had been carefully transported with her clothing and paint supplies. He was standing looking out the huge window, hands behind his back. He was not wearing the ridiculous wig he usually did at court. Without it he looked less pompous and effeminate and for a moment Summer was surprised to realize that he was actually rather a handsome man.

'Majesty,' she said curtsying.

'Don't worry about the formalities here, Summer,' he said. 'We are just two friends today.'

'I'm ready to start work,' she said.

'Good, I would like us to finish earlier so that we may go for a walk through the grounds later.'

Summer nodded and headed for her easel. She began to put out her paints. The winter light reflecting through the windows was magnificent – far more translucent than the light at Palais du Louvre. Louis was right about one thing – this place was far more inspirational. She set to work. The faster she finished this portrait the faster she could be with Tristan.

Tristan, I miss you my love.

⌘

Tristan was frustrated. They had watched the Francian shore for more than two days and besides a few fishing boats there had been no indication that the Hispanics were planning an invasion. He gazed out over the ocean through his telescope and saw nothing of concern. He sighed – this was a waste of everyone's time. He should have asked Lucas Beaumont to give him a more detailed account of where this information had come from.

What if this is Louis' ploy to get me away from Summer? No, it can't be – he doesn't know about our relationship. We've been so careful.

Still, Tristan felt a nagging sense that something was not quite right. His gut instinct was to go back to Lutèce, but as a Musketeer he was trained not to question orders and to follow the chain of command. Perhaps it was love that was making him anxious to return – to abandon his usual responsibilities. He fought the urge to find Summer and chided himself mentally.

Focus on the job at hand.

⌘

The evening sky was equally beautiful at the Château - pink and purple streaks painted across an orange canvas. Summer and Louis walked in the gardens that were not quite complete, snow crunching under their boots as they walked. It had been a productive day – Summer completed a large portion of the portrait and she was delighted with how it was looking. She felt happiness overwhelm her despite her circumstances. It would not be long till she could leave court and be with the man she loved. Even having Louis at her side did not thwart her optimism.

'You seem happy, Summer. I'm glad Château de Versailles has that effect on you. It's very important to me that you love this place.' He stopped and took both her hands in his.

'Majesty...' Summer said alarm in her voice.

'Shh, don't say anything. I may be a king, but deep down I am just a man. I have feelings for you and I want you as part of my life more than anything.'

'Majesty, I am flattered but you are a married man.'

She wanted to shout out that she did not love him, that she did not want to be with him, that her heart belonged to Tristan Chevalier, but something told her not to humiliate or goad him.

'Yes I am Summer, but that does not mean that I could not provide you with a very comfortable life of privilege. Maria and I have fondness for one another, as does a brother and sister. I need more than that – I need affection and intimacy with someone who has as much passion as I do. You are that woman. Stay with me in my chamber tonight. I will please you very well.'

Summer almost choked at his invitation.

'I appreciate your invitation Majesty, but I am not an object or someone who would give herself in return for position or possessions. I have reserved my heart for someone very special and I cannot just turn off those feelings.'

Louis sneered. 'You mean that sop Tristan Chevalier? Yes, I know all about your dalliances with him Summer.'

Summer blushed. 'Have you been following me?' she challenged.

'He's not man enough for you. I can show you what a real man is like.' He pulled her to himself, pinning her arms at her sides as his head descended and he claimed her lips. She could smell rich brandy on his breath and she felt repulsed. She struggled against him trying to turn her head away and he laughed into her neck.

'Stop it,' she begged.

'You don't really mean that Summer. I could have your head, your brother's and your cousin's too. Or maybe I should just have Tristan Chevalier killed in battle. It's quite easy enough to organize as king. In fact right now he is defending the border of Francia - a very unsafe place to be. I believe your brother and cousin are with him too.'

Summer was shocked at his revelation. She wanted to scratch his eyes out – she hated him, but instead she went limp in his arms at his veiled threats.

'That's better,' he said leaning in again for another kiss. Summer felt broken. She would do anything to protect the three men she loved the most, even if it meant kissing a repulsive king.

She closed her eyes and tried to pretend it was Tristan kissing her. He pushed her mouth open forcing his tongue inside. Her stomach threatened to heave and she fought down the urge to flee. Hurried footsteps interrupted them. Summer's relief was tangible. Louis pulled away from her as Lucas Beaumont approached.

'I've been looking everywhere for you, Majesty,' he said out of breath.

'What is it Lucas?'

'Queen Maria has sent for you – its Philippe Charles.'

'What now?' Louis said, irritated at Lucas' intervention.

'You are needed back at Palais du Louvre. The child did not survive the night. Queen Maria is distraught.'

Louis was torn in two. On one hand he was shocked to hear that his youngest son had succumbed to his chest infection, but on the other hand he did not want to leave Summer, not when he was making headway. His desire was rampant and he growled in frustration.

Damn the universe!

'Louis,' Lucas said seeing the man's indecision. He could read his king like a book. Louis was essentially selfish to the core. He had to be told what to do in this circumstance or he would make the wrong choice. 'You must return with me. The people will not look kindly on you as king if you desert Queen Maria at a time like this.'

Louis sighed. Lucas was right – he could not alienate his people. They might overlook his indiscretions, but if he put a mistress before his own son and wife they would not be so forgiving.

'All right let's go.' He turned to Summer. 'Don't forget what I said, we'll continue this back in Lutèce. You will return tomorrow with your lady-in-waiting, as it's too late for you to travel now. A carriage will be sent for you in the morning.'

Lucas and Louis left hurriedly and Summer sank down on a nearby stone wall, her knees weak. She felt mixed emotions. She felt desperately sorry for Queen Maria and even a little for Louis, but at the same time she loathed the man. He was rude, arrogant and selfish. She was grateful for the reprieve though – if Lucas had not arrived she dreaded what the night may have held for her. This was not over though; she had to get away from him. She would work through the night and get his portrait finished. It was her only option. He'd pushed her into a corner and now it was time to fight back.

⌘

LIONSGATE

Mac looked down on his great-granddaughter and he felt angry.

How dare he force himself upon her!

'Get away from there Summerbee, before it's too late.

He wished he could communicate with her – to make her realize her life was in danger. Perhaps the Great One could send her a sign.

She worked through the night like a woman crazed. Finally she laid her paintbrush down, satisfied with the huge canvas before her. It was one of the most magnificent works she had ever done. King Louis would be delighted with it. Her desire to get it done and to see Tristan again had given her the motivation she needed. She should feel exhausted physically, yet all she could feel was euphoria at the completed work. She knew she should catch a few hours of sleep before morning, but emotionally she was too wound up. It had been quite a day and Louis' declaration of lust and his subsequent threats had left her body with a fight or flight response. She doubted she would get much sleep. She selected a book of poems from Louis' library shelf and carried it to her chamber.

As she lay under the warm down quilt flipping through the poetry book, a letter fell out of the pages. She did not mean to pry but curiosity got the better of her. She opened the parchment and began to read, gasping at the contents; her anger fuelled again as she read the words. She felt something else too – terrible fear.

THIRTEEN

MOURNING

PALAIS DU LOUVRE

QUEEN Maria sat in Philippe Charles' room, dressed in black, her expression cold and angry. It had happened to her again – she had lost another child.

What is wrong with me as a mother? Why have you allowed this to happen to me Great One? Is this your way of punishing me for being a bad wife to Louis?

The questions went around and around in her head and she had no answers for any of them. All she knew was that her heart was crushed again.

Damn Louis. Where is he when I need him most?

The rumours at court had circulated when Louis left the palace with Summer. Maria tried to brush them off but it was becoming increasingly more difficult. She could ignore his dalliances with servants like Sophie – they were merely distractions, but someone like Summer Sveinsson came with a title. There was money and power behind her family name. She was a greater threat to Maria's children. She had seen the way Louis looked at the young woman. It was not simply a passing fancy. She not only wanted to be rid of Summer – she also wanted to hurt Louis the way he had hurt her and if removing Summer from his life was the way to do it, then she would see that it happened.

She picked up her son's little teddy bear and held it to her chest. She would never again hold him close or be able to tell him a story. She wiped away a tear and vowed she would do everything it took to protect the children she still had.

⌘

Summer leaped out the carriage and headed toward the barracks. She had slept on and off throughout the journey back from Château de Versailles. She wanted to escape from her emotions – they were too painful to analyse and if she gave in to them she would explode. She made her way through the alleys lifting her skirts to jump over puddles. She had never quite gotten used to the smells of the streets in Lutèce. She attracted her fair share of wolf whistles from Musketeers who were practising their sword fighting in the courtyard. Finally she entered the barracks headquarters through a large wooden door.

'Can I help you Mademoiselle?' a young Musketeer on duty asked.

'I am looking for my brother Griffin Sveinsson. He's a Musketeer in training.'

'Ah, the foreigner,' he smiled. 'I'm afraid he's not here Mademoiselle. He has been sent on a scouting mission west of Francia.'

'Is my cousin Cameron Hamilton here?'

'No, he too is on the same mission.'

Summer felt nausea well up. Louis had gone through with his threats. She'd hoped that he was just trying to scare her.

He's taken away anyone who can protect me at court. Please Great One, let them be safe.

'Have you had any word from them?' she pressed the musketeer.

'No Mademoiselle, it may be many days before we hear from them. Would you like to leave a letter for them?'

'Yes please, I will have one sent to you after I draft it.'

Summer made her way back to the palace feeling dejected.

Would Louis really be so vindictive and calculating?

She felt a prickle of fear. For the first time since she arrived in Francia she felt things would not be all right. She had no idea what would happen, but her gut told her that Louis would do anything to separate her and Tristan. She would have to do as he asked – she would never forgive herself if her rejection of the king caused their deaths.

Stay safe, all of you, she willed.

⌘

Louis paced up and down his chamber like a caged animal. He felt trapped – trapped with Maria, pretending he was a doting husband and grieving father. It couldn't be further from the truth. He had played this game before with his wife – many times in fact as each of their children succumbed to the chest infection the physician cited as the cause. He was beginning to wonder if this was the truth – perhaps the rumours of Maria suffocating their children were true. One child dying from sickness was a tragedy, two was a coincidence, but more than that left one asking questions. He did not feel bereft at his son's death. The honest truth was that he had little to do with the children other than Dauphin Louis. He had scheduled time with his oldest son, as he had to teach him the ways of being a king as he was next in line to the Francian throne. His thoughts were not with his wife at this time, but instead they were consumed with Summer and the kiss he had stolen from her.

How I want her – in my bed.

He remembered the smell of her robe. She had enchanted him and he would make sure he had her – no matter what the cost.

'May I come in,' Lucas said from the doorway.

'Yes, yes, I called for you. We need to handle that matter once and for all Lucas.'

'Majesty, do you really think this is the time for that? Your Queen needs you and the people will expect you to show some grief for Philippe Charles.'

'This cannot wait Lucas. Maria has dealt with this many times before – she survived then and she will again,' he said callously. 'It has come to my attention that Summer has completed the portrait and she will have no reason to stay, unless I give her one. Do you understand what I am saying?'

⌘

She stood outside his chamber her hand about to reach for the latch. She heard the words he spoke to Lucas.

Bastard she thought angrily.

Every bone in her body wanted to storm in there and slap his smug face, but she knew that she needed to be shrewder – to outwit him at his own game and the only way to do that would be to discover just what his plans were. So she listened, pushing down her anger and planning her revenge.

'Tristan Chevalier has to die. She will never let him go if he remains alive, but it has to look like an accident. We must impersonate the Hispanics. No one must know that we attacked our own men. Do you understand?

'It can be arranged, Majesty.'

Do you have men who will do the job for you?'

'I know of a band of mercenaries that will take on the task, but it will cost you in gold coin.'

'Whatever you need, it's yours.'

'What about the young men from Griswold? If we kill them we run the risk of The Northmen invading.'

'Not if they believe the Hispanics killed them. This could work in our favour Lucas. We could use the Northmen and men from Griswold to weaken the Hispanics in a retaliation attack which would open the door for us to take over Hispania.'

'Queen Maria will be furious Louis, if you invade her country of birth and her people.'

'All the more reason to do this now, Lucas. She is overcome with grief and won't care about the politics.'

'All right Majesty, I will set it up. It will take a few days to get the men together, to organize Hispanic uniforms and to get to the coast.'

'Just do it as fast as you can.'

⌘

She'd heard enough. She left before Lucas found her outside his door.

Louis' evil goes deeper than I imagined. He will kill anyone to get what he wants. I can't let him do this – to use people I love as the pawns. He won't have his way – not if I can help it. I have taken enough of his nonsense.

She drafted a letter of warning to Tristan and prepared to send it through one of the Musketeers. She had to ensure that nothing delayed it and that no one would open it. To ensure this she would need the King's seal but it would be a huge risk getting it.

I'll do whatever it takes, she thought angrily.

She waited till he left his chambers for his daily duties and she slipped in quietly. She rummaged through his desk trying not to disturb papers and documents, praying silently that no one would disturb her. She felt relief when she finally found his seal. She dripped warm wax onto the document and stamped his seal into it, smiling at the official looking document. Then she slipped it into her pocket and headed for the door.

Her hand reached for the latch but before she could pull it, it was yanked from her grasp and she came face to face with Louis. He looked surprised to see her in his chambers.

'What are you doing here?'

Her heart hammered in her chest, threatening to explode. She steadied her voice and said what she thought he would want to hear.

'I need you,' she said reaching for him.

Tristan, Cam and Griffin were feeling the frustrations of reconnaissance for different reasons. Tristan missed Summer and he worried about her safety. Cam just wanted to get back to civilisation to sleep in his own bed, have a square meal and maybe a dalliance with some pretty young girl at court while Griffin wanted to further his Musketeer training. Sitting on a hillside watching the ocean for endless hours hardly constituted training and he felt his skills could be better honed back at the barracks. There had been no sign of any ships and certainly nothing from Hispania. They all hoped that this mission would soon come to an end.

⌘

King Louis was making a rare visit to his wife's chambers. The grapevine worked exceptionally well in Francia, and he knew that the maids-in-waiting were the ones who kept it going. To appear empathetic to his wife he had to go along with the charade of being grief stricken.

'How are you my dear?' he inquired.

'How do you think I am Louis? Our son is dead and my heart is crushed. Why do you care how I feel anyway?' she said bitterly.

Louis wanted to scream but he saw how all his wife's ladies were watching and taking in their interaction.

'Now, now my dear queen, of course I care. You must not distress yourself so or you will make yourself sick. That would not do. We have two other children who need you.'

'They will be fine Louis. I need time to grieve and to let this sadness pass,' she said resigned.

'I have a wonderful idea Maria. Mademoiselle Summer Sveinsson has completed my portrait and it is truly magnificent. Why don't we get her to paint Philippe Charles so that you will always have his picture?'

Get out you monster. It was what she wanted to spit at him, to claw his eyes out as he smugly sat there patronising her. Instead she swallowed her hatred for him and smiled.

'What a lovely idea Louis, but I must decline. I want to remember my sweet child the way he really was and not as some artist's interpretation of him.'

'Think about it Maria – I want to remember our son too and this is a fine way of doing that.'

'I'm tired Louis – please let me rest.'

'Very well my dear, but think about what I said.'

He left the room and Maria sent her ladies out after him. Once alone she pulled out her little dagger and proceeded to stab her official royal cloak, leaving deep slashes down the beautiful fabric.

She growled as she ripped it, imagining it was Louis' heart she was destroying.

How dare he suggest his whore paint our son's portrait. He does not care about me – all he cares about is keeping her here at court. That will never happen Louis, I swear it, she silently vowed.

FOURTEEN

PLOTTING

THE messenger raced to the west of Francia. He had a letter in his saddlebag from the King himself. It had been implied that it was extremely urgent and that he waste no time in delivering it to none other than Tristan Chevalier. He wondered what was so important. Perhaps the Hispanics were on their way. It was his duty to make sure that whatever this news was, that it reached its destination, sooner rather than later.

⌘

Lucas Beaumont handed over the bag of gold to the mercenaries. There were twelve of them and he briefed them on their task. Together with the gold, he issued each man with a Hispanic military uniform. It had been quite a task to secure them, but money had a way of making even the most loyal of subjects less honourable.

'There are five of them and they must not know you are Francians,' Lucas stressed.

'They will not have time to worry about who we are,' the mercenary leader sneered. 'The job will be done thoroughly and quickly.'

'Be sure to leave one survivor to tell the tale. Make sure it is none of the three men we discussed.'

'You will have word of this in two days. We leave tonight.'

Lucas left the men as they readied themselves for their mission. He hoped Louis was not making a grave mistake.

⌘

Summer was still angry. She thought back to the letter she had found in Louis' poetry book.

It was Tristan's letter to her and he had somehow intercepted it. The fact that he violated her privacy and read Tristan's intimate words infuriated her. More than her anger was fear for the man she loved. Louis was determined to separate them. She was glad that she had finished the portrait and that she could leave court as soon as Cam and Griffin returned – *if they returned.* All she had to do in the meantime was try to avoid Louis. She prayed that Queen Maria would need him in her hour of grief.

Philippe- Charles, you don't know how you have helped me. Rest in peace, she silently thanked the child.

⌘

Tristan was on guard when he heard a horse approaching. He signalled to the men to hide. They all took their positions amongst the rocky outcrop, hidden by brush and foliage. The horseman came into sight, scanning the landscape as though somehow he knew they were there. Tristan let out a whistle. He waited. The horseman whistled back in response. Tristan grinned and then waved to the men.

'It's safe,' he called. 'He's one of us.'

The men scrambled out of their hiding places as the messenger dismounted his horse. He pulled the letter out of his saddlebag and handed it to Tristan who tore it open. His eyes scanned the parchment, his face draining of all colour.

So Louis is going to try and have us killed.

He felt sick to his stomach. He certainly was a clever man using every opportunity to get what he wanted. This had nothing to do with invading Hispania and everything to do with invading Summer. Louis was going to use this plot to win on two fronts.

How could he do this to me? I saved his life once.

Tristan felt betrayed. He loved Francia with all his heart and had chosen to put his king and country above all. After this there would be no return for him – he would have to leave forever, as once Louis discovered his plot had been foiled there would be a bounty on all their heads. He knew how it would play out. Louis would deny their story and instead spin it to the people that they had betrayed Francia to the Hispanics and they would be executed as traitors. Kings had a way of creating stories to suit their own needs. This wouldn't be the first time an innocent person had been accused of treason.

Tristan knew that Louis wanted not only his death but Cam and Griffin's too. *Should I tell them about the plot? What if they don't believe me?* Louis would certainly want a survivor to confirm that the Hispanics were to blame. That would mean one of his fellow men would die if he kept silent. He did not know what to do.

⌘

Summer was surprised to see Queen Maria at her door.

'Majesty,' she said surprised curtsying to the older woman.

'May I come in?' Maria asked.

'Certainly,' Summer said stepping aside. 'I just want to say that I am deeply sorry for your loss.'

Maria was surprised that she sounded so genuine.

'Thank you. Actually that is the reason I have come to see you. Louis wants you to stay longer at the castle and paint Philippe Charles' portrait.'

Summer looked dismayed.

'Don't look so horrified my dear,' Maria said genuinely surprised at the young woman's response.

'Oh I'm sorry Majesty. It's not that I don't want to stay or that I'm ungrateful. I simply miss my family so much. I was hoping to go home,' Summer lied.

'You don't have to pretend with me Summer. I know why you want to leave and I can't say I blame you. When Louis sets his heart on something he is very hard to dissuade. I've seen the way he looks at you and he will stop at nothing to bed you.'

Summer felt mortified by the queen's words.

'Queen Maria, I assure you I have done nothing to encourage him. The last thing I want is to become his mistress. This is why I want to go home.'

'I know, and I can help you, but we have to move before Louis becomes aware of our plan. I will convince him that you will be staying to paint Philippe Charles' portrait. We are having a wake for my poor boy tomorrow. That will be your opportunity. I have organized a carriage to transport you to a southern port. Your brother and cousin will meet you there where you will set sail for Griswold the moment you are aboard.'

'Thank you Queen Maria. I don't know how to repay you, but there is just one other thing,' Summer said cautiously.

'I have not forgotten your payment for the portrait. There will be sufficient gold to compensate you.'

Summer blushed.

Does this woman think I'm such a gold-digger?

'I wasn't talking about payment Majesty. I was talking about Tristan Chevalier.'

Queen Maria laughed. 'So the rumours are true? Yes Summer, he may go with you if he chooses to do so.'

'Thank you. I will be ready.'

⌘

Summer packed a small bag with her paint supplies. Finally she stuffed the beautiful wedding gown her mother and grandmother had worn into it. She was willing to leave everything else to escape Louis, but these few items she could not bear to part with.

She felt relief that Queen Maria had made a way for her to escape. She understood why the woman wanted her gone. She was a threat to her marriage – even as unwilling as she was. She would see Tristan, Griffin and Cam again. She felt a pang of guilt that their training would be cut short due to the circumstances she found herself in, but she hoped they would understand.

Perhaps it will be all right after all.

⌘

The mercenaries rode through the night. They wished to reach the western coast of Francia before first light. Then they would rest a few hours before completing their mission as soon as it became dark again. It wouldn't be a difficult task – after all the men would be totally outnumbered by them and they would be watching the coast, not expecting an attack from the rear. This would be the easiest money they had ever earned.

FIFTEEN

❧❀❧

TRAPPED

THE wake for Philippe Charles was well attended. Church bells rang throughout Lutèce as people crowded the streets in support of their King and Queen. It was the perfect day for thieves and pickpockets to line their coffers as the city came to a standstill. King Louis stood beside his wife who adorned black. He could not concentrate. On their way into the cathedral Maria had whispered to him, 'I saw Summer Sveinsson and she's agreed to paint Philippe Charles' portrait. You were right Louis, it will be a wonderful way to remember him.'

This was music to his ears. Summer would be staying longer and he would have her. She had sent him mixed signals up to this point, but he was certain that she would seek his solace and comfort when she heard that Tristan and her family members were killed by the Hispanics. He would vow to avenge their death and she would be eternally grateful to him. This plot of his would bring them closer.

He looked around the cathedral, searching for her beautiful face.

Where is she he wondered?

⌘

She looked back at the castle as the carriage rolled down the road, relief flooding her soul. She felt excitement at the thought of seeing Tristan again. She had missed him and her love had grown only stronger. Nothing would keep them apart now. She touched the silver medallion that hung around her neck, remembering his touch and kisses the day he gave it to her.

⌘

Tristan shared the contents of the letter with the men, however he did not divulge who the letter was from. He could not take it upon himself to sentence them unknowingly to their deaths. They had been shocked and angry at the King's plot. Anger had turned to confusion, as they did not understand what they had done to deserve it. Tristan felt guilty that he had brought this on them.

If I had only kept my feelings in check, kept Summer at a distance, none of this would be happening.

They readied themselves for the attack – the only thing they had going for them was the element of surprise and they had to make the most of it.

⌘

The mercenaries crept up the hill toward the glowing embers that flickered in the evening light. They had to move slowly as the ground was slippery from the light snow. They could see four men lying near the fire. The fifth had his back to them and kept watch out toward sea. An owl hooted in the distance. The leader signalled with his hands to move in. Slowly they crawled forward for their attack. Within a few metres from their target the unthinkable happened – the earth gave way beneath their body weight. They tumbled into the age-old animal trap, six feet below the earth. They scurried to find their feet, cursing loudly at their predicament, realising they had been outwitted. Tristan and his men ended the attack as quickly as it had begun. They left one survivor who fearfully looked up at them.

'How did you know?' he asked.

'Let's just say that King Louis has his enemies too,' Tristan replied. 'What does he expect from this attack?'

'He's waiting for one of you to return, declaring that all are dead and that the Hispanics are responsible for the attack.'

'It's as I thought then,' Tristan said nodding to his men. He turned away as the two Musketeers took care of the final man. They could leave no loose ends.

'What now?' they asked him.

'King Louis wants the three of us dead,' he said motioning to Cam and Griffin. 'We cannot return or we will jeopardize Summer's safety. For now Louis must believe his plan has succeeded, until we can get her out of Lutèce. One of you two will have to return.'

'I will go,' Pierre volunteered. 'I want to ensure my family are safe if Louis gets wind of what really happened.'

'What if he kills you?' the other Musketeer asked.

'He won't kill me because he needs me to verify his story that it was the Hispanics who attacked us.'

'Be careful,' Tristan said. 'Don't trust him.'

'Don't worry; King Louis betrayed all of us here today. I won't forget that.'

'Then let's head back to Lutèce. I don't feel comfortable leaving Summer there one more minute,' Griffin said.

Tristan nodded in agreement. He was terrified at the thought of Louis discovering that his plan had failed.

⌘

SOUTHERN PORT, FRANCIA

The carriage bumped its way down the rocky road to the crude little port. This was nothing like the port in Lutèce. It was barely a port at all. Still, Summer assumed that Queen Maria had chosen it for its obscurity. She craned her neck out the window but all she could see was inky blackness all around her. The journey had taken most of the day and she felt weary. She would be glad to be reunited with Tristan, Griffin and Cam and even happier to get off these shores.

The carriage finally came to a halt and the door was opened by a tall man with a huge moustache that curled out each side of his lips.

'Come Mademoiselle the ship is waiting for you,' he urged. He seemed nervous and in a hurry to get her out of the carriage.

'Where are my brother and cousin?' she asked. It was deathly quiet except for the lapping water as it licked the ship's hull.

'The captain will speak to you about that. We must get you on board before anyone sees you.'

'My luggage,' Summer said reaching for her bag.

'Leave it, I will get it for you,' he said quickly. Summer followed another man onto the boat stepping onto the wooden deck. She was surprised to see many dark faces looking at her. These men were not Francians.

THE GOLDEN CAGE

'I want to see my brother and Tristan Chevalier,' she declared loudly. She could not squash the feeling of anxiety that filled her belly. Something seemed strange.

'Welcome aboard Mademoiselle Sveinsson. I am Captain Firat. I see you are surprised that we are not Francians. Don't be alarmed. We are simply helping Queen Maria, as we believe that starting a war with Hispania would be a grave mistake on Louis' part. Since we had planned to sail today anyway we agreed to take you home. We are always looking to increase our alliances with other countries. You provide us with that opportunity.'

'Who are you?' Summer asked.

'I am who I say. I am the Captain of one of the Anatolian ships that brought the emissary of the Sultan to Francia. His ship set sail just a short while ago to return to Anatolia, but as I said, we have offered to help Queen Maria with her dilemma before we return home with a ship full of Francian treasures.'

'Where is my brother?'

'Come down to the cabin – they are already aboard thanks to a warning letter sent by Queen Maria. You will be more comfortable once you are settled in. It will not be long before we set sail.'

He ushered her down into the bowels of the ship.

'This way please.' He opened a door and waved her in. As she stepped over the threshold he pulled it closed and firmly locked it.

Summer spun around, pounding on the door with her fists.

'What are you doing? Let me out,' she screamed. 'Where is my brother?'

'No-one can hear you and soon we will be out at sea,' he replied through the wooden barrier 'I'm sorry but this is what Queen Maria wants.'

Summer slumped to the floor and sobbed.

What's happening? Why is Maria doing this to me and where are they taking me?

She had no answers.

⌘

King Louis was furious.

'Where is she Maria? What have you done?'

Maria stared at the man who was supposed to be the leader of a nation; a man who was supposed to command others and show some dignity. Now he just looked like a frightened child who could not get his own way. She pitied his demise as the great Sun King. Inwardly she gloated that she was the one who had brought him down.

What goes around comes around, she thought bitterly. *Now you know what it's like to have your heart broken Louis.*

⌘

LIONSGATE

Mac was distraught. 'Come away from the Mirror of Time,' the Great One said kindly. 'You will torture yourself if you watch her constantly.'

'She's been kidnapped – did you see that?'

'Yes, she has been betrayed by Queen Maria. Jealously has a way of making even the most rational people do horrific things.'

'Well we need to save her.'

'We...' the Great One laughed. 'Mac you cannot return – you have crossed over to Lionsgate.'

'But Ziah and Aedan cross over all the time.'

'Yes because they are able to – but it is different with those who leave their bodies before they come here. You've had a good life and you've left an incredible legacy – you cannot go back now – your body has long gone.'

Mac knew it was true but he still felt frustrated.

'Well what are you going to do to help her?'

'Nothing right now Mac. Summer is going to learn to help herself as all of you have done as you've navigated your lives. She will discover her true value. Don't worry, there will be people who will help her along the way, I promise.'

'I hope you are right.'

SIXTEEN

UNRAVELLING

ALBORAN SEA

SUMMER felt seasick again. She remembered how awful she felt when she travelled to Francia, but this time she could not escape the cabin to vomit over the side of the ship. Captain Firat kept her confined, except for an hour a day when she was supervised on deck. He was terrified she would throw herself overboard. All she had was a bucket to retch into, and the stench of her stomach contents pervaded every corner of the cabin. She washed her face in the small basin, trying to rid herself of the sour, rancid odour that clung to everything. She did not have Tristan to make her tea or give her a handkerchief and the thought that she might never see him again terrified her.

No one will ever know where I am. I'll never be found.

Her only hope was for Queen Maria to admit what she had done. Maybe if she confessed to Louis she would stand a chance. Louis would do everything in his power to rescue her. She had seen the way he lusted after her.

Please Maria, do the right thing.

⌘

The surviving Musketeer stood before King Louis. His uniform was bloody and torn and he had bruises on his face.

'It was horrible Majesty. They came out of nowhere and caught us completely off-guard. We did not stand a chance. The only reason I am standing before you, is because I had gone off to relieve myself and when I came back everyone was dead – Tristan Chevalier, the two men from Griswold and Pascal. They hit me from behind and tied me up. They instructed me to return here and tell you that they are coming.'

'Who did this to you? They will pay for killing my men. How am I going to explain this to The Lord and Lady of Griswold? The entire Northern clan will come down on us if I don't give them answers.'

'I don't know Majesty.'

'What do you mean you don't know? You must have some idea who they were, what language they spoke. Did their attire or accents not give them away?'

'They wore nothing distinctive that made us believe they were anyone other than Francian rebels Majesty; but I have no way of knowing that for sure.'

'We had word that the Hispanics were planning an attack. That's why you were out there in the first place. Are you certain it wasn't them?'

'The only thing I am sure of Majesty, is that it was not the Hispanics, unless they swam from their homeland. There was not a single ship that crossed the horizon from Hispanic waters.'

Louis sucked his breath in and turned his back.

Dammit, they have played me for a fool, taken my gold and not done the job properly. Without the Hispanics to blame I will have a war with the Northmen and Griswold. Tristan may be dead, but to what end? Summer is gone. This is your fault Lucas Beaumont. His mind raced with all these thoughts.

THE GOLDEN CAGE

'Leave me,' he said to the ravaged Musketeer. 'I need time to think.'

Louis was backed into a corner and he was not going to take responsibility for any of it. Queen Maria's admission to him that she had arranged for Summer to leave the castle after the young girl begged her to help her return to her family left him resentful and angry with his wife.

'She was afraid of you Louis and had no intention of becoming your mistress. What was I to say as your wife when she begged me for help? It would have seemed absurd to encourage her to stay and begin an affair with you. The whole court would have been talking within the week,' she defended. It was her only choice to make him believe that Summer had manipulated her actions. 'You know how fragile I am at the moment Louis. I am not able to deal with Francian cruelty right now. I'm still your queen,' she whined letting an effective tear roll down her cheek.

Louis was forced to condone her behaviour although deep down he wanted to shake her, slap her really hard to vent his anger. He could not, as she made him feel so guilty.

What will I do? he thought.

⌘

Tristan, Griffin and Cam listened to Pierre's account of his time with King Louis.

'He was very agitated when I did not identify the Hispanics as our attackers. He virtually tried to put the words in my mouth.'

The men laughed imagining his frustration. They had agreed not to blame the Hispanics for their disaster. Griffin knew that if word got to his family of Louis' treachery that the entire army of Griswold and Kaldakinn would invade Francian shores. At this point he was not sure that was a bad thing. They might yet need the armies if they could not secure Summer's freedom from Francian court.

'Let's keep it to ourselves for now. Right now King Louis has to find a plausible reason for our attack. That gives us time to decide what to do. We may even be able to negotiate Summer's release with this information. I still have the letter warning us of his intent. If it were released to his nobles and the people there would be an uprising.'

'Who was it who wrote the letter?' Cam asked curious. That was the one thing Tristan had not revealed to them.

'Queen Maria.'

There was shocked silence.

'Why would she betray Louis?' Griffin asked. 'It doesn't make sense.'

'I don't know, but I'm certain she did not want her own people accused of a crime they did not commit. This must stay our secret for now.'

⌘

Louis was concerned. If Summer returned home and told her father that he had pursued her relentlessly, he would be very angry. Then when he found out that Francians had killed his son and cousin, he would assume that Louis had a hand in it. Of course he would be right, but Louis could not allow that happen. War with Griswold and the Northmen would not bode well for Francia. He had to formulate a plan.

'Lucas,' he said to his confidant standing at the door. He looked afraid, almost sickly green, his pallor pasty with beads of sweat on his brow.

You should be afraid, Louis thought resentfully.

'What is it? You look positively ill.'

Lucas entered his chamber and closed the door.

'I have some tragic news Majesty.'

'I already know that your mercenaries fouled up the mission,' he said angrily.

'I am not sure what you mean. The news I have is not about their mission.'

'Well what is it then?'

'Summer Sveinsson's carriage was attacked enroute to the coast. It appears that she has been killed Majesty.'

Louis paled and then held his chest as though he had been stabbed.

'No, that is not possible. How do you know it was her carriage?'

'They found this in the woods near the carriage Majesty.' Lucas held up a dress that had once been truly beautiful. Now it was ripped and bloody. Louis recognized it immediately. It was the dress she had worn to the banquet held in honour of the Anatolian Sultan's emissary. It had been so beautiful that even he could not be angry that she had rejected his red velvet gown that night.

'They also found painting supplies tossed from the carriage.'

'Have they found her body?' Louis asked resigned.

'I'm sorry Majesty, there was the burned body of a female found in the carriage remains.'

THE GOLDEN CAGE

'They burned her to death in the carriage,' Louis said horrified. He turned away as he heaved, thinking of Summer's last moments of sheer terror and agony.

You sent her to her death Maria – your jealousy killed her!

'I need to be alone Lucas.'

After he was gone, Louis cried for the young woman he had developed feelings for. Everyone thought he was a lecherous fool who wanted nothing more than to satisfy his carnal nature. It wasn't entirely true. Summer had something in common with him. They both loved and appreciated art. She was someone he could hold intelligent conversations with. She knew what he meant when he discussed art works and she had an opinion about things. She taught him so much and challenged him to want to know more. It wasn't only that she was beautiful, but that she was unique. He had never met anyone like her before.

I'm sorry Summer. As much as I hate Maria for what she's done, I am truly the one to blame. I am the one who sent you running away. Please forgive me.

It was the first time Louis had ever admitted his guilt, if only to himself. He wiped away a tear that flowed. He had been unable to cry for his son, but now he wept for the woman he would never have.

⌘

'Is it done?'

'Yes, he has seen the dress. Lucas has just come from his chambers.'

'Does he believe it?'

127
THE GOLDEN CAGE

'Yes.'

'Thank you, now perhaps this will be the last time we have to clean up his indiscretions.'

Queen Maria paid her moustached accomplice and returned to her parlour. It was sheer genius getting Lucas to discover the carriage. She had known Louis would send Lucas after Summer in the hope of catching her before she sailed. She had set up the scenario perfectly. Lucas could never find out that she had left with the Anatolians. She knew Louis would believe it, if it came from his own man. It had taken some doing getting a cadaver to burn, but a few silver coins had done the trick. It had saved a poor family the cost of burial for one of their own and given them enough food for their table for the whole of winter. She thought of how close she had come to Louis catching her using his seal in his chamber when she had prepared the letter to Tristan. Her heart had almost stopped when he had opened the door and found her there. She reached out to him pretending to want him, but his rejection had been a slap in the face and had hurt her more than she believed possible. He sent her away citing a headache. This revenge would be sweet. Summer Sveinsson would never be mentioned again at court; unless it was in regard to the magnificent portrait she had painted of the king.

⌘

Summer lay on the bunk bed, pale and clammy. She had a fever and could no longer retch. There was nothing left to give. She felt as though she had vomited her entire soul into that bucket. She lay glassy eyed staring at the rolling wooden walls.

Just let me die, she silently pleaded!

'Land ahead,' a voice echoed from above.

The men cheered, jubilant that their journey was at an end. They could be cheerful – they knew where they were going and what to expect. Summer just felt hopeless.

SEVENTEEN

ASHES

ANATOLIA — LATE WINTER 1672

SULTAN Mehmed stood before his mother, Valide Sultan Turhan Hatice. Even though he was a man, he always felt like a child in her presence. She was a powerful woman, yet politics did not interest her terribly much. She favoured the arts and building projects. However, one area she ruled firmly was the harem. She was head of the imperial dynasty regarding the family and it was her responsibility to ensure there was a male heir to take over the sultanate. She was the one who selected suitable candidates who might catch the fancy of her son and she saw to their education and grooming. It was a vital role and one she took seriously. She herself had come from Ruthenia as a young woman. At twelve she was captured by the Anatolians and brought to the palace. She was groomed as a concubine to the then sultan, Ibrahim. Although he had never married her, she had been given the status of Haseki Sultan, which meant she was one of his favourites. She had played a vital role in preserving the royalty as she had provided Ibrahim with an heir.

Mehmed had ruled Anatolia since he was just six years old. As a result he had given up most of his power to his Grand Vizier, who ruled and made decisions until he was old enough to co-rule. It had been a mutually beneficial arrangement and the Anatolian empire had increased in wealth and power over the years. The Valide Sultan had to protect her son many times from other relatives. It was not

THE GOLDEN CAGE

uncommon for the heirs to be killed as the mothers of each of them jostled for their sons to be made sultan. That was the only problem having heirs from a number of women.

'Your emissary has returned from Francia. Their ship docked last night,' she told her son.

'Good, I trust that relations between King Louis and our country have been further strengthened.'

'They have,' she said cautiously as though she was finding a diplomatic way of broaching another topic.

'What is it Mother? I know you have something on your mind. Did something happen in Francia that has jeopardized our relations?'

'Certainly not. What the King does not know will not hurt our relations. Keeping the Queen of Francia happy is equally important Mehmed.'

'What have you done Mother?'

'Queen Maria had a problem she needed remedied. We simply agreed to help her. I think you will be very pleased in the long run Mehmed.'

'Just make sure this does not ruin our alliance with Francia.'

⌘

Summer was herded from the ship and into a wagon. She could not quite make out where she was, but she knew it was nowhere near home or Francia. The language was foreign and she felt all eyes on her as she climbed into the wagon. She gazed through the wrought iron window bars. The faces all around her were more olive in tone and the dock was alive with fisherman with weathered faces and no teeth. It was warmer here than Francia and there was no snow on the ground.

Where am I?

She felt afraid and completely out of her depth. No one would ever find her here. Her mother and father would believe she were dead. Tristan would think she was dead too.

Great One, only you can help me now.

The wagon began to move and she held on to the side to avoid being bumped and bruised as it rolled. She tried to work out where she was, but she had no clue and everything was so foreign to her. Finally she saw it – a palace, huge with many domes and turrets. The wagon rolled through the huge gates and into gardens that were breathtaking.

Perhaps this isn't anything to be afraid of, she thought hopefully.

The wagon came to a standstill and she waited. Finally the doors were opened and a tall man, with skin as dark as the night, stood in front of her. He nodded his head politely at her and gave her his hand to climb out of the wagon.

'Thank you,' Summer said and he smiled, his white teeth sparkling in the sunlight. He nodded again.

'Where am I?'

He smiled again but kept silent.

Does he not speak?

'He may not interact with the women,' a voice echoed behind him. A strikingly beautiful woman stretched out her hand to Summer.

'I am the Valide Sultan at Topkapi Palace. I will show you to your quarters.'

Finally it dawned on her that she was in Anatolia. Louis often talked about Topkapi Palace. He was obsessed with making Versailles grander than this place. He boasted about it when they had visited the chateau.

'Why am I here? I was told that Queen Maria was sending me home to Griswold.'

'You are our guest and although it may seem foreign to you, you will be very well cared for here. This place has many opportunities for you.'

'I still don't understand,' Summer persisted.

Summer followed the Valide Sultan who provided no further insight. She was more confused than ever. They passed through hallways, the vibrant mosaic tiles stretching from wall to ceiling, arches that were huge forming a canopy in each room. Finally they passed through enormous engraved doors and into a huge room. There were many women of all ages in the room. Some were dancing, some were braiding each other's hair. Still others read books but they all were beautifully adorned and attired, their eyes framed by dark liner and little jewels sparkling on their bright clothing. They stared at Summer as she entered, a few with compassion and but mostly with disdain. Summer smiled nervously but she felt extremely uncomfortable and out of place.

'Come,' the Valide Sultan said sharply. Summer followed her quickly. They entered a bathhouse and the steam rose from the water in hazy clouds.

'Get undressed, we must wash that stench off you.' Summer felt self-conscious once more of the sour smell she omitted from weeks of vomiting at sea. Servants pulled at her stained and torn dress, ripping at her dignity in the process. Despite her desire to be clean, she could not help but feel resentment that all her Mama's hard work to make

133

that dress was being destroyed, and although the dress was damaged she did not want to part from it – it was her last link to her family. As she sank into the hot water her situation dawned on her.

I've been sold into slavery.

She began to cry, softly.

⌘

FRANCIA — PALAIS DU LOUVRE

Tristan waited in anticipation. He hoped that Summer had received his letter. He had given the note to Pierre to pass on to her as he was returning to court at Louis' request.

Please let him find her.

⌘

'I have discovered who was behind the plot to kill you,' Louis said to Pierre. 'I am very disappointed to say that it was one of our own – Lucas Beaumont. He hired mercenaries to kill you in the hope of starting a war between Francia and Griswold.'

'But why Majesty?' Pierre asked. So this was the lie Louis was planning to weave.

'I do not know yet Pierre, but I think it is to do with the young men from Griswold. By killing them and the young painter he has ensured that they will set upon our country and that the Northmen will join them. Francia does not stand a chance unless we stop them by delivering the traitor who began this mess.'

'The painter, she is dead?' Pierre asked surprised.

'Yes, she was taken from the palace and burned in her carriage by Lucas' men.'

Pierre looked genuinely distressed.

'What are you going to do now Majesty?'

'Lucas Beaumont is being arrested as we speak. He will pay for his treachery.'

Pierre felt sick. Lucas Beaumont was not the one behind this plot. He may have set the ball in motion from the King's orders but he was not the mastermind. Now he would die for his loyalty to Louis. Pierre hated the man even more.

Why would he kill the young woman from Griswold? Did she discover his plan? Was she a loose end?

Tristan, Cam and her brother would be devastated to hear this news. He was not sure how he would break it to them.

⌘

Lucas Beaumont was dragged from a renowned Madame's House, half-clothed and protesting. He was thrown into the dungeons of the Palais Du Louvre, accused of treason and plotting to start a war. He was furious at Louis' betrayal.

I'm the last thing standing between Louis and his lies. All the mercenaries are dead and I'm his loose end, the idiot who takes the fall.

To say that he felt bitter was an understatement.

He cursed himself for his stupidity. He should have seen this coming. Only a miracle could save him now. It was his word against Louis'.

⌘

'I don't believe it,' Tristan said grief-stricken. Cam and Griffin hugged each other, too distraught to talk. They had been surprised to learn that Tristan and Summer had pledged their love to one another.

'Why was she in the carriage in the first place?'

'I don't know, but Louis is planning to pin this on Lucas Beaumont.'

'It doesn't make sense. I don't believe Louis would have Summer killed. Us, yes, but not Summer. He wanted her more than anything. Lucas Beaumont would have been following his orders so he would not have touched Summer. Someone else is behind this. I have to find out who.'

'I will ask around. My wife is one of the Queen's ladies-in-waiting. Maybe she can find out something.'

'Thank you Pierre, but don't let her take unnecessary risks.'

'I'm sorry,' the Musketeer said patting Tristan on the shoulder. 'We will find out who did this and they will pay.'

Tristan headed out into the woods. They were hiding on his sister's property. She had promised not to reveal their secret and they were staying in an abandoned cottage in the woods. He needed to be alone, to let his overwhelming grief out. As he crunched through the snow he brushed away tears that rolled down his cheeks. He felt as though his heart had been ripped out.

'Why don't I feel as though you are dead Summer? Surely I would know it in my gut if it were true. Perhaps I'm in denial because it's too painful to admit you are gone, but until I see your body with my own eyes, I will not believe it. I cannot because it will destroy me. I'm sorry I was not there to protect you- I failed you my love,' he sobbed. He muttered to himself as he reasoned with himself. As hard as he tried he could not believe she was gone. Then a thought came to him.

Perhaps this is Louis' way of hiding her away as his mistress. She certainly would not be a willing participant. If he hid her away from the palace then he could force her to comply without any repercussions.

His heartbreak was replaced by fury. This made more sense to him. Louis would never kill Summer, but he would do anything to make her his.

You haven't won yet Louis – I'm coming back from the grave and I will not let you do this.

⌘

ANATOLIA

Summer sat to one side watching the women. She was dressed in pure fine silk, a beautiful magenta colour that fell to her ankles. It was tight fitting showing off all her curves and a cashmere shawl covered her shoulders and head. Her thick brown hair fell in waves, the front pulled back and held in place by a jewelled headband. Her blue-grey eyes were thickly outlined in black liner. She felt like a stranger in her own body. She hardly recognized the young woman they had turned her into. The rich perfumes they had covered her body in assailed her senses making her sneeze periodically. The girls stared at her curiously but none of them approached her. Only one attempted to make conversation.

'My name is Anna,' she said shyly.

'Hello, I'm Summer. How long have you been here?'

'A few moons.'

'How old are you Anna?'

'I am fourteen,' she said proudly.

Summer gasped, shocked. She could tell she was young, but with her face made up she looked older than fourteen. She felt disgusted. She was no more than a child.

'Were you taken from your family?'

'Oh no, my parents sold me to the Valide Sultan. They thought it was a good opportunity for me to make something of myself. One day I will be his wife,' she added proudly. She seemed genuinely pleased to be here, a slave to a man old enough to be her father. Summer shook her head as though to shake out all the insane thoughts that assailed her.

How can this ever be all right? Surely not all these women want to be here, and if they do, then why am I here?

It dawned on her why they had glared at her when she arrived. This was a competition to see who would win the Sultan's favour. Well, they could relax – she had no intention of being the winner of this competition.

EIGHTEEN

DEAD CERTAIN

FRANCIA

'MY wife says it was not Louis' idea for Summer to leave the castle. She overheard a conversation between the Queen and the King. They were arguing. Louis was furious that Summer had left. It was Queen Maria who planned it. My wife believes that she was trying to escape Louis' clutches and Maria organized a carriage to take her to a southern port to catch a ship back to Griswold.'

'Maybe Louis found out that she left and sent someone after her. Perhaps it turned ugly,' Griffin said.

'No Louis had no idea – he was at the wake of his son and could not have sent anyone after her carriage.'

'Then who did this?' Tristan said angrily. 'I know it wasn't Lucas Beaumont.'

'I don't know, but my wife said that Queen Maria received a man in her parlour the day before Summer left and again a day after she was killed.'

'Who is this man?'

'She doesn't know. She's never seen him before at court but she promises if she sees him again she will alert me.'

'Thank you Pierre. I will not forget how you have helped us,' Tristan said.

'Oh one other thing,' he added as he was leaving. 'They have retrieved Summer's body. Louis asked for it to be brought back to the palace. It is in the cathedral being prepared for burial.'

'I have to see her,' Tristan said.

'Do you think that's a good idea? There is not much to see from what I've heard. Don't you wish to remember her the way she was? Besides, if you are seen, it will alert Louis that his plan to have you killed failed.'

'That is a chance I am willing to take.' Tristan said firmly. 'Louis thinks he can just bury Summer and hide the fact that he is equally involved in this mess somehow. He may not have killed her, but he still has blood on his hands. I need to know for certain that it is her body.'

⌘

Griffin had not yet broken the news of Summer's death to his parents. He had barely processed it himself and he did not know how to begin the conversation. It was not something he wanted to write in a letter – he had to tell them face-to-face and right now getting back to Griswold was a near impossibility until they sorted out this mess with Louis. After all, he was supposed to be a dead man. It was ironic that it was his sister who had succumbed instead. He felt sad, that what was meant to be an opportunity for them all, had turned into a tragedy instead. He also felt guilty that he had not protected her better.

I should have been there for her, not half way across Francia on some useless mission. This is my fault. Caring for Summer's safety was the main reason Mama and Papa sent me here.

⌘

Tristan slipped into the cathedral. He pulled the monk's habit further over his eyes, ensuring that he would not be recognised. It was not difficult to secure the clergyman's garb, and although he did not want to alert Louis of his presence, he had to see for himself that Summer was really dead. He moved through the side door of the sanctuary and headed to the rooms where he suspected her body would be. Cautiously he peered into each room as he went, finding nothing but robes and religious paraphernalia. Finally, he came to door that gave him some hope. The large rectangular box was crude and roughly made. Clearly the preparation of her body had not yet begun, as this was the box they would have used for transport. Louis would ensure she had a magnificent coffin as her final resting place. The lid was tacked down with a few nails. He quickly shut the door behind him and jammed a chair under the handle. He did not want to be caught red-handed. He attempted to lift the lid but the tacks held it firmly. He searched around the room for something to pry it open with. Finally he found a sharp silver artefact. He was not sure what it was meant for, but it would do for his purpose. He wedged it between the lid and the box and leaned his weight on it. The tack popped out with a splintering sound as the box shattered along the edge. He did the same all around the box till the rough wooden lid balanced on the box. Tristan took a deep breath, willing himself to open the lid. The smell hit him first – burned flesh, almost a sweet musky smell that made him gag. He forced himself to lift the lid. It was definitely a woman's body – charcoaled and shrivelled. Tristan was surprised at how serene she looked. Her eyes were closed and she looked as though she were asleep. Her hands were neatly folded across her stomach. It was a bizarre picture which set off alarm bells for Tristan. She was about the right height and size of Summer, but still he was convinced it was not her.

Am I going insane? Is this my way of denying that she is gone?

He shook his head as though to shake away any doubt.

Think Tristan. How will you know it's really not her?

It came to him suddenly – he could picture her smiling at him, fingering the silver medallion he had given her.

'I love it,' she'd said. 'I will never take it off.'

He looked at the corpse before him, and his hands moved straight to her neck. A fire as vicious as this one would have melded the medallion into her flesh. Silver did not melt easily and so it should still be intact. He had to swallow hard to stop the urge to vomit as he scratched at the woman's neckline. Her skin felt leathery and crackled at his touch, the black skin peeling under his fingertips.

I'm sorry, he mentally apologized to the corpse. He sighed in relief. *It's not here, there is no medallion. This can't be Summer. She wouldn't have taken it off.*

Something else bothered him too. He was certain it was not Summer, but why would they lie about her death?

Unless it was Queen Maria's way of protecting her from Louis? Perhaps they staged her death. Where are you really Summer?

⌘

Summer fingered the medallion. It was her only connection to Tristan and she felt incredibly sad. They had not even had time to begin their lives together and now the future had been snatched from them. He would never know where she was. The more she thought about him the more forlorn she became.

The other women interacted with one another, but Summer sat alone near the window looking out at the palace gardens. Despite their incredible beauty, she felt trapped and desolate. A hand gently touched her shoulder. She jumped slightly as she looked up. It was the dark skinned man who did not speak. He moved his hand quickly as though afraid she may cry out. Summer saw fear in his eyes. She smiled reassuringly and said quietly, 'Thank you.'

He nodded as though understanding her pain. Maybe she would have a friend after all.

It did not take Summer long to discover the true competitiveness of the women in the palace. Anna was the only person who befriended her and the others made it perfectly clear they despised her and saw her as yet another woman who could potentially win the Sultan's favour. Each day they underwent beautifying rituals that Summer found ridiculously tedious. She felt like a walking perfumery.

They made their way once again toward the baths. It wasn't a long walk to the steaming water and the other women did not seem to care about their nakedness, but she felt extremely exposed and vulnerable. She had never been ashamed of her body before, but this ritual stripped away her dignity and crushed her soul little by little each time.

143
THE GOLDEN CAGE

She felt as though every shred of privacy had been stolen from her, and with that every ounce of control over her own life. Summer shuffled through the mosaicked bathhouse, oblivious to the magnificent architecture that once would have delighted her. She realised something was amiss when she found herself surrounded by six women. A knot of tension settled in the pit of her stomach. She smiled reassuringly, but the women spat in her face. Shocked she wiped the slimy mucous away.

'Please,' she implored, but the women set on her pulling her long hair and flinging her to the paved floor. The tiles were cold on her naked body and she felt shooting pain in her arm as she landed. The women did not relent. They slapped and kicked her as she tried to protect herself with her arms. One beautiful dark-haired woman seemed to direct their aggression, shouting commands to kick and beat her. Finally, after what seemed like an eternity, they held her down as the instigator yanked at the silver chain, ripping the medallion from Summer's neck.

'No, please not that,' Summer begged reaching for the silver necklace, her final connection to a world she knew and was familiar with. The women laughed as she begged, mocking her. The one who had stolen it, picked up a sharp piece of broken tile and held it against her throat. Summer knew she was in trouble.

Why do they hate me so much? I've done nothing to threaten them.

'So, you think Mehmed wants you and that you are better than all of us?'

'No, I'm not better than you. I don't want to be here, I just want to go home.'

THE GOLDEN CAGE

'Yet you are here. If you really didn't want to be here, you would have slit your throat already, like many before you. Now, I guess I will have to do it for you.'

The women held her tighter as she began to struggle. Summer felt sharp, stinging pain under her right ear as the woman moved the lethal weapon across her throat. She whimpered, fearful that her life would end as a slave in some Anatolian bathhouse. She closed her eyes and focused on Tristan and his love.

If I'm going to die I want to be thinking of him and seeing his face, not this woman's.

'Let this be a warning to you all,' the dark-haired woman said to the others. 'I am Mehmed's favourite.' They were the last words Summer heard before she passed out.

Anna entered the baths. The young girl looked shocked, then let out screams that sent the assailants scuttling off to the other end of the baths.

She screamed continuously, panicking as Summer's blood oozed in thick red streams from the deep gash. 'Help,' she screamed louder. She rushed over to Summer and crumpled to her knees beside her lifeless body.

The Keeper of the Baths rushed in at the commotion, finding the two women on the floor. She cursed loudly then too called for help. Summer came to, opening her eyes as she tried to focus on the commotion around her. Anna sobbed in relief as she realised she was still alive.

Where am I, what's happening?

The dark skinned man, came to their assistance. He was forbidden from entering the bathhouse, but this day the terrified screams of the women overrode his fear of reprisal. Immediately he reached for a towel, covering Summer's nakedness and averting his gaze from her body. His eyes locked with hers and he could have sworn he saw

145

THE GOLDEN CAGE

gratitude reflected. He scooped her up and carried her through to the harem, laying her gently on the bed. Then he raced off to find the Valide Sultan.

'Who did this?' the Valide Sultan demanded to Anna. The young girl cowered afraid to say anything. Summer understood her reluctance. Living with a group of women was not easy, especially when you all were competing for the same man's attention. She reached out and touched the young girl's hand, squeezing it gently.

'She did not see who did this,' Summer whispered hoarsely.' She could see the relief in Anna's eyes. She would not put the young girl in jeopardy. Those women would not hesitate to kill her if she talked.

'You should not speak,' the palace physician chided her as he attended to her wound. 'You are very fortunate, if they had cut another inch, you would not be here to tell the tale. They just missed your jugular vein. As it is, you have lost a lot of blood.'

The Valide Sultan was furious. Summer was someone she had handpicked for Mehmed and now she would more than likely have a horrible scar across her neck – she would be imperfect for her son – damaged and ruined. She could never be his concubine – simply an odalisque in the wider harem – a slave and servant. She suspected who the culprit was, and she seethed inwardly. She had hoped Summer would become Mehmed's favourite and produce heirs for him, since his current wife was a spiteful woman with a temper. Even the Valide Sultan feared her.

She called the dark skinned man aside. 'Keep an eye on her. I want you to protect her and ensure she is safe.'

The man nodded. He knew the drill. He would watch over her as she recovered. The Valide Sultan was hoping that her scarring would not be too severe so that she could

THE GOLDEN CAGE

sell her or gift her to another government official. He had performed this duty before, but somehow this young woman stirred his heart – he felt pity for her and something else – admiration.

⌘

FRANCIA

'It's not her,' Tristan said emphatically.

'Tristan,' Griffin said, seeing the hope in the other man's eyes. 'She's gone. They found the dress and her paint supplies.'

'Yes but there was no medallion.'

'What are you talking about?'

'I gave her a silver medallion and she promised never to take it off. It wasn't there.'

'Thieves could have ransacked the carriage after it burned and taken it Tristan.'

'No, there is something else about the body that doesn't make sense. If she were burned alive, she would have been terrified, screaming. She would have fought to get out of the carriage. The body I saw is not the body of someone who died an agonizing death. The corpse is perfectly straight, the face peaceful and the hands folded on the stomach – almost as though the body was dead before it was burned. I looked inside the mouth too, and this corpse has some teeth missing. Summer definitely has all her teeth.'

Griffin and Cam stared at Tristan, shocked at this new revelation.

'So you're sure?' Griffin asked.

'I'd bet my life on it. I think Louis staged her death and has her hidden away somewhere. It makes more sense. Louis desired Summer more than anything, and if he could not have her, it would have driven him crazy. He would never have killed her.'

Griffin and Cam let out a shout of delight and hugged one another, slapping each other on the back.

'So how do we find her,' Griffin asked.

'We watch Louis and wait for him to make his move.'

NINETEEN

BETRAYAL'S STING

FRANCIA

LUCAS Beaumont pulled himself up against the rough dungeon wall. He rubbed the beard that had begun to grow, convinced that some kind of lice had made their home in it. He had been in the dungeon for what seemed like a few weeks awaiting his fate. He'd only had one visitor during this time, and that was Queen Maria. Louis had avoided him like the plague.

The dirty bastard doesn't even have the guts to face me. After all I've done for him over the years.

He had been surprised to see the Queen and begged her to help him. She had been less than sympathetic and even told him that it was his own fault for trusting Louis. It was clear to him that unless Louis had a crisis of conscience there could be no hope for him. He wondered why it was taking so long for Louis to sentence him. Surely the Northmen would be on their way to Francia to avenge the deaths of their young people? It would benefit Louis to have him killed immediately.

If only he had a witness to prove that Louis had set him up, but unfortunately every one of the mercenaries were dead – just as he would surely be in a few days.

⌘

'I have some news,' Pierre said excitedly to Tristan. 'My wife Clara has seen that man again at court. He is Hispanic and apparently a distant cousin of the Queens. I'm not sure why he is in Francia, but he certainly is consulting with Her Majesty. Clara had a servant boy follow him when he left. He is staying at a bordello in the city.'

Tristan slapped Pierre on the back. 'Thank you my friend.'

Hopefully they would find out some information regarding Summer's whereabouts. Their plan to watch and follow the king had yielded nothing, as Louis had not left the castle since his son's death. Tristan was beginning to doubt whether Louis had spirited Summer away to a secret hideout. If he had, he was certainly restraining himself and playing it safe.

The bordello was just as they expected – dark and sultry, with women draped all over the gentlemen of Lutèce. Its smoky, seductive atmosphere added a measure of the dramatic. As they entered, the Madame of the establishment pounced upon them, seeking their coin. She waved over three women who swayed their hips as they moved, their breasts eager to escape from their tight corsets. They draped their arms over the young men, rubbing their bodies invitingly against them. Cam laughed nervously. If Summer hadn't been uppermost in his mind, he might well have enjoyed the attention.

'We are here for information, that is all,' Tristan said trying to shake off the leech that had attached herself to him.

'This is a business gentlemen, and even information will cost you,' the Madame said matter-of-factly. 'If that is not to your liking you are welcome to leave.'

'Fair enough,' Tristan said reaching into his pocket for a bag of silver. 'We are looking for a man who is staying here – he is Hispanic.'

'Ah yes, he is upstairs in his room, third door on the left.'

'Thank you,' Tristan said as they made their way up the darkened staircase.

'Are you sure that will be all?' the young girl who had attached herself to Tristan said seductively as she winked at him and licked her full lips.

'Yes, that's all,' he replied shaking his head as he went up the stairs. 'Who knows what one would catch here,' he laughed as the others followed him. They knocked on the door and waited. A tall man with the biggest moustache they had ever seen opened it.

'Yes?' He looked surprised to see three strangers at his door. They pushed their way in, cornering him in the room. 'What do you want?' he asked nervously seeing no way of escape. They saw fear in his eyes.

'We hear that you were the last person to see Summer Sveinsson. Where is she?'

'I have no idea who you are talking about,' he denied weakly.

'That's too bad then – we'll have to tell King Louis that it was you who had the young woman killed in her carriage. Lucas Beaumont will be set free and it will be you that has his head removed from his body instead.'

The man paled visibly. He looked frightened.

'You have no proof of that.'

'If you think your cousin the Queen can save you, you are wrong. She's betrayed her husband and she knows if

Louis finds out the truth that both your heads will be on the chopping block. Louis would rather protect Francia than start a war with Griswold and the Northmen.'

The man looked terrified.

How did these men know who he was and about his arrangement with Maria?

'I did not kill the young woman,' he finally stuttered. 'She is not dead, I swear to you.'

The three of them looked at each other, delighted their suspicions had been confirmed.

'Where is she then?' Tristan asked. 'If you tell us the truth we will let you go and this will remain our secret. If not, this all goes back to King Louis.'

'I am not sure where she is. All I know is that I met her at a small southern port where I had instructions to place her on a ship at Queen Maria's request. I was to take her belongings and burn them together with a body we acquired from a local family. It was meant to look like she had been attacked by rebels during her escape from the palace.'

'So Queen Maria was trying to protect Summer from King Louis?' Tristan pressed.

The man looked cornered once again. His silence made Tristan feel uneasy.

What isn't he telling us?

'What can you tell us about the ship?' Griffin pressed.

'It was not a Francian or a Hispanic ship, if that is what you are asking. The captain had darker skin, like that of someone from the east. I think I heard him mention his name – a Captain Ferrer.... No Firth.... or it could be Firat.

Something like that anyway. I did not hear everything as I was on the dock but I think he mentioned an emissary.'

Tristan paled as the truth dawned on him. 'Oh dear Lord, it's worse than we thought. Queen Maria wasn't trying to help Summer escape. She is ensuring that Summer will never be a problem or a threat to her children ever again. She has sent her to the sultan in Anatolia.'

'What does that mean?' Griffin asked seeing Tristan's distress.

'Every year, the emissary of the sultan comes to Francia to build relations. You remember the ball we had in their honour? They bring us spices, fabrics and wealth, the king and the emissary discuss politics and in return the king sends women to Anatolia to join the sultan's harem. Usually these women consent to going – it is a way to improve their station in life and to become the wife or concubine of a powerful ruler, but I have heard stories of women being kidnapped and taken against their will. If Summer embarked on that ship, she had no idea where they were taking her and why. King Louis put her in grave danger when he pursued her.'

Griffin turned away, shocked at this news. His sister was a slave in a foreign land. They would need help to get her back if they were going to tackle the entire Anatolian sultanate.

'Everyone knows that King Louis has mistresses Tristan – even the queen. Why would Queen Maria do this to Summer, especially as Summer would never agree to be his mistress? It doesn't make sense to me,' Griffin said.

'It does to me though. Summer's refusal of King Louis' advances would have made him all the more determined to have her. Queen Maria tolerates dalliances with servants as they are no real threat, but Summer is titled and has an

THE GOLDEN CAGE

influential family and that would be a threat to Maria's heirs and position as Queen. We've all heard stories of kings who have beheaded their wives over some frivolous reason to enable them to marry again.'

Griffin realized the truth of his words. 'We must get word to my parents – we'll need help from the Northmen and ships to get to Anatolia.'

Tristan nodded in agreement. There were no Francian resources available to them – if Louis found out they were alive who knows what he would do. He still had to cover his plot to kill them and although he knew Louis would do anything to get Summer back, it would cause instability in Francia if he divided the King and Queen against one another by revealing the truth. He may loathe Louis, but he still loved Francia and his sister lived here with her family. He would not put their lives in jeopardy. It was better if they tackled this without involving the Francian military.

⌘

LIONSGATE

'Finally, someone is going to rescue her,' Mac breathed relieved. He was frantic for Summer and when she was attacked in the bathhouse he thought she would surely die.

'Come on boys, you can do this. Go rescue her,' he cheered Tristan, Griffin and Cam as he watched in the Mirror of Time.

The Great One smiled at Mac's devotion – he loved his great-granddaughter beyond words. Love like that was always a good thing.

THE GOLDEN CAGE

ANATOLIA

Summer gazed in the mirror. She ran her finger over the scar that crossed half her throat, stopping just short of her windpipe. It was beginning to heal, but was still red and tender. She felt ugly. It was not something that could be hidden unless she wore a veil or scarf around her neck. She hoped it would fade with time. Each day she put oil on it to aid the healing process. The dark skinned man had not left her side day or night and although he still had not said a word to her, she felt safe with him nearby. He communicated with his eyes and when she tried talking to him but he simply shook his head and put his fingers to his lips. She wished he would talk to her, as she felt so lonely. Even Anna stayed away from her and she wondered if the women had threatened her. Most of her days were spent drawing and painting now.

She tried to draw Tristan as she remembered him. She used charcoal to capture him – his eyes staring at her full of love and his lips, those beautiful lips she would never kiss again. A tear rolled down her cheek and she brushed it away as the Valide Sultan came into her room. She had separate quarters from the women after the incident, and although she was relieved not to have to watch her back continually, the loneliness was claustrophobic.

'Good morning. How are you feeling today?'

'I am on the mend, thank you.' Summer quickly folded the paper that had Tristan's face on it and placed it on the bench next to her.

'I see you have been drawing,' the Sultan Valide said. 'May I see it please?'

Summer reluctantly handed her the paper. The Valide Sultan looked at it for a while and then handed it back.

'You drew this?'

'Yes.'

'Who is he?'

'A friend.'

'Well, I suggest you forget about your friend as it will only make this much harder on yourself. I have come to tell you that you will be receiving your new name. Usually we wait till a girl has been in the harem a while before she gets her new name, but we want you to feel welcome here and a part of Topkapi Palace. From today you will become known as Süheyla.'

'Please, I want to go home. There are girls who want to be here, but I don't. You told me when I arrived that I was a guest. If that is true then please let me go.'

'I'm afraid it's a bit more complicated with you Süheyla. I cannot jeopardize my relationship with Francia or its Queen. We have an alliance and one young girl is certainly not going to destroy it. You will do well to stop fighting this and settle into life here. When we bring girls here who do not wish to be here, they have to remain for nine years. If they do not find a husband or become one of the sultan's wives in that time, then they are free to leave.'

'Nine years!' Summer exclaimed horrified. 'That is absurd. You cannot force me to be a part of this ludicrous system. It is nothing more than slavery.'

'Nonetheless it is our law Süheyla.'

'Stop calling me that. My name is Summer.'

The Valide Sultan slapped her so hard that Summer lost her breath. She held her cheek, tears welling up in her eyes.

'Don't ever address me that way again. Summer no longer exists, do you understand me Süheyla? Perhaps I should send you back to the harem with the other women,' she threatened. Her tone changed abruptly back to one of concern and care. 'I do however see that you have remarkable talent. If I remember correctly that is why you went to Francia – to paint the King's portrait. I think a portrait of the Sultan would be a wonderful way to take your mind off other things.' She picked up the parchment with Tristan's face, crumpled it and threw it in the fire. 'Yes, you can begin the painting tomorrow.' She exited the room leaving Summer sobbing.

I'm a prisoner; I'll never get out of here.

The dark skinned man draped his arm across her shoulders gently as she sobbed. Summer did not see the look of consternation that furrowed his brow.

TWENTY

❧❧❧

HUNTER & THE HUNTED

GRISWOLD

ERIK and Isabel scanned the message once again.

Dear Mama and Papa,

We find ourselves in rather a tenuous predicament. Francia has not been all that we anticipated and Summer has been taken by the Anatolians. We are without any support from Francia, as they have an alliance with the Anatolians and will not breach it. Cam, Tristan (the friend I mentioned) and I plan to rescue her, but we will need some ships and men from Kaldakinn to support us. The Anatolians are incredibly powerful and this will be no easy task. I am sorry that I could not protect Summer – I feel that I have let her and both of you down. I will not rest till we find her and bring her home to Griswold. Please send word immediately.

We will get her back, I promise.

Love Griffin.

Isabel looked stricken. Summer sounded so happy in her last letter. Tristan was the young man she had mentioned and now she was a slave in some foreign country. She felt anger stir.

Damn King Louis. He had not protected her children as he had promised.

Erik was shouting orders to his guard. 'Get Balfour now,' he barked. 'Don't worry Isabel, we will get her back.'

'I'm coming with you Erik,' she said defiantly.

'No, you must stay here – who will rule Griswold and protect it if we are both gone? We cannot leave ourselves vulnerable at this time. This is Griffin's inheritance and we have a duty to protect it for him. That is what Phoenix would want.'

Isabel felt frustrated. She knew Erik was right and that they could not leave Griswold unprotected.

'One thing Griffin hasn't remembered is that the fjords are frozen and Kaldakinn is landlocked,' Erik said.

'What will you do without the Northmen, Erik?' Isabel was concerned. She knew the Anatolians were one of the strongest kingdoms in the east.

'We have enough ships and I'm sure Struan will give us some men from Ebondeen. After all, it is his son who is heading into Anatolian territory.'

'What about Aedan and Ziah? Do you think they would go with you?'

'We can only ask.'

They drafted a message to Struan, Griffin and to the Great One. They dispatched a rider to Ebondeen and Monwings to Lionsgate and Francia. In the meantime they would ready an army to get their daughter back.

⌘

FRANCIA

Lucas Beaumont stood in the cobbled square, his hands bound behind his back. He was pushed toward the wooden platform by two of the King's dragoons. He felt humiliated. He was one of the best and most loyal musketeers in the King's Guard, now he was being portrayed as a traitor to King and country. He had tried to protest his innocence to the Cardinal when he came to give him his last rites. He had begged the priest to hear the truth behind his imprisonment. Initially the Cardinal had indulged him, but the moment King Louis was mentioned, he had shut down refusing to hear another word. It was in this moment that he realised his fate was sealed. No one would cross the King, not even the Cardinal.

He stumbled up the rickety stairs toward the executioner who stood waiting with the sharpened axe in his hand. He seemed disconnected from the task he was about to do. For him it was just another day at work. The crowd jeered and threw rotten food at him, the juice running down his face as it splattered on contact. It stung, but not half as much as the false accusations they yelled. He held his head high determined not to look ashamed.

I've done nothing wrong he reminded himself.

King Louis watched from the parapet with Queen Maria as Lucas ascended the platform. Before he was pushed down to his knees and forced to lay his head on the huge slab of stone in front of him, he stood his ground and looked up at the King he had served so faithfully. Their eyes locked and Louis could feel the intensity. He was the first to look away. Lucas was pushed down onto his knees. The last remnant of winter fell in light snowflakes turning his hair white. It was ironic really, as he would never grow old as he should, his hair would never turn silver from old age. He laid his head on the icy slab, closed his eyes and waited. It did not take long for the punishment to be enforced. One accurate blow from the executioner ended the life of Lucas Beaumont, severing his head swiftly from his body. He wiped the bloody axe on a cloth and nodded to his assistant who lifted the basket that caught Lucas' head. The crowd cheered, the atmosphere macabre. Pierre watched from afar, feeling sick knowing that Lucas was simply a scapegoat. He would only ever be remembered as a traitor for all of Francian history – all his heroic deeds in the Kings Guard counted for nothing now. It was a reminder that they were all pawns in a game controlled by Kings and Queens.

King Louis and Queen Maria left the parapet, each feeling a prickle of conscience at allowing the man to die for no reason. Neither one of them knew what the other was thinking. They each had their own awful secrets, and each was as guilty as the other.

⌘

Griffin tore open the message from Griswold. He let out a triumphant cry. 'They're coming, three ships and men from Ebondeen and Griswold.'

'What about the Northmen?' Tristan asked. He feared that three ships would not be enough to face the Anatolians.

'No, they cannot sail due to the ice, but Papa assures me that once the snow melts they will join us if necessary. They set sail two days ago and should be here within a few weeks.'

'How long will it take us to get to Anatolia?' Cam asked Tristan.

'I'm guessing it will take close to two moons, if the sea and weather are kind to us.'

Griffin looked dismayed. 'What will they have done to her by then?'

'Don't think about it Griff,' Cam chided his cousin. 'All we can do is find her, and we will. We'll deal with her state of mind once she's safe. She's strong, she'll be okay.'

Cam knew they were empty words to make Griffin feel better. He had heard stories of harems and they weren't always good. He too feared for Summer. Tristan left to clear his head. He had been thinking non-stop of Summer and what was happening to her, and their conversation fuelled his already overactive thoughts. He tried to keep thoughts of her being raped out of his mind, but it just would not leave him. The fact that it would take them so long to get to her ate at him, made him a little insane. It would be almost three moons by the time Erik arrived from Griswold and they then travelled to Anatolia – far too long. They could get there in fewer than two moons if they found a merchant ship to sail on. He knew what they must do. He headed back to Griffin and Cam, determined.

'We can't wait,' he said to them. 'We need to get there sooner. We must leave immediately for the port of Massalia.'

Tristan pulled out a map of the countries that surrounded Francia. 'This is the way we'll go. We'll cut down to south Francia to the port of Massalia. Then we'll catch a merchant ship to Anatolia. It's far quicker than sailing from Lutèce, which would take us around Hispania and into the Alboran Sea. That would take two moons.'

'It's over two thousand miles,' Cam exclaimed horrified. 'It's not a viable option,' he was concerned. 'Horses can only travel so far before they need rest.'

THE GOLDEN CAGE

'Not if we change horses every couple of days. We'll purchase fresh legs to cover the distance as fast as possible.'

'I'm in,' Griffin said, before he could change his mind. He would do anything to find his sister and if they could get to her even one day earlier it could make all the difference.

Cam kept silent. This was sheer madness – they could end up killing themselves before they even made it to Anatolia.

'We'll take our musketeer uniforms which we'll wear once we arrive in Anatolia. We can use the excuse that Queen Maria sent us to ensure that Summer was safely out of the way.'

'You're forgetting one thing Tristan. Griffin and I don't have full musketeer uniforms,' Cam said.

'Leave it to me,' Tristan said. 'Here's some coin – go into the closest village and secure us some horses. Make sure they are fresh and healthy and remember not to be seen by anyone who can identify you.'

⌘

AT SEA

Erik looked out to sea. It had been a long time since he had crossed the ocean to pick a fight. He thought of his daughter held captive and the irony of it hit him hard. Once he had stolen Isabel from her family and taken her captive. He had never regretted it. He had chosen to protect her and keep her safe from harm. He prayed that the Sultan of Anatolia had some conscience. Aedan joined him on deck.

'Thank you for coming with us,' Erik said to the red-haired man.

'Your family means a lot to us,' Aedan replied. 'We've conquered some difficult obstacles and we'll conquer this one too.'

'I hope we are in time.'

'The Great One will assist us. He has promised to send us good winds to aid us in the journey,' Aedan reassured Erik.

⌘

ANATOLIA — LATE WINTER 1672

Summer stood before the Sultan. She was afraid, unsure what to expect.

'Come in Süheyla,' he said kindly. 'You have nothing to fear here. My mother tells me that you have incredible talent and that you are willing to paint my portrait.'

'Yes Sultan Mehmed, it would be my honour.'

The Sultan was of average height but looked taller due to the large turban that sat atop his head. He had a dark beard that covered most of his face, the remainder of it dominated by a fairly large nose. His eyes were small and dark, but Summer could only see kindness in them. His upper lip was swallowed by facial hair. He was fairly athletic which surprised her. She had heard rumours in the harem that Mehmed's favourite sport was hunting.

'If only I were a gazelle,' one of the women had said. 'Then perhaps I could get him to hunt me down.'

'I would not wish for that, he would shoot you if you were a gazelle. Better to be a horse and ridden by him,' another laughed.

The women had giggled.

They also practiced dance routines of a hunting ritual to impress the Sultan in the hope that they would catch his eye. Summer thought it ridiculous at the time and she tried not to laugh thinking about it.

'So how do we go about this Süheyla?'

Summer hated the name, especially since she had discovered it meant gift or sacrifice. It was humiliating.

How dare they treat me as a possession? I'm not his gift and I won't sacrifice my soul for them, she silently vowed.

She tried to smile at the Sultan, to disguise her frustration. 'I will draw some sketches and you can choose which pose you like the best. I've heard that you enjoy hunting. Is this true?'

'Yes, Süheyla, I find it far more invigorating than politics,' he laughed.

'Perhaps I could come with you and do some drawings while you hunt. A painting of your true self is always better than a posed portrait.'

'What a marvellous idea, Süheyla. It would be unlike any other portrait in the palace. Let us arrange to go out today.'

Summer was delighted. It would get her out of the four walls of the harem for a few hours. She missed the freedom she'd had when she could ride Hawk and freely roam the hills of Griswold. She felt a tinge of heartache. The last ride she'd had was after she had spent time in Tristan's arms and given herself to him.

'Do you know how to ride Süheyla or do I need to organize a carriage?'

She snapped out of her reverie. 'I love to ride Sultan Mehmed.'

He clapped his hands in delight. 'Even better,' he smiled.

The Valide Sultan was furious. Mehmed seemed totally taken with the young woman. This was not good.

Süheyla is no longer good enough for my son – she's flawed and the other heirs will mock him.

She would have to keep watch over them and ensure that this portrait was painted quickly and without any distractions. The eunuch would help her.

⌘

Summer loved the ride. For the first time in weeks she felt happy. Her thick coat kept her warm, as did the unusual pants referred to as salvars. They were unlike anything she had ever worn – fitted at the waist but then they ballooned out on each leg till they became tight around the ankle once more. Although it was nowhere near as cold as Francia, the air was still crisp. She wondered what summer was like in this place.

She had lost sense of time on the ship – she knew a new year had come around - 1672, but it appeared that the Anatolians had their own calendar. They celebrated their new year at a different time. Everything here was so foreign.

She wished she had been with her family over their new year celebrations – she missed roasting chestnuts with them, the laughing and bantering as they ate roasted meats in the Great Hall at Griswold, her parents and brother, cousins and grandparents. They would all have been there.

She was surprised when the dark skinned man saddled a horse to join them hunting. She was expecting a retinue of hunters to join them, but it seemed the Sultan wanted to keep the party small. He looked annoyed at the eunuch's intrusion but his mother simply said, 'Ali is to be with Süheyla at all times. It is for her safety right now.'

At least she knew his name now. *Ali.* Summer felt relieved that she would not be alone with the Sultan.

Once they had found their target, a beautiful gazelle, the Sultan pulled out his weapon – a large rifle. Summer expected him to hunt with a bow and arrow, as her kinsmen did. She felt sorry for the beautiful creature. It did not stand a chance against this weapon. She reminded herself that she was not here to judge – simply to draw. She scribbled furiously as he took aim. She almost jumped out of her skin when he fired, the loud bang echoing through the undergrowth. The gazelle dropped to the earth. He smiled triumphantly at her and she tried to look excited for him but her stomach turned in disgust.

Just another egotistical, powerful ruler exerting his manhood.

She was by no means against hunting as a food source, but this creature had no chance to escape. The rifle enabled him to stand a good distance from his target and take aim. Where was the sport in that?

Ali had to carry the gazelle back to the palace. He hoisted the animal across the back of his saddle, tying it down securely. Then they started their journey back to the turreted prison. On one hand it had been amazing to escape the confines of the palace, but on the other Summer felt trapped even more. All she wanted to do was to go home!

As they handed their horses over to the stable hands, she became aware of the Sultan standing right behind her. She turned and faced him squarely.

I will not be the victim. These people do not own me, she thought firmly.

'Süheyla, I would be honoured if you would join me for dinner?'

Summer momentarily looked as alarmed as the dead gazelle had just before it was shot. The poor creature had known something was not right, that it was in danger, but it had been helpless to escape. Summer felt the same way.

'What will the Valide Sultan say?' she asked. If she feared this man, it was only a fraction compared to how much she feared his mother.

'I am Sultan,' he said indignantly. Then when he saw her blush he laughed. 'Don't worry about my mother Süheyla, I can make my own decisions too.'

'Thank you, I will bring my sketches and you can select one at dinner.'

'You do know that is not the reason I asked you to dine with me?'

Summer blushed again and looked down at the ground.

'Thank you Sultan Mehmed.'

She scampered back to the area of the palace that the women referred to as the golden cage. The first time she heard the harem referred to as this, she felt sickened. They were possibly the most beautiful of all of the living quarters in the entire palace, with stained-glass windows surrounded by beautifully coloured Iznik tiles, a huge seating platform, elaborate gilded fireplaces, and a spectacular painted dome over the innermost room. But as beautiful as it was, it was still a prison – her prison and although many of the women in the harem were there by choice, she was not. There was nothing golden about this cage.

She pulled off her clothes and readied herself to take a bath. She hoped she would not be alone with Sultan Mehmed at dinner and that Ali would be nearby.

She had dodged one ruler's affections only to be targeted by another. All she wanted was her life back – the days where she played in the woods with her brother and her cousin. Life was simpler then, light-hearted and safe.

TWENTY-ONE
FRIENDSHIP

FRANCIA

THEY pulled themselves into their saddles. Each man had food and water, a rifle, musket and a sword. They also had a blanket rolled up and tied to their saddles and full Musketeer uniforms that Pierre had secured for them.

'Take care Tristan,' his sister Louise said, touching his leg.

'Thanks Lou, I hope we have not put you or your family at risk,' he replied.

'We'll be fine. No knows that you have been living in the abandoned cottage. The servants have no idea and if King Louis gets word we'll simply deny any knowledge of it. This old place is isolated and no one ever comes here anymore. What will you do once you've found her?'

'I don't know, but I can't come back here. I will probably take her home to Griswold and we'll make our plans from there, but first we have to find her.'

'You will. Here,' she said pulling a ring off her finger and pushing it into his hand. He recognised it as his mother's ring – a beautiful large stone set in silver and surrounded by smaller gems. It had been in the family for generations.

'No Lou, you can't give this to me. Mother wanted you to have it before she died. It is your last link to her.'

'It's just a possession Tristan. Mother will always be in my heart. Use this ring to help you any way you need. Sell it if you have to, or give it to Summer when you find her and make her your wife. Godspeed Tristan. I love you.'

'I love you too,' he shouted as he kicked his steed and cantered off.

They flew across the countryside, walking their horses every now and again, watering their horses when they came to rivers.

'How long will it take to get to Massalia?' Griffin asked.

'If we keep us this pace, about a week,' Tristan said. Then it should take us another few weeks to sail to Anatolia from there. We can be there in just over a moon if all goes to plan.'

Both men thought of Summer and silently prayed that she would be alive. Neither had hope that she would be unscathed by her experience.

⌘

ANATOLIA

She sat opposite him and picked at her food.

'You do not like our food Süheyla? he asked concerned.

'Forgive me Sultan Mehmed. The food is delicious. I'm just not very hungry that's all.'

'You must eat or you will become ill.'

'I'll try,' she promised. Summer was still trying to figure out this man. She was not sure whether he was complicit with his mother in her abduction or whether he was unaware of her dilemma. She did not want to speak out in case he was behind it all. She would need to win his favour and learn more about the man if she was to ever get out of this horrible place. She glanced over at Ali who waited in the shadows – her silent protector and she smiled.

At least I have him to keep me safe.

The Sultan stood to his feet and held out his hand for her to take. She nervously took it.

'Come, let us look at some of the sketches you did today.'

Summer followed him to a large seat and took out her drawing parchments. She showed him a few of the sketches and he clapped his hands in delight.

'These are magnificent Süheyla. You have such talent as you have captured me at my best; in an activity I truly love. This one with my rifle raised, is my favourite. No other Sultan will ever have a portrait quite like mine.'

His childlike enthusiasm made her smile. That was the one thing about painting that gave her such great pleasure – seeing it bring joy to a person is all she ever hoped to achieve.

'I am glad you like it,' she said. 'I will begin work on it right away.'

He lifted her hand, kissing it and she could not help it as she snatched it away as though she had been stung by a bee. He looked confused.

'Süheyla? I have offended you?'

'I'm sorry Sultan Mehmed,' she mumbled. 'I am very tired – it has been a long day.'

He tried to hide his emotions and lifted his chin with dignity. 'Of course, I will have Ali take you back to your rooms.'

She did not know if he was offended or angry. His eyes became hard and a little cold at her rebuff. She did not mean to be so defensive, but after her experience with Louis she was on tenterhooks.

I must not alienate him, she thought as she followed Ali back to her rooms.

⌘

FRANCIA

Three horses thundered across Francia, tearing up the ground with their hooves. The animals snorted under the exertion, steam blowing from their nostrils. Their riders moved in sync with them, willing them to eat up the miles before them.

Darkness began to fall as the last rays of light dipped below the horizon in vivid streaks of colour. Tristan was grateful that the snows had melted which made the journey easier. At least they would not freeze tonight.

'There's a small village up ahead,' he said pointing to a few lights that twinkled in the distance. 'We'll water the horses and get a bite to eat, before we set off again.'

The meal was meagre – fresh bread and gruel, but it was welcome and hot after their long day in the saddle. The men ate lustily and washed it down with a light ale. Then they pulled themselves back into the saddle, muscles aching, before they headed down the road toward Massalia.

Summer brushed her long hair as she gazed out of the window. She looked up at the stars – sparkling gems that seemed to mock her captivity.

If I could just be one of them, she wished. She thought of Tristan and a deep sense of loss engulfed her once more. He had told her in his letter that the number of stars was just a fraction of his love for her. A tear escaped her lashes and rolled down her cheek. She began to sob, little noises escaping her as she tried to hold them back, but the flood of dread and loss was too much. She sank to her knees clutching her stomach as she rocked back and forth, moaning in anguish.

His touch was gentle and it startled her. She lifted her teary eyes and saw the compassion and concern written across his face. He nodded as though to acknowledge her pain.

'I understand,' he whispered.

Summer was surprised. She had never heard Ali speak before. She knew the risk he took. If the Valide Sultan heard him talking to her, he would be severely punished.

'Thank you Ali, you are the only friend I have in this place.'

He bowed and nodded his head in thanks. 'I can only speak when we are sure that no one will hear us. You understand that, don't you?'

'Of course, the last thing I want is to get you in trouble.'

'I will look out for you Miss Summer. You are not like all the other girls here. You did not choose to be here, as I did not. We have that in common. I know what you are going through.'

She smiled, 'you called me Summer. Thank you Ali, you don't know what that means to me.'

She felt reassured by the tall, thin ebony skinned man. His face bore the pain he had obviously suffered and yet he had a dignity about him that profoundly touched her.

How does he do it? She pondered.

It had been a day of emotional highs and lows. She had been delighted to escape the palace walls, but having Sultan Mehmed single her out, had brought all her memories of Tristan's courtship vividly back to her, highlighting her loss and yet this beautiful, gentle man in front of her had helped her feel safe once more, to not feel so alone. She hoped the women in the harem did not get wind of her time spent with the Sultan. All hell would break loose if that happened.

TWENTY-TWO

❦

EMOTIONS

AT SEA

THE Great One was true to his word – he sent winds to favour their journey and their boat cut through the waves effortlessly.

Erik stood gazing out to the horizon, remembering the years he had sailed to plunder other lands. It seemed like a lifetime ago. He had not missed the adventure as he had found everything he had ever wanted in Isabel and his children had been a delight. He wished he were embarking on this journey with as much confidence as he had years ago when they sailed to the South. He had been ambitious, full of hope and dreams for a new and exciting future. Now all he felt was dread and even fear that his beautiful daughter was dead, or even worse, raped. He still had mental pictures of women being raped by his kinsmen when he was a young man. It was one part of his culture he despised. He remembered their cries begging for mercy and pleading for the men to stop. The thought that Summer may be subjected to such treatment terrified and sickened him. He would kill any man who had touched his daughter without her consent.

⌘

The port of Massalia gleamed in the bright sunlight as the deep blue sea glistened, boats bobbing on the water like corks and seagulls screeching as they swooped looking for tidbits to eat. It was a pretty city, cleaner than Lutèce and buzzing with activity. It was one of the busiest ports in Francia, as many merchant vessels sailed between Francia and other nations to trade in spices, textiles and wares. The trio made their way down to the dock. They looked exhausted, as they'd barely slept the previous six days in their haste to get to the port. Tristan operated purely on adrenaline. His desire to find Summer consumed him and he had to force himself to eat and take care of himself. He knew they needed strength when they got to Anatolia. He hoped they would find her easily and that they would be able to rescue her or at least make a deal with the Sultan, but if that did not happen, he knew they would have to fight to get her back.

'Wait for me,' he said to Cam and Griffin as he dismounted his horse. 'I'll see if I can sell the horses and get us passage on a ship sailing for Anatolia. I will meet you at the Inn,' he said indicating the whitewashed double storey building across the wharf.

Cam and Griffin headed for the Hungry Pelican, an old waterside inn that serviced sailors and merchants. It was full despite the relatively early hour of the day and Griffin assumed it was because sailors sought food, rum or ale and the bosoms of bar girls in that order. He and Cam ordered some food and drink and flopped down onto a rickety wooden bench.

'Ouch,' Cam moaned as his rump touched down. 'I don't think I'll be able to sit for a week after riding non-stop for days.'

'I'll be sure to tell Summer of your sacrifice,' Griffin laughed seeing his cousin's grimace.

'Excuse me lads, but would you mind if I joined you?' The voice belonged to a very pretty young girl who could be no more than nineteen years old. She had a splattering of freckles across the bridge of her nose and her honey hair fell in waves around her shoulders. She did not look like any of the bar maids. She was well spoken and impeccably dressed.

'Certainly,' Cam said almost stumbling over his feet to stand. Griffin smiled at his eagerness and waved his hand.

'We'd be delighted,' Griffin said. 'I've been looking at my cousin's ugly mug for days now and a prettier change of scenery would be welcome,' he teased.

She smiled coyly at him and he blushed. He had always been a little reserved and shy and this young woman made him feel like a boy again. Cam on the other hand had no problem flirting with the ladies.

She flopped down on the bench next to Griffin and sighed. 'Bloody hell,' she mumbled. Both men roared with laughter. The cuss word did not sound right coming from such a refined young lady and yet Griffin detected that she was a rebel underneath the ladylike garb. She certainly had spirit.

'Do you have a name?' he asked amused.

'You can call me Lucy.'

'So Lucy, what is a lovely lady like you doing in the Hungry Pelican? I somehow don't believe this is your usual hangout.'

'I could ask you the same thing,' she said defiantly. You're not sailors.

'We're just passing through,' Cam interjected.

'So who are you hiding from?' Griffin chuckled.

'What makes you think I'm hiding from someone?' she asked.

'You haven't stopped glancing at the tavern door since you sat down.'

'It's not funny,' she punched him on the arm. 'It's not easy being a woman set up for marriage. I feel like a bloody item on display that some man can purchase if the price is high enough.'

'You're hiding from a suitor?' Griffin raised his eyebrows.

'Hardly a suitor,' she scoffed. 'Just another stupid imbecile my father has arranged to court me. I wish he would get it into his thick head that I will decide who I marry and when I will marry.'

'Well you are welcome to hang out with us for a while,' Cam chuckled. 'We promise not to match make you.'

She gasped and ducked her head behind Griffin's shoulder. 'Damn, he's here,' she muttered.

A young, well-dressed man in his late twenties scanned the inn, searching for the missing girl. He looked exasperated as he raked his hand through his thick red hair. Finally he spotted her and made his way across the crowded room.

'It looks like he's.....'

Griffin did not finish his sentence as she grabbed him, kissing him passionately. Her lips were soft and warm, her mouth seductively open just a little, as he felt her tongue touch his. He was simultaneously surprised and shocked. Strong arms ripped him from the bench and her lips, a fist hitting him squarely in the left eye. Cam jumped on the intruder and a brawl broke out. Cheers erupted as sailors joined in the fight, eagerly swinging at whoever was in their way.

'Are you all right?' Lucy said pulling Griffin to his feet as he held his painful eye. 'Let's get out of here,' she shouted over the chaos. The three of them fled the Inn, leaving the red-haired man under a pile of sailors. As they exited the Inn, they bumped into a stern looking man.

'Lucinda, what is the meaning of this?' he growled.

'Papa, I was just coming to find you,' she lied effortlessly.

'Who are these young ruffians and what are you doing in the Hungry Pelican?'

'Oh no Papa, it is not what you think,' she started to cry and Cam and Griffin glanced at each other astounded. She did not seem like the crying type. 'These two young men are heroes Papa. They saved me. That man you chose as a suitor brought me here and then suggested the most despicable things. These gentlemen overheard him and stood up to him. This fine young man even took a blow for my honour.'

Both Cam and Griffin tried their best to look serious so as not to ruin Lucy's incredible acting performance. She spun a story so believable that her father placed his arm across her shoulders and comforted her.

'I'm sorry Lucinda – this is awful. I don't understand why Fabien would act that way. It is so unlike him.'

'Just promise me Papa that I will never have to see him again.'

'I promise my dear. I want to thank you gentlemen for coming to my daughter's aid. I am indebted to you. If there is anything I can do for you, you just need to give the word.'

'There is nothing we want from you Sir,' Griffin said rubbing his swollen eye. 'We are just glad that Lucy.... Mademoiselle Lucinda is all right.'

THE GOLDEN CAGE

Tristan joined them, gasping when he saw Griffin's swollen eye.

'What happened to you?' he asked.

'It's a long story,' Griffin said.

'Do you two know each other?' Lucy's father asked surprised.

'Yes,' Griffin replied. 'We are travelling together.'

'You're the man from the docks who was asking about passage to Anatolia,' he said to Tristan. Tristan nodded.

'No luck,' I'm afraid,' Tristan said to Griffin and Cam.

'What are we going to do now?' Griffin asked dismayed. Their plans could not be thwarted after they had made such good time to Massalia.

'I am Chauncey Grainger. I own three of the ships docked here. My captains have strict instructions not to offer passage to travellers, no matter how much money they offer. Piracy is quite rampant these days and I am not willing to take any chances. However, since you came to my daughter's aid today, I will make an exception for you. I have a ship sailing for Anatolia in two days. I will organize passage with the captain. It's the least I can do.'

'Thank you Sir,' Griffin said shaking the man's hand. 'We appreciate your offer more than you can know.'

'I assume you have nowhere to stay in Massalia?'

'No Sir, we only arrived this morning and I doubt the Hungry Pelican will host us after that fight broke out.'

'Then I insist that you stay in my home till the ship sails. You can follow my carriage home.'

Chauncey Grainger's homestead was a huge sprawling apartment in the middle of the city. It overlooked a huge cobbled square and was three storeys high. The architecture was magnificent and Griffin felt a touch of sadness seeing it.

Summer would love this building.

It was not only the building that was beautiful and fascinating. Lucinda Grainger was an enigma. Griffin had never met anyone quite like her. She had a wicked sense of humour, a mouth a sailor would be proud of, and yet she was refined and rebellious at the same time. The moment they arrived at the apartment, she wasted no time pulling him aside.

'I'm glad you're here,' she said sweetly.

'Your father is very generous to extend his hospitality to strangers.'

'You do know that it's thanks to me that he feels indebted to you.'

'Yes, that was some performance you gave him. Outstanding, if I may say so myself.'

She smiled wickedly then touched his swollen eye. He flinched. It was beginning to bruise. 'Yes, sorry about this,' she said. She sounded genuine.

'Yes what was that all about?'

'It wasn't just to make Fabien angry if that is what you think. I wanted to kiss you from the first moment I laid eyes on you.' Griffin blushed and she laughed at his discomfort.

'You're not very experienced with women, are you? That's what I like so much about you. You seem different to other men – incredibly handsome, yet you don't seem to realize the affect you have on women.'

'Thank you – I think,' he laughed.

'Don't forget me Griffin,' she whispered in his ear before kissing him on the cheek and running off. She was an impulsive creature.

⌘

ANATOLIA — EARLY SPRING

Spring was beautiful in Anatolia. The days were warmer and the skies a brilliant blue. The portrait of Sultan Mehmed was well underway and Summer was thrilled with her progress. Every morning she spent hours of time working on her canvas, getting the textures and tones perfect. Even the Valide Sultan praised her.

'You have remarkable talent,' she said to Summer. Then she ruined the compliment by tearing her down again. 'It's a good thing you have something to offer now that you are scarred. If a man cannot have a beautiful wife, then he at least needs a woman with talent. Don't worry Süheyla, we will find someone who will want you.'

Summer shuddered at the thought. If the scar on her neck protected her from the unwanted advances of men then she would personally thank the woman who cut her. She still felt self-conscious about the angry red scar that covered half her throat, but for now it may just save her life. Each day before she went out into public she covered her head with a scarf and then tucked it into the collar of her gömlek, a chemise that went to her mid-calf, covering her pants. She did not want anyone's pity or stares or to see the horror in their eyes when her scar was visible. She was glad Tristan did not have to see her this way.

THE GOLDEN CAGE

Would he be repulsed by the awful disfigurement? Stop it Summer, at least your face is not scarred. Stop feeling sorry for yourself, she mentally chided herself.

She looked back at her painting and smiled. The Valide Sultan could say anything she pleased. She would not let them break her. Now that Ali was her friend she did not feel so lonely anymore. He knew all about her, yet somehow he had refrained from telling her how he had come to be at Topkapi Palace. She could see in his eyes that he had suffered greatly and she did not want to push him. She knew he would tell her when he was ready.

⌘

'Mehmed, you spend too much time with Süheyla. The other women are frustrated and jealous which means you put her at risk,' the Valide Sultan warned.

'Mother, it is work – she is doing my portrait as you well know.'

'I've watched you, and I know you my son. This is not just work, and you know it. You are becoming too attached to her. How do you think Emetullah will respond if she finds out that you are enamoured with Süheyla?'

Mehmed sighed. Emetullah was his wife, the mother of his son Mustafa II and until recently, his favourite. He knew what her jealousy could do. Years before a new young concubine had caught his eye. Her name was Gülbeyaz and she was beautiful. Emetullah had not been able to deal with the attention he had given the young woman. Usually he took his wife on hunting expeditions to the Balkans but this occasion he had taken Gülbeyaz.

'You can't humiliate me this way,' Emetullah had raged. 'Mehmed, please don't do this. I am the mother of your heir. She is nothing. While I know you have concubines, taking her on this trip tells the other women that I am no longer your favourite.'

He had ignored her pleas and taken Gülbeyaz on the hunting trip. This had led to tragic circumstances. One day while Gülbeyaz was sitting on a rock overlooking the Bosphorus Sea, she tragically fell to her death. Mehmed always suspected that Emetullah had pushed her, but none of the other women were willing to confirm his suspicions. He knew they feared her. He had to ensure that nothing happened to Süheyla.

'Ali is protecting Süheyla at your request Mother. Is there something you are not telling me?'

'No, I am simply ensuring she is safe while she settles in. Emetullah has been telling me of her desire to have another child, Mehmed. You need to have her in your bed more, as one heir is not enough. It will reassure her. Why don't you take her away on a hunting trip? The time together will be good for you both.'

Mehmed growled in frustration. He may be the Sultan of Anatolia, but his mother still ruled him with an iron fist.

'All right Mother, I will reassure Emetullah and we will go away for a few days, but I will not stop seeing Süheyla. This portrait is my excuse for spending time with her, and I expect you to convince the women of its importance.'

'I hope you will not regret this Mehmed.'

'Just ensure that Ali protects Süheyla mother.'

TWENTY-THREE

SHATTERED

MASSALIA, FRANCIA

THE ship sailed away from the dock, cutting through the blue water. The crew hoisted sails and prepared for the journey. Tristan, Cam and Griffin were given a cabin to share and although it was cramped, it was clean and more importantly, a way to get to Anatolia. They agreed to help with some of the chores on the ship even though Chauncey Grainger had insisted they were guests on board. Griffin thought of Lucy and his heart lurched. He had only met her three days previously and yet she had left an impression on him he could not shake.

Is this what love feels like? he wondered.

The night before they sailed she had sneaked into his bedroom at the apartment. He had woken with a start to find her curled up beside him on the bed.

'Lucy, what are you doing here? Your father will have me strung up if he finds you.'

'I just want to be near you,' she replied. 'You are leaving tomorrow and I'm terrified I will never see you again.'

Griffin was surprised at her vulnerability. He had seen how she flirted, how she made up stories and teased. He had not entirely taken her advances seriously. Now she looked like a frightened child and tears glistened on her lashes.

'Do you really have to go?' she asked.

'Yes, I do. My sister has been abducted and we have to find her Lucy.'

'Why didn't you tell me this before?' she said shocked.

'There are people in Francia who wish us dead. I promise you that I'll return and I will tell you all about it. The less you know in the meantime, the safer you will be.'

She'd looked wide-eyed at him and his desire to kiss her was unbearable, yet he held himself back.

'Are you ever going to kiss me, or do I have to initiate it again,' she teased. He pulled her close locking his lips with hers, giving all of himself to her as she did to him. Her taste was sweet and sensual and Griffin felt aroused as her breasts pressed against his chest. She ran her fingers across his bare torso and it suddenly hit him that he was shirtless. He moaned softly as his hands ran through her thick hair.

'I think I am in love with you Griffin,' she whispered between kisses. 'Is that even possible?'

'I believe it is,' he whispered back before claiming her mouth once more.

'I want you,' she begged. Finally he pulled away, her words sinking into his brain.

'No Lucy, not like this. Trust me, I would love nothing more than to make love to you, but I will not betray your father's trust or jeopardise my passage to Anatolia. Summer is counting on me to find her. Nothing can stand in the way of that, especially not my desire for you. This has to wait, but I will be back for you, I promise.'

Now they were on their way to Anatolia and he could hardly believe that he felt such happiness amidst such fear for his sister and the unknown. He knew he had to focus on what was ahead or his delirium would endanger them all. He understood how Summer had fallen in love with Tristan so quickly. Love did not wait for perfect timing or circumstances. It came when it wanted, hitting you as life thundered by. He understood too why Tristan was a man obsessed and in pain. Love would do that to you if it were taken. He willed the ship to sail faster and prayed to the Great One to send good winds.

We're coming Summer – don't give up.

⌘

ANATOLIA

'Kapudan Pasha, welcome to Topkapi Palace.'

'It is I who is honoured to be here Valide Sultan. I must say I was surprised that you requested to see me. Our men are delighted to be back from Galata. I was hoping to have an audience with the Sultan.'

'I'm afraid that won't be possible as Mehmed is away hunting with his wife. In the meantime he has asked me to ensure that you are well taken care of and that you have every pleasure at your disposal. I have organized a special performance of dancers and a feast for you and your officers tonight.'

'That is extremely kind of you Valide Sultan. We look forward to it.'

The Kapudan Pasha was the commander of the Anatolian navy. He and his men returned from Galata where they spent the winter months and the Sultan usually threw a party in their honour before they left on sailing missions during the summer months. Valide Turhan Hatice had planned this carefully. She knew that Mehmed would probably be furious with her once he found out what she had done, but in the long run he would be grateful. It was best for Anatolia and best for him. Tonight would be the turning point for them all.

⌘

Summer put the last touches on her painting. It was complete and she was satisfied with her work. She'd had nothing but time to work on the masterpiece, and as a result had completed it faster than she usually would have. She hoped the Sultan would like it. The last time she'd seen him he had thanked her for the beautiful work and she felt that she was gaining his favour and trust. Once she felt confident their relationship was solid, she would beg for her freedom. She would offer an alliance with Griswold and the Northmen. She would do whatever it took to be free of this prison.

'Miss Summer, I have to leave for a while,' Ali said in hushed tones. They had to maintain caution that no one hear them converse. 'The Valide Sultan has asked me to run an errand. Promise me you will not leave your quarters while I am gone.'

'I promise Ali. I will be right here when you get back.'

Summer sat on the couch and looked out at the sky. Dusk was just beginning and the night was clear and crisp. She had to admit the Anatolian sunsets and night skies were truly magnificent. There was rarely rain and so the stars always seemed so numerous and beautiful. Palms silhouetted against orange skies together with the palace domes and turrets made a stunning backdrop. She was startled when the door opened and the Valide Sultan entered.

189

'Get dressed Süheyla,' she said curtly. 'Wear your finest silks tonight.'

'Where am I going?' Summer asked alarmed. She had a bad feeling about this.

'The Sultan wishes to see you,' she said. 'Hurry up, you are not to keep him waiting.'

'I thought Sultan Mehmed was away hunting.'

'He was, but he's back now. Come on girl, you need to get dressed.'

Summer quickly bathed and changed into her silk attire. She selected an iridescent turquoise that highlighted her eyes and hair. The Valide Sultan added a thick silver choker that covered the scar on her neck. The jewellery was beautiful and for a moment Summer gazed at herself, remembering how she had looked before the attack. She almost felt beautiful again. Then her nerves hit her.

Why am I being adorned for the Sultan? She feared the answer.

'Follow me,' the Valide Sultan said, leaving the room.

If he wants to see me so urgently, he must favour me. Tonight I will ask him for my freedom, she thought.

⌘

The party was well underway when they arrived and Summer was surprised that she was being thrown together with some of the women who attacked her. She looked at the Valide Sultan, alarm in her eyes. She recognized one or two and they glared at her menacingly, daring her to give them up. She looked away.

I won't give them the pleasure by showing fear, she thought.

She glanced around the room, her apprehension growing with every second. She could not see the Sultan.

'Kapudan Pasha, this is Süheyla. She is one of the most beautiful women in Topkapi. She will entertain you tonight and meet all your needs.'

'Please,' Summer stammered, desperately afraid now. The Valide Sultan pulled her aside and hissed, 'Don't disappoint him Süheyla. I know the drawing you did of that young man was your love, and I know that he is a Musketeer in Queen Maria's dragoons. She told me all about him. It would be a shame if he were killed in battle. Maria can arrange it should you need motivation to be hospitable.' Her threat was clear and Summer let out a sob.

'Pull yourself together and entertain the Kapudan Pasha. You should be honoured to have the commander by your side. Who knows, if you please him well enough, he may even make a respectable woman of you.' She laughed an ugly hollow laugh as she pushed the girl toward the waiting commander.

He was not a bad looking man. He was taller than the sultan with big brooding eyes that looked like black pools. His most striking feature were his eyelashes that seemed far too long for a man and would leave any woman envious. He must have been in his late thirties Summer guessed, and he was well built, his military training obvious by his muscular frame. Under any other circumstances, Summer may have found him quite attractive.

They ate dinner and watched the dancers. Summer picked at her food and drank more raki than she was used to. The anise-flavoured drink dulled her senses and made her head feel as though it were somehow blissfully separate from her body. She felt herself relax despite the situation. She determined that it would be better to just not feel the pain in her heart.

She felt his hand on her thigh before she saw him put it there and she stiffened. He leaned over and whispered in her ear, 'follow me.'

She could not move, her legs were jelly and the world spun around her furiously. She did not remember anything more.

⌘

AT SEA

Tristan sat bolt upright in his bunk. Something was wrong. Sweat covered his brow and the rolling motion of the ship did nothing to calm him. He swung his legs over the side, pulled on a shirt and headed to the deck. The night sky was pitch black, a myriad of twinkling lights dancing across the heavens and a bright moon shining on the water. It was beautiful but it did not assuage his fears. He had a gnawing anxiety that was growing every minute. It felt as though he could sense what she was going through, as though they were somehow connected.

'Summer, I love you, don't ever forget that sweetheart,' he whispered to the stars.

⌘

She opened her eyes to find the Kapudan Pasha staring down at her. She felt the soft bed underneath her and she panicked pulling herself up unsteadily.

'Slow down. You gave me quite a scare,' he said.

'Where are we?' she asked.

'In your room. The Valide Sultan said I could bring you here. He stroked her cheek and Summer recoiled.

'Why do you find my touch so offensive?' he asked angrily.

'I'm sorry, it is not you that is the problem. It is my heart. It belongs to someone else.' She did not expect him to laugh at her disclosure.

'I'll show you Süheyla how to truly please a man and in return you may find it is not so bad.' He pulled her to her feet and caught her in his arms. She was unsteady, and she stumbled. He held onto her and she felt trapped.

'You are beautiful,' he said in his foreign accent. 'Don't worry you will get used to it all.'

'Please sir,' she said softly. 'There's been a mistake. It was not my choice to be here.'

He laughed, louder this time as though she had said something amusing. She looked confused.

'That is no concern of mine,' he answered. 'Choice is not something harem girls have in Topkapi. The Valide Sultan handpicked you out of all the girls and that is all that matters. You should be honoured to be with a Captain.'

Honoured she thought angrily. *To be a prisoner – a slave!*

'You cannot force me to stay here,' she challenged.

He slapped her hard across the face and her cheek throbbed as she held it. She was shocked. She had never seen a man treat a woman this way before. She held back the tears as she bit down on her lip. She would not give him the satisfaction of her fear.

'Don't ever speak to me that way again,' he growled cruelly. He looked her up and down and subconsciously licked his lips. 'You will do nicely,' he said sliding his hand under her robe, invading her personal space, touching her breast in a way that left her ashamed. Tristan touched her this way and it had been beautiful, special, but now this man cheapened it.

Don't let him touch you, her mind screamed but her body would not cooperate – it felt dead and incapable of retaliation.

Why won't my limbs work, her mind screamed to her functionless body?

'Please don't,' she whispered again.

He pulled her closer kissing her roughly on the lips as he held her arms pinned tightly to her sides. Then he spun her around and pushed her against the brightly tiled mosaic wall.

He lifted her chemise and she suddenly became aware that her salvars had been removed. She was furious.

How dare he!'

Pain shot through her abdomen as he penetrated her, rough and with grunting sounds. He pinned her arms to the wall, her face squashed against the cold surface. She thought how pretty the tiles were, how colourful and creative – she had to cling to something beautiful in this moment of pure ugliness.

THE GOLDEN CAGE

She closed her eyes and let her mind wander to happier times. She started to hum a lullaby her mother sang to her as a child, shutting out the horrible reality of what was happening to her as he thrust for what seemed like an eternity. She would not let him take anything more from her – she would separate her heart from her body – she had to or she would die in this place – this golden cage.

⌘

AT SEA

Tristan let out an anguished wail as he held his stomach. Something awful had happened to Summer – he just knew it, he could feel it. He could feel her pain.

TWENTY-FOUR

BROKEN

ANATOLIA

HE found her curled up on her bed in the foetal position, rocking back and forth as she hummed the same tune over and over, tears rolling down her face. He covered her with a quilt and sat beside her.

'Miss Summer, what have they done to you?'

Ali touched her gently and felt her pull away as she opened her mouth to wail – no sound came out.

'It's all right Miss Summer. It's only me. I am sorry, this is my fault – I should have been here for you. None of this would have happened if I had stayed with you.'

His distress brought Summer back to reality momentarily. She grasped his hand, vice-like as though she would never let go. She could not lose Ali.

'Not your fault,' she whispered hoarsely. He reached over and poured her a goblet of water, holding it to her dry lips. She took one sip and then vomited all over the floor.

'I'm sorry,' she sobbed, embarrassed by her reaction.

'Let's get you into a hot bath,' he suggested. He helped her to her feet, watching her hobble, each step agonisingly painful and he knew that the Valide Sultan had given her to a man who had not treated her kindly. He felt angry and disgusted that another beautiful young woman had been maimed both emotionally and physically in this harem. She groaned and he held her with one arm, supporting as much of her weight as he could.

'Wash, Miss Summer,' he said helping her into the steaming water. She did not care that he saw her nakedness or the blood stains on her thighs. Her dignity was stripped, gone forever by one act of violence.

'There will never be enough water to wash away what he did to me,' she sobbed.

'I know, but the water will soothe your wounds Miss Summer. I will be back in a moment,' he promised as he left her soaking in the steaming water.

He returned carrying a bowl full of seeds and a goblet of raki.

'Here, eat these,' he instructed dropping a small spoonful into her hand, which she looked at suspiciously.

'What are they?'

'They are seeds from a flower, known as wild carrot – they will ensure that his seed will not produce a child within your womb.'

Summer felt a wave of nausea engulf her. She had not thought of pregnancy. She and Tristan had been very careful when they were together, but this act had been brutal and the animal that raped her had not cared whether his seed spilled inside her.

Great One, I would rather die than have his baby!

She took the seeds, put them in her mouth, chewing as fast as she could, the flavour rather unpalatable. Then she washed them down with raki. The liquid burned her throat, but the pain was better than the pain she felt between her bruised thighs.

'You must eat these seeds every day for one week Miss Summer. They will work, I promise you.'

'Thank you Ali,' she said. He helped her out the bath and into clothes and then he tucked her into her bed like a protective father. She smiled weakly at him.

'Sleep Miss Summer, your body needs rest.'

⌘

The Sultan was delighted with his portrait. It was the first thing he noticed when he entered his rooms. The days he had spent hunting with Emetullah had made him certain of one thing – his wife whom he once doted on, bored him to tears. She had become predictable, whining about her station and how she needed him more, needed another child, needed more time with him; on and on she went until he wished he could just shoot her when they were out hunting. Still, he tried to please her, but even that had proven difficult. He just did not feel attracted to her anymore. Unbeknown to her, he had taken saffron and ginseng to help him function. He knew she would be furious if she even suspected that he had no libido around her. Fortunately the herbs had helped. He closed his eyes as he lay on top of her, imagining Süheyla beneath him and that seemed to work even better than the herbal remedies. Emetullah was spiteful and Mehmed knew that if she were threatened she would resort to any means to rid herself of competition. He would have to find a way to be with Süheyla without his wife knowing about it. The young woman was not only beautiful, but she was intelligent, cultured and talented and his fascination with her grew.

The first thing he did on his return was send an invitation to Süheyla to join him for dinner. He wanted to thank her for the portrait, but more than that, he wanted to see her again, drink in her beauty. He sat at the table, waiting for her to join him. It was a pleasant reprieve from Emetullah who'd returned to the women's quarters. He imagined how she would be bragging to all the other women that she was the favoured one, Mehmed's wife. She would certainly cut them down to size – it was in her nasty nature. He thought how different Süheyla was.

What is taking her so long?

Ali appeared in the doorway and knocked softly. He bowed his head until the Sultan invited him in.

'Yes Ali,' he said distracted.

'I have been sent to inform you that Süheyla is not well and will not be able to attend dinner this evening.'

'What is wrong with her?' the Sultan asked concerned. 'Has she caught a fever?'

'No Sultan Mehmed, she is just feeling under the weather and does not feel up to it.'

The Sultan narrowed his eyes as he looked at the dark skinned man. 'What are you keeping from me Ali?'

Ali looked down at the floor unable to meet the Sultan's gaze.

'Fine, then I will go to her if she cannot come to me,' he said pushing back his chair.

'Sultan Mehmed, that's not a good idea...' Ali muttered flustered as the Sultan strode past him toward Summer's quarters. Ali raced after him, but Mehmed was on a mission and it was hard to keep pace. He knocked and burst through Summer's door, not waiting for a response. He was shocked to see her lying in bed, her face pale and drawn. It was not her physical pallor that scared him. It was her eyes. They had a haunted look, a look he had seen in the women who were sold unwillingly into the harem. Mehmed was momentarily confused. He thought Süheyla had agreed to come here – an arrangement with Queen Maria and his mother to escape Francia.

'Süheyla,' he said shocked. 'What is the matter with you? Has someone hurt you?'

Summer looked dazed as she tried to pull herself upright. She tried to pull the covers up to her neck but she was not quick enough. He gasped when he saw the scar on her neck. Summer dropped her head and covered her hand over it. Mehmed sat on the edge of her bed.

'Who did this to you?' Summer kept silent.

'When did this happen? I have not seen this scar.' He realized that he had never seen her without a veil or scarf. He also realized that the wound was not old and must have happened when she first came to Topkapi.

Emetullah did this, he thought angrily. *But this is not why she looks so afraid, so sick. I've seen her since this happened and she did not have this look in her eyes.*

'What happened Ali?' he demanded. 'What has my mother done?'

'It is not my place to say, Sultan Mehmed. You need to ask her yourself.' Ali replied.

His face looked like thunder when it dawned on him what his mother had done. She was the only person with the authority to assign the harem girls and the only person who had tried so hard to dissuade him from spending time with Süheyla.

How could she do this?

⌘

200
THE GOLDEN CAGE

AT SEA

Tristan gazed out over the horizon. They had passed numerous islands on their journey, stopping for a few hours to trade at some of the little ports. He wanted to scream 'Stop wasting time, she needs us now,' but he knew that he had to bite his tongue and maintain an air of patience as Chauncey Grainger had done them a favour by giving them passage. His frustration would get them thrown off the boat if he didn't keep it in check. – they needed to get to Anatolia no matter how long it took.

'How much longer do you think it will take?' Griffin asked.

'I feel your frustration too,' Tristan said slapping him on the back. 'I guess if we don't stop at too many more islands it should take us another two weeks.'

They both knew that two weeks would feel like an eternity and that even another day could be too late for Summer.

⌘

COAST OF FRANCIA

Erik's ships sailed along the coast of Francia. They continued to the port of Bayonne, southwest of the country. They could easily dock there without King Louis getting word of their arrival. By the time he discovered their presence they would have acquired new supplies and left the shores to sail around the horn of Hispania and into the

Alboran Sea. Griffin sent word not to wait for them as they would cross Francia on horseback and would gain passage on a merchant ship. Erik felt relieved at the news as Griswold was further west and their journey had taken many weeks even with the good winds the Great One had sent. The men shouted as they saw the bay that would take them to port. They all looked forward to a square meal and some mead before they set sail again.

TWENTY-FIVE

WISHES

ANATOLIA

'HOW dare you Mother! She is not like the other girls in the harem. You lied to me about her willingness to be here. She was not ready for this. You knew how I felt about her and yet you spitefully did this to make a point.'

Mehmed could barely contain his anger. This was the first time his mother had ever done anything deliberately to hurt him. Usually he trusted her judgement to run the harem and to select the women, but this time she had blatantly ignored his wishes.

I am Sultan, this is my Kingdom, he thought bitterly.

'I know you don't understand Mehmed, but in time you will thank me. She is flawed, scarred and the women hate her. She is safer this way – what I did will ultimately find her a husband. I was thinking about her future as much as yours,' she lamely justified.

'Yes, let's talk about why she is scarred Mother? You just happened to omit to mention that she was attacked and almost killed. We both know who was behind it.'

'All the more reason to find her a suitor, Mehmed. Emetullah won't be so careless next time. She will kill the girl. Have you forgotten what happened to Gülbeyaz?' she added cruelly.

THE GOLDEN CAGE

Mehmed stiffened. It had taken him years to shake off the guilt he felt over her death. He would never want that to happen to Süheyla.

'Perhaps you did what you thought best Mother, but I don't care that she is scarred. I love her and I plan to make her my wife. If Emetullah objects, she will be detained in the golden cage and I will have no more to do with her. Your plan is wasted because I aim to court Süheyla till she believes that I truly care about her. I want her to trust me and learn to love me. She may have been brought here unwillingly but I hope to win her over.'

'You fool Mehmed,' she spat. 'You would jeopardise your whole kingdom for one girl. You forget that your brother Suleiman would be only too happy to take over your rule should you become weak. This girl will make you weak.'

'No more Mother,' he roared. 'I will not take further advice from you. The only weakness I have displayed is allowing you to manipulate me.' He stormed from his quarters leaving her seething.

He's going to throw it all away, the stupid, gullible fool. I cannot let him!

⌘

He visited Summer daily checking on her progress. He wanted to build a bridge of trust, but he could see fear and wariness in her eyes every time he approached her. She flinched when he took her hand and she found it hard to look him in the eye.

'Please,' she begged, 'please let me go home to my family.'

'I cannot Süheyla. It is custom for girls who do not wish to be here to stay for nine years. If I let you go, others will expect the same.' The truth was that he could not bear to let her go. 'I will ensure you are safe. What happened to you will never happen again, unless you consent to it, of course.'

'I don't ever want a man to touch me again,' she spat. Her bitterness stunned him. Instinctively she touched the scar. 'This is the best thing that's happened to me. I wish my whole face was carved up, then no one would want to touch me.'

He was shocked and pulled her hand from her neck. Then he gently touched the scar. She cringed and held her breath.

'This is not ugly to me,' he said. He lifted his turban and slid it backwards, revealing a large scar across the top of his forehead. 'I too have had horrible things happen beyond my control Süheyla. When I was just an infant my father got into an argument with my mother. He tore me from her arms and threw me into a cistern. I would have died had it not been for the harem servants who found me. It left me with this scar. We are more alike than you know. We are both victims of circumstance, but we are also both far more than our circumstances.'

Summer was horrified.

The way these people live is barbaric, cruel, horrible. She shuddered again.

'I know now is not the time Süheyla, but I want you to know that I care about you. I want to protect you and give you everything that Topkapi has to offer. I can make you happy again. All I ask is that you consider it.' He stood up from her bed and she flopped back against the pillow defeated.

'Think about it,' he said as he left her.

Summer felt her anxiety increase. She had ingested the wild carrot seeds that Ali gave her every day, and as a result her womanly cycle had come. The relief she felt had been enormous, but now after Sultan Mehmed's declaration, she felt that familiar feeling of being caged descending upon her again.

He's told me to think about it, but he doesn't really mean it. He knows that I have no choice, that what I want doesn't really matter. She felt despair creep up and latch its ugly hooks into her heart once again.

'You have to help me Ali. I have to get away from here.'

Her ebony friend stared back at her in response – lost for words. He too knew that she was trapped.

⌘

'Please Valide Sultan, you must help me,' Emetullah pleaded. 'Mehmed is losing interest in me because of that woman. I am the mother of his heir and I believe that I am carrying his seed and will produce another son in the near future. He cannot throw away what we have now.'

The Valide Sultan did not favour her daughter-in-law or agree with her often, but this time she had to admit that Emetullah was right. Mehmed was being a fool. He was going to throw away his kingdom, and if one of his brothers or relatives got wind of it, they would not hesitate to overthrow him. She was not ready to give up her role as the Valide Sultan. It was her future at stake too.

'Don't fret Emetullah. I will take care of this. No one is going to threaten your son's rightful inheritance. Mehmed will see this in time. Just be patient.'

THE GOLDEN CAGE

Valide Sultan Turhan Hatice paced up and down her quarters after the young woman left. Süheyla had been a threat to Queen Maria and now she understood why the Queen had been so anxious to rid Francia of the girl. King Louis had been won over by the painter and now her son had fallen into the same trap. She had believed Süheyla would be a perfect match for Mehmed as she disliked Emetullah so much, even feared the woman a little, but now that Süheyla was disfigured she could never be in the Sultan's harem. They had an image to uphold and only perfect women would be good enough for the ruler. Bringing her to Anatolia was a grave mistake, nonetheless not one they couldn't fix. Unlike Queen Maria, the Valide Sultan had no qualms about cleaning up her own household and getting her hands dirty. She would take care of Süheyla once and for all.

⌘

AT SEA

Tristan felt his spirits lift a little. They had left the Alboran Sea, heading into the Aegean Sea – they were getting closer to Anatolia each day. He could see islands and the shore, and the landscape was changing slightly as he saw rocky outcrops covered in foliage rising out of the iridescent blue sea. The contrast between water and land was startling and although it was so different to Francia, he had to admit it was beautiful. He had been unable to fall asleep after he felt Summer was in danger, tossing and turning until he eventually fell into a fitful sleep. He dreamed of her, her sweet trusting face looking up at him as she pledged her love for him. The dream had been so vivid, exactly as he remembered how it was when they made their promises to one another. The last thing she said before he woke with a start was, 'I love you.' It had given him new encouragement and patience to find her. No matter how long it took he would never give up. He felt hope stir, for the first time in weeks.

It will be all right; it has to be all right.

TWENTY-SIX

⚜

INSTRUCTION

SPRING 1672, ANATOLIA

'WHY is she doing this?' Summer cried as servants packed all her things together.

Ali just shook his head, unable to speak to her in front of the servants. She glared at him frustrated, wanting answers. The Valide Sultan had ordered her back to the harem, to the place her life had been endangered and Summer knew she was in trouble.

Why does she hate me so much? I have done nothing to anger her.

Ali looked equally annoyed but he could do nothing. The Valide Sultan had full control over the harem and he was just a eunuch. All he could do was protect Summer as best as possible. The move back to the women's quarters did not take long as she did not have many possessions. She was assigned her sleeping divan and she resolved to keep as far away from the women as possible. She did notice Anna glancing at her as though she wanted to say something, to connect; but then the young girl looked away every time the other women were nearby.

Summer lay on her bed quietly. She could hear the breathing of the other women as they slept, but she dared not close her eyes. If she gave them a reason they would kill her. The only relief she had, was that the beautiful dark-haired woman who slashed her throat was not in their

209
THE GOLDEN CAGE

quarters. She assumed that she must be one of the Sultan's favourites if she had her own apartment. Still, she had enough presence to get to her if she wanted to, or to have one of the other women take care of her problem. Summer would not go down without a fight.

⌘

Morning came and Summer felt exhausted. She had dozed on and off through the night, her instinct to protect herself had not shut down giving her no real rest. The light was just beginning to break and the other women still slept soundly. She decided to take her bath before they woke, not wanting to relive the experience of her last bathhouse visit with the women. She slipped out of bed and took her clothes, walking quickly along the tiled passage to the hamam, the name given to the bathhouse. Looking around to ensure no one had followed her she disrobed and slipped into the steamy water. The warmth enveloped her, making her sleepy and she briefly closed her eyes. A splash next to her brought her back. She gasped, relief flooding her as she recognised Anna.

'You startled me,' she said laughing nervously.

The young girl looked apologetic. 'I've been waiting to speak to you alone. Are you all right?'

'I am fine thank you,' she said unconsciously touching the scar on her neck.

'I also want to thank you for protecting me. The Valide Sultan frightens me, but I am even more afraid of the woman who did this to you. Thanks to you, I did not have to name her.'

Summer smiled understanding her dilemma. 'Yes The Valide Sultan can be quite intimidating.'

'It was Emetullah, Sultan Mehmed's wife who did this to you,' she blurted out.

'Why are you telling me this?' Summer asked.

'You should know.'

'Thank you Anna, I will be very careful of her, I promise.'

'If I don't talk to you, it is not because I don't want to,' she said guiltily.

'I understand.'

'I will write you notes – look in the concubine's garden. All the women write their dreams and hopes on scripts that are put on the gate. I will put my notes in a crack in the stone wall to the left of the gate. That way we can communicate without anyone knowing.'

'All right,' Summer said. 'It will be our secret.'

'I must go, before the women wake up,' Anna said as she slipped out of the water and pulled on a robe. She smiled and waved as her wet feet padded across the floor back to their quarters.

Summer waited a few moments, then she followed suit. She too did not want to be caught here when the women came for their bath.

⌘

Mehmed shook his head in disbelief. Emetullah had just sent word that she was carrying his child, a result of their time away hunting. He chuckled to himself, relieved that the herbs had enabled him to perform. This baby would keep Emetullah busy, she would feel sick for a few moons and then she would be too uncomfortable to want his advances. She would feel secure as the mother of another of his heirs, which would keep her distracted while he pursued Süheyla. The timing could not be more perfect.

⌘

Summer faced the Valide Sultan. She was summoned to a room she had never seen in the palace. It was beautifully adorned with luxurious fabrics, rich tapestries and golden statues. There were numerous couches and the lighting was dim. Summer felt alarmed.

What is she planning now?

Two women joined her, their hips and bodies showing seductively in their tight bodices. They smiled at her knowingly and Summer felt more confused than ever. Finally the Valide Sultan arrived.

'Süheyla, you've had more than enough time to adjust to life here, the portrait is complete and now it is time to learn how to please a man. The Kapudan Pasha was quite taken with you, but he felt you were rather unresponsive and cold when he made love to you.'

Summer almost choked in fury. *Made love to me! Don't you mean when he raped me?* She wanted to scream.

She bit her tongue in anger and could taste blood.

'Today you will learn how to please a man. Touch and kissing is essential to being a good concubine. You will be instructed by Safiye and Mihriban, two of our most adept concubines.'

Summer looked confused as the young women circled her, swaying their hips provocatively. They gently touched her skin, running their fingers up and down her arms, brushing her breasts lightly as Summer gasped, shocked. They smiled, keeping eye contact with her.

'See how they look at you Süheyla, as though you were the only person in the room, lust in their eyes. This is what a good concubine can achieve, no matter how repulsive the man before her.'

Summer stepped back, feeling uncomfortable. She was not offended because they were women, although this concept was foreign to her values, but it was the fact that she had no control over her choices that upset her. She felt angry that the Valide Sultan believed she could use her body this way, despite her feelings. She gasped as Safiye undid the buttons on her robe, exposing her breasts. The woman placed her hand over her nipple and expertly caressed it, causing it to harden under her touch. Summer blushed, ashamed that her body had responded. She pushed her hand away angrily.

'No,' she said defiantly to the Valide Sultan.

'Yes, it is all about learning' the Valide Sultan replied firmly. This was not entirely true. The Valide Sultan knew that their great book condemned sexuality between women, but she was determined to break this defiant young girl before her and she would do it by any means necessary.

Mihriban smiled at her reluctance, pulling her close and kissing her. Her tongue pushed into Summer's mouth and her hands ran up her body touching her in intimate places. Summer pushed her away so hard; the young woman stumbled falling backward.

'I said no,' Summer repeated, anger flashing in her blue-grey eyes.' They had taken her dignity once – it would not happen again. She would make her own choices regarding her body. The Valide Sultan slapped her so hard, she heard her neck snap, but she did not feel any pain. She realized they had taken away her capacity for pain and pleasure – they had taken everything away from her. She started laughing, uncontrollably, a hollow, eerie echoing sound, a little bit of madness escaping her inner turmoil. The Valide Sultan looked furious.

'You think this is funny Süheyla? You will not mock me. Take her to the cage,' she ordered two guards. 'The Kapudan Pasha will pay you a visit there and this time there will be no one to care for your wounds,' she threatened.

'Please no...' Summer screamed as they dragged her half-naked from the room.

⌘

The cage was a tiny cell, with a high barred window, a hole in the stone floor to urinate in, and a sleeping mat that had seen better days. Summer now understood why the harem was called the golden cage – it was a prison, but a luxurious one. This cage was simply a crude jail cell. She lay down on the floor, buttoning her robe up as tears slid from her lashes. She could not endure another session with the Kapudan Pasha. She would rather die than be raped and tortured again. She pulled the jewelled clip from her hair and straightened the sharp pin. Then she began to scratch at her wrist till a thin red line appeared. She cut deeper and deeper till the blood flowed freely. She began to feel light headed and the cell faded into black spots.

THE GOLDEN CAGE

It will be over soon, she thought, peace engulfing her. *I won't feel any more pain soon. I will finally be free.*

TWENTY-SEVEN

THE PLOT

ANATOLIA

'I WARNED you she was unstable Mehmed,' the Valide Sultan chided her son. 'See, she's tried to kill herself. She does not belong here and she cannot be your wife.'

'Why did you bring her to Anatolia Mother?'

'It was a grave mistake, I admit,' she replied.

Summer was found unconscious in the cage when the guard brought her dinner. He notified the Valide Sultan immediately. She knew Mehmed would be furious if he discovered Süheyla had been imprisoned without his consent. So she lied about the circumstances.

'She was found in her quarters by one of the servants.'

'Why do you think she did it?' he asked.

'I don't know Mehmed, but she almost succeeded. We cannot watch her every minute of the day.'

'Ali will be assigned to her full time, Mother. He will ensure her safety.'

'All right,' she agreed reluctantly. She could not raise his suspicions.

⌘

Summer's eyes fluttered open. She was surprised to find herself in a bed. Light streamed in the window and she squinted, the brightness almost blinding her.

Are you there Great One?

She had shut herself off from the Great One since she had been brought to this place. After all the atrocities she experienced, she found it hard to have faith in his goodness or his love.

'Süheyla, are you awake,' a voice called in the distance.

No it's not possible. I'm in Lionsgate. I must be.

She was not ready to face that she had failed and was still stuck in her prison, so she closed her eyes again and drifted into oblivion.

Tristan was there, smiling at her reassuringly and her heart thumped furiously in her chest, her legs weak when she saw him. She stumbled toward him and he caught her in his arms, kissing her deeply and holding her as though he would never let her go. She looked up into his face lovingly, but it was no longer Tristan – it was Mehmed caressing her cheek.

'No,' she cried pulling away. 'What have you done with him?' Mehmed tried to hold onto her as she turned away, as she came face to face with the Kapudan Pasha. She felt trapped, she could not scream as each man grabbed one of her arms. They began to pull at her like she was a possession, each growling that she was his. She felt that she would tear in two as she pleaded them to stop.

Summer sat bolt upright, sweat dripping from her brow. She looked terrified and the physician calmed her in a gentle voice.

'You are safe, you need to rest.'

'Where am I?' she asked confused.

'You are in the palace infirmary.'

She looked down at her wrists that were bound and remembered the cage.

Why couldn't they just leave me to die?

⌘

The Valide Sultan had been tempted to leave Summer bleeding on the floor, however one look at the young girl and she knew the cuts weren't deep enough to cause her death. She smiled; Süheyla had initiated the perfect plan without even realising it. Now that Mehmed was aware of her suicidal tendencies it would be easy to convince him her death was by her own hand.

She knocked on Emetullah's door before entering. Emetullah looked pale and the Valide Sultan noticed the bucket beside her chair.

'Not feeling well?' she asked.

'This is always the worst part of carrying a child and this one is determined to make it memorable.'

'They say that sickness is a good thing,' the Valide Sultan said. 'The sickness lets you know that the child is growing well within. I have come to ease your mind that Süheyla will no longer be a threat to you or your children. I have a plan to get rid of her once and for all.'

'Thank you,' Emetullah replied. 'I have heard the way Mehmed talks about her, and it reminded me of how he used to sing my praises many years ago. I know that if she stays, I will lose him to her.'

'That is not going to happen, Emetullah. You need to look after yourself and this baby in your womb. It is only a matter of time till Mehmed comes to his senses. Once Süheyla is gone, he will need comforting in his grief. Just one other thing Emetullah, Do not wear that medallion until our plan is carried out. The women know you took it from her and if there should be any questions about it, you could jeopardise everything we have planned.'

'I understand,' she smiled at her mother-in-law as she removed the necklace and put it in a silver box. 'I will console Mehmed after her accident and he will turn to me in his grief. Thank you Valide Sultan.'

The two women plotted, unaware that Anna stood just outside the doorway. She was instructed to bring Emetullah some ginger tea to ease the nausea. She almost dropped the tray when she heard their plan. She scuttled back to her quarters, fearing for her friend.

I have to warn her.

⌘

AEGEAN SEA

The ship sailed effortlessly through the water toward the land of Anatolia.

'How much longer?' Tristan asked the captain.

'If these winds continue we'll be there in about five days.'

Five days Summer, I'm coming my love. Just be patient a little longer.

⌘

Anna scribbled the note and tucked it into her chemise. She hurried down the tiled hallways toward the garden that was solely for the purpose of the concubines. It was a haven, a beautiful escape from the confines of the palace. She entered the gate looking at all the scripts that had been attached to the gate. One day she too might write of her dreams and desires to catch the Sultan's eye. She hurried, afraid someone might see her. She looked around before slipping the note between two stones in the wall. She prayed Summer would find it.

Eyes watched from a window that overlooked the garden. They saw her slip the note into the wall before she hurried away. Clearly she did not want to be seen. Emetullah was curious.

What is Anna up to?

⌘

Summer pulled herself upright in the bed. Ali sat quietly in the corner keeping a watchful eye over her. The Sultan had instructed him to ensure she never try to hurt herself again. Ali understood her pain, but he did not want her to die. He did not understand why he felt such a connection to this young woman. Many foreign women had come into the harem before, both willingly and as captives, and yet he had never felt the urge to protect them as he did this woman. It was almost as though he felt compelled to ensure her safety. He waited for the physician to leave before he whispered, 'Are you feeling up to a walk in the garden yet?'

She nodded. Getting out of the four walls would be good and sunshine on her body would lift her spirits. She

THE GOLDEN CAGE

pulled on a robe and some silk slippers. She brushed her hair and pulled it across her shoulders and over her neck to cover the scar. She still felt self-conscious about it. Then she and Ali headed for the Concubines' garden.

⌘

Emetullah watched from her window. She was curious to see who would look for Anna's note. Whoever it was, they would never find it as she'd hurried down soon after Anna left the garden and retrieved it. She was shocked to discover that Anna knew of the Valide Sultan's plans to dispose of Süheyla. If the Sultan found out about this or her involvement, he would disown her as his wife and cut their children out of his life. She had to make sure this information was never leaked. She watched Ali and Süheyla enter the garden. They walked around the little pond, its water bubbling cheerily. She sat for a while and soaked up the sun. A few other concubines came and went, but Süheyla seemed to be in no hurry. Emetullah gasped when she and Ali whispered to one another. The eunuch was forbidden from speaking to any woman in the harem other than the Valide Sultan. Ali crossed the lawn, heading for the stone wall alongside the gate. He searched up and down the rough stones, then turned and shook his head. Süheyla nodded and smiled weakly. Then they left the garden. Emetullah sighed; relieved she had taken the note. She'd been tempted to leave it till the person collected it, but then curiosity got the better of her. She was glad it had, or Süheyla would know of their plan. She pulled the note out and reread it.

Summer, you are in great danger. Today I overheard the Valide Sultan and Emetullah talking about you. They plan to kill you as they feel you are a threat to Emetullah's heirs. I don't know exactly what they are planning, but you need to be very careful. Do not let Ali out of your sight. I will let you know more should I discover anything new. Keep safe.

Anna

She tucked the note into her robe and headed for the Valide Sultan's quarters.

⌘

Ali stood before the Valide Sultan. He had been summoned to her quarters and he felt a little apprehensive.

What could she possibly want?

'Come in Ali,' she smiled at the tall Abyssinian eunuch. 'I have some matters to discuss with you,' Ali nodded politely and entered. He could not shake off the feeling that he was entering the lion's den and was about to be devoured.

'Your devotion and diligence in looking after Süheyla's wellbeing has not gone unnoticed by the Sultan or me. You have shown that you are trustworthy and that you take your job very seriously. Because of this I have decided to appoint you as Kizlar Agha.

Ali was surprised. This was not what he expected when she summoned him. To be Kizlar Agha, was to be chief eunuch in the harem – his influence and ability to help the women would be substantially increased. He wondered what had prompted this decision.

'Solomon is getting old,' she added as though seeing the questions running through his mind. It was true that Solomon, the current Kizlar Agha, was old in years, but he still managed to fulfil the role efficiently and the concubines respected him.

'I don't quite know what to say,' Ali stuttered. He was not sure he wanted the position as it would be impossible for him to watch over Summer constantly.

'It is settled then. I won't take no for an answer Ali. You can prove your loyalty to the Sultan by doing the best job you can. The concubines trust you, as do I. You are the perfect man for the job.'

Ali walked back to Summer's quarters. He felt ill at ease. Something was not right.

Why would Sultan Mehmed agree to me being Kizlar Agha? It doesn't make sense. He was the one who wanted Miss Summer protected but surely he knows that with this responsibility I will not be able to protect her sufficiently?

Still, one did not say no to the Valide Sultan or the Sultan. He would have to find a way to both jobs well.

⌘

LIONSGATE

The Great One looked in his Mirror of Time and his concern for Summer grew. He knew what Valide Sultan Turhan Hatice was up to. She was trying to separate Ali from Summer to execute her diabolical plan. Well he would make sure that it did not happen. Summer had a lot more to accomplish in her life – it was not her time to die.

TWENTY-EIGHT
DEEP WATERS

AT SEA

ERIK squinted, the bright sunlight off the blue ocean dazzling him. They had just entered the Alboran Sea and were heading toward Anatolia. It would take a few more weeks at sea, but he didn't care how long it took, as long as they found her. He missed Isabel and knew that she would be frantic, so he had sent word when they were in Bayonne. Aedan joined him and slapped him on his back, trying to encourage him.

'We'll find her, I promise,' he said.

⌘

ANATOLIA

He waited in the shadows of the courtyard, hidden. He recalled the conversation he had with the Valide Sultan.

'The Sultan has an urgent message that needs to be relayed, Ali, and you are the only one we can trust. I know it seems odd asking you to be a messenger but our Janissaries are all on patrol or in training. She handed him a sealed document. Hurry, this must get to the Kapudan Pasha – it is an opportunity that will ensure Anatolia's influence is expanded and we must act fast.'

Ali felt torn in two. He'd prepared to leave tucking the document into his saddlebag. He felt sick leaving Summer, but if this document was as important as the Valide Sultan said, then he had a duty to carry out the task.

She told him that the Kapudan Pasha was in Salonica on a routine sea patrol. It would take him a week to deliver the message by horseback. He left the palace with his supplies and headed into the hills of the Anatolian countryside toward Salonica. A few miles from the palace his horse stumbled over a rocky outcrop, becoming lame. There was no way he could continue, his only alternative to return to the palace to get a fresh horse. It took the entire afternoon to walk the poor beast back to the palace. He arrived as the sun was setting and he put the horse in his stable. It was then that he saw the Kapudan Pasha leaving the palace.

She lied to me?

He had a sinking feeling Summer was in grave danger. The Valide Sultan wanted him gone so that he could not thwart her plans. He knew the time had come to choose where his loyalty lay – with Summer or her captors.

He slipped quietly between the pillars, staying hidden as he navigated the corridors. He hid in a cove near Summer's quarters and waited.

⌘

LIONSGATE

Mac sighed in relief. 'How did you do it,' he asked the Great One.

'There is no such thing as coincidence my friend. Things happen for a reason. Let's just say that his horse becoming lame was no accident,' the old man laughed.

'What is she up to?' Mac asked referring to the Valide Sultan.

'I have my suspicions Mac, but I am not going to share them with you or you will become stressed. All I can say is that Ali is there to protect Summer and I am confident that he will. He may fully not understand his purpose but he does feel connected to her. I have ensured that. Now, time to stop looking in the Mirror of Time and for you to find other things to occupy your mind.' He chased Mac from his room and chuckled at the glare he gave him as he left.

The Great One chose to hide much of what happened to Summer from Mac. He was not aware of her brutal rape or the attempt to kill herself. He knew that it would be too much for him to endure.

⌘

ANATOLIA

Summer felt a warm hand clamp over her mouth and she gasped for air, struggling. Strong arms held her down as she squirmed. There was more than one man in her room. Fear and dread engulfed her again as she remembered the feeling of being held down by the Kapudan Pasha as he raped her. She tried to scream but the hand over her mouth only enabled her to let out a gargled noise. A fist smashed the side of her head as she struggled furiously and she felt herself slip into oblivion. They bundled her into a large sack and carried her down the dark corridor.

Ali saw them exit the heavy doors from the harem. Two of the Valide Sultan's bodyguards grunted as they carried the dead weight. His heart sank. He knew Summer was in the sack. His gut told him so. He prayed she was not dead.

'Where's the other girl?' one guard asked the other.

'They're fetching her.'

'Let's get her to the carriage. We'll wait for them there.'

Ali hurried to the stables and saddled a horse.

Where are they taking her?

He walked the horse out and waited in the shadows as they loaded the sack into the carriage. He thought he heard a soft moan as they bumped her against the door.

She's alive!

Another guard marched a terrified Anna to the carriage. She looked pale, her eyes huge in her head.

'Get in,' he ordered. She whimpered when she saw the sack.

The carriage rolled out of the palace and into the night. Ali kept his distance as the full moon lit the sky and the path ahead of him. They were heading for the Bosphorus Strait. The carriage pulled up alongside a deserted section of the strait. It was rocky and uneven. Ali dismounted and made his way to the shoreline. He slipped between two rocks and waited. He had a horrible premonition that history was about to repeat itself. The Valide Sultan was committing the same atrocity, her husband Sultan Ibrahim, had all those years ago. He was known as Ibrahim the Mad after he'd ordered two hundred and eighty of his concubines to be thrown into the Bosphorus Strait in

THE GOLDEN CAGE

weighted sacks. It was a mass drowning that shocked the Anatolian nation.

Anna was dragged from the carriage as was the sack containing Summer. The men carried it down to the water's edge and set it down on a rocky ledge. Summer squirmed in the sack, her muffled groans getting louder. Anna began to hyperventilate, huge sobs wracking her small frame as she tried to breathe. She looked around wildly as if hoping for a miracle or escape. Then she saw Ali. She opened her mouth to call out, then closed it again when she saw him put his finger over his lips. The guards untied the sack and opened it slightly, revealing Summer's head. She moaned, half conscious. Anna gasped, fear completely overwhelming her.

'The Valide Sultan wants you to know, Anna, that Süheyla did not receive your message. This is her warning to you. What you are about to witness will be what happens to you if you ever try anything like this again or if you ever mention what you have seen. Your loyalty is to her alone. Do you understand?'

Anna wiped the tears that ran down her cheeks and nodded numbly. She looked apologetically at Summer.

The men added a few loose rocks to the sack and tied it up again. Then they dragged it to the edge of the rocky outcrop and threw it into the black sea. The sack floated momentarily, then started to slowly sink as it became water-logged. Anna became hysterical.

'Get her out of here, before she alerts half of Anatolia,' the guard said. They dragged her away kicking and screaming as she craned her neck toward the sea. The last thing she saw was Ali running and diving into the water after the sack.

⌘

228
THE GOLDEN CAGE

Tristan let out a shout of delight – he could see the lights of Anatolia in the distance.

'We're here,' he shouted to Griffin and Cam who scuttled on deck to see. 'We've made it,' he said cheerily, 'and we are going to find her – I just know it.'

The three hugged each other. It had taken weeks to get here and their sense of relief was tangible. Tristan just hoped that the Sultan would be receptive to his offer. The last thing they wanted was a battle with the Anatolians. They were outnumbered by far.

'Time to get our Musketeer uniforms on, boys.'

'Finally we get to wear the real thing,' Cam teased. 'I'll have to thank Summer for this.'

TWENTY-NINE

CONSTANTINOPLE

ANATOLIA

ALI did not think twice before he dived into the dark water. Swimming was not his strong suit but his overwhelming urge to save Summer masked his fear. The water was black but the brilliant moonlight shone through it making it look almost navy blue. He searched for the sack but couldn't see it. He surfaced for air, taking a new mouthful before diving under again. He pulled with his arms and kicked his long legs as he went deeper and deeper. Then he saw it. The sack was entangled on a submerged log, which had prevented it from sinking to the bottom. He pulled at it but it would not budge.

Time is running out, for both of us, he thought frantically.

He placed his hands on the top of the sack straddling it each side. Then he pushed his feet against the log with as much force as he could muster. The fabric ripped and he pulled it up to the surface. It was heavy with her body and the added rocks, but somehow Ali felt he had a supernatural strength. He dragged it ashore, pulling himself onto the slippery rocks. The sack was a dead weight and there was no sign of life from within.

'Don't you dare die on me Miss Summer,' he gasped out of breath.

He ripped the torn sack open and pulled her out. Her wet hair was plastered on her forehead and her body felt cold and limp. He remembered what he had witnessed as a child growing up in Abyssinia. When he was eight, one of his friends had almost drowned in a lake. The child's parents had called for the witch doctor to revive him. The gnarly old man hardly had any teeth, a stare that could make you tremble and a raspy voice, but he had performed a miracle on the child's lifeless body. Ali followed the procedure he had used. He laid her on her back, tilted her head sideways then he began to rub her sternum, gently then with greater pressure. He blew in her face and tickled her throat, hoping to elicit response from her. Then he rolled her onto her side and covered her body and warmed her. All the while he spoke to her, 'come on Miss Summer, it's not your time to die.'

Ali also remembered the beating his father gave him when he found out that he had watched the witch doctor's work. 'He's evil, boy and he gets his magic from the devil.' Ali had never understood that.

Why would the devil save his friend?

⌘

Summer floated between worlds – she felt at peace for the first time in weeks. Her body longed to just relax – let it all go as she floated, but something held her back. She tried to ignore it, shrug it off, and she looked at the beautiful gates that were ahead of her. They opened as she entered and then she saw him – her beloved Papa Mac. She ran to him and he folded her in his arms, hugging her as though his life depended upon it.

'Summerbee, I've missed you so much.'

'Me too Papa Mac,' she sobbed. 'I'm so glad to be here with you.'

THE GOLDEN CAGE

'I want you to know,' he said earnestly, 'that I did see all those beautiful drawings you left for me at my grave. I just wish you had known it then.'

Summer smiled. She loved him with all her heart.

'There's something else. It's not your time to join me in Lionsgate, Summer. You must go back. You have your whole life to live.'

'No Papa Mac,' she pleaded. 'Living as a slave, my body not my own is no life. I don't want to go back. How can you want me to return to that place?'

He struggled to answer but he knew he must. 'Things will get better Summerbee – you'll see. Just have a little faith.'

He hugged her and then turned away. 'I love you, now you must return. There are people who love you, back there, who are waiting for you.'

'Papa Mac, no,' she cried as he disappeared and she was left alone in a misty cloud. She could hear a voice calling her and she moved toward it. 'I'm coming,' she said afraid.

Summer spluttered, then vomited up the salty water. She gasped in fresh air and Ali laughed, relief overwhelming him.

'You're alive,' he smiled, his white teeth gleaming in his thankful face. He hugged her close and whispered, 'I'm going to get you away from here, I promise.'

⌘

The ship docked in Constantinople and Tristan, Griffin and Cam were down the gangplank the second it was put out. They looked impressive in their uniforms and Griffin

THE GOLDEN CAGE

and Cam had to admit they were glad they had the opportunity to wear the full uniform at least once. They walked the winding streets. It was early morning and people were just beginning to surface for the day. Many looked at them curiously in their strange uniforms, but they seemed an amicable enough people. Finally they found a coffee house that was open. Rumours of the Anatolian coffee houses were well known. They were still a bit controversial. One of the Sultans had agreed for them to be opened to the chagrin of many who believed coffee was as bad as any form of alcohol. The religious customs of many in Anatolia forbade them to drink the dark, rich brew. They were surprised to see how full it was so early in the day. Groups of men sat together smoking tobacco and drinking coffee as they discussed music, art and poetry in animated voices. They momentarily stopped when the three entered, staring at their uniform, then they resumed their debates. They ordered coffee and sat at the counter.

'What brings you to Constantinople?' the man behind the counter asked.

'We are here on Francian business with the Sultan,' Tristan answered. 'In fact it's the first time we've ever been to Constantinople. Can you direct us to Topkapi Palace?'

The man laughed. 'Sure, but it's hard to miss. Just follow the cobbled street up the hill and the palace sits at the top. Now what do you think of my coffee?' he asked.

'Much better than the coffee we have in Francia,' Tristan laughed.

⌘

Ali and Summer made their way along the edge of the Bosphorus Strait. They headed away from Constantinople

THE GOLDEN CAGE

toward Marmara. Summer sat on the horse while Ali led the animal, carefully keeping an eye on her. He had taken a robe off a wash line at one of the fishing houses along the Bosphorus and Summer was warmly wrapped against the morning air. He was tired but knew they could not stop yet. They needed some distance from Constantinople and the palace. If anyone saw them or reported them they would be in trouble. They moved slowly but made steady headway.

'How did you end up at Topkapi, Ali?' Summer finally asked. She had waited for him to share his story but he had not. Now she felt that she should know him better. He'd protected her more than once.

'It's a long story Miss Summer.'

'We have time,' she smiled and he laughed. 'All right, perhaps my story will help the miles pass faster. Like you, I did not choose to come to this land. I come from Abyssinia, a place many miles from here. It is further south and it is a hard place to live. I grew up in extreme poverty – my family had very little food to eat and when the rains didn't come many people starved. When I was twelve, my sister and I were captured by the military. We were taken and imprisoned. The rulers of our country made their money and kept themselves in comfort by selling children to the Anatolians and other nations. My sister and I were sold to the Sultan.'

Summer was surprised to hear that Ali had a sister.

'What happened to your sister, Ali?'

'She was taken into the harem, like you were. She could not stand it Miss Summer.'

'I understand Ali,' she said softly touching his shoulder.

'She did what you attempted to do, but she was successful.' He let the implication hang in the air.

'I would have tried again if I had been given to the Kapudan Pasha,' she said earnestly.

'I know. I couldn't save her Miss Summer, but I was determined to save you.'

'It wasn't your fault. You do know that, don't you?'

She saw the guilt in his eyes and she said more firmly, 'you were just a child Ali – it wasn't your fault. Did they hurt you too?' She changed the subject hoping to take his mind off his sister.

Ali laughed cynically. 'You could say that. I wasn't always called Ali, you know. My name used to be Eli but that was not acceptable to the beliefs they follow, so they changed it to Ali which is the Anatolian expression of my name.'

'Yes, I know about that. They insisted on calling me Süheyla – I hate that name. It's as though they are determined to erase our previous lives by giving us new identities. As if it were that simple. Come to think of it though, they never renamed Anna. I wonder why?'

'Oh, she'll be renamed. She is still too young, but when they prepare her for the Sultan or some other man they will give her a new name. It is just a matter of time.'

'I feel bad leaving her there,' Summer said.

⌘

Anna was locked in her quarters after her return from the Bosphorus Strait. She cried till she felt her face would crack and her tear ducts could produce no more tears. She stared out the window at the horizon.

Why did I ever want to come here? These people are animals.

She was afraid, for the first time since she had come to Topkapi. The Valide Sultan had made it perfectly clear what would happen to her if she stepped out of line again.

'Before we throw you into the Bosphorus, I will gift you to the Kapudan Pasha. You saw what a night with him did to Süheyla,' she threatened.

Anna nodded demurely and promised she would try harder to please the Valide Sultan, but all it had done was strengthen her hatred for the woman.

As she gazed out her window she saw three men in their uniforms. They were not from Anatolia. She strained her ear against the trellised window to hear what they were saying.

'What can we do for you?' one of the Janissaries asked.

'We are here on the orders of Queen Maria of Francia to see the Sultan.'

'The Sultan is away hunting,' the Janissary said, 'but the Valide Sultan will hear your request. Wait here, we will fetch her.'

They stood in the courtyard, watched suspiciously by four Janissaries. They stood with their hands on their sabres, menacing and sending the message that Tristan and his friends were neither welcome nor trusted.

The Valide Sultan appeared and looked alarmed to see Musketeers in her courtyard.

'Why are you here?' she asked curtly. Tristan stepped forward and nodded his head in respect.

'Valide Sultan, we are here at Queen Maria's request. She sent you a woman and she wants us to ensure that this woman arrived here and will no longer be a problem to her.'

The Valide Sultan smiled. 'Do you really expect me to believe this? Queen Maria would have sent a messenger, not soldiers to find out the information she needs. I know who you are. You are the Musketeers that betrayed Francia, the ones who would be beheaded should she discover where you are.'

Thanks to Summer's sketch of Tristan, the Valide Sultan knew exactly who they were.

They looked surprised at her knowledge.

'We do not want trouble Valide Sultan. We just want to know that Summer Sveinsson is all right. We are willing to pay handsomely for her release.'

The Valide Sultan looked insulted.

'Do you think so little of us as a people – that we enslave women and drag them here against their wishes? There are many women in our harem, that is true; but none of them are forced to be here. The woman you refer to is not here at Topkapi Palace. Whatever yarn the Queen of Francia has spun you, I can assure you it is not true.'

'Forgive me if I insulted you Valide Sultan, but we have it on good authority that Summer was brought here on one of your ships from Francia.'

'I assure you once again that she is not here. You are welcome to look around if you wish. In fact we would be happy if you stayed as our guests tonight to meet the women in the harem. This way you can set your mind at ease that the woman you are looking for is not here.'

'Thank you we will accept your kind offer,' Tristan said nodding again at the Sultan's mother.

'Do you believe her?' Griffin asked Tristan when they were alone.

'No, but she didn't seem worried about us looking around the palace either, and that concerns me. We need to find evidence that Summer is here.'

'How are we going to do that?' Cam asked.

'I'm not sure,' Tristan said, 'but we'll make a plan.'

THIRTY

QUESTIONS

THEY found shelter in an old, deserted barn. A fierce storm blew in, streak lightning hissed furiously through the night sky, hitting the earth in angry strikes. Thunder rolled soon after, shaking the earth. Then the rain came. It was the first time Summer had seen rain since she had come to Anatolia and instead of sheltering from it she put her hands out catching the water that ran through the leaky barn roof. She drank it thirstily and splashed her face. Ali watched her, a smile on his face. She was enjoying the simplicity of rain.

'We need to rest Miss Summer, we have a long journey ahead of us. The sooner we get to Marmara, the sooner we can find a ship to take us away from Anatolia. They settled down on some old sacks and listened to the storm.

'We should be scared listening to it,' she said, 'and yet it's somehow comforting; as though a greater being is trying to communicate with us.'

'Yes, you're right Miss Summer.'

'Do you believe Ali?'

'Believe? What do you mean?'

'In the Great One, a god, some kind of supreme being.'

'I've always believed Miss Summer.'

'Why? You've seen some awful things. How can the Great One truly love us if he lets us suffer so much in this world?'

'He doesn't want us to suffer. I am a believer, but not in the same way others believe.'

'What do you mean,' she asked curious now.

'I don't believe the Great One, as you refer to him, is controlling us like puppets. I think more of him as a force that fills the universe, a supreme creative energy that is love and that his essence and nature is in each of us. It is not his job to make us happy or order our lives step by step. That is our job; our choice and we attain it when we realize that we are one with the universe, and ultimately him. We will all experience good and bad in this world, and yes some things will even be too horrible to bear, but it is our responsibility to take those awful things and use them for good. Kindness, love, happiness – all those are choices we make and a path we can follow. Evil only exists when good men do nothing.'

She kept silent. She understood what he was saying but she found it hard to believe that she could choose to be happy and she felt such a deep rage within her that she didn't want to love or show kindness to the people that hurt her. She hated them with a consuming passion. So she changed the subject.

'How did you become a eunuch?'

He was surprised by the question, but he had expected it at some point. 'I am Sandali.' He could see the blank expression on her face and knew she had no idea what that meant. 'That means, every part that makes me a man, has been removed.'

She looked shocked when she realized what he was saying. She had assumed that only a portion of his manhood had been removed.

She shook her head, shocked. 'They took my dignity and used my body without my consent Ali, but what they've done to you is unforgivable.'

'No Miss Summer, this wasn't done by the Anatolians. It was the Abyssinians who castrated me, long before I went to Anatolia. They knew that I would fetch a higher price if I was a Sandali eunuch.'

'I'm sorry Ali. Would you prefer me to call you Eli?' she asked suddenly.

'Yes, I think I would. It's time we both had a fresh start, a new life with a new future. Now get some rest, we have a big day tomorrow.'

Summer leaned back against the sacks and closed her eyes. It wasn't long before she heard him gently snoring but she could not sleep.

I know Eli thinks that nothing is your fault, that we have to be kind no matter what, but I just don't understand it Great One. Why can't you just do your job? You owe it to us to keep us safe. This world is a horrible place. What did Eli, his sister or I ever do that was so bad? Why did you let us all suffer so much, yet the really evil people get away with it? There's no point having faith in you because you are a let-down, a farce and a coward. Her thoughts fuelled her anger.

⌘

LIONSGATE

He wasn't disappointed or angry with her. She had a right to question, to make sense of why life was so disappointing at times, why people were so evil and she had a right to question her faith. He was pleased she was asking questions. Those who followed blindly never really saw, they never developed true faith – they simply developed the ability to follow what they were told. She was progressing beautifully. The Great One smiled. 'Question all you need Summer, for it will heal your soul and lead you to true freedom.'

⌘

TOPKAPI PALACE

The food was excellent and the Valide Sultan ensured the men's glasses were filled with raki constantly. The dancers swayed to rhythmic music and the atmosphere was heady, lustful. The concubines were brought in one by one for them to see. Summer was not amongst them. Tristan was surprised to see such a young girl amongst the women.

'How old is she?' he asked pointing to Anna.

'She is fourteen,' the Valide Sultan replied.

'Yet you say no girl is here against her will?' he asked suspiciously. 'Is a fourteen year old even capable of making that choice?'

'Ask her yourself,' the Valide Sultan said confidently. 'Anna, this gentleman has a question.'

Tristan was shocked when Anna confirmed her desire to be in the harem. He swore that her eyes had more to say when she was escorted away. He was not convinced by her words alone.

'Finally, I would like to introduce you to the Sultan's wife,' the Valide Sultan said. The three men had to hold back their mirth at this statement. They had just met numerous concubines before finally meeting his wife. It seemed almost comical. 'This is Emetullah.'

Emetullah stepped forward. She had dark hair and eyes and was truly beautiful, however there seemed something hard and cruel about her. The three men nodded out of respect. Tristan could see that the other women were wary of her. He wished he could ask her a thousand questions about Summer, but the Valide Sultan presided over them anxiously. Instead he smiled and drank the raki.

Griffin leaned over and whispered. 'We have to find evidence of Summer being here.'

'I know, but she is watching us like a hawk.'

'I have an idea,' Cam said.

'Valide Sultan, you certainly have some very beautiful women in the harem. I have to confess I am rather jealous of the Sultan and his good fortune,' Cam laughed waving at the myriad of women. The Valide Sultan smiled.

'Yes, I pride myself on selecting only the best for Sultan Mehmed.'

'And that you have certainly done. I don't suppose you have any second best women for a weary soldier who is in dire need of some company?' Cam asked. Griffin's eyes widened and he shook his head at his cousin who deftly ignored him.

'Hospitality is certainly something I pride myself on here at Topkapi Palace,' the Valide Sultan said. 'I certainly do have a young woman who would be more than happy to satisfy your needs.' She waved her hand to a young woman swaying her hips in dance a few metres away. 'She will take care of you. Would any of you other gentlemen like to retire?' she asked suggestively.

'No thank you,' Griffin and Tristan echoed in unison.

Cam and the young woman exited the room and made their way toward Cam's quarters. She draped her arm across his shoulders and Cam felt sorry for the young girl. He wondered what it was like being sent off with a stranger to be a pawn in whatever game he chose.

Is she afraid or does she feel nothing – are her senses and personality so crushed by this system that she has died inside?

He did not know.

'This is a beautiful palace,' he remarked as they made their way down the mosaic-tiled hallway.

'Yes, it is,' she whispered seductively.

'How long have you been here?' he asked, genuinely curious.

'Five years,' she replied and he gasped. She would have been a child when she arrived, as she could be no more than eighteen. She smiled at the shock on his face.

'Do you like it here?'

'There are worse places for a woman to be,' she replied evading his actual question.

'Before we retire I would like to see something of the history of this place. Can you show me where the Sultan stays?'

She gasped at his direct request. 'I cannot,' she said afraid. 'The Sultan's quarters are off-limits unless the Valide Sultan invites us to spend time with him. If we get caught I will be punished.'

'Who will catch us?' Cam teased. 'The Valide Sultan is entertaining and the Sultan is away hunting, so I believe.'

'No we cannot.' She insisted.

'It would be a pity for me to report to the Valide Sultan that her hospitality had not been satisfactory,' Cam manipulated the young woman. He felt a twinge of conscience when he saw the fear in her eyes.

'Please no,' she begged. 'If you do that I will become nothing more than a servant in the harem. My chances of ever finding a man to marry me will be over.'

'Just one quick tour of the Sultan's quarters,' he implored.

'All right, but we will have to be very careful,' she said. Cam followed her through the darkened passageways toward the Sultan's quarters. They hid in the recesses when Janissaries passed them, but mostly it was quiet and abandoned. They slipped through a large wooden door and into a beautifully ornate room that had books from floor to ceiling. The furnishings were luxurious as heavy velvets and silks cascaded from the arched windows to the floor.

'This is the Sultan's library,' she whispered, the fear in her voice was tangible.

'It's magnificent,' he whispered back as he gazed around the room. He was certain now that the Sultan was indeed away hunting, as he knew she would not have brought him here had the Sultan been home. It was the answer he wanted as he had not believed the Valide Sultan when she insisted Mehmed was away. They heard voices outside the door and the young woman froze, her eyes huge in her ashen face. Cam grabbed her by the wrist and pulled her behind a large freestanding bookshelf. It was a small space, but obviously one the Sultan used for storing things.

They stood face to face and he could see the young woman trembling as the door to the room opened.

'Where should I put it?' the voice asked.

'Just stand it against the bookshelf,' the other voice said. 'The Sultan can select where he wishes it to go when he returns from his trip.'

The young girl in front of Cam looked as though she were about to faint. Her breathing became ragged and he feared she would get them caught. He had only one thought in mind to keep her quiet. His head descended as he pulled her close and kissed her. She did not resist or fight him; instead she leaned against him as she returned his kiss. They did not hear the door close as the two men left, their lips locked and their breathing becoming more passionate. Finally Cam pulled away and apologised awkwardly.

'I'm sorry,' he said blushing.

'I'm not,' she said breathlessly. He took her hand and pulled her out from behind the shelf. It was then that he saw it – the Sultan's portrait. He would recognize her brush strokes and technique anywhere – it was Summer's work. He rushed over to the painting and looked in the bottom right hand corner and there he saw her signature. She was here, or had been – this was the proof.

'Thank you,' he said to the young woman, 'but I must get back to my friends.' She looked disappointed and then upset.

'The Valide Sultan will be very angry if I have not satisfied you,' she said and Cam smiled.

'I would like nothing more, but you are worth more than a man using your body for one night. You will find a man who loves you and who will treat you with the respect you deserve.'

Her eyes grew wide again and then misted over. 'I wish you were that man.'

Cam smiled and kissed her hand. 'The Valide Sultan will be told that you were magnificent,' he smiled and she laughed, relieved.

'Thank you.'

They made their way back to the feasting hall and Cam kissed her on the cheek as they entered. Then he made his way over to Griffin and Tristan, a sparkle in his eye.

'Hope you enjoyed yourself Cam,' Griffin said sarcastically to his cousin. He was annoyed that Cam had gone off to relieve his sexual frustration when he should have been focussing on Summer.

'She's here,' he exclaimed 'and I have seen the proof.'

THIRTY-ONE

ESCAPE

SUMMER and Eli hid on the outskirts of Marmara. No one seemed to be following them and they both assumed that the Valide Sultan believed she was dead. Eli had time on his hands, at least another week since she had supposedly sent him on that farcical trip to Salonica. It would give them enough time to escape Anatolia before she questioned his whereabouts. They rummaged in a bin in an old alleyway looking for food scraps. They ate hungrily when they found bread crusts and even the rats that competed for the food did not put them off.

'Dinner with vermin,' Summer sighed. 'Believe it or not, this is the best meal I've had in Anatolia.' Eli raised his eyebrows and she laughed, a tinkling, happy sound.

'No I mean it Eli. This is the first free meal I've had in a long time and it tastes better than the sumptuous food of captivity.'

He understood what she meant. 'Come, we must make our way down to the docks. The sailors will be heading to the taverns for dinner and it is the best time to stow away.'

Summer paled. 'Do we have to stow away?' she asked dismayed. 'Can we not offer to pay for our passage on my safe return to Griswold?'

Eli shook his head. 'No Miss Summer, no ship will take us on board in Anatolian waters. They will take one look at us and know we have escaped from the Sultan's harem. I stand out like a sore thumb as a eunuch and you are a foreigner with me. They will put two and two together. The reward they would receive for our capture would far exceed the promise of payment on your safe return. We cannot chance it.'

She nodded her head. 'All right, I trust you Eli.'

⌘

TOPKAPI PALACE

'You saw the portrait?' Griffin asked in disbelief.

'Yes,' Cam reiterated for the second time. 'It was her work. I saw her signature. She's here, or was here. What are we going to do? We can't mention the portrait as it was in the Sultan's quarters and if they discover I was there it will cause trouble for the girl I was with.'

'I have an idea,' Tristan said excited. 'Let's go for a walk in the palace gardens and I will tell you all about it. I don't want to talk here – it feels as though these walls have ears.'

⌘

Anna watched the men from her window. They were deep in conversation. She heard the one man refer to himself as Summer's brother and she knew they were here to find her. She wondered if Ali had managed to save Summer. Somehow she had a good feeling about it. She had to get a message to them. She slid off her bed and tiptoed down the passage to Emetullah's quarters. She knocked gently on the door and awaited a response. When she heard nothing, she slipped into her rooms and headed for her dressing table. She found the medallion in the silver box and she took it out. This did not belong to Emetullah and she had no right to it. It belonged to Summer's brother and she would ensure that somehow he received it. He had a right to know his sister had been here. She tucked it into her pocket and headed for the door. It was pulled open before she could grab the handle and she gasped in fright.

'What are you doing in my quarters Anna?' Emetullah growled suspiciously.

'Oh you startled me. I came to see if you would like some tea Emetullah. I know how unwell you have been feeling lately.'

Her heart pounded in her chest but she kept a smile on her face.

Please let her believe me, she thought.

'Thank you Anna, that is very kind but I have just had tea a short while ago. I am really tired and just want to rest.'

'Let me know if I can do anything for you,' the young girl said as she made her escape. She scuttled back to her room and wrote a note. Then she sealed the medallion inside and climbed up on the window ledge.

⌘

Tristan heard the tinkle of a small bell as it bounced off the gravel beside him. He bent down to pick up the small shiny object. He shook it and it tinkled once more. It looked as though it had come off a piece of jewellery or clothing. He looked up at the huge stone wall beside them. Way up he saw the young girl they had met at the feast. She waved at him and placed a finger over her lips. He nodded.

'She's trying to tell us something,' he said to Cam and Griffin. 'I knew there was something not right.'

She dropped something out of the window and it fluttered to the floor. Tristan scooped it up and when he next looked up she was gone. He held the parchment in his hand and pulled it open. The medallion slithered out onto the floor at his feet.

'My medallion,' he exclaimed picking it up and fingering it as though it would somehow magically bring Summer to him. 'Summer never would have taken this off.'

He looked at the parchment and read her note.

Meet me at midnight in the stables.

Finally, they would have some answers.

Summer, please be safe, Tristan pleaded.

⌘

They huddled amongst the cargo, cramped but comfortable. Eli found some old sacks and made a makeshift bed for them both. The old boat creaked and gently swayed against the dock. They hoped it would not be a long wait before the ship sailed. More than that they hoped no one would discover them before they set sail. Summer could literally taste her freedom and she was glad that Eli was with her. This would have been terrifying if she had been alone.

She fell asleep with the rocking motion and for the first time in days she dreamed of Tristan. He was there, in front of her, smiling and reaching out for her. She wanted to take his hand but somehow she just could not grab hold of him as hard as she tried. Each time something would hinder her and she was becoming frustrated. She whimpered and just as she thought she could take hold of him, she found she was looking up into the Kapudan Pasha's face. She woke with a start and a muffled cry. Tears ran from her eyes as Eli shushed her. He held her hand and reassured her.

'You are safe, Miss Summer. It was just a dream.'

'Will the bad dreams ever go away Eli?'

'One day they will, I promise you.'

'Do you feel that?' Summer asked suddenly.

'Yes,' he smiled, his white teeth gleaming in his dark face. 'We are moving, the ship has set sail.'

They hugged one another – another milestone reached in their great escape.

'We are free Eli,' she said. 'We are free.'

⌘

Tristan, Cam and Griffin made their way to the stables. It was almost midnight and they hoped that no one would see them. They knew Anna was taking a big risk by meeting them and their first concern was that she be protected at all costs. They found her huddled in one of the stalls.

'I'm here,' she called anxiously.

'Anna, where did you get this medallion?' Tristan asked.

'It was Miss Summer's medallion, but Emetullah stole it from her when she cut her throat.' She saw the horrified look on the men's faces and realized what they were thinking. 'Oh no, don't worry she didn't die,' she assured. Tristan breathed out in relief. 'Where is she now?'

'I'm not sure,' Anna responded tentatively. 'I think she's alive, but I don't know for sure. Emetullah and the Valide Sultan had her thrown into the Bosphorus Strait.'

'They drowned her?' Griffin asked horrified.

'They tried to, but I saw Ali jump in after her. I think he may have saved her.'

'Who's Ali?' Cam asked.

'The Chief Eunuch. He liked Miss Summer for some reason and he has been protecting her while she has been at the palace.'

'Where would he take her if he rescued her?'

'I don't know, but they would have to escape from Anatolia. He would not bring her back here.'

'Where does he come from Anna?'

'I don't know, I've never heard him speak, although I have heard the Valide Sultan talk about his sister as the Abyssinian whore who killed herself. Does that help?'

'Yes it does, thank you. We must leave immediately before you are discovered and before the Valide Sultan discovers our plans. Let's get our horses saddled.'

'Please,' Anna implored, 'you have to take me with you. When Emetullah discovers that the medallion is gone she will know I have taken it, and the Valide Sultan has sworn to kill me if I step out of line again.'

'I thought you wanted to be here? Tristan asked.

'I did, in the beginning, but I have seen what they have done to Summer and I don't want that to happen to me – please.'

The three men looked at one another, each terrified by the girl's words.

What did they do to Summer? Each man was too afraid to think about it.

'All right, let's saddle up and out of here.'

⌘

Erik sailed into Constantinople in remarkable time, thanks to the tailwinds the Great One had sent. It was past midnight and the city was quiet. Lights flickered like stars on the horizon and the boat lurched and swayed. It had been a long journey but they had finally arrived. He hoped that it would not be too difficult to find Griffin and Cam. The boat sailed into the harbour and bumped gently against the wharf as ropes were thrown over the side and secured to the moorings. The men bounced over the side like rats abandoning ship and headed to the local tavern that was still in full swing. There was not much they could do tonight except refuel and refresh themselves. Tomorrow he would search for Griffin and Cam. Erik strode down the gangplank toward the inn with Aedan on his heels. It always took him a few moments to get rid of his sea legs and to feel normal again.

'Papa is that you?'

Erik swung around and broke into a smile when he saw Griffin and Cam. They were accompanied by another young man and a tiny slip of a girl.

'Well that was easy,' Erik said hugging his son. 'I've missed you.'

'I've missed you too Papa. We need a place to hide Anna before anyone sees her.'

'What have you got yourself into this time?' Erik smiled. 'Come along Miss, let's get you onto the ship.' Anna was settled into a cabin and Griffin filled Erik, Aedan and the others in on what they knew about Summer's whereabouts.

'Seems to me that we need to leave Anatolia as soon as possible,' Erik said earnestly. 'You believe she is heading for Abyssinia?'

'It seems logical to me that that is where they will go. Trying to get back to Griswold is too far to travel. I believe that this eunuch will try to find her passage from his homeland.'

'Then Abyssinia is where we will go. Let's get the ship replenished and we sail at first light.'

'I'm glad we found you Papa,' Griffin said.

'Me too.'

'I'm sorry Papa, I feel this is all my fault. I should have protected Summer better.'

'None of this is your fault. We'll find her Griff, I promise,' Erik said patting his son on the shoulder.

⌘

The dreadful nausea returned and Summer recalled how sick she had been on her journey to Anatolia. Now she was trapped in this small space, the air stifling and stale and she felt the urge to vomit.

Stop it! she mentally chided herself. *Now is not the time to fall apart. Your freedom and life depend upon it.*

She willed her body to behave, to conform and she fought the nausea down. She nibbled on some of the dry crackers that Eli found and it helped her. They had been at sea for a week and she knew that Anatolia would be far behind them. She just wished she could stand up on deck and breathe in the fresh salty air and feel the wind blow through her thick chocolate hair.

Not long now – your freedom is just around the corner.

THIRTY-TWO

SANDCASTLES

LOUD SHOUTING woke her from sleep. Rough hands pulled her to her feet and dragged her from behind the barrels of food. Eli was dragged behind her. Her half-awake state did not register that they had been found, that stowaways were not welcome on ships. Finally she felt the cool wind on her face – the wind she had been desperate to experience but now it was fear that filled her belly.

What will happen to us now?

The captain of the ship looked furious. He eyed her and Eli up and down, shaking his head angrily and cussing in another language.

'You have put me in a very difficult position,' he shouted.

'Please Captain,' Summer tried to placate the man, 'my father will pay you handsomely for my safe return.'

'Money is no use if my head is absent from my body, ' he shouted at her waving his fist. 'I am not stupid. I know you are from the Sultan's harem. No woman ever travels with a eunuch unless she has come from the harem. If word gets out that we helped you to escape I will be banned from ever trading in Anatolia again, or worse, have my head removed. No, this will not do. Get the boat,' he commanded one of the sailors.

They watched as two sailors lowered a rough wooden boat. It had two rickety oars and it bobbed alongside the ship's side. Then they threw a rope ladder over. 'Go, before I change my mind and throw you overboard.'

THE GOLDEN CAGE

Summer clambered over the side before he changed his mind. The descent to the little boat was terrifying. The rope ladder swayed in the wind. She clung to the ladder, her knuckles white as her wobbly legs took her lower and lower. Finally she dropped into the little rowboat and her stomach lurched at the motion. Eli dropped into the boat alongside her. Then the men lowered a small bag of food and some fresh water. The sailor cut the ropes that kept their boat attached to the ship and within seconds they began to drift away from the enormous vessel. Eli rowed the boat. The sun beat down and Summer felt her lips begin to dry and crack. She took tiny sips of water, terrified that they would run out. She did not want to die from thirst in a rowboat on the ocean.

'We're going to die, aren't we?' she asked him.

'Not if I can help it Miss Summer. We haven't come this far to be defeated.'

'You still have faith and believe, even though we are in a mess?'

'It's good to always believe the best. Negative thoughts can't change our reality but positive thoughts can certainly make a bad situation feel better. You were wishing for fresh air in that hold, now you have plenty of it,' he smiled.

'You're right Eli. Let's think happy thoughts,' she agreed.

I must be more careful what I wish for, she thought.

⌘

'Are you serious Great One? They are stuck in a rowboat in the middle of the ocean. Can't you give them a break?'

The Great One smiled at Mac's frustration.

'Relax Mac, they will be fine. Summer is finding herself throughout this ordeal. She is tougher than you think. Eli will protect her.'

'Will Aedan and the others find her?'

'Have a little faith Mac. You used to have a lot more faith when you were the one facing trials and tribulations,' the old man teased.

'Somehow it is easier living through it than watching it, and you still haven't answered my question,' he bellowed after the old man.

⌘

'Eli,' Summer shook him awake. 'Land,' she pointed in the distance and he laughed. It was land indeed. He grabbed the oars and began rowing. They took turns and the more they rowed the further away the land seemed.

'I thought it was much closer,' Summer huffed as she handed over the oars to Eli.

'Yes, it's deceptive,' he admitted.

Finally they hopped over the side and pulled the boat ashore. Summer felt like crying. All she could see in every direction was the same – sand – red, gold sand.

259
THE GOLDEN CAGE

'Out of the frying pan and into the fire,' she muttered forlorn.

'What does that mean Miss Summer?'

'Nothing, we must have positive thoughts,' she reiterated to herself. 'Do you have any idea where we are?'

'My guess is Eber-Nari judging by the desert.'

'Eber-Nari, never heard of it,' Summer said. 'Is there anything else in Eber-Nari besides desert and rocky outcrops?'

'No,' so let's get moving. We need to find water.

They wandered parallel to the shore, over sandy dunes toward nowhere. As far as the eye could see there was nothing and no one. Just more sand dunes. Their water was almost at an end and Eli was beginning to feel alarmed. He did not know what to do. Then he saw it, marks in the sand that appeared to be camel hooves.

'Miss Summer, come we must follow these trails.'

They followed the prints in the sand heading further inland and away from the shore. Every now and again Summer would let out a squeal of delight, her legs running toward the water she saw in the distance, only to discover it was her mind playing tricks on her in the heat of the sun.

'I'm tired,' Summer said. 'I can't do this anymore Eli.'

'Sit, rest for a while,' he said seeing her weariness. They sat in the sand but it only served to make them hotter.

'Leave me Eli,' she said as she flopped backward, squinting her eyes in the relentless sun. 'I am not going to make it.'

'That is not true Miss Summer. You have survived far worse than this. We must keep following the camel tracks.'

THE GOLDEN CAGE

She pulled herself upright. 'You're right Eli. She looked at the tracks that meandered over the dunes. Then she saw it. She shook her head convinced it was yet another mirage but it did not go away. Instead it seemed to be advancing in a hazy fury.

'What is that?' she asked pointing in the distance. Eli looked and cursed when he saw the red cloud.

'Quickly Miss Summer, come here. He wrapped his long tunic around them both and pulled her close. Then he turned her back to the approaching cloud and made her sit in the sand alongside him. He tucked all the edges of his tunic in, making a makeshift tent around them.

'What are you doing Eli?' Summer protested, alarmed.

'It's a sandstorm Miss Summer. Cover your nose and mouth with your tunic and keep your head down.'

She heard the roar of the storm before she felt the first sting of the sand as it descended on them. Eli dug his heels in and held her tight, shielding her body with his. The sand beat their bodies relentlessly, getting into every gap it could and Summer felt both dirty and afraid. She plugged her ears with her fingers trying to keep out the noise and she buried her face into her knees. She wished it would be over. It seemed an endless onslaught but eventually the wind died down and the storm passed over. They were semi-buried in the red sand and it permeated every pore on their bodies. Eli stood and shook all the sand from the outside of his tunic. Then he wrapped it back around him. He pulled Summer up and she too tried to rid herself of the sticky sand. She looked around and moaned. The entire landscape had changed, the camel prints nowhere to be seen.

'What do we do now?' she asked forlorn.

He too felt a measure of fear. He had no idea which direction to go. He looked up at the sun and tried to gauge which way would return them to the coastline.

'I don't know, but my guess would be this way,' he said pointing to nothingness. Summer nodded and they began to walk, hoping they would find some water or human inhabitation. Both felt hopeless but decided to think of good things.

⌘

The ship lurched and rolled as it cut its way back through the Aegean Sea. They were heading to Abyssinia and the journey would not be easy. There was no direct route to get there, and to travel by sea would take many moons to circumnavigate the large landmass that Abyssinia was a part of. Their only option would be to sail to Alexandria and then up the river Nile. Thereafter they would have to travel across land till they reached the Sea of Reeds. Then they could catch a ship to Abyssinia. Erik worried about Summer. This journey was not for the faint-hearted and it would involve many dangers along the way. She was a beautiful young woman and he had heard of many women being captured and enslaved in this part of the world. He just hoped that the eunuch would protect her and that they would find her quickly. He thought of his daughter and remembered her as a baby – Griffin had always been his son, but Summer held a very special place in his heart. She was his flesh and blood, the embodiment of his and Isabel's love. He could not bear to think of anything bad ever happening to her. He liked Tristan too, from the moment he met him, and he understood why Summer had fallen in love with him. He just hoped that she was not too damaged to find her way back to love again. It broke his heart thinking of what she may have experienced.

We're coming sweetheart, he willed. *We'll never stop looking for you. Don't give up!*

THIRTY-THREE

REPRIEVE

SHE passed out, face first into the sand, little black dots dancing before her eyes. She thought she heard Eli calling her name, but she didn't want him to rouse her – she just wanted to slip into oblivion and enjoy the peace for a while. She closed her eyes and drifted off to a better place and time. She was running through the grounds with Cam and Griffin, they were throwing acorns at one another, giggling and laughing. Then she found herself flying across the meadow on Hawk's back, the wind whistling through her hair, a sense of freedom that made her smile and shout out with joy. She could feel the stallion's strength beneath her and for a second she felt invincible. She was home, at Griswold and she felt happy for the first time in ages. Yes, she would stay here forever – this was where she belonged.

⌘

Tristan fingered the medallion once more as it hung around his neck. He felt anxious and his fear for Summer had not abated. Anna's words haunted him – how Emetullah had attacked her in the bathhouse and how she had been fortunate to survive the attack. He knew there was more, but for some reason Anna refused to talk about it.

'It is not my place,' she said. 'Summer will tell you when she is ready.' This had not quelled his fears but had increased them.

What if she never wants me near her again? What if she hates all men?

He knew that things would never be the same between them again – that the carefree young woman he met and made love to in Francia was not the same young woman he would find in Abyssinia. His heart ached at the thought that he might find her, only to discover that he never would truly find her soul ever again.

He looked up at the sky and whispered, 'I love you Summer.'

⌘

She thought she was dreaming. She opened her eyes and looked up into a dark, starry night – a myriad of sparkling gems that twinkled in the black sky. It was beautiful.

'You're awake,' Eli said relieved.

'Where are we?' she said trying to pull herself upright, but dizziness overwhelmed her and she sank back.

'You are very dehydrated and weak. I thought you were going to leave me to fight this desert alone,' he scolded. 'Fortunately for us, we were found by a Bedawi tribe who brought us to their camp. Here, drink some water.' He tipped the flask and the wet liquid was a welcome reprieve on her cracked, dry lips.

'Best water I've ever tasted,' she joked.

'Now get some rest – you need to get your strength back. The Bedawi are making their way to Damascus and they have agreed to take us with them. Once we are there we will make our way to Alexandria.'

'We are not going to Abyssinia?' she asked surprised.

'No, I've thought about it and it doesn't make sense Miss Summer. Abyssinia is too far from Griswold and if I take you there it will be near impossible to ever get you home again. I don't know how much more of this travelling you can endure. Alexandria is a busy port and we will be able to buy you passage to Hispania quite easily. We will send word to your family and they can sail to Hispania to meet you. It is the best way.'

'Thank you Eli, I could not have done any of this without you.' She kissed him on the cheek and he looked embarrassed.

⌘

GRISWOLD

Isabel felt she would go mad if another day passed without word from Erik. She knew he was right to leave her to protect their lands, but it was the not knowing that was driving her crazy. Not a moment passed when she was not thinking of her beautiful daughter, son and husband. Then there was Cam too. She worried about them all. She had not been able to tell Struan or Catriona much when they had come to visit. They were equally concerned about their son. She had last received word from Erik when he was heading toward Anatolia, but she had no idea whether he had arrived safely. She drafted a letter and sealed it in a pouch. Then she called for a messenger.

'Send a Monwing to seek out the Master's ship. He is somewhere in the Aegean Sea,' she instructed. She had no idea if the creature would find them, but she had to try. The messenger nodded and took the pouch with him.

Isabel felt better. At least she had done something and she hoped the winged creature would succeed in its quest to find Erik. She picked up the sketch Summer had done of their family. She gently ran her fingers over it, remembering how long she had worked on it to get everyone's expressions just perfect. She did not realize she was crying till a tear dripped on the sketch, making a smudge at the bottom of the parchment. She wiped it dry and placed it back on the mantel.

'She'll be fine Isabel,' she reassured herself. 'Erik will bring them all home.'

⌘

EBER-NARI

Summer was grateful they had set up camp at an oasis. She was not accustomed to the harsh desert conditions as the Bedawi were. The few palm trees and water hole gave her a measure of comfort in the vast mass of sand. She sipped the water as she sat in the shade of a tree.

The Bedawi who found them were a group of nine families, about fifty people in all, made up of adults and children. They lived in camel and goatskin tents and they raised livestock and lived in the desert, moving, as they needed.

It must be a harsh life Summer thought as she watched the women milking the goats. Children played alongside the water, giggling and jostling one another.

'Here,' one of the women said handing Summer a scarf. 'It is for your head,' she indicated her own head that was wrapped in fabric, just leaving her eyes exposed. 'The Bedawi woman must cover herself.'

Summer nodded and wrapped the fabric around her head and face. The woman smiled and nodded her approval. Summer felt trapped under the fabric.

How do they expect us to breathe in this heat?

Living in this sandy prison reminded her of Anatolia. She had simply traded one golden cage for another – her experience of both had left her desperate to find freedom once more.

Still, this golden desert was better than the prison in Anatolia. She recalled the night the Kapudan Pasha raped her and she shuddered. The thought of ever being in that situation again made her vow silently that she would rather die before being used that way again. Eli was her only friend, the only person she trusted right now. She felt safe with him because he treated her with respect and saw her as valuable. She was a person when she was with him, not a possession. Her ordeal had left her confused. She often thought of Tristan and yet somehow she felt sadness – as though that ship had sailed and they would never have the dream life they had planned. She wasn't the same heady young woman he met – she was broken now, scarred and damaged beyond repair. He deserved better than that. Besides, he probably thought she was dead and it was better that way. Too much water had passed under the bridge and she could never turn back the clock. All she wanted now was to get back home to Griswold – to be with her Mama and Papa. She was unsure whether she would ever paint again. Even that joy was stolen from her when King Louis and Sultan Mehmed had treated her as something they could own. They had used her talent to manipulate her. She pulled the scarf tighter around her face. If this piece of fabric could hide her fear, her pain and her attractiveness to men, then she would gladly suffocate beneath it. She wondered whether the Bedawi women felt the same way. It made her feel angry and safe simultaneously.

⌘

ANATOLIA

Mehmed paced up and down his quarters. He was angry, heartbroken and confused. His return from hunting had been met with the news that Süheyla was dead. He did not believe the story his mother had concocted but no one contradicted her version of the events.

'She just did not want to be here Mehmed. I tried to make her feel welcome – I even let her leave the palace with Anna and Ali. She wanted to paint the scenery along the Bosphorus and I thought it would be good for her to get away from here for a while, to do something she loved. I had no idea that she would throw herself into the river. I am deeply distressed Mehmed. I lost my best Eunuch when Ali jumped in to save her. They both drowned and Anna was left hysterical along the banks of the river.'

'I want to speak with Anna,' he said.

'That is not possible. The young girl was so distraught that I sent her back to her family. She was traumatised by the events. Süheyla was one of the few friends she had here in the palace.'

Mehmed knew his mother was lying but he had no way to prove it. Süheyla, Ali and Anna were all gone and he had no other explanation for it.

⌘

'Does he believe you Valide Sultan?' Emetullah asked.

'I don't know. He is angry and upset and that is where you come in. You need to distract him and give him comfort.'

The Valide Sultan felt sick to her stomach. Her carefully laid plans had gone horribly awry. She discovered that Anna had escaped and since the three young men had left abruptly, she assumed the young woman had gone with them. She worried what they might do or what Anna would tell them. If Mehmed found out about their visit it would all unravel. Then she received word that Ali had not gone to Salonica. A stable boy had reported that his horse was returned to the stable lame. Since then, he had disappeared and her contact in Salonica had sent word that he had not arrived looking for the Kapudan Pasha. She felt uneasy. Ali would never leave unless he suspected her plans and found a way to thwart them. He must surely fear for his life. She had no idea whether Süheyla was dead or alive. Her men assured her that the sack had submerged, but what if Ali had rescued the young woman? Mehmed must never know any of this. Süheyla and Ali would both be far away if they had escaped – all she could hope was that they never darkened the door of Topkapi Palace again. She doubted Süheyla would ever return to Francia and it was this hope that made her believe it would all be okay. In the meantime she had to win her son's trust back as she could see the distrust in his eyes. If she were to control him and the harem, he would have to believe her story. It was imperative.

THIRTY-FOUR

THE BOOK

EBER-NARI

THE tents were erected and Summer rested in the shade of a large palm tree. The intense heat left her feeling debilitated and exhausted. She'd spent the morning learning how to milk goats and it was not as easy as it looked. Her hands slipped off the animal's teats and she realized it took skill to work out how to squeeze the milk out into the pail. The Bedawi women laughed as she struggled, which made her more determined to master it. Her hands felt sore and stiff as a result, and even the poor goat became annoyed with her after a while, bleating in frustration as she did her best to milk it.

'Don't worry, you will get the hang of it,' one of the women encouraged her.

Summer smiled and nodded her head.

Damn goat, just give me some milk, she silently pleaded.

Finally she lifted her pail, which was a quarter full, in triumph. The Bedawi women clapped and Summer did a little dance which made them laugh.

Eli joined her in the shade as she waved flies from her face.

'I hear you conquered the goats this morning,' he said.

Summer laughed. 'I would hardly call it conquering anything, but I did manage to get about a cup of milk.'

'I know this is hard for you Miss Summer. This is not the life you are accustomed to, but we must do our bit while we are with these people. They are our only hope for freedom.'

'I agree Eli. I will take my turn at the chores, even if they are unfamiliar to me.'

⌘

Summer soon became familiar with the Bedawi's way of life. They were a religious people, praying a few times each day and giving thanks. They would wash themselves with water before prayers and if there was no water, they would cleanse themselves with sand. She was surprised at how rich their culture was. They were not simply ignorant nomads travelling through the desert. Instead she discovered that they had a love of poetry and story telling, which the older members of the tribe shared each evening around the campfire. The children would listen attentively as the men shared stories of their ancestors, weaving history into their tales. Summer realized how vital this was considering none of the children went to school and the women too were illiterate. Only the men read from the large religious book they carried.

It was this book that began a chain of events that snowballed into a gigantic mess.

Summer was assigned to sweep out the tents one morning. She took her woven palm frond, which she used as a broom and she began in the first tent, sweeping with over-exaggerated movements. It was harder than she imagined it would be, and her back ached from bending over. She grunted as she exerted herself. Then when she was finished she moved on to the next tent.

The book caught her eye in the third tent. She tried to ignore it but it seemed to beckon her and she could not resist flipping through the pages, the parchment old and beautifully scripted. She did not understand the language but just seeing the words on the page gave her some hope, or rather it inspired her to fight for her old life – a life that was full of books and art and culture. She missed those things.

'What are you doing?' an angry voice jarred her from her daydreaming.

'I'm sorry,' she slammed the book shut as though it were red hot and had scorched her fingers. She felt herself blush at being caught out by the sheikh. 'I meant no harm; I just wanted to feel a book in my hands again. I've missed reading.'

'You read?' the Sheikh asked horrified.

'Yes, I was taught to read by my mother and Friar Thomas when I was a little girl.'

The Sheikh shook his head. 'It is not a woman's place to read,' he muttered.

Summer was shocked, but more than anything she felt indignant. 'Why not?' she challenged, her eyes flashing.

The Sheikh seemed taken aback by her brazen challenge. He was not used to a woman addressing him in such a manner.

'The Bedawi women know their place and their function. It would not do for you to put ideas in their heads,' he warned.

Summer felt like screaming.

What is wrong with the men in this part of the world? Why do you see women as possessions, as less than human?

It frustrated her beyond measure, mostly because she saw just how hard the Bedawi women worked. They were clothed from head to toe in this infernally hot desert, yet they cooked and raised children as well as fetched water from the oasis, kept the tents repaired and clean, made new tents from goat and camel skins. This was just a fraction of their busy day.

Summer backed down despite her inner anger. She must not upset the Sheikh. This was not her battle to fight and she had to get to Damascus, to some form of civilisation and these people were her answer.

'I am sorry I touched your book,' she replied dropping her eyes in submission. She had learned something from the women here.

The Sheikh nodded curtly and Summer took that as a dismissal. She grabbed her palm frond and made a hasty retreat to the next tent.

Later that night as she sat with Eli around the oasis she mentioned her encounter.

'Why do men seem to look down on women so much in this culture? It is like that in Anatolia too.'

'It is their way, their belief system. Just as you follow the Great One, they believe in their god too.'

'What kind of god would demand that one gender of humanity has more value than another? I don't understand it Eli.'

'That large book you were paging through declares that women are inferior Summer, and they believe it. They believe that women have to be told what to do, that they do not have the intelligence to learn to read or write. They are simply here to provide satisfaction and to produce children.'

'It disgusts me,' she said passionately and Eli smiled.

'It is not the world you come from, but it is their world and their reality. When one does not know any different, then it is possible to live with all kinds of atrocities. It is only when people become aware that there are choices out there, that they become dissatisfied with their reality. You see it as injustice because you have had a different experience Miss Summer. To these women it is simply their destiny.'

Summer shuddered. She knew what he said was true but still she could not believe it was acceptable to treat women this way. She remembered her mother telling her stories about how hard it was for her when she had first gone to Kaldakinn. She'd been horrified by their beliefs and rituals, their brutality to women when they raided, and yet she had fallen in love with her father despite it all.

Does love totally blind a person?

⌘

AEGEAN SEA

Will Summer's awful experiences blind her to what we have together?

Tristan often worried about this and as he gazed up at the sky standing on the deck of the gently undulating ship, he once again pondered over this. He was desperately afraid that the brutality she had experienced would kill anything they had and although he did not know the extent of it, he knew she had suffered.

He willed the ship to sail faster – to reach their destination. He wanted this uncertainty to be over – to know that she was alive and safe and to realise that people loved her. He stroked the medallion around his neck and his heart ached as he thought of his great love.

Where are you Summer? Look up at the stars and guide me. Give us a sign.

⌘

She gazed up at the sky and laughed as she tried to count the millions of sparkling beads above her.

'I've never seen so many stars Eli.'

'I always think of them as people who love us, watching over us,' he smiled. 'There are many people who love you watching over you right now Miss Summer.'

He was surprised when he heard her sob. Her shoulders heaved and she buried her face in her hands.

'Don't be sad,' he said softly. 'It is good to be greatly loved.'

'I know, and this place makes me even more grateful to have my family, but I miss them. Eli, I am afraid.'

'What is there to be afraid of Miss Summer? The worst is behind us. Now we just have to find our way back home.'

'I am afraid that when I get back home I will be different; that what the Kapudan Pasha did to me will haunt me the rest of my life. I have lost someone I love because of Queen Maria's deceit. What if I never love someone this way again?'

'The heart has a way of mending Miss Summer, despite tragedy. It may not look or function the same, but it does heal. Usually it becomes tender and better able to understand others. It also discovers gratitude for life. Tragedy has a way of showing us the value of kindness in this world. You have lost much, but you will also gain much from your experiences. Don't be afraid to embrace what you gain.'

He left her with her thoughts. She wiped her eyes and considered what he'd said. She wanted to desperately believe that she would find herself and happiness again, but a lingering sadness at losing Tristan made her heart ache. She wondered if he were safe, whether he was even alive after Louis' plan to kill him.

She looked up at the stars again and hoped that one of them was Tristan loving her.

I will always love you, even if we can never be together.

THIRTY-FIVE

DÉJÀ VU

EBER-NARI

THEY were on the move again, miles and miles of desert sand as the caravan of camels, goats and people moved over the yellow-red landscape like a giant caterpillar. They moved slowly as children and animals dictated. It was hot and Summer brushed at the flies that attempted to sit on her face. She did not know what was worse – the annoying insects or the suffocating headscarf she had to wear. Her long thick hair clung to her neck in a sweaty mass and she wished she could wash all the dirt off her body.

'I heard what you said to my husband,' Ashira said to her as they walked. It was the Sheikh's third wife and she was younger than his first two wives.

Summer smiled and nodded. She did not want to engage the young woman in this conversation. The Sheikh had made his feelings clear that she could not influence the women's thinking.

'So you can read and write?' Ashira pressed.

Summer knew she could not ignore the woman completely. 'Yes, my mother taught me to read.'

'What is it like?'

'It is magical,' Summer smiled, forgetting her promise to the sheikh. 'Reading takes you to another world, a different place. It shows you how others live and what the rest of the world is like.'

'I would love to know what that is like,' she said wistfully. 'Will you teach me to read?'

Summer was horrified. She hadn't meant to inspire the young woman. She had simply been honest about what reading meant to her. Now she had piqued the Sheikh's wife's curiosity.

'No Ashira,' she replied shaking her head. 'It is not wise for you to learn to read. Your husband will get very angry. I cannot teach you. It is not the way of the Bedawi,' she added to convince her.

'He does not care,' she said. 'I am his third wife and he is planning on taking a fourth soon. When that happens, I will no longer be his favourite.'

Summer felt sad for her. She wondered what it must be like to share someone you loved with other women. She thought of Tristan with another and it made her feel sick.

'I'm sorry,' Summer repeated more firmly, 'I cannot teach you to read.'

They walked a full day before they set up camp again. Judging by the men's talk they were still a couple of days away from Damascus. Summer wiped away the perspiration that dripped down her forehead. Setting up camp was always a tedious task. As the women sat in the shade of the scattered palms, Summer noticed that Ashira was not among them. She felt alarm bells. Her sense of danger had heightened since her experiences in Anatolia and her naïve innocence was long gone. She headed toward the Sheikh's wives' tents. Ashira was not there. She scouted the entire camp to no avail. Finally she asked the children who were playing one of their stone games if they had seen her. A child pointed to the sand dune east of the tents.

THE GOLDEN CAGE

Summer checked no one was watching her before she scrambled over the dune. What she saw made her heart stop. Ashira was tied to a stake by a rope that circled her neck. She lay in the hot sun and Summer feared she was dead. She ran over to the young woman calling her name.

'Ashira, Ashira, speak to me,' she said as she cradled her head in her lap. 'Who did this to you?'

Ashira's eyes rolled back in her head and her dry lips tried to mouth some words but her swollen tongue could not form the words.'

Summer pulled her water pouch from her belt and tipped the liquid down the woman's throat. She gulped thirstily. Then she tried to loosen the rope that had left chafe marks on her neck. She was appalled at the treatment of this woman and she had no answers as to why she had been tied up outside of the camp.

'Are you all right?' she asked the woman once she had finished drinking. She nodded her head. 'Why are you tied up like an animal Ashira?'

'My husband saw me talking to you and when I asked him if I could learn to read he became very angry.'

'Ashira, I told you it was a bad idea.'

'I know, but when he told me that he is marrying my younger sister I got so angry that I wanted to hurt him, to make him pay. Instead he told me that I would learn my place and that maybe the hot sun would bring me to my senses. He believes you are Jinn.'

'Jinn?' Summer asked confused. 'What is that?'

'Jinn is the presence of spirits. He believes you are a malevolent spirit that has taken on a human form to interfere in our lives and cause mischief.'

'You don't really believe this, do you?' Summer asked. She was seething. 'You could die out here with no shade and water. I am taking you back to my tent.'

'No Summer, he will kill us both if we defy his orders. He will never allow a woman to humiliate him in front of the whole tribe, even a woman who is a guest. I know you aren't Jinn.'

'I can't just leave you here Ashira.'

'You have to. I've had some water and the sun is already sinking. I doubt he will leave me here all night and I will beg his forgiveness when he comes. If I am not back in the morning you can bring me some more water.'

'I don't like it,' Summer said, but she knew that Ashira was right. The Sheikh's pride would not suffer ridicule and he would make both of them pay for it. 'I will check on you later,' she promised.

⌘

Summer found it hard to concentrate during the story telling around the fire. Her mind kept wandering to Ashira who still had not returned. She could barely look at the Sheikh without feeling the urge to wring his neck. She tried to think about Damascus and what it would be like. She wished they were already there. She wished she was more like Eli – accepting of all people, even those who did the most horrific things; but it wasn't in her nature to turn a blind eye to injustice.

Soon the children were all asleep in their tents and the men talked around the fire. A young girl of no more than seventeen sat nearby the Sheikh and he displayed her as his latest trophy for all the men to see. Whenever he required

THE GOLDEN CAGE

anything she would jump up and serve him. Summer assumed this was Ashira's sister and his next wife. She wanted to shake the young girl and tell her to *run!*

The moon shone brightly in the night sky and Summer tiptoed around the camp. Everyone was asleep as she made her way over the dune.

'Ashira,' she whispered urgently. There was no reply.

'Ashira,' she called again but the landscape was deserted. The Sheikh must have taken her back to camp. Summer felt both relief and dread simultaneously. She shuffled back through the soft sand. She had to be sure Ashira was safe. She made her way to the young woman's tent. Each wife of the Sheikh had her own living quarters that she resided in with her children. Ashira, as yet had not provided any children for her husband and Summer assumed this was one of the reasons he had decided to take a fourth wife. The Sheikh had a separate tent that was more luxurious, where he was able to bed his chosen wife for the night in privacy. It was a system that baffled Summer. Ashira was not in her tent, so she tiptoed over to the Sheikh's tent.

She heard his voice coming from within the tent, angry and cruel.

'Don't ever cross me again Ashira,' he growled.

'I'm sorry,' she mumbled.

'That woman is not one of us. She is Jinn and fills your head with nonsense. Can't you see she is trying to bring disorder to our tribe? You are a Bedawi woman and your place is serving me. The sooner you accept your station in life the better.'

He tugged at her headscarf, ripping it off before grabbing her by her long black hair. Ashira yelped in pain. He slapped her hard across the face.

'Bend over and lift your tunic,' he barked. She whimpered. Summer heard shuffling as she did as she was told. She could also hear Ashira trying not to cry. Then she heard her beg, 'Please be gentle.'

He laughed and slapped her again on the back of her head and this time Ashira's sobbing could clearly be heard. He grunted as he entered her and Summer was transfixed to the spot. She was instantly transported back to the room she was trapped in as the Kapudan Pasha raped her. She recalled the grunting sounds as he ravaged her. She could picture the Sheikh's face as he pleasurably forced himself on his wife and her anger boiled over – she snapped. She bent down, picked up a rock and entered the tent. The Sheikh's back was to her as he thrust himself deeper into his sobbing wife.

He's an animal, Summer thought as she raised her arm. She did not think of the consequences of her actions as she smashed the stone down on his skull. He grunted a final time before he slumped to the floor. Summer was lost in a trance and she continued to smash the rock over his skull – two, three, four times. Ashira cowered in the corner terrified. Finally Summer fell to the floor exhausted, the reality of her actions finally hitting her. She stared at the glassy open eyes of the Sheikh, his bloody and matted head lying awkwardly sideways in an unusual position, an expression of both pleasure and surprise on his face.

Summer groaned. There had been only one face in her mind as she smashed the rock, backwards and forwards, time and again. It was the Kapudan Pasha's face.

'What are we going to do?' Ashira looked panic stricken. 'They will kill us both for this.'

'Find Eli,' Summer croaked weakly. Shock was setting in and she pulled her knees up to her chin and rocked back and forth. 'No, no, no,' she whispered over and over to herself.

Eli found her in this position. He was horrified at the mess he discovered. 'Miss Summer, can you hear me?'

She did not look at him as she rocked.

'It was the Kapudan Pasha,' she murmured. 'He was hurting Ashira, like he hurt me. I had to save her,' she sobbed. Eli picked her up and carried her to her tent. Then he washed away the blood on her hands and face. She looked like a terrified child and Eli felt the urge to protect her. Her trauma had finally caught up to her and this was the result.

Ashira was frantic. 'They will find him in the morning and they will kill us all,' she said afraid.

'No they will not,' Eli said calmly. We'll leave tonight. We will take a camel and you will tell them in the morning that the Sheikh forced himself on Miss Summer and that I killed him to protect her.'

'No Eli,' Summer wailed. 'This is my doing. I must take responsibility for it.'

'Miss Summer, we have to leave. Ashira is right; they will not show mercy or be interested in the details. It is their leader that is dead. If the men don't kill us then the wives just might. It is safer for Ashira if we leave – this way she will not be implicated. Do what I have told you Ashira.'

Ashira nodded. 'Take a smaller camel. And head southwest. You will get to Damascus ahead of us.'

Eli secured their water pouches and placed the rough bread that she handed him in the saddle bag attached to the camel. Then he placed Summer on the animal and pulled it to standing position. It snorted, making it clear that it did not appreciate its sleep being disturbed.

THE GOLDEN CAGE

'I'm sorry about this,' he whispered as they turned to leave.

'He was hurting me,' she said to Eli as they parted and he nodded his head in acknowledgement. 'May favour be upon you.'

'And you. Look after her,' she said as they disappeared into the dark night.

Eli used the stars to navigate as they rode through the night. It was certainly cooler and almost peaceful as the camel trudged through the sand. He wanted to get as much distance between them and the Bedawi camp as possible before daybreak. He had a feeling this was not the end of their challenges. Once they got to Damascus they would have to make their way to the nearest port. They had to find passage on a ship to get them to Alexandria. Crossing this harsh land was no longer an option and too dangerous for Summer in her current mental condition.

He leaned back against the camel saddle and shifted a sleepy Summer who reclined against him. He would enjoy this peace while it lasted.

Is this intense desire to save Summer my way of making up for my sister's death? Do I still feel responsible for not saving her?

It made sense and yet he had seen many women enter the harem over the years and none of them had made him feel this protective.

There is a reason for everything, he thought. *Perhaps her Great One is guiding me too.*

He thought about Summer's anger toward her Great One. He understood how she felt. He had been so bitter when he was snatched from his family as a child. He remembered the day they castrated him – the pain and the humiliation as they took his identity as a man. He had vowed revenge and he had allowed it to brew in his heart. He had been angry with his god too. *Why had he allowed this to happen to him and his sister?* It took him years to realize that hatred only hurts the person who feels it. He became tired of stoking the fires of bitterness and feeling poisoned by it. He knew that he could never regain what was stolen from him – it would change nothing. He also realized that being a man was more than his manly parts – it was about his heart and his character and if he forfeited those because of hatred then he would truly lose himself completely. He'd made a conscious decision to fight for himself. It had taken years, but he had done it. Now he recognized the spiral that Summer was in and he was determined to save her the years of pain he had suffered. If he could help her to discover her true self again, then he would have accomplished something good.

THIRTY-SIX

CITY OF FIGS

DAMASCUS

DAMASCUS was a bustling city, full of noise and life. The markets were alive with trade amongst the stone buildings. A number of different languages could be heard, as it was a melting pot of cultures. Camels and livestock roamed through some of the streets and vendors shouted out their specials of the day. It was a good place to get lost temporarily and Eli felt some relief as they wended their way through the busy streets. The city was also known by another name – the 'City of Figs' as it had numerous fruit trees on the outskirts. Eli and Summer ate their fill before entering the city. They found a well and filled their pouches, drinking deeply to quench their thirst. Most of their travel was during the night and they'd arrived in Damascus in good time.

'We cannot stay long Miss Summer, in case the Bedawi people come for us. Fortunately they will travel slower than us with all their livestock and children. You rest and I will go and ask for directions to Beyrouth. From there we can buy our passage to Alexandria.'

Summer nodded and settled in the shade of a large fig tree that bordered the market. She closed her eyes and drifted off to sleep. Her dreams were a mixture of longing for home and Tristan, interspersed with terror and fear and her crashing a rock down on the Sheikh's head. The Kapudan Pasha always seemed to be the last face she saw before waking up in terror each time. Sleep was bittersweet for her. She longed to see Tristan in her dreams but then she had to deal with the fear that always sabotaged her sweet place.

⌘

LIONSGATE

'Will she ever sleep peacefully again?' Mac asked the Great One.

'She will, but it will take time Mac.'

'Can't we just send Aedan a sign where to find her?'

'Relax Mac, there will come a time where their paths will cross, when they will find each other, but that will take time. Have some patience.'

⌘

ALBORAN SEA

The ship cut its way effortlessly through the azure water. Constantinople was way behind them and they were entering the Alboran Sea once more. Erik estimated they would arrive in Alexandria in a week. They'd faced some challenging weather as the winds dropped causing their ship to lose speed. It was frustrating.

'Why?' Tristan raged to the skies as he stood on deck watching the lifeless sails. 'Damn the universe,' he raged. Aedan patted him on the back.

'Don't despair, I've often found that things happen for a reason, even when we don't understand why.'

'Don't patronise me Aedan. What's happened to Summer did not happen for a reason. It was not for her good or for developing her character. I've heard all this mumbo-jumbo before and I just don't believe it. Bad stuff happens to good people and frankly I don't understand why.'

'I'm sorry, you're right,' Aedan said. Tristan looked surprised. He expected the Great One's sidekick to offer more arguments and encouragements. 'There is simply no excuse, but despite all the tragedy in the world, good can come from it.'

'What good can possibly come from what has happened to Summer?'

'Time will tell Tristan, but you have to believe in her. You know who she really is and you have to help her find herself again.'

'What if she doesn't want me to?'

'Then you have to make her see that she needs you – and she will need you more than ever. You will find a way to show her, I am certain.'

'Why do bad things happen to good people Aedan? You've lived with the Great One. Why doesn't he just put a stop to it?'

'The Great One isn't a puppet master Tristan. People make poor choices and sometimes good people get swept up in them whether they like it or not. Life embraces us all everyday – both the good and the bad. Good people are not immune to bad people's actions. We all have to face the hard and the ugly in life, as well as the wonderful and good things that come our way.'

'I should have been there to protect her,' he hung his head with guilt. 'If I had, none of this would have happened.'

'You will have a lifetime to protect her. Guilt is a wasted emotion. It evokes shame and pity – both useless in moving forward. You will be of no help to Summer if she sees your guilt. Your guilt will increase her guilt and anxiety. You must let it go Tristan, if you are to ever help her.'

Tristan was surprised. He had not seen it from this perspective.

Maybe Aedan is right, but what if Summer blames me? What if she can't forgive me?

⌘

DAMASCUS

'There she is.' Voices woke Summer from her sleep under the fig tree. She sat up, startled to find four Bedawi men surrounding her.

It's not possible her mind screamed. *They cannot be here. Where's Eli?*

She recalled Eli telling her to rest before he left. The men grabbed her, pulling her roughly to her feet.

'Where's the eunuch?' they growled.

'He's gone,' she lied. 'Please, he did not kill the Sheikh, I did.' It was her turn to protect Eli, besides it was the truth.

Her parents had taught her to own her mistakes and to face the consequences.

The men looked confused. 'Ashira told us the eunuch killed him when he accosted you.'

'No, I killed him because he was hurting me.' She would not implicate Ashira or Eli after all they had done to protect her. They looked at one another and the man standing in front of her slapped her twice across the face. The men spat at her as she cowered and covered her stinging face.

'It was Jinn who killed our Sheikh. An evil spirit took our leader.' They spat at her again. 'You will suffer for this,' they promised.

'We should kill her.'

'No that is too quick – she deserves to suffer. Perhaps we could take her into the desert and leave her to die a slow and painful death.'

'I have a better idea. She came to us in the form of a woman, now it will be the thing she regrets the most. Let's sell her to harem traders and get some compensation for our Sheikh's death.'

Summer let out a sob. 'Please no,' she begged. 'Kill me rather than that.' She could not believe she had come so far only to find herself full circle and about to be sold back into a harem.

The men smiled. 'You will be sold to harem traders. You will remember the Sheikh every day of your life when men are using you. It is a fitting punishment.'

Summer let out a wail as they dragged her from the market square. She did not see Eli hiding behind the rough stone wall.

He was shocked to see the Bedawi in Damascus. They must have left the tribe to hunt them the moment they discovered the dead Sheikh. He followed them to a house where they disappeared with Summer. She was locked in a room that only had a tiny sliver of light through a small opening in the wall. Then the men refreshed themselves with food and goat's milk.

Eli kept watch, right through the night.

⌘

Early the following morning they were back in the market square. The Bedawi men made enquiries and found some traders who sold women and children as a living. They agreed upon a price for Summer. Silver coins were exchanged as she was roughly bound and dragged away with the men who would sell her back to a harem. She felt hopeless. She determined she would find a way to kill herself before she allowed any man to use her body unwillingly again.

'We should take her and the other women to Alexandria,' one of the men said.

'Why can't we just sell them here?'

'Alexandria will fetch us a much higher price as it is the busiest market for not only Anatolians to buy women, but also Sheikhs from surrounding countries. We have good merchandise and it would be a waste to get less than it's worth.'

The men agreed to make the trip to Alexandria. Summer counted six other women beside herself and three children. Each of them looked alone, frightened and uncertain of what the future held. She dared not tell them. She tried to shut out the memories that flowed fast and furiously. They began their journey to Beyrouth, taking turns riding camels and walking. The men did not want them too worn out, as it would affect their sale price. Three days of continuous travel brought them to the seaside city. The smell of the salty ocean and the cool breeze that blew off the water was a refreshing change from the dry desert and rocky landscape with bushy scrub they had travelled through. It felt like an oasis. Summer reminded herself that their surroundings did not reflect their reality – they were slaves, merchandise as the men called them.

It did not take them long to secure passage for them on a ship to Alexandria. Silver is a language all men understand.

Once out at sea, Summer thought about throwing herself overboard, but she was never left alone long enough to follow through. Every few hours they were brought onto the deck to exercise and get fresh air. The one good thing about being merchandise was that they were well cared for so that the men could receive top price for them.

The third day at sea Summer found her opportunity. She was alone on deck as the man watching her rushed off to the side of the ship. He was not a sailor and the rolling motion of the large vessel did not sit well with the breakfast he had consumed. As he retched Summer took the distraction as an opportunity to head to the opposite side of the boat. She climbed up on the wooden railing and sat with her legs over the side of the ship. She gazed at the water below and willed herself to just fall forward into it. She recalled the feeling of being tied in the sack and thrown into the sea. Initially fear had been overwhelming and water had filled her nose and mouth as she tried to claw her way out of the sack. It had not taken long for the feeling of suffocation to leave as she began to drift into unconsciousness and finally it just felt peaceful.

Just do it Summer. The frightening part only lasts a few minutes and then you will be free forever, she convinced herself.

She leaned over, her eyes closed, about to let go when she felt a hand on her wrist. She gasped, her eyes flying open in fear. Eli looked at her with sad eyes that implored her to have a little faith.

'Eli,' she gasped. 'What are you doing here?'

'Shhh...' he whispered as he helped her back onto the deck. 'I saw them take you and I followed. I sold the camel in Beyrouth and bought myself passage on the same ship. They must not discover we know each other. Once we get to Alexandria, I will free you Miss Summer. Promise me you will not try this again,' he said pointing to the water. She nodded.

'I promise.'

'Do you trust me?'

'I do,' she said.

'Good, then we must not speak again. If they discover I know you, then we are both in danger.'

He left her and she headed back to the man who was still retching over the side of the boat.

'I hear that weak tea with ginger and lemon really helps with sea sickness,' she said. He lifted his grey face and smiled. 'Thank you,' he said before gagging again. Summer was surprised to discover that she did not feel sick this journey. She had finally found her sea legs.

She felt hopeful for the first time in days. She had no idea how Eli would rescue her, but she trusted him. He had saved her hide more than once over the last few moons. He would make a plan – she was sure of it.

THIRTY-SEVEN

WHERE THE WINDS GO

ALEXANDRIA — LATE SUMMER 1672

THEIR ship berthed against the dock and they disembarked as soon as possible. It was good to be on solid ground once more. Erik scanned the city, taking in everything around him. Travelling and discovering new cultures always enthralled him. He just wished it were under better circumstances. The dock was close to the main street – a road that travelled from one side of the city to the other. He soon discovered it was called the Via Canopica, an east-west boulevard that spanned the city and was an impressive one hundred feet wide. Massive gates, set in limestone walls sat at each end, the Gate of the Sun in the east and the Gate of the Moon in the west. Royal palaces and grounds took up a large portion of the city. Alexandria was located on a sliver of limestone between the sea and a large lake. Erik marvelled at the buildings – he imagined they would be crude and rough and yet the architecture was refined and almost classical. There must have been some influence from the City of the Seven Hills. It was well known that this culture, like the Anatolians had influenced much of the world around it and the evidence was here in Alexandria too. He'd read books about these civilisations, but never thought he would ever see them.

'Let me guess, you are lost in wonder,' Griffin slapped his father on the back.

'Don't tease Griff. You should be drinking in everything you see on this trip. I know our focus is on finding Summer,

296
THE GOLDEN CAGE

but you may never get another chance to return here. Let every image be imprinted on your brain. A great leader knows about other civilisations, and I know you will be a great ruler.'

Griffin was surprised by the earnestness of his father's words. He was right. He should live in the moment, enjoying every moment of every day. He would learn as much about this place as he could while he was here. He had spent too many days thinking about Lucy and what the future could possibly hold for them. He hoped he wasn't just an idle distraction for her. He missed her and longed to see her again.

'Come let us find some food and drink,' Aedan bellowed. He chuckled when he realized that he was gaining a fair amount of attention. Alexandrians were not used to seeing men with fiery red hair and he was quite the attraction. Children followed them and screeched in glee and fear when he pulled faces at them or made scary noises. A few concerned mothers pulled their children away, distrustful of the stranger.

They found an inn on the Via Canopica and settled down with some food and coffee.

'This brew is so good,' Cam said sipping the hot, rich liquid. 'We have to take some of it back with us to Griswold.'

Erik enquired where the market was. They would need supplies for the next part of their journey. They would sail up the large river canal as far as they could and then they would travel to the Sea of Reeds. The innkeeper gave him directions and advised them to barter.

'Don't pay what they ask you,' he warned. 'They will ask for far more if they know you are strangers to Alexandria.'

THE GOLDEN CAGE

Erik thanked the man for his help.

'The market is on the west end of the Via Canopica and it runs every day. We will head there tomorrow and replenish our supplies.'

⌘

Another ship was just a few miles from Alexandria. Suddenly the winds picked up and the sails billowed out, urging the vessel to the finish line. The captain of the ship shook his head.

'I don't understand it,' he said. 'I've never experienced this at this time of year - no winds and then suddenly a gust that will make up time in a few short hours. It won't be long till we get there if these winds keep up.'

Summer and Eli communicated with their eyes. Eli nodded and reassured her that it would be all right and she responded with a smile of confidence. Summer had taken it upon herself to try and encourage the other women and to tell the children stories. She had no idea if they understood her, but she did it anyway. The scar on her neck was no longer a bright, angry pink. It was still visible but scar tissue had formed causing a slight ridge where the tile had cut. She still kept it covered with her scarf – it was a reminder of a time she did not want to think about and she avoided thinking about what would happen if Eli's plan failed.

It would not be long now and they would know one way or another.

⌘

THE GOLDEN CAGE

A third ship sailed the Alboran Sea, heading for Alexandria. There would be brief calm before a storm that none of them foresaw.

⌘

The winds carried both vessels across the waves at great speed. It took the remainder of the day for both ships to berth – one in the eastern port and the other in the western port. The sun started to sink low in the sky as the brilliant colours shone off the water, reflecting on the beautiful buildings.

It is almost beautiful Summer thought, *if only it were under different circumstances. Think happy thoughts* she reminded herself.

THIRTY-EIGHT

BATTLE OF SILVER

THE market buzzed with activity as people spilled out into the streets. Erik pushed through the throng as the others followed behind. It helped to have a huge Northman leading the way. Bodies scattered like skittles as he towered over them. They had covered their heads with the traditional kaffiyeh, a cloth that was tied on with a cord. They wore tunics as the locals did; as they did not want to appear obvious as foreigners. They further looked the part as they had agreed to grow beards at sea so as to blend in with the locals. It had created much hilarity, as Cam's beard was wispy and rather sad. The others teased him mercilessly about it.

'Laugh all you like,' he replied, ' but when it is time to come off, you will all wish you had as little hair as me.'

The only one who did not grow a beard was Aedan as his red hair was a giveaway. 'You'll have to cover your hair and face,' Erik said. No one paid them much attention as they made their way through the market.

'We only have a certain amount of silver,' Erik reminded them, 'and we have a lot of supplies to buy, so we must bargain shrewdly.'

'Is the market usually this busy,' Aedan asked one of the vendors.

'No, today is a big day at market. Every week on the first day it is slave day at the market.'

'Slave day?' Cam asked horrified.

'Yes, it is one of the most popular days in Alexandria. If you wish to purchase a woman to keep you smiling, then today is a good day to do so. They will bring out the women soon and display them for you to see. Don't pick the old ones, they are no good and if they are too young it is not good either. Make sure your woman has strong bones and some meat on her body' He winked at Cam.

Cam was at a loss for words for once in his life, so he just nodded his head as though he understood.

'It's barbaric,' Griffin mumbled under his breath.

They could barely move as the street filled up with eager traders.

'We'll have to wait till the slave trade is over before we get our supplies. There's no way we can carry anything through this crowd,' Erik said. They watched as women, children and men were paraded through the streets and placed on a platform. It was an auction of human trade and it sickened them all.

'Det var som faen,' Erik cursed in his native tongue. 'I can't tolerate this anymore. I'm going back to the ship.'

The others agreed and followed him down the street back toward the port.

They just missed her, as she was part of the last group of people brought forward. Summer looked tired and afraid as she was herded onto the platform.

The auctioneer began his sales pitch. 'We have a beautiful woman here from far across the seas. She is fair and has beautiful long brown hair.' He ripped her headscarf off and Summer gasped. Her hand flew to the scar on her neck instinctively. The auctioneer looked dismayed. He stumbled momentarily before continuing.

'She has a slight flaw, but nothing that can't be covered up with a beautiful piece of jewellery. Who wants to purchase this rare and beautiful woman?'

Summer's eyes raked through the crowd desperately looking for Eli. She could not see him and she began to panic.

'Two pieces of silver,' a voice cried out and the crowd cheered.

Summer looked for the voice that had placed the bid. Finally she saw him, a man with a Sheikh's head covering. He stared at her intently and she felt fear creep up her spine. She looked away.

Eli, please don't let them take me!

'Four pieces of silver,' another voice challenged. This time Summer did not have to look – she knew that voice. The Kapudan Pasha stepped forward to the front of the crowd, in direct challenge to the Sheikh.

Summer felt the blood drain from her face.

What is he doing here?

Her mind went into turmoil as she remembered the last time she was alone with him. She felt like vomiting.

He smiled at her knowingly and she thought her legs would buckle under her. She would die before she became his slave.

'Eight pieces of silver,' the Sheikh countered. The Kapudan Pasha looked annoyed at his persistence.

'Twelve pieces,' he responded.

The crowd started to murmur in excitement. They loved a good battle in the market square. Summer pleaded with her eyes for the Sheikh to make another offer.

Even being with him will not be as bad as being the Kapudan Pasha's slave. Great One, if you really are there and you care about me even a little bit, please don't let this happen to me again, she mentally prayed.

'Twenty pieces of silver,' the Sheikh offered.

The Kapudan Pasha started to sweat. He had not planned on buying slaves in Alexandria. He was simply on a scouting mission for the Sultan – the last one before he and his troops returned to Galata for the winter. The moment he had seen her across the market square he knew he had to have her, but now he was running out of silver coin. He took a deep breath and made his final offer hoping that it would be enough.

'Forty silver pieces,' he called.

The crowd went silent. It was unusual for a slave to be sold for forty silver pieces. The men who brought Summer to the market rubbed their hands in glee, hoping the two men would drive the price higher.

The Sheikh looked momentarily worried. Then he rummaged in his pocket and brought out an item, which he held up.

'Forty pieces of silver, plus this.' He waved something in the air. Summer could not make out what it was.

'It is worth far more than any offer you will get,' he added.

The Kapudan Pasha looked furious. The traders who brought Summer to market inspected the treasure before accepting the Sheikh's offer.

'Sold to the Sheikh,' the auctioneer shouted and the crowd cheered. It was too much for Summer. Her legs gave way and she toppled off the platform. The Sheikh scooped her up, paid the men and carried her away from the crowd. He did not see the eunuch following him.

Eli watched as Summer was carried away. He had remained hidden during the auction because if the Kapudan Pasha recognized him there would be no way to save her. He would follow the Sheikh and find a way to help her escape. They headed toward the port and Eli kept his distance.

⌘

It was hot and she was becoming heavy. The Sheikh shifted her weight and she moaned. She was beautiful despite the angry scar that crossed her neck. He turned into an alley where it was shady and set her down on a low wall. He held her against his side so she would not fall over. She moaned again and opened her eyes.

'Where am I,' she mumbled holding her bruised head from her fall. She suddenly became aware of the arm around her and she stiffened, pulling away. Fear was reflected in her big grey eyes.

'Please don't hurt me,' she whimpered as she wrapped her arms around herself to protect herself from him.

'Shhh...' he whispered soothingly. 'You are safe now Summerbee.' He did not know why he called her that, but it just slipped out. He felt her shock as she looked at him.

'Papa Mac,' she said softly. 'Is that you? Am I in Lionsgate?'

She's lost her mind, he thought worried.

'No Summer, it's me, Tristan.' He felt fear engulf him. She did not even recognize him.

304
THE GOLDEN CAGE

She looked at him and then touched his face tentatively, sure he were a mirage, a figment of her imagination.

'I know you're not really here,' she said to herself. 'My mind used to do this to me all the time in the desert.'

'I am here Summer and no one will ever hurt you again. I am taking you home.'

She shook her head and closed her eyes. When she opened them he was still there.

'No, you are the Sheikh who bought me. You are trying to confuse me. I would know Tristan if I saw him and you don't look anything like him.'

Tristan sighed realizing that his face had tanned at sea and his beard covered most of it.

Of course she doesn't recognize me.

'I am Tristan,' he said pulling the medallion out from his tunic and pushing his head covering back. I gave this to you in Francia when I told you that I loved you and that this was a sign of my commitment. You promised you would never take it off, but someone snatched it from you. I have been searching for you for many moons and now I have found you. I dressed as a Sheikh so that I would fit in here, but I never expected to find you here. We thought you were in Abyssinia. As we were leaving the market I heard the auctioneer mention the girl from across the seas with the long dark hair and somehow I just knew it was you. It was me who was bidding on you in the market. I could not let that other man win.'

Finally the tears came as she sobbed, deep heart wrenching sobs. He wrapped her in his arms and let her cry till there was no more to come. He wanted to kiss her and tell her he loved her, but somehow he knew she was too raw and it was too soon.

THE GOLDEN CAGE

'You're safe,' he whispered again. 'Do you want to see your father and brother?'

'They're here?' She started to cry again and nodded her head.

They stood together but a shadow blocked the alley. Summer gasped and Tristan pushed her behind him.

⌘

Erik rolled out the barrels ready to have them filled with fresh water. Griffin and Cam prepared others by washing them out ready to receive fresh food. The sails were checked and ropes tested.

'Where is Tristan?' Cam grumbled after carrying the fourth barrel from below deck. 'We could use his help.'

'Didn't he return with us from the Market?' Cam asked. 'Now that you mention it, I don't remember him being with us.'

'Perhaps one of us should go and look for him,' Aedan said dropping the rope he was working on. 'It's not a good idea to wander the city alone, especially if they get wind he is a foreigner.'

'Maybe he went to get some more coffee' Cam said. 'I know I would sneak off for another taste of it.'

Aedan headed down the gangplank but came to a dead halt when he saw Tristan. Beside him stood Summer and a dark skinned man.

'Summer?' he said incredulous. 'SUMMER!' He grabbed her in a bear hug and then danced a little jig on the dockside. 'Erik, Griffin, Cam, get down here now,' he yelled.

They looked down at the group on the dock and Erik let out a yell of joy, his limbs carrying him down the gangplank as fast as they could move.

'Summer,' he stopped and looked at his daughter who looked overwhelmed and tearful. 'Oh Summer, I can't believe it's you. Your mother and I have been frantic. Thank you Great Odin that she is safe.'

Summer laughed through her tears. It was a family joke that her father always referred to the Great One as Great Odin. It was his culture meshing with her mother's and his way of expressing himself. He held out his arms unsure whether she wanted to be touched. He had seen women ravaged by his own kinsmen and he knew that many of them struggled with any intimacy after their ordeal. He was unsure of what she had experienced.

'Papa,' she flew into his arms and sobbed as he held her tight.

'It's going to be all right sweetheart,' he murmured. 'You are safe with family now and we love you.'

Summer pulled herself free and beckoned to Eli.

'Papa, this is Eli, my protector and someone who has saved me more than once the last few moons.'

Tristan smiled and confirmed her words. 'He almost had my head on a pike when he caught me in the alley with her. I thought he was going to kill me.'

Summer laughed remembering how Tristan had pushed her behind him as an act of protection. Eli had seen it as an act of dominance and aggression. His face had been cold and murderous – she had never seen him that way. She had dashed in between them and put her hands up defensively. She smiled thinking how confused they both looked. She also remembered how afraid she had been when his shadow had blocked their exit from the alley.

307

THE GOLDEN CAGE

Initially she thought it was the Kapudan Pasha who had followed them. Once she assured Tristan and Eli that they were all on the same side, things had improved.

Erik looked at the eunuch who humbly nodded his head.

'Eli, how can I thank you for keeping my daughter safe. Anna has told us how you saved her from drowning.'

'Anna, you met Anna?' Summer said incredulously.'

'We did and it is thanks to her that we knew you were alive. The Valide Sultan had no intention of owning up to the fact that you were a prisoner in her palace. Anna got your medallion back,' Tristan said.

'I wish I could thank her,' Summer said. 'It makes me so angry that she is trapped in that harem. She doesn't realize that it is a prison and that it will kill her soul eventually,'

I think she does,' Griffin said, 'and you can thank her personally.'

He indicated the ship. Summer looked up and saw the young girl waving excitedly from the boat. 'Summer,' she yelled as the two ran toward each other.

THIRTY-NINE

FINDING COURAGE

SHE sat with him in his cabin and she felt awkward. Once she would have yearned for him to take her in his arms and make love to her, but so much had changed, she had changed. She felt mixed emotions. She remembered his touch and his taste and how their bodies had fitted so perfectly together as they gave themselves to one another; but then she also remembered how painful it was when the Kapudan Pasha had forced himself into her, over and over again. She feared that if she allowed Tristan to become intimate with her that those memories would assail her and kill the feelings she had for him. She would rather remember what they had as sweet and beautiful than ruin it now. She watched him as he finished shaving. She smiled. He was incredibly handsome and now he looked as he did in Francia, only more tanned. It suited him. Her heart lurched as he patted his face dry and smiled at her.

'How's this?' he asked.

'Much better,' she replied. She touched the medallion that was back around her neck and plucked up the courage to tell him the truth. She undid the necklace and put her hand out to him, the medallion shining in her outstretched palm.

'I can't keep this,' she said softly. 'It wouldn't be right.'

'Why? Nothing has changed for me Summer. I still love you. What I said then stands true for me now.'

'But I am not the same person you fell in love with Tristan. I am different, broken and I am not sure I will ever be whole again. You deserve better and I can't give you what you need.'

Her face crumpled and she shoved the medallion into his hand.

'What happened to you in Anatolia, Summer? Tell me so I can understand. Nothing you say will ever change how I feel about you.'

'I can't talk about it,' she said. 'Please don't ask me.'

'All right, but I will wait for you, for as long as it takes,' he said. 'I made a commitment to you that day in front of the fire, and I will keep my word.'

'Don't, I won't change my mind,' she sobbed as she ran from his cabin.

Eli found her on deck crying softly.

'I assume those are tears of happiness?' he said.

She wiped her eyes and looked at him. 'Things will never be the same. I can't go back to the way things were before this all happened. I can't forget what has happened to me.'

'Of course you can't go back Miss Summer, but that doesn't mean you can't move forward either. There are people who love you, a man who loves you. I know you love him too because I have seen the way you look at him.'

'I do love him and that is why I have to let him go Eli. I am not sure I will ever be able to have a man touch me again. He deserves a woman who loves him in every way possible. I am not that woman anymore.'

'Miss Summer, you have been through trauma and you need time to heal and to accept. You cannot make this decision now. Poor decisions are always made in haste.'

'But I must, so that he does not sacrifice his life for a wasted cause.'

'Of all your characteristics, I never imagined cowardice to be one of them Miss Summer.'

Summer was shocked. The eunuch had never spoken so directly and cruelly to her before.

'How can you say that, Eli? You know what I have been through. I have faced it all, even when I have wanted to die. I could have flung myself from that ship, but I didn't.'

'I am not talking about how you have overcome challenges Miss Summer. I am talking about your reluctance to open your heart and share the truth with the people who love you. You have not told anyone what has happened to you.'

'I can't,' she whispered.

'Why not?' he challenged. 'What are you really afraid of?'

She hesitated. 'I'm afraid they will look at me differently, that every time they see this ugly scar on my neck they will blame themselves, or me for it. I'm afraid that people will only ever look at me with pity. I'm afraid that I will never know what it is like to know the touch of the man I love without seeing the Kapudan Pasha's face. I'm afraid Eli, of everything.'

'Oh Miss Summer, don't you see how fortunate you are to feel afraid – to be uncertain, because that uncertainty means it is not cut and dried. You are worried about what may possibly be, but unless you take a leap of faith you will never truly know. I wish I'd had the chance to be afraid after they castrated me, to wonder whether I would feel like a man again or ever father children, but I didn't because there was no second chance for me, no hope to undo what was done. You have the opportunity at a second

311
THE GOLDEN CAGE

chance, to be loved the way you should be. Don't let the Kapudan Pasha take that from you, otherwise no matter where you are, he will always have power over you.'

Summer nodded numbly. There was truth in his words but it was easier said than done.

'What did he do to you Summer?' Tristan asked.

He had come to find her and overheard the end of their conversation. Summer looked as though she wanted to flee but Eli nodded encouragement to her.

'Find your courage,' he whispered, 'and move forward Miss Summer.'

He left them to talk and Tristan sat beside her on the wooden deck.

'I just want to go home,' she whispered.

'I know, and we sail at first light. Who is this Kapudan Pasha Summer?'

'He is the man who was bidding against you in the market.' Tristan looked shocked. She continued. 'He is the captain of the Sultan's navy. He came to Topkapi Palace and the Valide Sultan decided that I would be the one to accompany him that evening. She tricked me by telling me the Sultan wanted to see me. I was painting his portrait so I went willingly with her. When I realized what she was doing I refused to do as she asked, and she told me she would ensure that Queen Maria had you killed. I couldn't live with that so I agreed to have dinner with the Kapudan Pasha. I drank too much raki and must have passed out. When I woke I was in my room, but I was not alone. He was there.'

She could see the shock on his face and she stumbled momentarily. Then she dropped her head in shame and spoke so softly that he could barely hear her. 'He raped me.'

'Merde! Le batard, I'll kill him,' Tristan growled, inner rage and pain piercing his heart. Summer placed her hand on his arm. 'It wasn't all his fault,' she murmured.

'What do you mean?'

'If I hadn't drunk too much raki and passed out, it would not have happened. I wasn't able to protect myself, to stop him. He was too strong.' She was sobbing now, deep painful sobs that came like rivers.

'Summer,' Tristan groaned as he too was crying. 'None of this is your fault sweetheart. If anything I'm the one who let you down. I promised to protect you but I let Francia come before you. I failed you and I am so sorry. Can you ever forgive me?'

They sat holding one another, crying in each other's arms.

'You did not fail me,' she said. 'You found me and saved me.'

He looked into her watery eyes and wiped a tear from her cheek. 'I would have spent the rest of my life looking for you.'

He ran his finger gently across her scar and she shuddered. 'I am no longer beautiful,' she said. 'This scar will always be a reminder of that place.'

'You are so very beautiful and this scar doesn't have to remind you of pain – it can remind you of your strength and courage, remind you that even though something awful happened, that love is greater than evil. I meant what I said Summer. I love you and I will wait till you are ready. I don't want to be with anyone else.'

She nodded. 'All right, we will see how it goes.'

THE GOLDEN CAGE

'That's all I ask,' he replied.

⌘

Early the next morning they prepared to set sail. The men rallied about loading the final provisions. Summer stood on deck with Eli.

'Are you sure you don't want to come with us?' she asked sadly.

'No Miss Summer, I've done what was required of me. I have seen you safely back with your family and now it is time to find my own family. My parents deserve to know what happened to my sister and to know that I am alive. I must return to Abyssinia.'

'I will miss you. Who's going to keep me on my toes and prevent me from getting into trouble?' she teased.

He smiled. 'I think you have enough protectors to ensure you are safe. Remember what I told you Miss Summer. Fight for your future. Don't let your past define you.'

'I will do my best,' she said hugging the eunuch. 'I can never repay you Eli for all you have done for me. I would not be here, had it not been for you.'

'You are a strong woman Miss Summer. One last piece of advice, give your Great One another chance. I was there to protect you because he put me there.' He winked at her and she laughed.

Is that true Great One?

⌘

The ship creaked as it made its way slowly out of the port. Summer waved to Eli who stood on the shore, his body getting smaller and smaller as they moved out into the ocean. Finally she could see him no more.

'Keep him safe Great One and I'll consider giving you another chance,' she murmured.

FORTY

REVENGE, BEST SERVED COLD

PALAIS DU LOUVRE - FRANCIA

QUEEN Maria stared at her cousin. She was furious with him. 'Why did you wait so long to pass on this information?'

He shuffled awkwardly as he faced her anger.

'I was afraid,' he said. 'They told me that unless I gave them the information they wanted, they would tell Louis what you did. They also said I would have my head removed as a traitor.'

Maria paled. If Louis found out that she had Summer shipped off to a harem in Anatolia there would be no recourse for her. She would face the axe man as sure as Lucas Beaumont had.

'What are you going to do Maria?' he asked.

'I will convince Louis that Tristan Chevalier was plotting with Lucas Beaumont. I need to put a price on his head so that he can never return to Francia.'

'Doesn't the king believe he's dead already? How will you explain that he lives?'

'This might yet work in my favour cousin,' she replied. He could see her mind scheming, turning like a cog. 'If I tell Louis that Tristan Chevalier escaped because he worked with Lucas Beaumont and that he is set on returning to avenge Summer's death, he will agree to put a bounty on Tristan's head.'

She smiled. She had formulated a plan and Louis would go along with it, if only to cover up his part in the conspiracy to kill Tristan and the other men he sent to west Francia. They both had reason to want Tristan Chevalier out of their lives for good. Once they placed a bounty on Tristan's head they would win either way – he would leave or be captured and beheaded. She was not averse to either plan.

'As for you cousin,' Queen Maria said, 'I think it best you return to Hispania and our paths never cross again.'

He understood the insinuation.

⌘

ALEXANDRIA

After Summer sailed, Eli made his way across the port. Although he was anxious to return to his family in Abyssinia, there was something he had to take care of first. He searched for something in particular, scanning the ships that were moored as he watched them being loaded and unloaded. There were ships from various countries but he was only interested in one. Finally he saw the familiar Anatolian flag flapping gently in the breeze, the ships huge mast punching a hole into the heavens. He waited and watched.

⌘

AT SEA

The return voyage was less stressful as the ship made its way through the Alboran Sea. Summer and Tristan spent hours talking. Many times he had to hold his tongue from interrogating her. He wanted to know it all, but he also wanted her to share only that which she was comfortable doing. He longed to take her in his arms, kiss her, but he knew it would be a mistake, that it was too soon. He knew that she had nightmares about her time in Anatolia. He watched her sleep and fear and terror plagued her rest. All he could do was be patient. The ship headed to Massalia where they would restock their dwindling supplies before heading to Griswold. Griffin could barely contain his eagerness for the vessel to reach its destination. He had only one person on his mind – Lucy.

⌘

ALEXANDRIA

His wait finally paid off. The Kapudan Pasha descended the gangplank, making his way up the cobbled street of the city. Every now and again he glanced over his shoulder as though he knew he was being followed. He seemed nervous.

You should be, Eli thought as he followed making sure he was not seen.

The Kapudan Pasha turned into an alley that led to a courtyard. It twisted and turned as it followed a narrow cobbled street. He knocked briefly on a door and was ushered in by a man. The door shut quickly and Eli waited in the shadows. It was a long wait. It was nightfall when the Kapudan Pasha exited the building. He was unsteady on his feet, his eyes glazed. Eli knew instantly that he had been in a hashish den. He stalked him down the dark streets, hiding in the shadows as he stumbled back toward the port. The Kapudan Pasha stopped; turned sideways and pulled down his pants, urinating on the whitewashed wall of a building. He grunted as though deriving pleasure from emptying his bladder. Eli caught him by surprise as he pulled his trousers up. The eunuch pushed him up against the wall and murmured in his ear, 'Not a sound.'

He leaned his weight against the unsteady man as he pulled a sack from his pocket, pulling it over the Kapudan Pasha's head. Then he bound his hands with rope. Finally he lifted the sack and stuffed cloth into the man's mouth. He gurgled in rage when he recognised Eli, but he was too affected by hashish to put up a fight. His habit would cost him dearly. Eli dragged him into a dark side alley that was deserted. The hour was late and most people had retired for the night.

'You are probably wondering what I want?' Eli whispered menacingly. The sack bobbed up and down in response. 'Well it's not money. What I want you can't give to me – no one can because it was cut out of me. However I can ensure that you never again hurt another woman the way you have in the past. My sister was not a piece of meat for a man's pleasure. She was a person, a beautiful, intelligent woman with her whole life ahead of her. Anatolia took that from her and as a result she lost the will to live.'

The head shook vigorously as the Kapudan Pasha tried to growl something.

'Yes, I know you had nothing to do with her death, but it is men like you who abuse women and treat them as nothing but objects for your own pleasure and gain. This is not only for my sister. This is for Miss Summer too. You raped her.'

The Kapudan Pasha growled again, shaking his head vigorously.

'You would deny it?' Eli scoffed. 'You did not even know her real name. Perhaps you knew her as Süheyla.' The Kapudan Pasha stopped squirming as her name was said. Eli had his full attention.

'Yes, I thought you might recognize that name. You almost broke her, but she is strong and she knows that wasting her life hating you is not worth it. The man who bought her is not a Sheikh. He is the man who loves her and has been searching for her. That is why he would have paid any price for her return. She could have asked him to kill you, but she chose to walk away and put this behind her, but I cannot. It's really ironic because I am the one who told her all this time that she has a future and that she needs to look forward and forgive what has been. She will not seek justice, but I will seek it for her.'

The Kapudan Pasha began to growl as loud as he could, his terror evident.

Eli punched him in the face. 'Settle down,' he said. 'Death is too good for you Kapudan Pasha. You should suffer as much as the women you have raped have suffered. Did she beg you the way you are begging me now? Did you laugh at her pleas? Somehow I imagine you did. Yet you ignored her pleas for mercy. Your pleas leave me equally uncompassionate.'

⌘

She sat bolt upright in the bunk, sweat dripping from her brow, confused. Tristan reached out to her, but did not touch her. Instead she reached for him and he wrapped her in his arms. She began to sob softly and he made cooing noises of reassurance in her ear.

'It's over,' she said at last.

He looked enquiringly at her, uncertain of what she meant.

'The Kapudan Pasha will never hurt anyone ever again,' she said firmly.

'How do you know?' he asked.

'I just do. Eli told me so in my dreams. He told me it's over. Eli has never lied to me.'

Tristan could see relief flood her face. He did not care if it was just a dream. If she believed it were truly over then she would begin to mend and regain her life.

'Stay with me. Lie next to me and just hold me please,' she whispered.

Tristan held her in his arms as he lay behind her. He remembered the smell of her hair and the sweetness of their lovemaking and he ached just her know her this way once more. He truly hoped she was right – that it was over.

⌘

The Kapudan Pasha lay bleeding in the alley. The old man who found him was shocked by what he saw. His trousers were down around his thighs, but it was the bloody mess he saw between the man's legs that horrified him the most. His genitals had been crudely and callously removed. He raced to get help.

Eli washed the blood from his hands in the fountain. He shook slightly but it was his inner rage that had given him the resolve to see the deed through. He had not lied to Summer when he told her to reach for her future, that it was each person's responsibility to be happy. He wanted to save her from suffering the way he had, of living with bitterness and he felt he had helped her. It was the Kapudan Pasha's abuse of the young woman that brought back all his own bitterness and rage. For so many years, he had pushed it down and now it had resurfaced, boiling in his heart. He never imagined he was a violent man, until the moment he had castrated the Kapudan Pasha. It had not felt evil; instead it felt cleansing for him.

'I'm not sorry Miss Summer,' he murmured to the starry heavens. 'He deserves it, and sometimes even those of us who have forgiven, stumble once again. Sometimes forgiveness is not enough, sometimes retribution is what it takes to truly set one free. It's over – he will never hurt you or another again.'

He knew she would understand and for the first time in years he felt like a real man once more.

FORTY-ONE

WANTED

THE ship docked as seagulls screeched overhead and the sun shone down through blue skies. Griffin was the first off the boat as he raced to find Lucy. He had missed her and although he hardly knew her, he did know that she was the one he wanted to wake up to every day of his life.

She saw him running up the cobbled street before he even got to their apartment. She tore down the stairs almost knocking a maid off her feet and out the huge wooden door.

'Griffin,' she yelled, rushing to him.

He folded her in his arms and she felt smaller than he remembered. He did not want to let her go.

'Don't squeeze the life out of me,' she giggled breathlessly. 'Let me look at you,' she said stepping back and eyeing him up and down. 'You look like you could do with a bath and a haircut,' she laughed.

She ushered him inside and gave him something to eat. Then she handed him a towel and a fresh set of clothes and ordered him to bath.

'Father won't mind,' she said as he raised his eyebrows.

When he was clean and tidy they sat in the parlour and he smiled at her.

'I've missed you Lucy,' he said blushing.

She laughed. 'Still a little shy of me,' she teased. 'I missed you too, more than you realize. Griffin there's something I need to tell you.'

She sounded so serious that his heart dropped. Had she fallen in love with another while he was gone? He waited for her to continue.

'The Francian man you sailed with, has a bounty on his head.'

'What do you mean?' Griffin asked.

'Tristan Chevalier is wanted dead or alive by King Louis and Queen Maria. Musketeers came to Massalia a few days ago and posted his picture all over the city. Did he return with you?'

'Yes, but why is he wanted? King Louis believes he is dead.'

'Well, that is no longer the case. He knows he's alive and he is being accused of treason, of conspiring with Lucas Beaumont the traitor, to start a war between Francia and Griswold. They are also claiming that he killed your sister.'

'This is absurd. We must go to Lutèce and clear this up. He cannot be accused if Cam and I are alive and with Summer safe it will surely exonerate him.'

'No you cannot,' Lucy blurted out. 'This is a conspiracy by both King Louis and Queen Maria that will not end well for any of you. Our monarchy has determined that he is the scapegoat for deeds they are trying to cover up. They will ensure that none of you ever get to tell your story.'

'How do you know all this Lucy?' he asked.

'My mother's brother was beheaded a few moons ago as a traitor.'

She saw the shock on his face as he put two and two together.

'Yes, my mother was a Beaumont before marrying my father. None of us ever believed that Lucas betrayed the crown. He was loyal to King Louis – too loyal if you ask me, and that became his downfall. Tristan must stay out of the city and hidden till you sail. Your life is at risk just by association. I hate to say this, but the sooner you leave the safer you will all be. Promise me that you will not go anywhere near Lutèce.'

He could see how worried she was. 'You must get back to the ship and warn them.'

'Come with me Lucy,' he said suddenly. She could see the fear in his eyes, the longing, but she had to hear him say it.

'Why?' she asked.

'Because from the moment you walked into that tavern and coerced Cam and me into protecting your honour, I wanted to know you more. The few days I've spent with you made me realize that I have been looking for you my whole life. I love you Lucy, it's crazy I know, because we barely know one another, but I don't want to leave without you and clearly I cannot stay in Francia.'

She silenced him with her lips, soft and warm as she pushed herself close to him. She rested her hands on his chest and could feel his heart beating furiously as she explored his mouth. She pulled away before he could become too aroused.

'I'll come with you,' she promised, 'but right now we need to get back to the ship and warn the others.'

⌘

Summer was too afraid to leave the ship. She had no desire to explore Massalia and once again she became aware of how much she had changed. Her old self would have jumped at the opportunity to explore the bustling port city and to marvel at the beautiful architecture, but now it all seemed superficial to her. There were more important things to worry about than art and buildings. All she wanted to do was get home to Griswold, to feel Hawk beneath her as she rode carefree across the plains. Tristan refused to leave her and remained aboard the ship with her. Anna begged Cam to take her to see some of the port and the two of them had left together to explore. Erik and Aedan and some of the crew carried empty barrels ashore to secure new and fresh supplies.

'Why don't you help Papa and Aedan?' Summer said to Tristan. 'You need to get out of this cabin and get some fresh air. I'll be fine alone for a while.'

'I don't want to leave you,' he said worried.

'Please Tristan, don't treat me like a child. Pity is one of the things I feared the most about telling you what happened to me. I cannot live my life being treated as porcelain china about to shatter if not handled delicately. If we are to rebuild our relationship then you need to let me have my space.'

He nodded, surprised at her determination. He had his own fears to deal with and suffocating her was clearly not the answer.

'All right, I will give the men a hand, but if you need me just give me a shout.' He left the cabin and headed to the deck.

'What can I do?' he asked Erik.

'Head over to the Hungry Pelican and purchase some salted pork, smoked fish, cheese and hardtack? A barrel of wine would be good too,' he added smiling. 'After all, we are celebrating.'

Tristan strode toward the tavern, his mind still on Summer. He wanted things to be the same as they were before, but what she had endured in Anatolia had damaged them both and he wondered if it could ever be repaired. He entered the interior and it took a moment for his eyes to adjust to the dark room. It was not overly busy as it was early in the day, but there were still sailors and a few drunkards who had obviously not made it home the night before. He went to the counter where a young woman was drying tankards.

'I'm looking to purchase supplies,' he said. She looked him up and down.

'Let's see your silver,' she barked. Tristan pulled out a bag of coins.

'Follow me,' she said moving through a curtain to the back of the tavern. They found themselves in a large storeroom that had barrels stacked to the ceiling.

'Pull out what you want and I'll be back shortly,' she said. Tristan began to roll barrels of salted pork and smoked fish to the middle of the floor. He searched for the hardtack, a hard biscuit that made up most of their meals at sea. They would need a few crates to see them to Griswold. He found a few rounds of hard cheese and added them to the pile of goods he had accumulated. As he struggled with the last barrel of wine, he noticed he was no longer alone.

'I told you boys,' the woman said holding up a wanted poster with his face on it. 'It's him and I will share the reward with you if you apprehend him.'

The three men advanced cornering Tristan in the back of the room.

'What's this about?' he asked surprised by their antagonism.

'It says on this poster you are a traitor to Francia and that you're wanted dead or alive,' one of the men said.

'That's ridiculous, I am a Musketeer in King Louis' army.'

'Yes, and a conspirator with Lucas Beaumont to begin a war in Francia.'

'That's not true,' Tristan said, eyeing around for something he could use as a weapon. He backed up further as the men advanced.

'Actually it's not our problem,' the young woman said. 'You can plead your case when you have been delivered to Lutèce.'

The men lunged at Tristan and he punched the first hard in the jaw. As the man stumbled backward the second made his move. Tristan grabbed his outstretched fist twisting his arm and thrusting him toward the third, who was caught off-guard. He made a dash for the door but did not manage to get through it. A sharp pain in his skull rendered him unconscious as he slipped to the floor, blood seeping from the gash on his head. The young girl gasped, holding the broken bottle in her hand.

'Bloody useless lot,' she said to the men who gathered themselves up. 'Make yourselves useful now and tie him up.'

⌘

Griffin and Lucy arrived back at the ship, breathless from running. Griffin held out the poster.

'They're all over the city,' he said to his father.

Erik looked shocked, Tristan's image staring back at him as he read the words that sealed the Musketeer's fate. Half of Francia would have his head on a pike if they discovered him on Francian soil.

'Save the gods,' Erik muttered. 'I sent him to the Hungry Pelican to get supplies. 'Come, we must find him.'

'Lucy, will you stay here with Summer?' Griffin asked. 'She will be distraught if she discovers he is wanted.' Lucy nodded her head and the men raced off down the wharf.

Lucy looked at the poster in her hand. If anyone recognized Tristan he would have very little chance of escape. She crumpled the poster as Summer alighted on deck, holding it behind her back.

'What's all the commotion about? Who are you?' she asked surprised to see the ship deserted, save for a strange girl.

'I'm Lucy, Griffin's friend.' She held out her hand to shake then realized the crumpled poster was in it. Quickly she tucked it into her pocket and offered her hand once more. Summer smiled, realizing this was the woman her brother had been mooning over.

'I'm Summer, Griffin's sister. It is lovely to meet you, but where is everyone?'

'They have gone to get supplies,' she lied effortlessly. 'Griffin asked me to stay aboard in case you thought everyone had deserted you,' she added. 'I'm glad you're safe,' she added.

'Well in that case Lucy, come down to my cabin and have some tea.'

'I tell you again sir, that no one matching your description has come in here to procure supplies,' the young woman in the Hungry Pelican said. 'I resent the insinuation that I would lie to you.'

'This is where he was headed and our ship is just across the wharf. He could hardly have gone missing between here and there.'

'Perhaps he made a stop at one of the bordello's along the way,' she said. 'Men usually have one of two things on their mind after a long journey at sea and clearly a tankard of ale or rum wasn't uppermost in his mind or I would have seen him.'

Erik glared at the woman. He knew she was lying but he had no way to prove that Tristan was here.

'Come lads,' he said to the others. 'Let's be on our way.' They turned to go, Erik stopping momentarily as though deep in thought. Then he strode out of the Hungry Pelican back to the ship.

'What do we do now Papa,' Griffin asked.

'She's lying, Tristan's there.'

'You're right,' Aedan said. 'I know when a person is lying. She offered us every possibility of where he could have gone. She was trying to assuage her guilt. She also would not look you directly in the eye Erik. She knows where he is.'

'We watch. If Tristan is there she will want to get him transported to Lutèce. We'll wait till they take him from the tavern and we'll follow.'

'What if he's dead, Papa? The poster said he's wanted dead or alive.'

'She doesn't strike me as the murderous type Griffin. Greedy yes, but she will not dirty her hands.'

⌘

Anna and Cam arrived back at the ship and they both looked slightly green.

'What's the matter with you two?' Summer asked. 'You look as though you have seen the ghosts of Massalia.'

Cam held out the poster and Summer snatched it from his hand. She read it, her face paling.

'No, oh no...' she muttered. 'Tristan's gone ashore and he's been gone a long time. I must go and find him.' She pushed her chair back so forcefully that it crashed to the floor.

'No Summer, wait,' Lucy said. 'Your father and brother have gone to look for him.'

'And you didn't tell me,' Summer shouted at her. 'When will everyone stop treating me as fragile? I have a right to know.'

'I'm sorry Summer, you're right. I should have told you.'

'This is my fault, this is all my fault,' she said before storming out of the cabin. Cam followed her to the deck.

'Don't worry I'm not leaving the ship, but I do want to be alone,' she snapped. He nodded before leaving to look for the others.

Summer felt inexplicable anger. Eli wanted her to give the Great One another chance, to open her heart to him

331
THE GOLDEN CAGE

again, but what he didn't understand was that she was the one who needed another chance. The Great One had left her because he was trying to teach her a lesson. She had given herself to Tristan before they were wed and this was her punishment. It was why she had been abducted and raped by the Kapudan Pasha and now it was why Tristan had disappeared. She believed her protection was gone.

'Please,' she whimpered to the Great One, 'please let him be all right. You can heap as much pain on me as you wish, just let him be safe,' she pleaded.

⌘

LIONSGATE

'Did you hear her?' Mac asked mortified.

The Great One nodded his head sadly. 'Yes I did.'

'She's not right thinking you're punishing her, is she?' he asked.

'You have been with me for years Mac and you actually have to ask that,' the Great One smiled surprised.

'I'm sorry, but it does seem that wherever she goes, trouble follows her and it is only since she and Tristan have been together.'

'I do not heap pain on people to teach them lessons. Summer has been caught up with some evil people and this evil is playing itself out. It has absolutely nothing to do with her obedience or behaviour. She's a grown woman Mac, with her own choices to make. Even I respect that. She'll find her peace I promise you.'

'But she believes that you are doing this to her. She will lose her faith and belief in you because of this.'

'No Mac, she will find her faith again because of this – just wait and see.'

⌘

MASSALIA

Tristan groaned and his head ached when he moved. It was pitch black. He was on his back and as he tried to sit up he bumped his forehead hard.

'Ouch.' *Where the hell am I?*

He extended his hands out in front of him and they hit wood. He felt all around him, his dread mounting as he did so.

I'm in a coffin. He panicked. *Dear Lord, they've buried me alive?*

He wanted to scream out, then he remembered there was a sizeable bounty on his head. They would not bury him if they meant to collect it. He sighed, relief flooding him. He heard footsteps and felt the box moving. He lay as quietly as possible.

The men moved the coffin from the tavern to a waiting wagon. They surrounded it with barrels of wine and covered the box with a large canvas cloth.

'Take him to the old mill on the outskirts of the city. I will meet you there after the tavern closes. In the meantime I'll send word to the local barracks that we have him in our custody,' the young woman said. 'Don't think of crossing me,' she warned them.

The wagon moved and Tristan was jostled from side to side as it rattled across the bumpy cobblestones. It took a while for them to reach the old mill and his shoulders and legs felt bruised. He thought of Summer and worried that she may believe he had deserted her, given up on them.

Why is this happening to us? When will it all end?

⌘

They crouched in the trees along the edge of the old mill. Cam had joined them in their search for Tristan and they had followed the wagon when it had left the Hungry Pelican. They watched the men unload the large wooden box and drag it inside, grunting with the exertion. The rickety door shook on its hinges, as it slammed shut behind them.

'What now?' Griffin asked his father.

'We are going to get him back,' Erik said.

'How?' Cam asked.

'I have a plan,' Griffin said suddenly. 'It might just work.'

FORTY-TWO

CORNERED

IT took a while for Griffin and Cam to return from the ship. They were wearing their Musketeer uniforms.

'What if this plan doesn't work?' Cam said.

'Did you see those idiots who brought him here?' Griffin asked incredulous. 'They would believe a round of cheese was the moon if someone told them that.'

'Are you sure you are able to pull this off?' Erik asked concerned.

'We'll be fine Papa,' Griffin said. He felt nervous but this was the best plan they had and time was running out. Before long actual Musketeers would be arriving.

'We'll be outside if you need us,' he said patting his son on the back.

Cam and Griffin made their way to the old mill door. They banged hard on it and waited. A young, terrified man opened the door, looking around.

'We're here to verify the prisoner's identity,' Griffin said boldly.

'Where's the woman?' the young man asked nervously.

'She'll be here shortly. There's a delay at the tavern,' Cam reassured.

'I don't know,' he murmured. 'She warned us about anyone seeing him before she got here.

'All right then,' Griffin said shrugging his shoulders and turning as though to leave. 'You can explain to King Louis why you denied his dragoons access to the prisoner and perhaps he will let you keep your head if he's in a generous mood, but I wouldn't count on it, if this is the right prisoner.'

'As we said we need to verify his identity,' Cam interjected 'If it is Tristan Chevalier, he's a traitor to Francia, but if you're afraid of the little woman who runs the local tavern more than King Louis then I guess we'll have to leave.'

The young man paled at the mention of losing his head.

'Wait. Come in,' he said ushering them through the door.

'Where is he?' Griffin asked, knowing full well he was in the box.

'In there,' they pointed.

'Well it's a bit hard to check his identity through the wood, don't you think?' Their sarcasm was lost on the men.

'Open it,' Cam said frustrated.

They cranked the box open slightly and they peered in. They could just see Tristan and he looked bewildered and confused.

'You fool,' Cam said angrily. 'This is not Tristan Chevalier. This is someone who looks very similar, I grant you, but it's not him.'

'How do you know?' the second man challenged.

'Tristan Chevalier trained us. We completed a mission with him before he turned traitor and almost had us all killed. He was cut across the face with a sword and has a large scar across the left side of his face. This man does not.'

The men looked confused, unsure what to believe.

'His poster does not show a scar.'

'No, it wouldn't because it's not common knowledge that he was injured before he fled. Only those of us who survived his traitorous dealings are aware of this. Trust me, I of all people would love to see him lose his head, but this man is not him,' Griffin said.

'Maybe we should wait for Mallory,' the young man said.

'Oh is that the little woman from the tavern,' Cam mocked. 'You do know that she plans to keep all the reward for herself. That's the only reason she doesn't want you turning over the prisoner. You forget though, that there will be no reward for this man – he is not Tristan Chevalier and if he is going to charge anyone with kidnapping and assault it will be you boys who take the fall.'

'What should we do?' they asked each other.

'Let us take him and we will convince him to forget any of this happened,' Griffin said.

They all looked afraid and nodded.

They lifted the lid and helped Tristan out of the wooden casket.

'This has all been a misunderstanding,' Griffin informed him. 'We will get you home sir, if you are willing to forget all about this.' He glared at Tristan, urging him to play along.

He nodded, unsure about what was happening, but wise enough to let them take control. They made it halfway to the door when it was flung open and Mallory and four Musketeers entered the mill.

'Who are you?' she asked Cam and Griffin. 'Why are you letting these men take him?' she growled at her three co-conspirators.

THE GOLDEN CAGE

'We have the wrong man,' they defended.

'Don't be an idiot,' she spat furious. 'These are Musketeers straight from the barracks in Massalia. These men are imposters.'

'But they are dressed as Musketeers.'

'They are not from our barracks,' one of the Musketeers confirmed. If they are attempting to free the prisoner then they are equally treasonous. We will take them all to Lutèce and let King Louis decide what their fate will be.'

⌘

Erik and Aedan watched as Tristan, Griffin and Cam were herded from the mill and shackled to the back of the wagon. Griffin scanned the tree line looking for his father. He knew it would not be possible for them to attempt a rescue. They were outnumbered and would have to bide their time. Griffin hoped it would not be too late for them all. He thought of Lucy back at the ship and wished that this would all be over. He just wanted to go home to Griswold.

⌘

Lucy and Summer had been alarmed when Griffin and Cam returned to the ship to put on their uniforms.

'Promise me you'll be careful,' Lucy had said clinging to Griffin.

'I promise,' he said kissing her before hurrying back to the mill.

Now they waited, and when Erik and Aedan returned alone to the ship they both fired questions at the men.

'What are we going to do Papa?' Summer asked anxiously. 'King Louis can be vindictive when he is cornered. He will kill them all, I know it,' she said tearfully.

'It will take them more than a week to get back to Lutèce via horseback. If we set sail now, we can get there before them.

'What then Papa?'

'I will go and see King Louis and demand that he release them.'

'What makes you think that he will listen to you?' Lucy asked.

'King Louis and Queen Maria are not stupid. I may be the ruler of a small kingdom, but they know that every Northman from Kaldakinn as well as every soldier from Ebondeen and Griswold will be on their shores in no time if they kill Griffin and Cam. Three kingdoms that are allies are stronger than their Francian army alone. They will not wish to start a war with us.'

'Do you think it will work Papa?' Summer asked.

'It is the only card we have to play Summer. Now let's get going. The sooner we set sail the sooner we get to Lutèce.'

FORTY-THREE

PATHWAYS

PALAIS DU LOUVRE, FRANCIA

QUEEN Maria paced up and down as she read the message that had been delivered to her. Tristan Chevalier was in custody and in the process of being escorted back to Lutèce. It appeared that the two foreigners were with him and they were the ones who posed a problem. They were the ones who could start a war. Francia could not afford another war. Louis was away fighting against the Holtlanders who were threatening Francia's trade and Maria had been made Regent during his time away. The fate of Francia was in her hands with the decisions she made.

This mess was her problem and she cursed thinking about it. On one hand she was relieved that Louis was not here – at least she would not have to explain why the foreigners and Tristan had returned to haunt them. She'd managed to convince him of Tristan's complicity in Summer's death, but it had taken much cunning. She recalled his scepticism.

'Why would he kill her, Maria? He loved her and wanted to wed her. He would even have killed me at the first opportunity to be with her.'

She had to think quickly.

'Word got out that she spent time with you at Versailles. The moment you left rumours circulated in Lutèce that she was sharing your bed and that you were showing her the chateau as it would be her future home as your mistress.'

'I am still loathe to believe that he did not trust her.'

'I'm sure he did not know what to believe, Louis. He was on a mission in the west of Francia and was attacked. It's quite possible that after he escaped he found out that Summer went away with you, and his jealousy just spiralled out of control. She was travelling in one of our royal carriages with our insignia. Perhaps he thought she was with you and wanted you both dead.'

She let the accusation hang in the air.

'I suppose it is possible,' he concurred. He had been shocked to discover that Tristan was not dead. He had called for Pierre to offer an explanation. The Musketeer had sworn that he knew nothing of Tristan's survival.

'I would never lie to you King Louis. When I was ordered to bring you the message, I saw them lying in the snow. They were dead so I believed. Are you sure he is alive?'

Louis believed the soldier. He had no reason not to.

Still, he had to tie up any loose ends. If Tristan Chevalier discovered that he was behind the plot to assassinate them, it would discredit him and his guard would never trust him again. So he and Maria agreed to implicate Tristan by charging him with treason. Just two days later, Louis had to leave for northern Francia to ward off the Holtlanders.

Now she was left to deal with this quickly and quietly. Her secrets would remain intact and Louis would never have to find out that she had sent Summer to Anatolia.

What Louis does not know will not harm him, she thought.

She scribbled a note and stamped the royal seal on it. Then she handed it to the waiting messenger. 'Make sure you get this to the men before they arrive in Lutèce.'

⌘

It was a long and slow journey back to Lutèce. The wagon creaked and groaned as it followed the dirt road and a few times they thought it might just shatter apart. Six Musketeers, and Mallory escorted them. She was determined to claim her bounty from the crown.

'It almost worked,' Cam whispered to Griffin. 'We were so close.'

'I know, but now this gets complicated. I know Papa and Aedan will come for us, I just don't know whether it will be while we are travelling or when we get to Lutèce.'

'He will travel by ship, I am sure of it,' Tristan said. 'It will be quicker and I doubt he will leave Summer in Massalia alone after all she has been through.'

'Why have King Louis and Queen Maria done this?' Griffin asked. 'I thought they were playing on opposite sides. It just doesn't make sense.'

'It makes perfect sense Griff. When the object of their conspiracy surfaces or threatens their secrets then even Louis and Maria would work together to protect themselves and their thrones.'

They sat in silence for a while, each with their own thoughts as the wagon rambled on toward Lutèce – toward the axe man's blade.

⌘

THE GOLDEN CAGE

The three women sat on deck staring out at the blue sea. Lucy insisted on coming with them even though her father had been unhappy with her decision. She had issued him an ultimatum that if he did not give her his blessing, that she would leave regardless and he would never set eyes on her again.

He had seen her determination and there was something else there too – concern for Griffin that he knew was more than friendship. His daughter was in love. He knew that she could marry worse. He was the heir to a kingdom that was rising in the world, which had strong allies with the Northmen and Ebondeen. This could be a beneficial situation for them both. Lucy would marry for love and her new alliances would open up new trade routes and opportunities for his business. It had been a quick and a tearful goodbye. Lucy's mother was still grieving for her brother, and losing her daughter was an added blow. He promised her that when this was all over they would sail to Griswold to see their daughter and to build a relationship with Erik and Isabel.

Anna played with the bead bracelet that Cam had bought for her when they explored the city. She twisted it as though willing them to be safe. She'd told no one, but she had a crush on Cam. Everyone treated her as a little girl, as someone who still had to grow up, but the truth was that she was far more mature than her young years. Her body was transforming under her garments, her curves forming and her breasts swelling.

She had seen life in a harem and was being groomed to please a man. Although she had yet to be with a man, she knew how they thought and what they wanted. She had learned a thing or two in her time at Topkapi Palace. Her heart lurched every time she thought of him. He was eight years older than her but she did not feel the difference when they were together. He teased her and they laughed together. She dreamed of a future with him one day. She hoped that he would feel the same way one day too.

Summer gazed out over the water.

How can it be so calm and perfect, when everything else is tumultuous and breaking apart?

She could not shake the knot of tension in the pit of her stomach. She prayed they were all right. She felt responsible for Tristan's capture. She had pushed him away, told him to leave her alone and to give her space. She had sent him straight into danger.

She realised that she felt responsible for everything that had happened to him. She almost got them all killed because Louis was jealous of their relationship. She was equally responsible for his predicament now.

How can love be so destructive? If I truly love him, I have to stay away from him.

Her heart ached and she felt resentment build up within her.

I hate you Great One, she thought.

⌘

LIONSGATE

'She's in a bad place,' Mac said sadly to the Great One.

'Yes and no,' he answered.

'What do you mean? You know what she is thinking. She hates you, she believes that she is being punished and she is giving up on love. I would say that is pretty bad.'

The Great One smiled. 'Yes, you could look at it that way, but I see potential.'

'Potential?' Mac asked incredulous. 'Sometimes I really don't understand you.' He shook his head.

The Great One laughed. 'Yes, clearly we don't think the same way.'

'All right, enlighten me then. How do you see potential in all the evil that has happened to her?'

'Sometimes it is only when we are truly honest with ourselves that we are able to let go.'

'I'm not following,' Mac said.

'I am not offended that she hates me right now Mac. She is being true to her feelings, to her frustrations and she is letting them out. Bottled up emotion is far more dangerous than angry outbursts. When she truly acknowledges her pain and fears, her disappointment and rage; that is when she can begin to heal.'

'I understand what you are saying and I know you are right, but I cannot bear to see her in pain. Once, you sent Nuada to us to show us the path to take when we were lost. We would have abandoned all hope, had it not been for your help. Please can we send her a sign that there is hope for her?'

'All right Mac, I will send Ziah to her because your love for her is so great, and my love for you both is even greater.'

⌘

The ship cut through the water effortlessly as it rounded the tip of Hispania. They were leaving the Alboran Sea and heading toward the Francian coast. The winds were good but there was a heaviness of heart on board. The unknown is a difficult place to be and not one of them could predict the future. They could simply hope for the best.

FORTY-FOUR

VISIONS

PALAIS DU LOUVRE — FRANCIA

QUEEN Maria received word that the prisoners would be arriving in the morning. She had sent word that they were to be kept outside the city and brought into the palace grounds in the dead of night. She did not want to announce their arrival for all of Lutèce to see.

She also did not want the prisoners getting wind of the fact that most of their soldiers were fighting in Holtland. They had to believe that she and Louis were united in this plan.

A few more days and it will all be over. Just a few more days.

⌘

Erik threw the anchor overboard and the ship nestled against the side of the wharf. Summer remembered the first moment she had arrived in Francia. It seemed like an eternity ago. She had been standing on board in anticipation, marvelling at the bustling city and architecture, expectation and excitement for the future. Now she felt dread and she hid in her cabin, away from the porthole. She no longer felt safe here any more.

'We're here,' Anna said trying to distract her.

'I know and I plan to stay on board. This place is where it all started.'

'It's also the place you met Tristan,' Anna reminded her. 'Not everything that happened here was bad Summer.'

Erik knocked on her door. 'It's late. I cannot go to the palace now. I'm going to find us some fresh food and I will see the King first thing tomorrow.'

She nodded and he pulled her close. For a brief moment she stiffened as though she had been scorched, but then she relaxed against his broad chest and she returned his hug. He towered over her, and she felt so fragile. His heart ached for her. He had not missed the tension she had felt in his hug.

'They will be okay Summer,' he whispered. 'It will all be over soon and we can go back home to Griswold.'

She wanted to believe him, but a part of her was dead. It was the part that had hope. It had been snuffed out time and time again and she was not sure how she would ever get it back. She nodded numbly, more for his benefit than her own.

'Can I come with you to get something to eat?' Anna asked. 'I need to get off this boat for a while before I go mad.'

'Me too,' Lucy admitted.

'Summer, will you be all right with Aedan?' her father asked.

'Of course Papa.'

They left and she settled down on the bunk bed. She pulled a blanket over her legs and closed her eyes, listening to the creaking and groaning of the wooden ship, the lapping water against its hull. It should be peaceful but somehow she still felt anxious.

Aedan knocked at the door and she smiled at him.

'Can I come in?' he asked. She nodded and patted the end of the bunk.

'Sit,' she said. He carried over two steaming mugs and handed her one.

'What is it?'

'Something to warm you up and take away your anxiety,' he said. She could smell the rich rum as he handed it to her.

'This is not a good idea,' she said alarmed. 'The last time I had too much to drink it did not bode me well.' She recalled how the raki had affected her and how she had been unable to protect herself because of it. She never wanted to be in that position again.

'It wasn't the raki that was the problem, you know,' he said.

She gasped. 'How do you know what I was referring to?' She feared Tristan or Anna had betrayed her by revealing her secret. She felt anger stir.

'Neither of them told me,' he smiled.

Now she looked truly afraid. He reassured her quickly sensing her fear increase.

'I know what happened to you in Anatolia Summer. You've forgotten that what the Great One knows, I know too. He knows how hard this is for you, and he is heartbroken it has happened.'

'Then why didn't he save me?' she yelled angrily. He was not offended at her outburst. 'Do you really expect me to believe that he cares?'

'He has saved you Summer, but that doesn't mean he could prevent evil happening to you throughout your journey, because sometimes bad men make choices that hurt good people. He sent Eli to watch over you, to keep you from drowning and to help you find us again. Think about it,' he continued, 'how many times could you have died? What were the chances we would ever meet up in Alexandria?'

She knew he was right; it was almost unbelievable that their paths had crossed, that she had even made it this far alive.

'What do you mean when you said the raki wasn't the problem?' she asked. He knew too much and she wanted answers. She needed answers.

'They drugged your drink Summer. It wasn't the raki that made you lose consciousness. It was the concoction they put into your drink that affected you. The Valide Sultan does this to all the women when it is their first encounter with a man. It lessens their anxiety and resistance to what is about to happen to them.'

She looked shocked. 'She drugged me so that the Kapudan Pasha could rape me,' she whispered hoarse. She felt bile rise in her throat and she pushed down the urge to vomit.

'Yes, it never was your fault. She sent Eli on an errand, as she knew he was watching over you and she waited till Sultan Mehmed was away hunting. Believe it or not, the Sultan actually liked your company and was concerned about your safety. She did something so terribly evil.'

'All this time I have blamed myself. I believed that if I was only more careful, it would never have happened.'

'I know, but nothing could be further from the truth. There is more you need to know, but I am not the one to tell you. The Great One is sending Ziah to you, but you need to trust me and drink this to enable it to happen.' He handed her the warm liquid once more.

'What will it do to me?'

'It won't harm you if that is what you are worried about. It will relax you so that you are able to really see and feel for a moment. You can trust us Summer.'

She knew that she could, as it was common knowledge in their family history just how the Great One, Ziah and Aedan had helped them; but still she hesitated, fearful he would take advantage of her. She had to let go at some point and learn to trust again. She knew it was now or never.

'All right, I will trust you.'

He left her to drink the liquid. It did not take long for the rich drink to begin its work. She felt herself slipping into a place that was not quite another world, nor was it the boat cabin any longer. It was a dreamy place but she knew she was completely awake. Her body felt weightless and for the first time in moons she felt carefree again. Then she saw him drifting toward her.

'Are you real?' she asked as he held out his hand.

She was surprised that she felt no anxiety at taking it. She sensed she could trust him, she sensed he was love in bodily form.

'So we finally get to meet face-to-face Summer. I'm Ziah, the Great One's son.'

'I've heard all about you from my family. My great-grandfather Papa-Mac used to tell me about you all the time when I was a child. How come you or Aedan haven't aged?'

'Let's just say that living in Lionsgate keeps us eternally young. Your Papa-Mac sends his love by the way,' he added.

She gasped and he nodded. 'He's been worried about you and it's thanks to him I'm here. He insisted my father send me.'

She laughed. 'Yes, anyone would be afraid to refuse Papa-Mac.'

'We want you to know that it is okay to be angry about what happened to you, even to blame us; but it is never okay to blame yourself or those closest to you. This was never your fault and it wasn't Tristan or your brother's fault either. Evil men and women who want their own way, who are hungry for greater power, have taken advantage of you all. I wish it were different. Sometimes I wish we could make people do what we want them to, but then none of you would ever know what true freedom is if you were controlled by us. It hurts us deeply when good people are hurt by evil actions.'

She knew he was being genuine, she could tell by his face. She believed he could truly feel her pain and understand it.

'I understand what you are saying, but how do I move on from this? Queen Maria, the Valide Sultan and the Kapudan Pasha don't deserve forgiveness for what they have done to me. Please don't tell me to forgive them Ziah – I just can't do it.'

'I understand how you feel. I've been there you know-tortured and beaten for doing nothing wrong. In my case they actually killed me, but thanks to my father I was given a second chance. You are getting your second chance too. Don't waste it on hatred.'

'Why should they get a reprieve?' she said angrily.

'Many people think they need to forgive in order to receive forgiveness in life. This is not the truth about forgiveness Summer. Forgiveness is never about helping

THE GOLDEN CAGE

the person who wronged you. It is about helping yourself. Forgiveness will enable you to move on, to make a life with Tristan and to trust and love again. This is the way to heal yourself. Life has a funny way of catching up with those who do evil deeds. They will reap what they have sown.'

'I need to know something? Did I bring this on myself because I gave myself to Tristan before I was his wife? '

Ziah looked perplexed but his eyes held deep compassion. 'Summer, no! My father does not punish and hurt people who make their own choices. I've already told you that you are free to make your own decisions.'

'There's more,' she said hanging her head. 'I killed a man, Ziah. There can be no redemption for that? This is my punishment for becoming a monster. The Great One will never forgive me for the terrible things I have done?'

'Summer, redemption is always possible. No one is beyond it. My father looks at a person's heart. Yours is a little battered and bruised, but it still understands right from wrong. You killed a man to protect and save another, because your heart still knows love and what it means to protect. I see that you love Tristan, but you've built a wall around it to keep it from breaking again.'

'I am afraid that if I let Tristan back into my life I will never be able to love him the way I did before. I am afraid that I will only ever see one face again when we are together.'

'It will take time,' Ziah said, 'but you have to open your heart and take risks Summer. Tristan is not the Kapudan Pasha, nor will he ever be. He loves you.'

'I'm afraid I will push him away eventually. What If I can't get over it?'

'What if you can, but you are too afraid to try? You will miss out on a lifetime of love if you let fear hold you back.

THE GOLDEN CAGE

Did you know that your grandmother, Aislinn, had a ring that saved her many times?'

'The truth ring? Yes I have heard of it. Without it she would have never escaped from the Dark Lord.'

'What if I told you that a ring saved you, was your escape from the Kapudan Pasha in that market.'

'What do you mean. Tristan bought me with silver.' He could see she was curious.

'Yes he did, but he ran out of coin. He only had one thing left of value to trade with, and that one thing had sentimental value that can never be replaced. It was his mother's wedding ring.'

'He gave away his mother's ring for me?' She knew the ring Ziah spoke of. She had admired it more than once on Lou's finger when she visited their country chateau. Tristan had shared the story of how his mother had died and how Lou had inherited her ring. They had both sacrificed for her freedom.

'It wasn't a hard choice for him to make? It's easy to give up things of value when the thing you want is of utmost significance to you. Tristan's love for you is far greater than his mother's ring.'

'I've been so selfish. All this time I've convinced myself that I am protecting him by pushing him away, but really I've been protecting myself from getting hurt again.'

'I wouldn't say you've been selfish, Summer. You've been through an ordeal and building a wall to protect yourself is a natural thing to do when trauma happens. Sometimes it takes others to show us a different perspective. When we see things differently it gives new courage to bring walls down, little by little. Have patience.'

'I'm not sure how to be brave, but I'm going to try.'

'I might have something to help you.'

He took out a band that was intertwined with silver and red gold. The metals could not be separated and although they were vastly different, they complemented one another.

'It's beautiful,' she said as he placed it in her hand.

'It's time you had your own ring. Whenever you look at this ring remember that although you and Tristan may not always be on the same page, your lives are intertwined. When you feel afraid and weak he will give you the strength to face your demons. There will be times when he will doubt he can help you or give you what you need, and it will be in those times that you will encourage him. You did not meet him by accident Summer. Trust what you have and trust your heart, above all.'

'You have given me a lot to think about Ziah, thank you.'

'Don't leave it at that Summer. Tell Tristan that you love him. There is no time like the present to love.'

'Will I see him again?' she asked but before he could answer he was gone.

'Ziah, Ziah,' she called.

She drifted back into her bunk bed. The whole experience had been surreal. She looked at her hand and sure enough, there was the ring on her finger – a tangible reminder that her experience had not been a dream. She touched it and whispered, 'Let me have one more chance to tell him I love him.'

FORTY-FIVE

MALICIOUS

THE wagon bumped over the cobbles. It was late and the streets of Lutèce were almost deserted. A few sewer rats ran across the road searching for leftovers and waste.

The wagon pulled into the palace grounds, its wheels rattling as it rumbled over the cobblestones. It made its way to the rear entrance as Queen Maria had directed. Tristan, Cam and Griffin were herded downstairs toward the dungeon. They were pushed into a dark cell, the large iron door echoing as it banged closed behind them.

'How are we going to get out of this?' Cam asked despondent.

'Francian prisons are not made for escape,' Tristan agreed.

She watched the three men through the peephole for a while before she opened the grate and spoke. Her voice echoed eerily in the hollow jail.

'Why have you come back here?'

The men were surprised to hear her voice. Tristan faced Queen Maria through the metal bars. 'You and King Louis lied to us. You played us for fools. The only flaw in your plan was that you and your husband were playing on opposite sides, trying to control lives and destinies for your own gain.'

'You are rather sure of yourself, which is ironic, since you are the one behind bars. Remember who you are addressing Tristan. I am a queen and you will show respect.'

'Respect is not a right Majesty, it is earned. Why have you done this to me? I've been nothing but a loyal Dragoon all these years, serving a country I love, and yet this is how you repay my service. I would hate to see how your enemies are treated.'

'This was never personal Tristan. Unfortunately, you became my enemy when you delved into Summer Sveinsson's disappearance. This would have all been over, had you not insisted on raising her from the dead.'

'How do you sleep at night?' Tristan growled through clenched teeth. 'I am sure King Louis would love to hear the truth about Summer's disappearance. I am correct in assuming you haven't enlightened him?'

'Sadly he will never get the chance to hear the truth. He's away fighting the Holtlanders and I am Regent. Your heads will be long gone by the time he returns. He will thank me for cleaning up this mess and protecting Francia.'

'You won't get away with this.' Tristan gritted his teeth.

'I already have,' she said as she slammed the grate closed. They could hear her footsteps as she left.

'What now?' Cam asked. 'There'll never be a fair trial. She has condemned us already, to save her own neck.'

⌘

Erik wore his clan colours. He looked formidable, his height and stature sending a message of strength. He tucked his sword into his belt. This was the moment of truth where he would face the King. He strode into court where he was halted by guards who eyed him suspiciously.

'I am here to see King Louis.'

'The King is unable to see you. You must leave immediately.'

'I will not be leaving till I've had a word with the King,' he persisted more forcefully.

'Do you wish to be removed from here as a corpse?' a guard asked him.

'No, but should anything happen to me, the entire armed forces of Kaldakinn, Griswold and Ebondeen will be tearing these palace walls down, so I suggest you get in there and tell King Louis that Erik Sveinsson is here to see him.'

'It's all right,' a voice echoed from the parapet above. Queen Maria waved to the guards to let him past. 'Come through and we will discuss any business you may have Monsieur Sveinsson.'

She was trembling, but she put on a brave face. He was a man with immense presence, but she reminded herself that she was Regent of Francia and this was her turf.

'What can I do for you?' She got straight to the point.

'I don't wish to seem rude Your Majesty, but the business I have is with the King.'

'That is not possible, I'm afraid. He is presently indisposed.'

Erik smiled. He had heard rumours in the city that the king was away fighting a war. Queen Maria had just confirmed it, which provided him greater leverage.

'I believe you are holding my son and nephew captive in your dungeons.'

'Where on earth did you hear such nonsense,' Maria feigned amusement. 'I assure you; it is impossible since your son and nephew were killed in an attack on the west

THE GOLDEN CAGE

coast of Francia a few moons ago. I thought you had come to retrieve their bodies or ensure that the culprit responsible for their deaths was punished. I can assure you, Lucas Beaumont, the perpetrator of this horrible crime has paid with his life. I am deeply sorry for your loss but these insinuations are ludicrous.'

'Queen Maria, don't patronise me. I have seen my son and nephew. In fact, we have just returned from a trip to Anatolia.' He watched her face drain of all colour.

'An....Anatolia?' she asked composing herself.

'You know why we were there, and before you throw me into the dungeon with my nephew and son, you need to know that I have sent word that should anything happen to any of us, three kingdoms will breach your shores and burn Francia and this palace to the ground. My men are waiting for my reassurance that this will not be necessary. I am sure you will be willing to come to some agreement that will benefit both of us.'

Queen Maria looked afraid for the first time. She was cornered and she knew it.

'What do you have in mind?'

'I want Griffin and Cam released immediately.'

'Then you will leave and never return to these shores?'

'Yes, you have my word.'

'It is done.'

'There is one other thing.'

'You request more? I should have your head removed. What more do you want?'

'I want Tristan Chevalier released as well.'

'That is out of the question. He is a Francian traitor and must pay as one.'

'We both know he did not betray you, and neither did Lucas Beaumont. Let's just say I am aware of more than you think and I have witnesses who will attest to it. I am sure the Cardinal would love to send word to The City of Seven Hills about your dealings.'

Queen Maria knew her hands were tied and she was livid. They relied on support from the City of Seven Hills to help Francia in times of need.

'If I agree to this, then I have certain conditions. Tristan Chevalier may never set foot on Francian soil ever again. I want him as far removed from here as possible. Even Griswold is too close for comfort. I will release him on condition that he sail to Acadia.'

'Acadia? Where is that?'

'We have Francian men who are travelling across the huge ocean to explore new lands far to the west. Acadia is one of those places. It is a tough place, but also a land of opportunity. If Tristan agrees to go there, then I will release him.'

'No, I cannot agree. You cannot afford another war on top of the one you are fighting, which is what you will have if you don't release him. It will sink you.'

Queen Maria looked annoyed but she stood her ground.

'Perhaps, but Louis is at this very moment forming an alliance with the Anglo-Saxons as they fight the Holtlanders. Do you wish to take that chance? Perhaps we should put this to Tristan. He might see things a little differently. It is a generous offer. He will have the opportunity to start afresh and make a new life. It is an opportunity that far exceeds having his head removed by the axe man.'

'All right,' Erik concurred. 'I will let Tristan make his own decision.'

Queen Maria had the three prisoners escorted to her parlour. They stood shackled in front of her.

'Papa,' Griffin looked alarmed, but pleased to see his father.

'It's all right Griff. We are in the process of negotiation. Queen Maria has agreed to release you, but she has some terms she wishes to discuss with Tristan.'

'I am willing to release all three of you if Tristan agrees to go to Acadia. This is my final offer.'

'Acadia! You may as well send me to the ends of the earth. Why would I ever agree to that.'

'I was hoping you would see it as a new beginning, a fresh start where you could have new opportunities. There is of course one other matter to consider,' she added slyly.

'What other matter?' Tristan asked.

'I have it on good authority that your sister Lady Dubois aided you and your friends in your escape. If this were true, it would be considered treason to the crown. It would be a shame to return their lands to the crown and have her tried as a traitor. She has such a beautiful head, don't you think?'

Tristan was seething. He wished he could place his hands around Maria's throat and squeeze the life out of her. Lou had nothing to do with this, but Queen Maria would use any means to get her way. He would never endanger his sister, especially after all she had done for him.

'All right,' he conceded. 'You have my word. I will go to Acadia, but only after I have seen Summer home to Griswold and said my goodbyes. Will you give me at least two moons to do that?'

Queen Maria raised her eyebrows. 'So you rescued her, did you? All right, it is the least I can do to make up for this mess. You have two moons Tristan, and then I expect to hear that you are on your way to Acadia. I have Francian troops there who will confirm your arrival. In the meantime I will have documents drawn up that pardon you from the charges brought against you and your friends. I will also draw up a document ensuring your sister's safety as long as you keep your word. If you go against it, she will be charged with treason and will stand trial. I want it in writing Monsieur Sveinsson that you will not attack Francia after they are released.'

Erik was angry. She'd won the final hand. He had been unable to prevent Tristan from agreeing to going to Acadia. He knew Summer would be devastated. Still, they would deal with it all the best way they could. He understood Tristan's decision to protect his sister. Her family and whole life was in Francia and he would not put them in danger. Erik would have done the same for his own family. He respected the young man even more.

Documents were signed and deals were made and the four of them left the palace together and headed for the ship. They all had a heavy heart. Instead of it all being over, it was only just beginning. Erik felt sick to his stomach. He had told his daughter it would be all right, but that had become a lie and there was nothing he could do about it. How would he explain to her that the man she loved was being banished to a colony that would separate them by a vast ocean.

FORTY-SIX

SACRIFICE

THE journey back to Griswold was sombre. Little was said regarding Tristan's plans as each individual was dealing with their own demons. Tristan convinced Erik and the others not to tell Summer till they were back in Griswold. He wanted to be the one to break the news to her. He wanted her to have her mother's support and love when he broke her heart.

He noticed that she seemed different since his return. She seemed more at peace and less anxious and angry.

He joined her on deck as she sucked in the fresh air. Her nausea had returned and he held out some ginger tea to her.

'This feels familiar,' she smiled and patted the wooden platform next to her. He sat down.

'Clearly you are not a sailor, Summer Sveinsson.'

She laughed and he thought how good it was to hear her happy again.

'I've spent enough time at sea to last me a lifetime. Give me land and horseback as my mode of transport any day. I've missed riding Hawk.'

'It won't be long till you are tearing up the meadows again,' he teased.

'Yes, it will be good to get home.'

She twisted the ring on her finger then looked up at him.

'I was terrified when they took you. I know that I said I felt broken and there would be no hope for us, but I wasn't being completely truthful, Tristan. I still love you, but I'm afraid I might damage us in the long run. I'm afraid I will hurt you and it would break my heart.'

He was torn in two. How he'd longed to hear her say these words, to finally be vulnerable and admit she loved him. But that was before Queen Maria's ultimatum. It would be easier leaving if she did not want him. He wanted to hold her and never let go, to turn back the clock when it was just the two of them. He did not respond. How could he say anything without revealing that their time together was coming to an end?

'Say something,' she urged.

'Thank you for your honesty,' was all he could manage.

She stood, shook her head and left him sitting on the deck. Tears stung her eyes as she descended to her cabin.

I bear my heart and he thanks me for my honesty. No emotion, no reciprocation of his feelings. Maybe he no longer loves me or maybe I am just a burden to him, so damaged that he can't deal with it.

She sobbed quietly into her pillow unaware that he stood outside her door listening to her, his heart breaking. He wanted to pull her into his arms and kiss her so badly, but he knew that it would be harder for her in the long run if they rekindled their romance. It was better she believe that his feelings had changed. He could not expect her to go to Acadia with him. He'd heard stories about it – cold and unforgiving in winter, with local savages who massacred the foreigners. He would not put her life in danger again. She had been through enough and he loved her too much. It was better she move on without him, that her family surround her while she healed.

⌘

GRISWOLD - EARLY AUTUMN 1672

Isabel saw them coming from her window. She raced down the stairs and out into the courtyard.

'Open the gate,' she yelled at the guard.

Her legs flew across the bridge toward them. Erik reached her first and swung himself from his saddle wrapping her in his arms. He kissed her longingly.

'I've missed you,' she gasped. 'I've been so worried. Where is she?'

'Mama,' Summer called and Isabel raced to her daughter who finally crumpled in her mother's arms sobbing all her shame and hurt away.

'My sweet girl, you're home and safe and no one will ever hurt you again. I'll kill them first,' she declared.

Summer laughed through her sobs. 'Thanks Mama.'

'You're all in one piece, that's all that matters. Thank you for finding her,' she said embracing her son.

'How did you know to send horses for us,' Erik asked.

'I've been driving Balfour crazy every day sending him to the river with horses. I knew that one day you would need them.'

THE GOLDEN CAGE

Balfour grinned. 'I was beginning to think it would never happen. Of course the farrier was delighted – he's never had to shoe so many horses. Business has been booming for him.'

Isabel became aware of a few extra faces she did not recognise. 'Who have you brought home with you?' she asked.

'Mama, this is Tristan, a good friend,' Summer said. She did not know how to introduce him since things had been awkward between them since she had bared her heart.

'Welcome Tristan, and thank you for bringing Summer home safely. Who are the young ladies?'

'This is Lucy,' Mama. 'I hope that she will agree to become my wife,' Griffin blushed.

Lucy's eyes widened in surprise. 'Is that your way of proposing?' she asked teasingly.

'Enough already,' Cam interjected. 'Cousin Isabel I've missed you.' He swung her around and she slapped him.

'Put me down Cam,' she ordered. Sometimes she forgot that he was her cousin and not her nephew, since Struan had married so late in life. 'We need to send a message to your mother and father. They have been frantic about you. There is still someone I haven't met. Who might you be?' Isabel asked turning to Anna.

'Anna was in Anatolia with me,' Summer said. 'She helped me more than once.'

'Not as much as you have helped me,' the young girl smiled coyly.

'Thank you Anna, you will always have a home here with us,' Isabel said. 'Now come on everyone, it's getting

THE GOLDEN CAGE

cold out here. Let's go home and warm up by the fire. I think this calls for a celebration.'

It did not take Isabel long to realise that Summer was different. Her carefree spirit was broken and she seemed wary and distant at times. She prayed that she would find her daughter in there somewhere. Every time Isabel suggested painting to her, Summer withdrew and shook her head sadly.

'I don't know that I'll ever paint again Mama,' she said.

'But you love painting.'

'That was another life Mama,' she said sadly.

Isabel felt her heart break.

⌘

'What do you mean you have to leave?' Summer asked incredulous.

They had been home for a week and she and Tristan had taken their first ride together across the moors. The wind whistling through her hair as she cantered gave her a sense of freedom and joy she had not felt in a long time. Even Hawk remembered her, and they had ridden as one. She felt happy for a brief moment once more, until they stopped and Tristan had told her the truth.

'I have to leave Summer. It is not my choice, but it is the terms of Queen Maria's agreement.'

'She'll never know if you stay Tristan. She can't hurt you here.'

'Yes she will. Acadia is a Francian colony with many troops and word will get back to her if I don't go.'

'What can she do to you if we protect you. She wouldn't dare attack us. We have the Northmen and the army of Ebondeen to fight with us, you will be safe here...'

He placed his finger over her lips to silence her desperation.

'You don't understand. It's not about me Summer. It's about Lou and her family. Queen Maria has vowed she will have them tried as traitors if I don't keep my agreement. I am doing this for them. I can protect myself, but they shouldn't be forced to choose between Francia and me. It is their home and they have done nothing wrong.'

Summer remembered Ziah's words. Lou gave up her mother's ring to save her from the Kapudan Pasha. Now it was her turn to save Lou. It meant she would have to give up her most precious thing – a life and love with Tristan.

'When do you leave?' she asked.

'In the next moon before winter sets in.'

'Were we ever meant to be together?' she asked looking at the ring Ziah gave her. Somehow it taunted her now. All that nonsense about their lives being intertwined. She had not told Tristan about her encounter. There seemed no point to it.

'I don't know. All I know is that I loved you Summer, more than life itself. Maybe in another time, another place....'

I loved you Summer – past tense. He doesn't love me any more, she thought sadly.

'What will you do in Acadia?'

'Most of the men are fur trappers and traders. I guess that is what I will do.'

She nodded numbly, turning away as she was unable to look at him another moment, fearful she would break down and that her tears would never cease to flow.

'We should get back,' she said hoarsely pulling herself back into her saddle.

FORTY-SEVEN

LOVE AND FAREWELL

SHE woke crying, her pillow wet from tears and sweat. The nightmares still visited her, but this one was different. Although the Kapudan Pasha still filled her dreams he had somehow lost his power. Her fears were new now, different. Now she dreamed she was alone, that Tristan was gone and she was stranded on an island. She would call out to her family and although they would assure her they were there, she could never find them and the loneliness and fear she felt would engulf her in waves. Then Ziah would appear in her dreams urging her to take a leap of faith, but when she jumped she could not see where she was landing. She always woke up at that point terrified she would die.

She slipped out of bed and walked to the window. He was in the courtyard, staring up at the stars. He looked so lonely, sad.

She pulled on a robe and went to find him.

'I remember telling you once that every time you looked up at the stars you would know how much I loved you,' he said when she sat down beside him.

'King Louis stole that letter from me,' she blurted out. 'When I found it, that's when I truly feared he would kill you,' she continued.

'I had no idea.'

'Those words meant a great deal to me,' she said. 'When I was walking through the desert with Eli, believing that we would never make it, I would look up at the stars. There were so many because it was so dark and I would think of you and how I wished I could see you again. You helped me to fight, to survive.'

He took her hand in his. It was warm and comforting.

'I'm glad,' he said.

'So you are leaving tomorrow?' she sounded sad.

'Yes, my ship sails at noon.'

'Tristan, I understand why you have to go,' she said, 'but I will miss you.'

He looked at her and for the first time he saw regret. There was something else there too – love. Not love masked by fear, or love suffocated by pain or brokenness. It was pure, trusting love. This was the way she looked at him the day they pledged their love and had hope for the future. His heart skipped a beat.

She took his hand and placed it over the left side of her chest.

'You will always have my heart Tristan Chevalier.' She dropped his hand and kissed his cheek before turning back to the castle. 'Take care and stay safe.'

She had taken no more than four steps when she heard him call her name.

'Wait Summer.'

He strode over to her and took her in his arms, kissing her as though he could never let her go. She melted into his body and held him tight, shaking from the emotion that welled up in her. She kept expecting to see his face morph into the Kapudan Pasha's face, to feel afraid but it didn't happen. Instead she was surprised to feel the familiar stirring in her belly as she had the day she had given herself to him. He still made her feel safe and loved.

He pulled away and looked into her eyes. 'Is this all right?'

She nodded.

'I cannot bear the thought of leaving you and that you may believe I no longer love you. Summer, I have never stopped loving you and I believe I never will. I pushed you away because I didn't want to hurt you any more than you already were. I knew I had to leave and you've been through so much already...'

'Shhh... it's all right. We've both been guilty of hiding our feelings. Let's just enjoy tonight. Will you spend it with me Tristan?'

He nodded.

⌘

It was as beautiful as the first time. He was tender and took it slow, knowing that she may have flashbacks or memories that would overwhelm her. He did not want to do anything she did not want, but she initiated their lovemaking as she touched him and melded her body to his. Her passion surprised them both. She gave herself to him without reservation, gasping at the delightful sensations as his hands and mouth moved over her body. When he entered her she felt complete and loved. A tear rolled down her cheek and she felt surprised that she was feeling again, that her emotions were not completely dead. It was sweet and poignant, but it was also sad. They lay side by side as he held her and kissed her.

'I love you,' she said.

'I love you too.'

'Let me come with you?' she begged.

'I can't Summer. It's too soon. Acadia is a brutal place to live, dangerous and you are still healing. You need your family around you to mend. You need to feel safe right now. I cannot give that to you if you come to Acadia, at least not until I am settled and can provide a future for us. I won't endanger you ever again. Will you trust me?'

She nodded and knew that he was right. She had come a long way, but she still had to find the old Summer, to laugh again and feel carefree once more. Only time could do that for her. She would find herself again. She felt hopeful for the first time in many moons. She could see a future with him.

⌘

He left the following day and Summer felt her heart would break. She tried to put on a brave face but the tears escaped as his ship sailed down the river and into the ocean. She sat for a long time until she could no longer see the boat. The day grew cold and the light began to fade. Her father picked her up and carried her like a child back to the castle as she nestled her head against his broad chest, tears wetting the front of his tunic.

He knew it would take her a long time to get over her love. She was like her mother. Isabel needed time to grieve for Phoenix when he died, but eventually she had learned to love again. He was sure Summer would love again in time.

EPILOGUE

SPRING 1673

SHE stood on deck with the other families, looking out to the horizon. They had been at sea for over a moon and they were all searching for that first piece of land. They should be sighting it any day now. She had made some good friends on this journey. A few of the families were heading to the colonies to start a new life. It was an adventure but it was also terrifying not knowing what to expect when they arrived.

Her decision to come was made when she realised that her heart was entwined with Tristan's despite the distance. The pain of being apart became greater than the pain of the past. She knew that she would never give her heart to another and it had taken her a while to convince her parents of this. She knew something else too – that he was a part of her.

It had taken a while for her to put her ordeal behind her, but Cam, Griffin, Lucy and Anna had all helped her to laugh again and find a part of her that had not wholly been consumed by Francia or Anatolia. Her mind was also taken off the past by the wedding celebration of Griff and Lucy. They married soon after their return and Griffin officially became Lord of Griswold. Erik and Isabel would remain in the castle and advise him as he ruled.

She knew that she had found herself again when she started painting once more. She'd found the incomplete family portrait in the glasshouse her father had built. It was

374

to be something special for her family and she had not finished it. She felt that it was important for her to complete it, to have a painting that could be passed down their family line, something to hang in Griswold castle. She had painted for a King and a Sultan but this would be her finest work ever, the piece that gave her new memories and hope for the future. Her last masterpieces should not be of the people who had caused her so much pain.

She'd worked on the painting day after day and found that it kept her from longing for Tristan constantly. It brought healing to her as she saw her family come to life on the canvas.

Once the painting was complete she felt ready to face her future, and that was when she knew it could not be without Tristan.

The wind off the sea ruffled her chocolate locks. It would not be too long now. She felt butterflies in her stomach as she thought of him and their new life together. Would he be glad to see her or would he be angry? She had not told him she was coming, as he would have tried to dissuade her. They had been writing letters to one another and it sounded as though things were as tough as he imagined they would be. Many times she wanted to go to him but the winter seas were icy and treacherous, the journey to Acadia impossible.

Now it was warmer once more and she was taking that leap of faith Ziah had urged her to take. No longer did she have nightmares that she would die.

She knew she had survived the worst of her life and that anything else that came her way would be possible to face too. Eli was right; she was strong. She thought of the eunuch daily and hoped he had found his family as she had found hers.

She'd also decided to give the Great One another chance. She understood things better now. At no point had he ever left her. When she was in Francia, she had Tristan, Cam and Griffin to watch over her. Even in Anatolia he sent people to help her – Eli and Anna and even Sultan Mehmed who had been kind to her. In the desert Ashira protected her from a certain death. Summer thought of the times she could have died and they were numerous, yet here she was, alive and able to move forward despite all the horrific things she had endured. She had that second chance that Eli had urged her to take and she would use it well, she would live each day with gratitude and love.

The boat lurched and her stomach flipped. She gagged and smiled. She never had been much good at sailing and this time was no different. This time however, she was sailing to her one true love and expectation filled her heart. She held her queasy belly with one hand while holding the rail with the other.

This time she had a good reason for feeling nauseous – a very good reason. She could not wait to tell Tristan that he was going to be a father.

ALSO BY CAROLINE HEMINGWAY

⌘

THE AWAKENING

BOOK 1 OF THE DESTINY CHRONICLES

One Family, One Tyrant, One Truth...
Mackenzie Hamilton and his wife Imogene always did what was expected of them. Leaving their homeland to fulfil the prophecies spoken over them by the Elders of the Clan, they journey to Griswold with their four children. There they encounter a power hungry tyrant who rules his people with fear and manipulation. When tragedy strikes and all is stripped away, tearing their family apart, they have to dig deep to find courage within to take back what is theirs and to discover who they really are. Will the mistakes of their past be their undoing or will their faith in the Great One be enough to conquer an evil that threatens to consume them? A novel where tragedy confronts belief and victory depends upon it.

THE RECKONING

BOOK 2 OF THE DESTINY CHRONICLES

One woman, Two men, Many secrets ....
Four years have passed since the Hamilton family escaped the clutches of the Dark Lord to make a new life for themselves. Aislinn Hamilton, now a young woman, is on the brink of following her dreams with a desire to change the world. As she embarks on this new journey she meets someone who will change her life, challenge her values and

beliefs and will capture her heart. Love takes her on a road
back to the awful past she has tried so hard to forget – a
past she does not want to relive.

Aislinn will discover shocking truths about herself, her
beliefs and the relationships she has developed.

A novel where love and trust are challenged to their
limits.

THE RISING

BOOK 3 OF THE DESTINY CHRONICLES

Young...
Carefree...
Wild at heart...
Isabel Williams yearns for a life of adventure. She
unexpectedly finds her world turned upside down when
she's thrust into a culture she does not understand. Every
value she holds dear is challenged as she begins to
experience life from a new perspective. Will she be
courageous enough to open her heart to embrace new
truth, to rise above the circumstances that threaten her
long-held beliefs; or will she allow her intolerance to
threaten her chance at happiness?
A novel where prejudice confronts acceptance – only one
will rise to conquer the other.

ABOUT THE AUTHOR

Caroline Hemingway lives in Melbourne Australia with her husband Hamilton and their four children. The Destiny Chronicles were birthed when she undertook putting pen to paper as a therapeutic exercise, discovering in the process a love of writing. This was followed by short stories and children's books she hopes yet to publish. She and her family are Foster Carers to children who are at risk in the community and she is passionate about human rights. She is also an enthusiastic blogger and loves all things cereative and adventurous.

THE GOLDEN CAGE is Book 4 of the Destiny Chronicles. Other Titles in this series are THE AWAKENING (Bk 1), THE RECKONING (Bk 2) and THE RISING (Bk 3).

To follow Caroline's blogs visit her websites:

www.carolinehemingway.com

www.simplelivingbigadventures.com